THE SUMMONING

Axabara was large, so big he had little room to move within the circle. His head and torso were those of a jackal. The bottom half of his body was that of an enormous scorpion, and he moved about on six multi-jointed legs. The combination of fear and fatigue nearly made Jafar pass out, but he clung tenaciously to consciousness with the knowledge that all his friends were depending on him for their very lives at this moment.

Axabara raged against the walls of his tiny cell, and each time he battered against the rim of the circle, it was like a physical blow to Jafar. Time and again Axabara battered, and each time the walls held. With each blow Jafar's strength ebbed that much lower, and he prayed fervently to Oromasd that he could hold on long enough to do what must be done.

The Parsina Saga
Book 3

CRYSTALS OF AIR AND WATER

Stephen Goldin

BANTAM BOOKS
TORONTO • NEW YORK • LONDON • SYDNEY • AUCKLAND

CRYSTALS OF AIR AND WATER
A Bantam Spectra Book / February 1989

ISBN 0-553-27711-1

Published simultaneously in the United States and Canada

Bantam Books are published by Bantam Books, a division of Bantam
Doubleday Dell Publishing Group, Inc. Its trademark, consisting of
the words "Bantam Books" and the portrayal of a rooster, is Regis-
tered in U.S. Patent and Trademark Office and in other countries.
Marca Registrada, Bantam Books, 666 Fifth Avenue, New York, New
York 10103.

PRINTED IN THE UNITED STATES OF AMERICA

O   0 9 8 7 6 5 4 3 2 1

This book is dedicated to all the wonderful people of the Lothlorien discussion group . . . may their frivolity reign forever.

CONTENTS

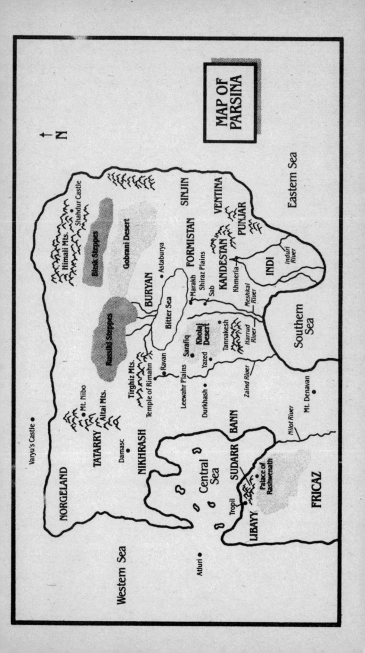

1

The Royal Nuptials

The tale is told of Shammara the plotter, the queen of corruption, the woman who betrayed good Prince Ahmad and despoiled the fabled sacred city of Ravan, holiest city in Parsina; Shammara, whose name drips like a curse from the lips; Shammara, who trailed misery and destruction in her wake; Shammara, who, from her position of ultimate power within the City of a Hundred Temples, strove for still more power by traveling secretly into the mountains to traffic with the dreaded rimahniya, those worshipers of darkness and the lie.

There in those frigid caverns did she bargain with Abdel ibn Zaid, high priest of evil, and make him swear his strongest vow to kill Prince Ahmad wherever the exiled prince might be. Then, satisfied with her unholy compact, did she return to her palace, with no one knowing of her absence but the trusted servants who guarded her secrets with their lives.

Having the personal oath of Abdel ibn Zaid to kill Prince Ahmad, she could now put all thoughts of the prince aside and concentrate on the business of ruling Ravan. She found much work yet before her. Prince Ahmad's coronation plans had already been under way when he left Ravan on his ill-fated journey to Marakh to wed his intended bride; those plans could now be modified to accommodate the new heir instead. In a few more months her son, the prince Haroun, would be officially crowned king of Ravan.

Her most immediate concern, however, was the imminent wedding of Prince Haroun and Princess Oma of Marakh. Shammara's agent Rabah—concubine of King Basir and confidant to Princess Oma—had sent many messages explaining that the princess was vehemently opposed to marrying Haroun; Shammara, though, knew how to manage a headstrong princess. King Basir was actually the weakest link in the

1

chain of her plan, being so indecisive that the wrong gust of wind could always change his mind.

Under intense prodding from his wazirs—most of whom had long since been bribed by Shammara—King Basir would certainly carry out his pledge to send his daughter to Ravan for the wedding. Princess Oma might be a spoiled brat, but she was also intelligent; she wouldn't run away from her wedding procession once it had left the gates of Marakh, for she had no experience in surviving the common world without a handful of servants, and would soon starve left to her own devices.

Then, once Princess Oma was safely in Ravan, Shammara could keep her in line long enough to have the wedding consummated. After that, the future queen of Ravan would be of little consequence. Shammara knew from Rabah's reports that the princess had little interest in politics and would not challenge Shammara for control of the city. Rabah had also stressed that there were ways to distract Oma should she show any inclination to politics. Shammara would let the sybaritic princess do as she pleased once she'd performed her official responsibility of marrying Prince Haroun.

In Marakh, the beautiful Princess Oma kicked and screamed, sulked and pouted, but her efforts were to no avail. Though her father wavered a bit in his determination and had to be reconvinced by his wazirs, all the court insisted that she marry the prince of Ravan. Nothing she did could sway their decision.

The servants and chatelaines of the palace spent three weeks preparing Princess Oma's train and wedding party, weeks in which Oma herself kept to her rooms and refused all company except that of her father's favorite concubine, Rabah. King Basir, heartbroken that his beloved daughter should be so unhappy over an unavoidable situation, ordered Rabah to do everything in her power to console the princess and ease her grief in these trying days. Rabah obeyed the king's command, and though many sounds were heard to emanate from the princess's chambers while the two were together, rarely were they the sounds of sobbing.

At last the royal train was prepared and the time for final parting came. Princess Oma emerged from her rooms dressed in her finest silken robes of gold and white, and surrounded by the handmaidens who would accompany her to Ravan. As Oma left her rooms, Rabah threw over her a red embroidered sharshaf. This shawl traditionally symbolized the protection of her parents' home, and would totally engulf her until she entered her husband's. In a sulk Oma started to throw it off, but Rabah restored it with a caressing gesture and a plea for Oma to remember her regal duties. Oma left it on as custom dictated, but her mouth could be seen pursed in a tiny pout behind her sheer milfa.

Oma walked stiffly through the women's section of the palace with Rabah and the rest of her train. When she reached the end of the last corridor and Rabah could accompany her no farther, the princess broke through her air of reserve and embraced her dear friend. There was much weeping and wailing, and each woman promised the other to write often.

With this emotional display out of her system, Princess Oma remained coldly aloof as she passed through the outer court, ignoring all the wazirs who had conspired to send her to this horrid fate. King Basir wept at the thought he might never see his daughter again. He embraced her warmly with tear-stained cheeks, while the princess returned the gesture with a formal and passionless embrace of her own. Then, with the farewells over and the speeches made, the princess's expedition went forth from Marakh with a loud blaring of horns, beating of drums, and flying of pennants.

Throughout the journey to Ravan, Princess Oma rode on a gilded palanquin with embroidered purple satin curtains to conceal her from public view. Her retinue comprised more than two hundred of her father's finest soldiers, since the king was willing to risk no repeat of the ambush that overtook Prince Ahmad. In addition to the soldiers there were fifty slaves and twenty maidservants to attend exclusively to Princess Oma's wishes, plus a small herd of asses to carry all the supplies needed to clothe, house, and feed this contingent upon the road.

Princess Oma sulked and complained throughout the journey. Nothing was ever quite right: the slaves carrying the palanquin jostled it too much, the dust from the road sent her into coughing spasms, the food was ill-prepared and tasteless, the sanitary provisions were barbaric, the days were hot, the nights were cold, the insects were a plague, the nighttime noises were too loud, the horses smelled bad, the soldiers were insolent, there was no privacy—the list of complaints went on endlessly. The princess's piercing voice became familiar, if unappreciated, music throughout the trip, and more than one member of the retinue harbored the wish to silence it permanently if only he could be sure of escaping King Basir's wrath.

With the only threat to the princess's safety coming from her own retinue, the expedition passed an uneventful time upon the road, making the long journey from Marakh to Ravan in just over two weeks. Their arrival at the Palace Gate of Ravan was widely heralded, and throngs of people were on hand to provide the princess with a welcome even more elaborate than her send-off had been.

Prince Haroun and the regent Kateb bin Salih came personally out of the palace to welcome the princess to her new home. Using the excuse of maidenly modesty, Princess Oma remained within the palanquin and peered cautiously through the curtains at her intended spouse. She was not greatly impressed by what she saw.

Prince Haroun was a paunchy young man, flabby and slack-jawed. His complexion was oily and his beard looked as though it had spawned like mold randomly around his jaw. His stance was slouched, and he had the irritating habit of shifting his weight awkwardly from one foot to the other while standing, never quite remaining still. His clothes were of the richest fabrics and the finest styles, but his poor posture defeated even the noblest tailor's ambitions. Everything hung at wrong lengths and odd angles, making him appear a poor parody of a prince rather than the genuine article.

The regent, Kateb bin Salih, was an old man with a high, frail voice and a perpetually perplexed look in his eyes. He gave the princess a welcoming speech that rambled aimlessly for more than half an hour before finally trailing off into nothingness without ever having made its point. Then Prince Haroun gave a speech in croaky, uncertain tones. While his speech was more coherent than the regent's, and mercifully much shorter, it nonetheless filled Oma with a tremendous despair that she, a royal princess of acknowledged beauty and wit, would have to submit to the sexual advances of such a nothing of a man.

Finally the ceremonies were over. Princess Oma's palanquin was carried to a side entrance of the palace where she entered and was escorted to the chambers that had been prepared for her within the harem. So relieved was she to be in properly luxurious quarters once again, far from the rigors of the road, that she did not bother to find fault with her new accommodations.

Once ensconced in her new quarters she continued to brood over her dismal fate as her maidservants bustled about unpacking her belongings and setting up a new order within her rooms. Although she knew the rules of diplomacy, Princess Oma had never really believed they applied to her; she made her complaints known loud and long that Prince Haroun was uglier than a camel's testicles and less desirable than a Malembari ape. She explained in great detail to anyone who would listen that under no circumstances would she let herself be forced into a marriage with such a despicable and worthless lump of humanity, no matter what contracts her father had signed.

That evening, as the palace was getting ready for sleep, Shammara paid a call on Princess Oma's chambers. The young woman was surrounded by attendants laying out her sleeping silks, perfuming her sheets, and combing out her long, beautiful tresses—but at a glance from Shammara the servants all vanished quickly, leaving Shammara alone with the recalcitrant princess.

"Welcome to Ravan, O beautiful princess," Shammara said with deceptive gentleness. "May your days here blossom like the flowers in the royal gardens. I am Shammara, mother of Prince Haroun. I've come to personally offer you the hospitality of the harem."

Princess Oma had heard many tales of Shammara, and was uncertain how to reply. On one level she was frightened by this slender, dark-haired woman who wore her age with power and dignity, and her mature beauty like a cloak of ice; but other parts of her knew no fear. Having been raised as a princess with no serious challenges to her authority, she found it hard to believe anyone could threaten her. She tried to steer a safe middle course. "Thank you for your fine welcome, O noble lady. This palace is most beautiful."

"It's only fitting that a beautiful palace should house a beautiful queen, as you shall become."

"That's most flattering, but I shall not become queen in Ravan. I find I cannot marry your son."

Shammara moved in two long, graceful steps to the princess's side and picked up a hair brush one of the servants had set down beside Oma's chair. Standing over her from behind, the older woman began brushing her young rival's hair with an experienced touch.

"I'm afraid you must marry him, my dear," Shammara said very quietly. "The arrangements have all been made, the contracts have all been signed, the dowry has been paid. A failure now would be an intolerable breach of both etiquette and diplomacy."

"I mean no disrespect to you, O noble lady, but I find your son as unappealing as week-old fish. He is unsightly, ungainly, and unkempt. I'd sooner give my maidenhead to the lowliest camel driver than . . ."

Shammara gathered a large handful of the princess's long hair and yanked down on it hard. Princess Oma's head was jerked back so she looked straight up into Shammara's eyes with her throat completely exposed. She started to cry out, but stopped when she saw the cold glare of Shammara above her.

"Now you will listen to me, O pampered cat of a mixed litter," Shammara said in the same quiet, icy tones. "Your opinion of my son is your own affair, though it could scarcely be lower than mine of you. Your lower-class, harping complaints and petty tyranny show a lack of intelligence and breeding which I trust you'll correct. Whether you love him or not, whether you honor him as a husband, is your concern and I will not interfere. But I've worked long and hard to arrange this marriage, and it *will* come about. You will wed my son and the union will be consummated, and thus will our two nations be allied. After the wedding night you can sleep with the asses in the stables if that's your desire, but you will become queen and you will sit beside Haroun on the throne."

Princess Oma was whimpering from both pain and fear, but from some unknown depth she found a tiny fragment of courage. "What if I spoil your plans and refuse to go through with the ceremony?" she asked. It was hard to talk with her head pulled back, but she choked the words out as best she could.

Shammara gave a sharp tug on the girl's hair, pulling her head even farther back, and Oma had to grasp the seat of her chair to keep from spilling on the floor and breaking her neck. "You'll marry him," Shammara said. "You may have to be carried into the temple with both legs and both arms broken, and you may have to nod your head in response to the vows because your tongue has been cut out, but the ceremony will take place. Your condition depends purely on your cooperation. After the wedding and the coronation, you will be queen. It's not so terrible a thing, to be queen of Ravan; there are many who will envy you. You can even look forward to a lengthy and prosperous reign, just as long as you don't interfere with my plans for the city. But you will live only so long as you mind your own business and don't displease me. Is my point understood?"

Princess Oma couldn't nod, and she could barely gag out a noise that sounded vaguely affirmative. Shammara smiled down into the princess's beautiful face and released her hold on the hair. Princess Oma leaned forward in her chair, coughing spasmodically.

"I'm so glad we understand one another," Shammara said as she glided across the room and out the door again.

Princess Oma had never been so frightened in all her life. For the next ten minutes she sat silently in her chair, her body trembling uncontrollably. No one had ever threatened her or abused her this way, and there was a touch of rage mixed in with the fear, anger that Shammara would so boldly insult her this way. Oma knew she dared not challenge Shammara's authority again if she valued her health, but she vowed to do everything she could to thwart the woman's will.

Every day she dispatched a letter to her father, pleading with him to void the marriage contract and declare war on Ravan for slights against her person. Shammara routinely intercepted and destroyed each missive. When Princess Oma realized there would be no help coming to her from Marakh, she closeted herself with her handmaid Hinda to help ease her mind. She gave great thought to Shammara's words and started to make some plans of her own as the days passed and the date of her wedding drew nearer.

The Holy City of Ravan, City of a Hundred Temples, was a city that rejoiced in celebrations—and a royal wedding was one of the greatest and most joyful that could occur. Catching the festive spirit, the citizens bedecked the outer walls of their homes with fabrics of the brightest colors. Women sewed gifts for the bride-to-be, and the city's artisans fashioned wedding presents of the highest quality.

Word of the royal wedding spread with the royal messengers Shammara dispatched to the neighboring kingdoms, and from these lands came gifts and ambassadors from royal houses, and common people flocking into Ravan to witness one

of the foremost events of their age. The bazaars did a brisk
trade and the many caravanserais were filled beyond their capacity. Seldom since the days of its founding had Ravan known
greater splendor.

Admitted through Merchant's Gate with a large group of
other pilgrims was a certain priest from the far kingdom of
Khmeria. All about him as he walked through the city were
merchants hawking their wares, jugglers and street magicians
playing to the crowds, brightly colored streamers blowing in
the afternoon breeze, the dialects of a dozen different regions
being shouted, spoken, and sung. A man could easily lose himself in the gaiety of the moment and not recover his senses for a
week.

But the priest paid no attention to the festivities around
him. At the first temple he reached, he entered and asked for
directions to the Royal Temple, then made his way pur-
posefully through the city until he reached it. At the Royal
Temple he asked to speak to Alhena, wife of Umar bin
Ibrahim. He was directed to Alhena's home, where he introduced himself to the servant answering the door as a man who
knew Umar bin Ibrahim. The servant ushered him into the
qa'a and went to announce his presence to Alhena.

After a few moments Alhena joined him in this beautiful
room with its arched recesses, high ceiling, and wooden
screens. A tall woman with intelligent, if sad, eyes, she bade
him welcome to her husband's home and offered him the hospitality of her kitchen. A servant brought in a plate of dates and
figs, and the priest gratefully accepted a date. Alhena sat cross-
legged on one of the mats beside the durqa across from this
stranger, and asked him what he had known of her late husband.

The priest did not reply aloud but instead took from his
sleeve the letter he'd been told to deliver to no other hand but
hers. He walked around the durqa and handed it to her.
Alhena had but to look at the writing on the outside to recognize it as her husband's, and swooned back on her mat in
shocked surprise.

The priest called for a servant, and together they brought
her around within a few moments. Once the initial surprise
was over, Alhena became her clear, rational self again and dismissed the servant so she could read the letter solely in the
company of the priest who had brought it. The priest guided
her to a diwan in one of the arched recesses, where Alhena

could sit more comfortably, then stepped back a few paces so the lady could read her note in privacy.

Alhena opened the letter with utmost delicacy, as though it were made of spiderwebs instead of sturdy parchment. She read the words with the glisten of a tear ever in the corners of her eyes and with the faintest tremble of her lips, scarcely daring to believe what had been placed before her.

In concise terms, the letter told how Prince Ahmad's wedding party had been ambushed upon the road by minions of King Basir dressed as brigands, and how they had learned that this perfidy was inspired by the treacherous Shammara; how the miraculous appearance of the daeva Aeshma had saved them from certain doom, and how they had chosen to travel to the oasis of Sarafiq; how they had encountered the wizard Jafar al-Sharif, and how the prophet Muhmad's strange vision was now sending them around the world on a dangerous quest for the pieces of the Crystal of Oromasd. Umar concluded the letter by telling Alhena to trust in his love for her and in Oromasd's wisdom that goodness would yet prevail in Ravan.

By the time she finished, Alhena's eyes were so filled with tears she could no longer distinguish the words on the page. She walked slowly to the small altar with the Dadgah fire always kept burning there, knelt before it, and thanked Oromasd and all the Bounteous Immortals, one by one, for the kindness and mercy they'd shown to her and her beloved Umar.

When she'd finished her prayers and regained some of her composure, she returned to the kind priest who had brought her the blessed news. The man had stood silently all this time, respecting the woman's emotions; now he asked whether there was any other service he could perform. Alhena said no and offered him a reward for all he had done already, but the man would accept nothing from her but her blessing. He merely smiled and said he was pleased to do Oromasd's work, which this obviously was.

Alhena offered him hospitality and a place to stay, but again the priest demurred. He would spend this night, he said, praying in the Temple of the Faith, something he had never expected to do in his lifetime. In the morning he would begin his travels back to his native Khmeria. Alhena showered him with her blessings as he departed the house, and for the next several months said extra prayers every day for the welfare of this kind and generous priest.

Being a wise woman, Alhena knew the value of keeping confidences. She knew she could tell no one else in Ravan of this news; to do so would mean their death as well as her own, and would merely alert Shammara to the truth of what was happening in the world beyond the city's walls. Better to let Ravan's evil, uncrowned queen gloat in ignorance over her petty triumph; it would give Umar and the prince more time to work their own triumphs in the world. The silence would be a heavy burden, but she could bear it better knowing her beloved Umar was yet alive and carrying out the will of Oromasd.

She reread her husband's letter many times, until she'd memorized every line and every word of its pages, extracting from it all the love he had mixed with the ink of his pen. Then she placed it in a small dish and set it alight, letting the sacred flame of Oromasd consume it so there would be no evidence of its existence to warn Shammara of the forces gathering against her.

The day of the royal wedding came at last, amid much noise and merriment. Handmaidens from the palace strewed petals of roses, orangeblossoms, and desert lilies throughout the bazaars of Ravan, while billowing stretches of colorful silk and linen cloth were draped from building to building so the sun shone through to the ground in a variety of colors and patterns. Hundreds of musicians paraded through the streets, playing their festive tunes on lyres and lutes, on cymbals and tymbals, tempting the citizens irresistibly to dance. Street vendors sold stuffed dates, garlic-flavored lamb wrapped in flat bread, melons, and hundreds of delicacies to the waiting crowds. Children ran and played in and out among spectators' legs, men smiled, and women came out of their homes to line the paths in hopes of catching a glimpse of the wedding procession. Evidence of the dyers' trade was everywhere as people wore their brightest clothes, and household gardens were stripped bare of flowers to add to the festive atmosphere.

Princess Oma was carried on a litter through the main bazaars of the city surrounded by her handmaidens dressed in all colors of the rainbow. The princess's gown was in the traditional cerise, adorned with other colors of Oromasd as befit a bride in the Holy City. Her kaftan was white silk shot with gold. Heavy gold, cerise, and sapphire embroidery in the intertwined symbols of Marakh and Ravan bordered the hem and sleeves. Over this was a cerise abaaya with gold, white, and sapphire cord edging it and tassels of the gold and white accenting the edges. Floating over this, lifted by the slightest breeze, was a silk gossamer thawb; it gave a rosy fog that kept the technical layer of modesty while showing the beauty of the princess to her soon-to-be subjects. From its edges dangled a thousand tiny antique gold coins that chimed and glinted with every move. Little bells dangled from the servants' clothing, and the women beat on tambourines, dancing in high spirits around their mistress as she was borne on the shoulders of six priests, symbols of her purity.

Prince Haroun wasn't nearly as spectacular as his bride-to-be, and rode his horse through King's Bazaar accompanied by an elite honor guard of soldiers all dressed in their finest armor with their horses groomed to perfection. Haroun's outfit was mostly white and gold, with touches of sapphire blue embroidery. His cloth-of-gold hizam held a saif in a gem-encrusted scabbard. The sunlight threw prismatic reflections from these jewels onto his clothes and face. He squinted to avoid the reflections, and this only made him seem more loutish.

Even though Haroun was less well loved by the populace than his half-brother Ahmad, a royal wedding was a time when such minor matters were put aside, and the people cheered him as though he were the most popular man in Ravan. The roar along the length of the bazaar was deafening, making it impossible to carry on normal conversations several streets away.

The two processions met at the main entrance to the Temple of the Faith, where they were admitted among a crowd of well-wishing nobility, all of whom had arrived early to assure themselves of a good place in the sahn. Prince Haroun dismounted his horse and Princess Oma stepped down from her litter. Bride and bridegroom walked down opposite sides of the riwaq to the front of the temple. They stopped and knelt before the minbar, and Princess Oma was unveiled before her husband for the first time. Prince Haroun was pleased by what he saw, while the princess was dreading her ordeal to come. Nevertheless, heeding Shammara's warning, she was prepared to be brave and make her painful sacrifice—at least for this one night.

As newly appointed high priest, Yusef bin Nard officiated at the ceremony. He was resplendent in his priestly robes of gleaming white delicately accented with silver threads, shining with dazzling brightness in the midday sun. Behind him, in a temporary altar, burned the Dadgah fire to symbolize the purity of Oromasd, which it was hoped would sanctify this royal marriage. Yusef bin Nard read the ancient wedding ceremony in his deepest tones, and Princess Oma responded appropriately—but through clenched teeth.

In little more than an hour it was over and Princess Oma was now the official wife of Prince Haroun. A cheer went up in the sahn and was echoed through the streets of the Holy City. Wine began flowing freely in all the taverns while the singing and dancing intensified. By sundown there was hardly a soul in the city who was not either drunk, dizzy from dancing, or at least hoarse from all the cheering throughout the day.

The bride and groom were escorted from the Temple of the Faith into the palace, where a banquet had been spread in their honor. Musicians played their finest compositions and poets recited their rhymes of love, both tender and erotic. Gifts were presented to the honored couple, so many they couldn't all be seen or counted in an afternoon, as the heads of neighboring states made contributions to the new couple's welfare. The horses, falcons, hunting cats, and other exotic animals raised a din, and there were problems getting them through the crowds safely. The jewels, coins, clothes, and luxuries were heaped in the hall; it would take several scribes weeks to inventory it all. Goblets were refilled liberally, until there was scarcely a person in the wedding party capable of standing without assistance. Finally, when the sun was well down and the stars were glittering like wedding jewels in the black night sky, the prince and princess were led with great ceremony to their official bedchamber.

The next morning Prince Haroun emerged from the room in a foul mood. His face, shoulders, and back were covered with scratches and bite marks, and he walked with a noticeable limp. While both prince and princess agreed that the marriage had been consummated, Prince Haroun declared loudly to all who'd listen that he'd have no more to do with the woman he'd married, and would sire his children by lesser wives and concubines instead. Shammara bought him a few new slave girls as consolation and his spirits were eased.

When Shammara next passed Princess Oma in the palace corridor, she gave a curt nod to acknowledge that their uneasy bargain had been made and kept. As long as the princess stayed out of Shammara's hair, she would be free to do as she wished within the palace. Shammara even assigned a pair of twin, young, lovely, and specially trained handmaidens to her as earnest of their agreement.

Three weeks later, news came to Ravan that King Basir was dead. He had been sleeping that night with his favorite concubine, Rabah, who woke up in the morning screaming that the king had died in his sleep. There were no signs of violence or traces of poison, so the doctors certified the death as being natural. There was certainly no reason to suspect foul play from Rabah. She was only a concubine, she had slept with the king many times before, and she had nothing to gain from his death. The pillow she'd used to smother King Basir left no marks.

The king's death left the succession to the throne of Marakh very much in doubt. There were no sons. Princess Oma was his oldest child, and there were three more daughters entirely too young for either marriage or rule. The wazirs of the realm argued and debated, each trying to grab the crown for himself, but the solution came imposed upon them from Ravan.

Since Prince Haroun was married to King Basir's eldest daughter and would soon become a king in his own right, Ravan's ruler seized the opportunity to claim the kingdom of Marakh as well. An army was sent from Ravan to quell any signs of nervousness on the part of the Marakhi. The wazirs couldn't unite effectively enough to dispute Haroun's claim, and the most powerful of them were quickly dispatched by agents in Shammara's employ.

In due course, young Prince Haroun was declared king of Marakh even before he attained his majority and the kingship of Ravan—and Shammara was well on her path of dominion and conquest in the name of her son.

2

The Path to Conquest

The continent of Fricaz had long been considered the most primitive and unknown region in all of Parsina. With the exception of its northern coast, which bordered on the Central Sea and had trading contacts with the rest of the world, Fricaz was a place of mystery. Geographers had not mapped its contours, nor had naturalists cataloged its animals and plants. Most inhabitants of Parsina thought about it little if at all, and when they did it was simply as a faraway place where nothing of importance ever happened.

True, great things had once happened here. The emperor Rashwenath had founded his far-flung state in Fricaz and used its soldiers to launch his expeditions against the rest of the world. But that was in another time far divorced from the present, and no one thought of it now. For all the rest of Parsina cared, Fricaz was simply a hole in the map, a place to fill up the emptiness on the bottom of the navigators' charts.

Fricaz was considered a place of strange and exotic animals, and indeed there were creatures here that lived nowhere else in the world. Traders would occasionally bring out cheetahs, crocodiles, strange monkeys, hippopotamuses, rhinoceroses, and other bizarre beasts, as well as stories of even stranger creatures left uncaptured. There were rumors, too, of great treasures, and plants that produced medicines to cure all diseases. Storytellers told tales of vast empires ruled by the black men who lived exclusively in this region of the world. But ultimately, Fricaz was of more interest to the storytellers than to the rest of the populace, for few ever bothered to learn of these things for themselves.

In truth Fricaz was a richly varied yet very simple land. Its climatic regions included both deserts and vast fertile plains, mountains and jungles, farmland and grazing land. It was a place of such abundance that its people never faced the same challenges as the rest of the world, and as a result they had never risen above a simple level of civilization.

Most of the people of Fricaz lived in small tribal units, each totally autonomous and independent of the others around it. A few of these had banded into loose nations, mostly to simplify the trading of wives and other goods. Each tribe had its own customs, its own rulers, its own language, its own way of life. Other than in the nations, trade occurred on a limited basis, as each tribe was usually self-sufficient; wars also occurred occasionally when one tribe tried to expand its influence into the region of another.

Most of the people still used implements of wood, clay, bone, or stone the way their ancient ancestors had done. Knowledge of metalworking was almost nonexistent except for the soft, easily worked copper and bronzes, but the rare contact with traders from more advanced parts of Parsina had brought some steel knives and other utensils into the region. These items were regarded as objects of great magic and power, and highly valued by the tribesmen.

Religion, too, was in a much more primitive form than in the rest of the world. Though knowledge of Oromasd had spread even here, the tales and the legends were garbled, and the practices adapted to suit the local needs. The fire of Oromasd was regarded with awe and reverence, but the individual tales of the Bounteous Immortals and the yazatas had been embroidered to the point where they had become deities in their own right independent of Oromasd, and were worshiped separately from him. Though all the people technically subscribed to the principles of performing good deeds, thinking good thoughts, and speaking good words, different tribes had different definitions of what was good and proper. Still, the infinite benevolence of Oromasd ensured that the truly good among the people would not be condemned unjustly at the Bridge of Shinvar, no matter what their definitions or beliefs were.

Such was the state in a certain village on a fateful day in late summer of this momentous year. The village had no name; it was simply "the village," the only one that mattered in the life of its inhabitants. They knew there were other villages in the lands around them, but those were outsider places not even worthy of names. The people referred to themselves as the K'lona, but that word simply translated as "villagers." They had names for their neighbors, too, which were far less complimentary.

The K'lona arose expecting this day to be no different from the one preceding it. The men would tend the herds of cattle, while the women would work in the home gardens or mend the simple huts. The men and boys carried spears and slings to protect their herds from the maraudings of lions, jackals, and other tribes; other than that they wore only loincloths and ornamentally carved pieces of bone in their ears and noses. The women wore simple skirts woven of grass and leaves, and necklaces of feathers, lions' teeth, and ivory. They had no defense against the disaster about to befall their village.

Shortly after the sun came up, a hot wind swept through the village, seeming first to come from the south and then from the west. It blew so hard that tall trees snapped and the huts shook with its force. The hot wind carried with it the sulfurous stench of the Pits of Torment, and it whipped up the dust so fiercely that the people had to cover their eyes and shield their faces from its fury. Women shrieked and men fell victim to fits of coughing, and the beasts in the fields fell over in a faint as though dead. The howl of this savage wind pierced through the peoples' ears like a spear, scattering reason before it like so many bits of straw.

Then, as quickly as it had come, the wind died again and the air became still. The men and women of the village shook their heads to clear the dust from their eyes and the ringing from their ears. When again they could see and hear, they were stunned by the sight that greeted them in the open center of their village.

Standing there was Hakem Rafi the thief, master of the daeva Aeshma—a small, wiry man dressed in a rich kaftan of deep purple and a turban of violet, in the center of which was an enormous canary diamond. Even without his fine garments the sight of Hakem Rafi would have caused a stir within the village because none of the K'lona had ever seen a man with skin so lightly colored.

"I am Hakem Rafi, your new king," said the blackhearted thief, and the invisible Aeshma translated his words so all the villagers could understand him. "Bow down and pay me the homage you owe your master." Hakem Rafi's words rang loudly through the open air with a timbre that bespoke power and dignity.

The chief of the tribe stepped forward defiantly. He was an older man, powerfully built, with scars across his chest from the time he had fought a marauding lion armed with nothing but a stone knife. He had seen much in this life and feared little—especially not the rantings of some stranger whose skin was so pallid he must obviously be ill.

"We know you not," said the chief. "Why should we bow to you?"

In response, Hakem Rafi merely clapped his hands together, and suddenly there appeared behind him the fearsome apparition that was Aeshma, king of the daevas. His hideous figure, with skin blacker even than the villagers', towered over the buildings and people standing before him. Some of the locals fainted dead away at the sight of him, while others shrieked or wailed in fear, certain the end of the world had come upon them. The bravest of the men grabbed their spears and hurled them with all their might at the giant standing before them. They could scarcely have missed, but Aeshma deflected the oncoming missiles and the spears landed harmlessly on the ground in front of him.

"Bow down before me," Hakem Rafi repeated, "or my servant and I shall visit death and destruction upon your village such as has never been seen by any of your ancestors. Your houses will be razed to the ground. Your women, children, and old men will be killed, and only your warriors will be left alive to serve as soldiers in my army of conquest."

Most of the women and some of the men, not daring to doubt the power of this stranger with the hideous giant for a servant, did indeed bow to Hakem Rafi. But the chief and the bravest of his warriors stood their ground. "The K'lona bow to no outsiders," the chief said bravely, even knowing the hour of his death might be at hand.

"Then the K'lona are fools," said Hakem Rafi. "Since some of them have bowed to me, O Aeshma, just destroy the village as a warning to those who would disobey my orders."

"I hear and I obey," Aeshma said. The king of the daevas waved his hand before him and the devilish wind sprang up once more, stronger than before. It swirled around the people standing in open ground and hardly touched them at all, but no building could withstand its force. The village collapsed to a heap of rubble, and then the wind passed. The K'lona blinked in stunned silence at the devastation around them.

But the chief of the K'lona was a good man. He sensed powerful evil in this haughty stranger and his huge servant, and he was determined not to yield to it whatever the price. Even though he had little knowledge of Oromasd and the judgment at the Bridge of Shinvar, his instincts told him that to accept this horror would damage him, his tribe, and the entire world.

"You may kill me if you can," he told Hakem Rafi, "but I will not accept you as my king." Several of his strongest warriors gathered behind him to support his decision.

Hakem Rafi said nothing, but made a slight gesture with his right hand. In obedience, Aeshma lifted his arms and a new terror was unleashed.

The ground shook and a fissure opened at the chief's feet. Out of the hole flew a horde of Aeshma's offspring, the hairy demons, moving so quickly their forms were scarcely more than a blur. They shrieked and jabbered in their high-pitched voices, so fearsome that most of the villagers fell to the ground cowering in fright. The hairy demons circled the village three times, laughing hysterically into the faces of the terrified K'lona, before finally centering on their real target.

First one, then a second, then a third of the hairy demons flew at the chief of the K'lona. The first one flew directly at the man's face and disappeared up his nostrils; the second flew into his mouth when he tried to scream; and the third flew into his ears. They vanished into the body of this valiant man and began working their evil magic within him.

The chief screamed a scream that no mortal voice should be able to produce. His body shook with uncontrollable tremors, and he danced around for a moment as though trapped amid a swarm of angry bees. Then he fell to the ground, still shaking, and writhed in the dust. As his horrified people watched, his eyes were eaten away from the inside until his skull showed empty sockets. His tongue stuck out from his mouth, swollen and black, and the skin of his lips dried, cracked, and split apart. His belly swelled and suddenly burst open to reveal a mass of wriggling maggots oozing from the wound. His skin sprouted red, festering sores, and pus began to seep over his limbs. Still his legs kicked and his arms waved about in his agony, even though he could no longer make a sound to convey his pain. In some ways that was more merciful to his people.

His body shriveled a bit, the skin becoming as dry and wrinkled as a raisin in the sun. In less than a minute the ordeal was over and the chief lay dead on the ground, mummified with a ghastly expression on his face that, for months afterward, haunted the nightmares of all who saw it.

After witnessing the gruesome death of their chief, the rest of the K'lona offered no further resistance. Those who had not yet made obeisance now knelt on the ground before Hakem Rafi, and all the villagers proclaimed him their king and total sovereign. Hakem Rafi the blackhearted smiled and accepted their vows, and as a token of his benevolence and magnanimity he ordered Aeshma to rebuild their village, with houses larger and grander than they'd been before. So relieved were the people to be spared further tragedy that they cheered their new king and praised him for his kindness and generosity.

The women, children, and old men of the village were allowed to stay behind to tend their herds and their garden crops. All the warriors, though, were conscripted as soldiers into their new king's army, to fight such battles as he would direct—and die, if necessary, in his cause and his name.

Thus did Hakem Rafi, the one-time petty thief who had chanced to steal the urn of Aeshma, begin his campaign of conquest across the face of the world. He chose first the easiest victims, the tiny settlements in primitive Fricaz, going village by village and terrorizing the inhabitants into submission with such tactics as he had used against the K'lona. Although his army grew as each new village came under his dominion, he did not have his troops fight just yet, preferring to let Aeshma and his hairy demons do the initial work. There would be plenty of combat ahead, and Aeshma advised Hakem Rafi not to waste his soldiers in foolish campaigns when other methods would work faster and more efficiently.

Aeshma had told Hakem Rafi that these tricks would be most effective in the primitive lands, where knowledge of Oromasd was slight. In the civilized nations, where the priests of Oromasd held sway and worship was stronger, the hairy demons would be more limited in their powers. It was there that an army would prove more useful, and there would Hakem Rafi's forces meet their true tests.

Over the course of the next few weeks, the empire of
Hakem Rafi grew until it covered the plains and jungles of
southern and central Fricaz. Nor did Aeshma and the hairy
demons have to terrorize every village and town throughout
the region in order to gain obedience. Word of their existence,
and of the sorceror who used their powers to hammer all opponents into submission, swept before their advance like a grass
fire in summer. Many were those people who fled their homes
in terror at the news of the new emperor's approach; and of
those who stayed in their villages, most simply yielded to his
authority the instant Hakem Rafi appeared without needing
demonstrations of his vast and terrible powers.

With each village he captured, with each people he subju-
gated, Hakem Rafi's army grew in size. Soon he had a force of
well over two thousand warriors at his command, all ready to
obey his slightest order lest they taste his displeasure. Initially
they were armed only with spears, slings, and blowguns, but
Aeshma provided them with more modern weaponry. Each
soldier had a fine steel sword, glittering armor, and a shield on
which was embossed the symbol Aeshma had designed as the
insignia of Hakem Rafi: the initials of his name, ornately cal-
ligraphed in silver and set in the center of the circular adarga.
The troops had well-crafted leather boots and helmets, and
were fed regularly on better provisions than most of them had
known in their lives. At Aeshma's suggestion, Hakem Rafi in-
stituted a training program to drill the warriors into an efficient
troop of combat soldiers, readying them for the day they would
have to fight against live opponents rather than depending on
Aeshma and his demons to conquer new territory.

At the end of a month, the empire of Hakem Rafi reached
from the southmost tip of Fricaz all the way to the southern
edge of the great deserts in the north of the continent. This
marked the transition between the first and second phase of
Hakem Rafi's campaign of conquest. The cities lying along the
northern edge of Fricaz, between the desert and the Central
Sea, had well-developed trade routes with the rest of the
world. Their priests knew the ways of Oromasd too well for
them to fall easy victim to Aeshma's demons. Such lands as
Libayy and Sudarr were sophisticated centers with armies well
versed in the skills of war. These nations would not submit to
Hakem Rafi without a battle—though, with Aeshma's help,
there was no doubt they would eventually succumb.

Aeshma provided the army of Hakem Rafi with horses, camels, and food for their trek across the great Fricaz desert. Most of the warriors had never seen a horse before, much less ridden one, and most of them preferred to walk, saving the beasts for carrying their supplies and equipment. Even though Aeshma provided clouds to shade them from the ravages of the desert sun, the heat was still oppressive. Many warriors complained—though none so loudly that the words would reach their emperor's ears.

Walking across the desert was hard work; the shifting sands provided a treacherous footing that the jungle and plains tribesmen were unaccustomed to. Even though all were in good physical condition, their legs ached at the end of each day's march from fighting against the unsteady terrain.

Aeshma provided large skin bags of water for the troops, and gave them food every morning and night to keep them strong. Although many in the army were tired, no one became sick and no one died on a trek that would otherwise have killed at least half the men attempting it.

Since Hakem Rafi's troops came from many different villages, most of them spoke dialects that were unfamiliar to the others. Aeshma translated Hakem Rafi's orders so each man could understand them, but other than that he left the languages alone. If the men couldn't speak to one another, they couldn't conspire against their emperor. As a result, the warriors congregated in small groups with others from their own village or nearby areas, and developed a simple sign language for dealing with everyone else.

But despite the problems with communication, the northward trek was not a silent one. Each tribe had its own songs, and the men were constantly singing to take their minds off their terrible plight. The desert air rang with conflicting, yet interweaving, music as Hakem Rafi's troops marched ahead, its pattern of march constantly changing to the many different rhythms of the singers. After three weeks in this wilderness—during which many despaired of ever seeing grass or trees again—they reached the fertile lands of the kingdom of Libayy.

A caravan of desert traders had warned the Libayyan king about a vast army approaching his borders, and he rallied his own forces to face them. An army of two thousand men had never attacked Libayy from the south before—the desert had always

formed a natural barrier to safeguard the southern border—
and the soldiers of Libayy were well impressed by the stamina
of the opposition they were now facing. Nevertheless, as loyal
sons of their homeland they were prepared to fight bravely to
defend their king and their country against the oncoming army
that slightly outnumbered them.

The defenders, knowing the territory better than the warriors from the south, picked the spot for the battle carefully—a
narrow pass between some tall, steep hills and an unfordable
river. It was their intention to lie in wait for the invaders at the
top of the hills, thus catching them between the slopes and the
river and decimating them with arrowfire; with their numbers
cut severely, the enemy would either retreat or try to run
ahead out of the fire—but in either direction they would find
fresh Libayyan troops ready to cut them off. Thus would the
Libayyan general deal with these invaders.

At first the plan looked as though it would work. The invading army, as though with supreme arrogance, sent no
scouts ahead of it to check the territory it was approaching. The
Libayyan bowmen waited patiently at their positions, prepared
to launch a storm of arrows the instant the enemy marched
through the valley below them and into their range.

From that point, however, the situation changed dramatically. The ground shook and the very hill beneath the archers
began crumbling away. Suddenly, instead of holding their
bows, the men were scrambling merely to stay upright as the
earth around them went through a violent upheaval. And even
through the sound of the earthquake, they could hear the deep
rumbling of inhuman laughter.

Before the Libayyan archers knew what was happening,
the enemy soldiers were running at them with swords drawn,
yelling their battle cries. Many of the Libayyans were slaughtered, and many others fled for their lives. The rest, seeing the
hopelessness of their position, threw up their arms and begged
for mercy. Hakem Rafi accepted their surrender generously—
not because he felt any trace of compassion, but because he
wanted as many trained soldiers as he could get to serve in his
own growing army.

After losing the element of surprise and his elite unit of
archers, and with the rest of his army split into two sections
and now vastly outnumbered, the Libayyan general had little
choice but to surrender to Hakem Rafi in the hope his men
would not be massacred. Hakem Rafi made the general swear

allegiance to him on pain of death and took command of these new forces.

Hakem Rafi now commanded the largest army in Fricaz. Despite the rearguard action of the king's finest, most loyal troops, he marched easily into the seacoast capital of Tropil, executed the king, and extended his own realm. He lost less than a tenth of his men, and those were the untrained Fricaz tribesmen. In exchange he had gained three times that number in new, well-trained soldiers. The entire land of Libayy lay at his feet, and he scarcely rested here before turning his forces eastward to march against the kingdom of Sudarr. With Aeshma's help, that kingdom, too, fell before his advance.

Hakem Rafi had now done what no man before him had ever accomplished: he had united the entire continent of Fricaz under a single rule. With Aeshma's aid, the vast distances were no problem; Hakem Rafi could issue a command from wherever he happened to be, and word of it would be carried wherever in his realm it was needed. No ruler in Parsine history had ever had an administration this efficient, but Hakem Rafi accepted it as the norm and turned his vision elsewhere.

Aeshma had advised Hakem Rafi to begin his conquests with Fricaz, since it would be the easiest continent to capture and hold, supplying good soldiers and a base against which no rear flank attacks could be mounted. All Parsina lay ahead of him, and his army grew in size with each new land he conquered. Soon, Aeshma assured him, Hakem Rafi would rule all the land between the Eastern and Western Seas—and there was nothing, not even the power of Oromasd himself, that could stop him.

3

The City of the Apes

Jafar al-Sharif, the storyteller kismet had cast into the role of a wizard, lay on the top of a hill in the Buryani countryside, retching. He had used his wits, and the magic cloak of invisibility King Armandor of Khmeria had given him, to kill the evil wizard Kharouf and thus defeat the army of corpses the yatu had brought against the impoverished kingdom of Buryan. But far from feeling triumphant, Jafar felt only nauseated. For the first time, he had killed another human being—an evil, damned soul, yet still a man created by Oromasd. He'd told many tales of heroes and slaughter in battle, but he found the reality far more grim than he could possibly have imagined.

When eventually he overcame his sickness, his mind began to work at its usual efficiency once more. Rising shakily to his feet, he walked over to his fallen enemy and looked down at the body. He knew it was an impure thing to touch dead flesh, but he also knew there were important things to be done here. Turning the corpse over gingerly, he examined it more closely.

The first thing he noticed was a small silver medallion hung around the wizard's neck on a silver chain. The medallion was disk-shaped and imprinted with strange occult symbols Jafar couldn't fathom despite all his recent reading lessons. This must be the amulet Kharouf had placed so much trust in, the one that protected him from enchantments. As a man totally engrossed in the practice of magic, Kharouf had forgotten that other things, like a simple sword, could kill him as well.

Jafar wondered whether the amulet would work for anyone else. Touching the dead flesh as little as possible, he took it from the dead man's neck and placed it around his own. There was a certain glowing warmth to it much as there was to the ring of the Jann Cari he wore on his finger, so he assumed it would still perform its appointed task. He wished he'd had the

24

amulet when he and Selima were escaping from the wizard Akar's castle; he could have given it to Selima while Cari protected him, thus sparing them the dangers of the quest they were now on. But at least it was comforting to know he would henceforth be safe from magical forces and spells; he merely had to avoid growing overconfident as Kharouf had done, and realize there were other threats than magical ones.

He looked up and saw Cari standing before him. The beautiful young Jann, slave to the ring Jafar had stolen from her former master, said, "When Kharouf died, the spell against djinni he'd placed on this hilltop died with him. I can be here safely and help you now, O master, if you need me."

This raised an interesting point that Jafar had been curious about. "Why do some spells last when separated from their creators, while others don't? I don't understand this. The ring that controls you didn't stop functioning when I took it from Akar, nor did his magical carpet. The cloak of invisibility still works though its creator is long dead by now, and this amulet I just took from Kharouf feels like it may be working. Yet Kharouf's soldiers stopped fighting the instant Kharouf was killed, and the spell that kept you away from here is now gone."

Cari shrugged her shoulders. "I know only a little of such things, but it depends on the sort of spell being cast and the use to which it's being put. If the spell is being used to make a tool—like your cloak of invisibility, for instance—then magical energy is poured into the implement. The magic becomes part of its very essence, like dye becomes part of a cloth, which is why it can survive a change of ownership. Such spells are much, much harder to do; that's why magical tools are so highly valued. The wizard places a part of himself into the tool permanently, so even if he isn't there, the magic is.

"Other spells are just temporary things, made to achieve limited purposes. Kharouf didn't want to put part of his will permanently into those soldiers; an effort that great would have killed him. Instead he just animated them with his will of the moment, which I'm sure was a hard enough job. At the same time he was maintaining the spell to keep djinni away from him, and probably several other minor spells. A strong wizard like Akar or Kharouf can juggle dozens of temporary spells and still have energy left for other things—but when a temporary spell is no longer being maintained, it ceases to function."

Jafar al-Sharif accepted that explanation and continued his delicate search of the dead wizard's body. There were no other amulets or tools, but in one capacious pocket of the yatu's purple kaftan he found an old book awkwardly handbound in black leather; its pages were yellowed and tattered, and filled with diagrams and formulas as well as with words. He showed his find to Cari, who looked at it with widened eyes.

"This must be Kharouf's grimoire," she said, "his book of magical formulas and incantations. With that to guide you, you could learn some real magic."

Jafar al-Sharif took another look at the book in his hand. Weathered and tattered, well read and well used, it looked far older than the pristine volume of Ali Maimun's journal, even though it had to be far newer. Once again, power was falling unbidden into his lap. Perhaps the prophet Muhmad was right; perhaps Oromasd did have some great design for a humble storyteller.

"Maybe I could at that," he said as he tucked the book away under his robes.

His business on the hilltop completed, Jafar al-Sharif told Cari to make herself invisible once more and then had her fly him down to where Princess Rida, the warrior princess of Buryan, and Umar bin Ibrahim were kneeling over the supine figure of Prince Ahmad. The young man's handsome face was drawn and pale, and he had lost a great deal of blood from the wound in his leg suffered during the battle with the army of the dead. "How is he?" Jafar asked.

Umar's face was grim. "He'll live," the old priest said, "but we have a hard road ahead of us, and it will be quite some time before he's well enough to travel. Unless . . . is there anything you can do?"

"Possibly," Jafar said. "Give me a moment to think about it."

He walked off to one side alone and whispered, "Cari, can you heal him the way you've healed me before?"

"It's just a sword wound, a simple cut," Cari whispered back. "There should be no problem."

"Can you remain invisible and make it look like I'm the one doing it?" Jafar asked her.

Jafar could almost hear the smile in her voice. "Hearkening and obedience, O master."

The storyteller turned back to the others. "I think I have the spell to do the job," he said. He walked to the prince's side and knelt beside him. Passing his hands over the prince's body as he'd seen Cari do, he closed his eyes and began intoning nonsense syllables in a low voice. All eyes were on him as he waved his arms about, and then suddenly, when he saw the prince react to Cari's treatment, he gave a final spectacular gesture and exclamation.

Ahmad's eyes were wide with the abrupt departure of his pain. "You are indeed powerful, O Jafar," he said, his voice brimming with youth and energy. "More than ever I'm glad we're traveling with a wizard as a companion."

Ahmad stood up and tested the leg. He winced slightly as he said, "There are a few mild twinges, but it's easily bearable."

"The bone must have gotten chipped," Cari whispered in Jafar's ear. "There's nothing I can do to cure that."

Meanwhile, Jafar's attention was demanded elsewhere. "There are others of my men also wounded," said Princess Rida. "Could I beseech you, O wizard, to heal their wounds as well?"

"I can manage a few, but not too many," Cari whispered in her master's ear.

"My powers are low after the fight with Kharouf," Jafar said aloud, "but I think I can tend to a few of them. Let me see the worst cases; the rest will have to be treated by your own physicians."

Jafar al-Sharif spent the next half hour going from one wounded soldier to another, stopping by the ones Cari said she could help and performing the same arcane ritual he'd performed for the prince. In all, he healed twelve of the Buryani fighters before Cari told him her powers were depleted and she could do no more this afternoon. The army's physicians were binding and cleaning wounds all around them. The astringent herbs these medical men sprinkled on worked quickly and well to stop infection and slow bleeding. Those soldiers with minor wounds would be able to walk home from the battle. The rest of the wounded men would be carried back to the capital in litters and have their wounds tended by more experienced doctors—but since Jafar and Cari had tended some of the worst cases, all the fighters who were not killed outright in the battle could be expected to survive.

Jafar's ghostly daughter Selima and their other companion, Leila, had ridden down from their observation point a few hills away to join the rest of the party by the time Jafar was finished with his rounds. Prince Ahmad was pale, looking very sober and obviously still strongly affected by his battlefield experience. "This is the first time I've ever been wounded in combat," he told his friends. "I don't know how to describe the difference. I always thought of battle as a glorious adventure; that's the way the histories all tell of it. Even the fight against the brigands in the woods, frightening as it was, didn't make me *feel* the effects. This did. Battle is real; it hurts. People bleed and die. I knew all that intellectually before, but now . . ." His voice trailed off thoughtfully.

White-bearded Umar was watching his pupil with a careful eye. "Many men shrink from combat after such an experience. Will that be so with you?" If Prince Ahmad lost his will to fight, it could spell the end of their mission.

But the prince shook his head. "I know some fights are necessary. We must always fight to defend ourselves and our honor, and we must always fight in the cause of Oromasd. But I think I'll choose my fights a little more carefully from now on. I'm responsible for the welfare of my soldiers; I must plan my campaigns so as few of them as possible will be injured."

Umar nodded with relief. His young student was maturing at a very rapid rate, and the priest was delighted with his progress. He was now more convinced than ever that Oromasd could not have made a better choice to lead the armies of mankind against the legions of Rimahn.

Princess Rida had sent a messenger back to Astaburya to relay the good news the instant the battle was over, and so the city was partially prepared to welcome them. The army's triumphant return was an occasion for the wildest celebration ever known in that simple mountain town. Many people, fearing the worst, had already fled early in the day, but there were still enough citizens left to drink down the city's stock of wine. Bonfires were lit around the walls, and the noise of the laughter and the revelry could be heard more than a parasang away through the still night air.

King Brundiyam himself led the celebration by singing a repertoire of bawdy drinking songs, many of which even Jafar al-Sharif had never heard, though he took great pains to memorize them as the king sang. The quantities of wine being passed around the royal table were truly prodigious, and by the early morning hours there was no one in the hall who could stand on his own feet. An enemy of Buryan could have attacked at that moment and caught the entire palace defenseless—but Buryan's only known enemy already lay in defeat that afternoon.

Now that the strain of what she'd thought would be a tragic defeat was lifted from her shoulders, the heretofore somber Princess Rida relaxed and enjoyed herself in the company of Prince Ahmad. Not only could the Buryani princess fight as well as a man, but she could drink like one, too. She and Prince Ahmad spent the night trading drinks and ribald stories, and talking about arms, armor, and the feel of battle. They had been raised with similar training and each regaled the other with incidents from their upbringing, although Prince Ahmad still kept secret the fact that he was of royal birth. The two young people laughed and joked until they passed out in one another's arms and lay entwined together on the floor, still wearing the heavy padded cotton garments they'd worn under their armor; Ahmad's injury was totally forgotten in the heat of the wine.

It seemed the only person who couldn't partake of the celebration was Selima, the poor phantom girl who, suffering from the wizard Akar's curse, could neither eat nor drink. She stood off in a corner watching everyone else drink themselves into a stupor, and particularly watching Prince Ahmad become such intimate friends with Princess Rida. Selima remembered all the quiet nights she and the prince had shared along the trail—but Prince Ahmad seemed to have forgotten them. Finally, unable to bear the sight any further, young Selima wandered off to another room where she lay down on the floor alone and sobbed herself to sleep.

And Leila watched Selima with knowing eyes, but kept her silence for the moment. As the celebration wore down, she and Jafar slipped away for a more private celebration—though she ended up spending most of the night holding Jafar and consoling him from the nightmares that followed the shock of his first killing.

The next day was spent recovering from the celebrations of the night before. Most of the Buryani court was ill from the wine they'd consumed; heads were aching, stomachs were queasy, and tempers were short for most of the day. Ahmad regretted his excess the most; the night spent on the hard floor had inflamed and stiffened his sore leg. Though Cari's spell had speeded the healing process, the blood loss and deep scarring still had to be overcome. Jafar al-Sharif was not feeling very well, either, and spent most of his time in the room he had been given, conferring with Cari and Leila about what to do next.

The first thing they did was pick up the handsomely bound journal of Ali Maimun, hoping it would give them some clue to their new destination. As always, though, the book remained stubbornly closed to them except for the pages they had already seen many times before. Jafar al-Sharif reluctantly put it aside and turned to his new treasure, the grimoire of Kharouf the yatu.

Since Cari could still read much faster than he could, Jafar asked her to skim through the book, looking for anything she thought might help them in their present circumstances. After an hour of careful perusal she looked up and said, "Here's a spell that might help you, O master."

Jafar al-Sharif took the book from her and looked where she was pointing. Kharouf's handwriting was far less precise than Ali Maimun's, which was the only one he was used to, and it took him a long time to make out what was written on the page amid ink stains and crossed-out words.

This was a spell to dramatically increase the speed and endurance of an ordinary horse. If certain ingredients were prepared with the proper procedure and incantations, and then mixed in with the horse's regular feed in the morning, the horse could run up to 150 parasangs a day, or less depending on how heavily it was laden. Considering all the traveling they had yet to do, this would be a miraculous time saver.

Jafar al-Sharif looked at the list of ingredients required. "We'll need cinnamon, pepper, and myrrh," he said aloud. "I'm sure King Brundiyam can supply us with those—but these others! The wing feathers of an eagle. The claws of a cheetah. Teeth of an orca. I've never heard of an orca, even in all the stories I've told!"

"I have," Leila said. "My mother told me about them when I was a girl. An orca is a monstrous black-and-white fish that swims off the coast of her native Norgeland. It's bigger than a fishing boat and it likes to follow the fleet, eating the fish they catch in their nets. Some of the Norgelanders hunt them with spears. They take the teeth and carve designs on them.

My mother had a little piece she showed me once. It was very beautiful and delicate."

"But how can we get all these exotic things?" Jafar wondered. "I'm sure even a rich king like Armandor doesn't have them on stock, let alone a poorer one like Brundiyam."

"Leave that to me, O master," Cari volunteered. "If you'll but give me your khanjar, I can sneak up on any cheetah in Fricaz or any eagle in its nest, kill them, and obtain the parts you need."

"The orca sounds like quite a job, though," Jafar said.

"For that I need only steal the teeth the Norgelanders use for carving. I won't endanger myself."

"But all this flying . . . to Fricaz, to Norgeland—"

"It's but the work of a day, O master. If I start now, I could return by nightfall."

"Very well," Jafar said, "but be careful. Don't take any unnecessary risks. Even if you can't find these things, we can still travel at our normal speed."

And Cari took off on her mission, secretly pleased that her master was so concerned for her welfare.

By late in the afternoon the worst effects of the night before were wearing off and people were returning to their normal dispositions. King Brundiyam ordered a banquet in honor of the heroic strangers who had saved his realm from the evil wizard. Because of the recent chaos the fare would be rather poor, but there would still be plenty of ham, chicken, and lamb, with the ever-present rice and many vegetable dishes and salads. Buryan was not a wealthy country, but they still knew how to treat honored guests properly.

Now that the threat to Buryan was over, King Brundiyam was more disposed to listen to Prince Ahmad's plea for military aid in the upcoming battle against the forces of Rimahn. The king was an honorable man, and though his army was not large, he offered it to Prince Ahmad as repayment of the debt he owed. The prince accepted the offer graciously, telling King Brundiyam where his army should rally with the others on the Leewahr Plains south of Ravan by the first thaw of next spring.

When the dinner was finished, as the guests were being escorted back to their rooms, Jafar al-Sharif walked over to Umar bin Ibrahim and asked if they could speak privately. Noting the troubled expression on Jafar's face, Umar agreed. The two men went to the priest's room, where no one would disturb them, and they sat down cross-legged on the floor to talk.

"I'm afraid I must consult you in your professional capacity," Jafar began. "Yesterday's events left me very disturbed. While I've been all over the world and seen and done many things with my sorcery, and while I've been in several feuds with other wizards, I've never before had to kill a man. It weighs heavily on my conscience. I know Kharouf was evil and that he'd long ago given his soul to Rimahn—but he was still a man, a creation of Oromasd. I'll have to answer for his death at the Bridge of Shinvar, and I'm worried I'll be deemed unworthy of the House of Song."

Umar gave him a reassuring smile. "The very fact that you feel this guilt is a good sign. A truly evil man would give it not a thought. But then, the prophet Muhmad wouldn't have chosen you for this mission if you weren't someone worthy to fulfill Oromasd's plan."

The priest spread his hands apart. "The fear you're feeling is one that's faced all soldiers from the beginning of time—how to reconcile the killing of the enemy with the divine law not to kill. There certainly is no easy answer, other than becoming a hermit and living apart from all men forever. I myself killed several brigands in the ambush in the woods, so my sins are many times yours. I know the moral dilemma you face, because I've dealt with it myself.

"For one thing, you must realize that the ultimate decision is not in your hands. The righteous Rashti stands at the Bridge of Shinvar, and it's he who makes the judgments on Oromasd's behalf. He is a stern judge, but fair, and he looks not just at the actions themselves, but at how you intended them. He sees your thoughts as well as your words and your deeds, and he judges you by all three standards. What were your thoughts when you killed Kharouf? Did you intend to commit an evil act for selfish purposes?"

Jafar considered his answer carefully. "No. Mostly I just wanted to keep him from killing me and stop him from using his army to conquer Buryan. I tried to avoid killing him, but he gave me no choice. It was either him or me."

"Then your thoughts, at least, were good, even if your deeds were technically a sin. You must remember that Rashti judges you on the entire span of your life. He takes all the thoughts, words, and deeds into account and weighs the good ones off against the bad. Oromasd knows no one is perfect, and he's infinitely forgiving. So long as the balance of your life is for the good, you'll be admitted to the House of Song.

"Besides," Umar added with a twinkle in his eye, "there's always the possibility your action was a good one rather than an evil one."

Jafar al-Sharif cocked his head and looked at him, perplexed. "I don't understand. How can murder be good?"

"Let's assume Kharouf had led a blameless and worthwhile life until a short while ago, and only recently fell under Rimahn's sway. Certainly if he continued on this current path he would end up in the Pits of Torment—but by cutting his life short, you may have done him a favor, since the balance of his life would still be good."

Jafar paused to consider that argument. "That's a dangerous game to play, O priest. Extending that reasoning to its conclusion, I'd be doing babies a favor if I murdered every infant I saw, since I'd prevent them from leading sinful lives."

Umar bin Ibrahim laughed. "Yes, theologians have a great deal of fun debating dubious premises—but there's still a serious point at the root of all that. You can't know what Kharouf's life was like before; you can only judge him by what you see him doing and hear him saying, and then you must act in the most righteous way you can. Leave the ultimate judging to Rashti. If you can keep to the path of good thoughts, good words, and good deeds and leave that path only when circumstances force you from it, you can trust to the goodness of Oromasd to see you safely to the House of Song. You can only be responsible for *your* salvation; other people ultimately take care of their own."

He looked deeply into Jafar's face. "Have I answered your questions?"

Jafar nodded. "I think so. If nothing else, you've given me plenty more to think about."

"Then go get some sleep," Umar told him as he raised his aged bones to stand up once more. "You'll have plenty of time for thinking along the trail."

Jafar al-Sharif returned to his room to find Cari waiting for him. All the necessary items for the spell were spread out beside the bed and Cari herself looked none the worse for wear. There was a troubled expression on her face, though, that worried him. "Is everything all right?" Jafar asked her. "Did you meet any trouble along the way?"

"No trouble," she said slowly. "It's just . . . When I was in Fricaz looking for a cheetah, I sensed a great deal of magic in the air. It was a little like a smell—or more precisely, a stink. Something is happening in Fricaz, something powerful and something bad. I didn't stop to investigate because I had my other task to do—but frankly, it scared me."

Jafar al-Sharif was thoughtful. "The prophet Muhmad told us Aeshma was on the move, and that we would need to counter him. That's what you may have been feeling. If so, it makes our mission all the more urgent. We may have great need of this spell before we're through. Come on, help me prepare for it. I'll need all the advice you can give me."

With the Jann's help, Jafar al-Sharif set about preparing this strange spell listed in Kharouf's grimoire. Cari flew through Astaburya until she found the shop of an ironsmith, where she took an unused brazier and left a dirham as payment. Then she went to the shop of a man who sold cooking implements, taking a brand new mortar and pestle and paying a handful of fals for it. Back in Jafar's room they set the brazier up in the center and mixed into it the articles called for by the spell: the eagle feathers, cheetah claws, and orca teeth Cari had gotten, plus pepper, cinnamon, and myrrh from the king's stores. After summoning up the feeling of power as he had the day before on the battlefield, Jafar mixed the items in the proper order and measured amounts, chanting incantations each step of the way as directed by the book. When all the ingredients were in the bowl and Jafar had spoken the magic words, the mixture sprang into flame of its own accord, so startling Jafar that he jumped backward and almost lost the concentration he needed to make the spell work. He recovered quickly, however, and continued bravely on with the process— though part of his mind was wondering what other surprises the spell might have for him.

The flame lasted only a few seconds, then flared out as suddenly as it had come. Left in the brazier was a pile of coarse, blackened ash. Transferring this residue to the mortar and pestle, Jafar al-Sharif ground it down to a very fine black powder, speaking more incantations as he worked. After half an hour of grinding, the powder looked as fine as it was going to get. Jafar announced the job finished. There was nothing more he could do tonight; the rest of the spell would have to be done in the morning when the horses were fed. Meanwhile, the working of even such basic magic had drained his energies more than he realized. He practically fell into his bed, and not even Leila could waken him until sunrise.

The next day was time to say farewell to their hosts. King Brundiyam generously filled out the travelers' depleted supplies and gave them copies of the best available maps for the region to the north and west of Buryan. Prince Ahmad spent a long time saying good-bye to Princess Rida. Selima was polite but formal, deliberately staying on the other side of the group from the prince.

Now was the moment of decision for Jafar al-Sharif and the spell he was attempting. He took a small handful of the powder he had made the night before and sprinkled it over the fodder they'd be giving the horses, all the while saying the incantation as listed in Kharouf's grimoire and summoning up the feeling of power within him. He continued to chant while the horses ate the food. When they were finished, he said, "Now we'll have to wait and see exactly how good a wizard Kharouf was. Sometimes wizards don't list every step of a spell in their grimoires for fear some rival may steal it. If Kharouf left something out, this probably won't work."

Jafar al-Sharif put the remainder of his magical powder in a leather pouch for later use, and the travelers walked their horses out past the main gate of Astaburya; they didn't want to run their horses at this incredible speed within the city's narrow streets. When they were out on the open road they remounted, and Prince Ahmad gave the signal for them to set out at a full gallop.

Kharouf's spell worked better than any of them expected. One moment the horses were standing still, and the next they were speeding across the countryside at a rate that took the travelers' breath away. The acceleration nearly knocked them from their saddles, and the fierce wind in their faces made them squint so severely they could scarcely see. Their supplies, which they had packed as carefully as ever, fell off the packhorse, and were left somewhere on the ground behind them. Only the insubstantial Selima, riding the packhorse, was unaffected by the great speed.

As the riding became unbearable, each rider made the individual decision to rein in his horse. Because of the horses' great speed, though, even slight differences in timing meant that the riders were separated by hundreds of cubits when they drew to a halt. They all dismounted and began walking

their horses back along their trail to retrieve the packs that had
fallen to the ground.

"It looks like the spell works too well," Leila said as they
all came within earshot of one another again. "I've never felt
anything like that wind in my face."

"We'll have to find some way to overcome our problems,
or stop using the spell," Umar agreed. "It's a shame, because it
could really help us on our travels—but we can't make any
progress like this."

"All great spells have their drawbacks," said Jafar al-Sharif.
"We just have to learn to cope with it."

As they picked up their gear that was scattered over the
ground for many cubits around, they discussed the problem.
The wind, they decided, could probably be dealt with by taking a trick from the Badawi of wrapping cloth tightly around
their faces so that only their eyes showed through narrow slits.
The people of the desert could travel even through heavy sand-
storms when their faces were protected this way; it should suf-
fice for the needs of Prince Ahmad and his party. Jafar showed
the wrapping method to Leila, who was unfamiliar with the
Badawi, and soon she was as adept at it as the rest of them.

Learning how to pack their gear upon the horses was a
more difficult problem to overcome. If they tied the bundles
too tight, the horses complained and chafed; if the bundles
were too loose, they fell off at high speeds. After spending all
morning and half the afternoon in experimentation, they finally realized that the decisive factor was the way the bundles
were arranged on the horses' backs. It was the wind, again,
pushing at the bundles, that made them fall off; if the bundles
were arranged in a way that offered minimal resistance to the
wind, they stayed on without being tied so tightly that they
injured the horses.

And yet another problem had to be solved before they
could continue. When they had been riding slowly, it was easy
to talk with one another and discuss the question of when to
stop for rest breaks or to make camp for the night. At these
magical speeds, however, speech between one rider and another was impossible; the wind would carry their words away
even if their faces weren't tightly wrapped and their voices
garbled—and if they didn't stop as a coordinated group, they
could end up scattered all over the landscape very quickly and
lose a great deal of time trying to find one another again.

They decided on a set of hand signals as the best way to deal with the problem. Prince Ahmad would be responsible for the major decisions of slowing down and stopping, and he would give the signals for those operations. Members of the party could relay other signals to him, such as danger warnings and requests to stop for a rest, but the prince alone had the authority to make commands. His would be the lead horse, and everyone would have to watch him for their cues.

By the time they'd finally worked out all the details, it was late afternoon, and they were almost tempted to return to Astaburya and start afresh tomorrow. Prince Ahmad finally decided, though, that they should push ahead, reasoning that any progress was better than none. They rode for only an hour before the gathering darkness compelled him to halt the ride for the day—but in that hour they traveled as far as they would have in one day of ordinary riding. Despite the initial problems, the travelers were pleased that Kharouf's spell would indeed help them on their mission.

Every morning Jafar al-Sharif gave the horses his magical powder mixed with their food, and the party traveled northwest toward the range of the Altai Mountains. Moving as quickly as they were, they ran beyond the edge of King Brundiyam's best maps by the second day of their journey. Even the maps provided by Muhmad and the priests of Sarafiq were of little help to them; most of the northern lands were unknown to Parsine mapmakers. The travelers resigned themselves to passing through large tracts of strange territory, but they were comforted by the fact that, with their horses able to run at these magical speeds, they could outrace most dangers they might encounter along the way.

The one thing no maps listed was the location of Varyu's castle, their next destination. The travelers only knew they had to head north toward the Altai Mountains and hope to find some clue that could direct them farther. Each morning Jafar al-Sharif would pick up the journal of Ali Maimun, hoping some previously sealed page would fall open and he could read a new section that would tell them more of what they needed. But for the first few days, the book remained stubbornly silent about their destination.

On their third morning out from Astaburya, as Jafar went almost listlessly through the now-familiar ritual of trying to elicit new information, the journal of Ali Maimun suddenly decided to cooperate, and opened to a new page farther back in the book than ever before. Jafar al-Sharif shivered with the unexpectedness of the act, then brought the book up to his face so he could better read the ancient script.

"Varyu's castle," Ali Maimun had written, "lies not upon the face of the earth, but in the sky well above Parsina's northernmost perimeter. It can be reached only by standing on the peak of Mount Nibo and summoning the djinni of the air to carry you to the castle gates."

When Jafar al-Sharif read those words, his heart went cold, for he had already had more dealings with the djinni of the air than he'd ever wanted. He recalled those tall, powerful Afrits playing with the magical carpet he rode upon—taunting him, despising him for intruding in their domain. Had there not been a protective spell placed around the rim of the carpet, they probably would have assaulted him and killed him; as it was, they used the air currents to knock him from his perch and steal the valuable carpet away.

How could he be expected to summon those powerful spirits to him, let alone control them and make them do his bidding? True, he had worked some minor spells with a great deal of assistance, but this was an entirely different manner. He'd seen these Afrits in action, he knew how dangerous and deadly they could be. He was more frightened of them than of anything else he'd ever seen.

After a moment the wave of panic passed and he opened his eyes—which he hadn't remembered closing—and read on in the journal, hoping it would give him further advice for dealing with those malicious djinni.

"Mount Nibo," the account continued, "is the northernmost peak in the Altai chain. Approaching it, as I did, from the east, there is only one way to reach its summit, and that requires passing through the city of the apes. I found that the city is best traversed during daylight hours, for the apes are vicious beasts, fiercely protective of their property—as indeed are many beastly men. I'd learned from my previous studies and travels that a man can become their king and bring them to his command by uttering the secret phrase, 'Sallah koda bin jemah,' but that of course brings hazards of its own which are best avoided."

Jafar al-Sharif came to the bottom of the page and tried to turn to the next, to read further about traveling to Varyu's castle—but the page would not turn. These tantalizing few sentences were all the book would tell him about the path to the citadel of the king of the wind.

Worried, he talked the situation over with Cari before mentioning it to anyone else. She had heard some talk about the yazata Varyu, and part of the rumor was that he did indeed live in a castle floating high above the earth, but she had never been there or known anyone who had. Visiting a yazata was not something one did casually. Nor could she offer any suggestions for dealing with the Afrits of the air, her distant cousins; she admitted they terrified her almost as much as they did him.

As for the city of the apes Ali Maimun mentioned, she had never heard of it. "Remember," she said, "Ali Maimun made his journey many centuries ago. Perhaps this city has vanished and the apes have all gone elsewhere. All things are possible with time."

Realizing there was nothing more he could do, Jafar al-Sharif told the others what he had read about their destination. Umar and Prince Ahmad continued to have a naive faith in Jafar's magical abilities to cope with the situation; Leila and Selima would follow Jafar no matter where he went; and Jafar himself knew he had to continue on this insane course if he wanted to save Selima's life. Therefore the group continued toward their destiny, with at least a slightly better knowledge of where they were going.

Even with Kharouf's spell to help them, they still took a great deal of time as they moved westward through the fields and forests of this high plateau region. Autumn had arrived in this part of Parsina as they reached the eastern base of the Altai Mountains and turned northward along the foothills. The weather now became an inhibiting factor in their travels. The winds, always fierce when traveling at their magical speeds, turned bitingly cold as well, and their thin summer clothes provided little protection. They had to slow down to avoid freezing, and eventually stopped at one town along their route to purchase fur coats to keep them warm—all except Selima, who could feel no cold, and Cari, who had her own magical protection against the elements.

The rain conspired with the wind to slow them down. The horses could run like lightning over solid ground, but moved slower over mud and ice. As they moved northward along the foothills of the Altai chain bordering the lands of Tatarry, they were beset by bitter storms of rain and sleet that slowed their passage still further. Sometimes they had to slow down just so they could see, as the sleet, driven by the great wind of their passage, got in their eyes and blinded them to what lay ahead. Some days they had to eat their food cold because it was impossible to find dry firewood. Other times, though, when there was a break in the storms, the air became crisp and fresh, invigorating to the lungs and body, and the travelers could see snow on the mountain peaks to their left as they moved northward.

Even to the companions who saw her every day, it was obvious that Selima was growing fainter with time. It was now almost impossible to see her in the dark, and her friends had to look closely to make out her form in the brightness of daylight. Selima had to speak more loudly than usual to make herself heard, and it was becoming readily apparent that time was working against them. The threat from Aeshma and the legions of Rimahn was simple to put out of mind, an intellectual menace that had little basis in their daily reality—but Selima's desperate plight was something that couldn't be easily ignored.

The hurt Selima had felt at Prince Ahmad's liaison with Princess Rida continued to eat at her soul. Intellectually she knew a prince would find a princess more desirable than a storyteller's daughter, but in her heart she still felt betrayed. She spent no more evenings sitting with Ahmad by the fire and reading, preferring to sleep in her tent alone. The prince was puzzled by her sudden coolness, but attributed it to her worsening condition and did not speak to her about the matter.

After more than a week of traveling at their magically accelerated pace, as the land around them turned to barren tundra, they reached the northern edge of the Altai chain and spotted a city nestled in the hills at the base of the peak that must have been Mount Nibo. From a distance it looked like many another city, with stone walls surrounding a cluster of houses and other buildings, but it was Umar bin Ibrahim who pointed out a crucial difference between this and most human cities—there were no minarets here with their flames eternally burning to symbolize the welcome of Oromasd. Either this was a city of men who did not worship Oromasd or, more likely, it was the city of the apes foretold by Ali Maimun's journal.

With sunlight shining upon it through the gathering clouds, it didn't look particularly foreboding, but the travelers well knew how deceiving appearances could be. Jafar recalled what Ali Maimun's journal had said, that the city was best traversed in the daytime, so the expedition came to a halt about a parasang away from the city and camped on level ground for the night. The wind, as though warning them not to visit, was particularly fierce that night, chilling the travelers to their skins, but the rain that was threatening held off and the cold air was dry.

Jafar al-Sharif spent the evening beside the fire with his two books, searching them for clues of what he should do next. The journal of Ali Maimun refused to open any further, giving him no more information than he already had. Kharouf's grimoire contained no mention of the city of the apes, nor did it have any advice for conjuring and controlling the Afrits of the air. Jafar would be totally on his own in dealing with both problems.

With daylight, the party set off toward the mysterious city. Jafar al-Sharif sent Cari on ahead to scout the area, and she reported back that the city appeared deserted. She couldn't tell whether all the apes had gone somewhere for the day or whether the city had been deserted for many years. The travelers would have to take what precautions they could and hope for the best.

They traveled on horseback up a rocky defile until the path became so treacherous that they had to dismount and lead their horses along the way. They moved single file between the high craggy rocks towering above them until, by early afternoon, they reached the city's walls. The sky was leaden and the first droplets of rain began to fall, with the promise of a torrent to follow shortly.

The gate was barred, but Cari flew inside and easily unfastened it so the travelers could enter. They passed the gate, leaving it open behind them, then remounted their horses and wandered down the central street of this strange settlement.

The houses and buildings on either side of them were crudely built, mostly stacks of rocks piled together with wooden timbers for ceilings and an opening in the front to serve as a door. The openings were lower than would have been seen in human dwellings, adding to the impression that these were the homes of subhuman creatures. Nonetheless, there was an order to the city that bespoke intelligence. If the builders were indeed apes, they were certainly smarter than any apes the travelers had heard about.

None of the houses was more than one story tall, and the open doorways made it look as though the inhabitants had just stepped out momentarily, to return at any second. The travelers rode quietly on their horses at normal speed, afraid to break the stillness and alarm the citizens, wherever they might be.

The rain was beginning to fall heavily now, beating down in large drops with increased frequency. As they came to a crossroads in the town, Prince Ahmad and Umar bin Ibrahim stopped to consult with Jafar al-Sharif.

"Exactly what are we supposed to do here?" Umar asked.

Jafar shrugged. "I don't know precisely. The journal merely says we must go through this city in order to reach the peak of Mount Nibo. Maybe there's a road on the other side of the town that leads up the mountain."

They continued along their way, but when they reached the far wall they confronted a sheer cliff rising hundreds of cubits above their heads. The escarpment was totally unscalable, and the town backed right up against it. Aside from returning out the gate they'd come in, there appeared to be no way of leaving the city or going up the mountain to its summit.

The group stopped dead in the middle of the street, staring at the impassable obstacle before them. They scanned the cliffs looking for some way around, but there was none. Ahead rose the mountain face; to either side were the crude houses, and beyond them were craggy jumbles of rock that looked equally forbidding.

It was Umar who finally voiced their disappointment aloud. "I guess we'll have to leave the city and try some other way. If there was a path here in Ali Maimun's time, it's vanished by now."

They reluctantly turned their horses around and were starting back toward the gate when Cari suddenly whispered to Jafar al-Sharif, "I sense danger, O master."

The storyteller was instantly tense. "The apes?" he asked.

"Yes," Cari replied, "plus a very human danger as well."

Jafar's hand instinctively reached for the hilt of his saif, and as though that were some kind of signal, danger exploded all around them. The air suddenly filled with the high-pitched shrieking of a thousand unhuman throats, an ululating wail that surrounded the travelers and echoed from the walls of the mountains. There was an indignant anger behind the sound,

and so piercing was its intensity that the travelers looked
around to find the cause of the noise.

In the craggy rocks overlooking the town on both sides
were the apes who lived in this city—thousands of them, with
fur of rusty brown and ugly faces staring at the humans with
uncontrollable fury. They averaged three-quarters the size of a
man with powerful muscles and sharp claws. As they shrieked
their anger down at the interlopers, they bared their teeth,
revealing sharp, white fangs that could rend a man's flesh.

But this was not the only menace here. Coincidental with
the appearance of the apes, a group of people popped up,
seemingly from nowhere, along the path leading back to the
gate. These other humans had swords drawn and murder in
their eyes as they ran toward Prince Ahmad and his party, their
blades slashing through the rainy air.

The apes stood on the rocks for a moment observing this
scene and shrieking, the sounds growing louder as their anger
built to a fever pitch. Then, as though on a single cue, they
bounded from their perches and came straight at the humans
in the street below them. With the apes coming from the sides
and behind, and with these strange swordsmen charging them
from the front, Prince Ahmad and his friends were caught in a
trap from which there appeared to be no escape.

4

The Secret Door

Abdel ibn Zaid, fanatical leader of the fearsome rimahniya assassins, led his band of rimahniya from the oasis of Sarafiq the morning after his discomfiting interview with the prophet Muhmad. Even though Muhmad had known ibn Zaid was stalking Prince Ahmad as a lion stalks an antelope, he had still been open about the prince's destination and itinerary. If what Muhmad had told him was true, the rimahniya had far to go to catch up with the prince and his entourage—and somehow, even though it would have been in the prophet's best interests to lie, Abdel ibn Zaid felt intuitively that the man had indeed told him the truth. He hated relying on his sworn enemy for help, but in a matter as important as this he couldn't afford to be proud; he'd take assistance wherever he found it.

The rimahniya crossed the fearsome Kholaj Desert, taking care of their horses but ignoring the hardship to themselves. Riding hard toward the east, they eventually reached the kingdom of Punjar. Even with all their fabled subtlety and ability to hide, the desolate land around that underground kingdom offered them little in the way of cover. They were captured in a fight with the Punjari soldiers—a fight that left one of the rimahniya dead—and were brought before King Zargov for interrogation. Their interview was much more favorable than the prince's had been, for when Zargov learned that the rimahniya's mission was to kill Ahmad, he was eager to help them. He was still smarting from the loss of his Crystal and his wife Leila (he was never sure from moment to moment which he valued more highly), and he let the intruders leave with his blessing. He wanted to give them the additional task of killing the wizard Jafar al-Sharif as well, but Abdel ibn Zaid said his oath to his employer precluded him from accepting any other commissions until Prince Ahmad was killed. He did, however, accept a rich pouchful of jewels and said he would be glad to kill this wizard once the prince was disposed of.

Even the rimahniya didn't know the exact location of Varyu's castle, but legend had it somewhere in the north. In that direction did the assassins ride, so rapidly that even though Prince Ahmad's group originally had a several-week head start on them, the rimahniya arrived at Astaburya just a few days after Prince Ahmad had left it. The town was full of stories about these marvelous travelers and the wonders they had performed in defeating the yatu Kharouf. Pretending to be old friends seeking to reunite with the prince, Abdel ibn Zaid and his people learned that their quarry had gone northward, aided by wizardry that enabled their horses to move at a magically fast rate.

This was frustrating news for the rimahniya. With the prince moving so quickly, and with the head start he already had, the rimahniya would have little, if any, chance to catch him simply by following his trail. Somehow they would have to find a method of either catching up all at once or else anticipating his moves and getting ahead of him to lie in ambush. But neither way would be easy.

Abdel ibn Zaid meditated on the problem for an entire night, and finally concluded that if Prince Ahmad was using magical assistance, the rimahniya would have to do the same. The rimahni priest was not himself a practitioner of those arts, but the rimahniya had wide connections among such circles and he knew of a wizard named Ptessen who lived not far from here. This yatu was by no means as powerful as either Akar or Kharouf, but he was devoted to the cause of Rimahn, which gave him access to resources that neither of the other men would have touched.

The rimahniya rode for three days and finally found Ptessen living in a simple wooden shack with a thatched roof, far removed from any town or possible neighbors. So entranced was the yatu by Rimahn's deception that he thought these accommodations palatial and did not choose to live in a wealthier style. The rimahniya, with their own disdain for luxury and comfort, saw no reason to enlighten him.

Abdel ibn Zaid introduced himself and was greeted with honor by this evil sorceror. He explained his problem in general terms and asked the yatu whether there was any way the rimahniya and their horses could be instantly transported to a spot near the prince's current location, where they might more easily kill him. Ptessen pondered the problem for some hours, consulting his books of spells, until he at last reported his findings.

"There is a way," he told ibn Zaid, "but it bears a high price."

"The rimahniya will pay whatever toll to cross the bridge that leads us to our goal," replied Abdel ibn Zaid.

"I can conjure the Marid Zarfun, and he will take you where you wish to go," Ptessen said, "but he is a particularly ravenous djinn and he dines exclusively on human flesh. Before he will take you anywhere, one of your people must serve as a sacrifice to appease his hunger."

"My followers will do what is needed to further the cause of Rimahn," Abdel ibn Zaid said staunchly.

He gathered his people together and explained the situation to them. They greeted the news with stony silence, and ibn Zaid knew then that he had chosen his companions wisely. These were people unafraid to lay down their lives in the furtherance of Rimahn's cause. He walked up and down their ranks inspecting them carefully, and finally chose one man to serve as the sacrifice. The man accepted his selection with stoic dedication, and Abdel ibn Zaid told Ptessen to proceed with his spell.

The yatu went about the task of gathering his herbs and amulets, setting braziers about the room burning the proper incense, and drawing mystic signs and symbols upon the bare stone floor of his hut. When, long past midnight, he had finished with these preliminaries, he gathered together with him all the rimahniya except the sacrificial victim, and the group stood within the perimeter of a large circle marked out upon the ground. The lone victim stood outside, chanting his dedication to Rimahn, his face glowing with fanatical devotion. He swayed slightly in rhythm to his prayers, awaiting his fate and prepared to do his duty on behalf of Rimahn.

As the room filled with smoke from the braziers, Ptessen waved his arms about his head and moved his fingers in a pattern seductive to watch. His voice started low, barely a whisper, as he began his incantations, but rose gradually until it was a roar that echoed back within the walls of his hut. An eerie breeze sprang up within the room, swirling around the circle and ruffling the clothes of the victim outside, while leaving the people inside the circle untouched. The smoke made the light from the lamps grow dim, and everything outside the circle became faint and indistinct.

Then came a sudden roar and a dazzlingly bright light erupting from the floor of the hut. Up from the ground came a blurry form taller than two men, like an enormous ox standing upright on its hind legs. Bathed as it was in this unearthly light, no man could look directly at it without squinting, and none could see it distinctly.

"Who dares summon Zarfun?" bellowed this ferocious creature in a voice that shook the very walls of the yatu's hut.

"It is I, Ptessen," the yatu replied in even tones. "I conjure thee to perform a service for these men who serve our mutual master, Rimahn."

"Zarfun is slave to no man!"

"It is not as slave that I conjure thee. We offer in payment of thy work the body and blood of our fellow who stands awaiting thy pleasure."

The Marid turned slowly and his glowing amber eyes beheld the assassin who stood outside the circle. With a sudden fierce cry that deafened all inside the hut, he fell upon his victim and tore away at the living flesh. The victim stood in stoic silence as his chest was ripped open by one of Zarfun's razor claws, nor did he cry out in pain as the Marid reached inside him and began pulling out his entrails. For a while the only sounds within the hut were of Zarfun chewing on the unfortunate assassin's flesh and cracking the bones with his powerful jaws. The other rimahniya looked on, displaying not a hint of emotion as they watched their comrade devoured by the fearsome djinn.

When Zarfun was finished with his meal, so that not even the least drop of blood was left to stain the floor, he turned back to the yatu who had summoned him. "What service need I render to these humans?" he asked, making even this concession sound bellicose.

It was time for Abdel ibn Zaid to speak up. His own eyes were glowing with the heat of this blood sacrifice, and his voice was in a state akin to holy rapture as he said, "You must take my people and myself and all our horses and our gear safely to within a few thousand cubits of wherever Prince Ahmad of Ravan and his followers are camped for the night. You must bring us there without detection, so we may fulfill our vow to kill him."

"As spoken, so shall it be done," Zarfun agreed. "I so
swear it in the name of our master Rimahn, lord of the lie."

Thus assured, Ptessen made a break in the perimeter of
the circle so the rimahniya could exit safely. The band of assassins went outside the hut and assembled their horses together in one place. The Marid Zarfun grew in size until he
was as big as a barn, but still indistinct in the dim starlight.
Bending down, he gathered the group of rimahniya and their
horses within his massive arms and lifted them all together into
the air. Without further word he took off, carrying his passengers northwest through the nighttime sky.

True to his promise the mighty djinn flew the rimahniya to
within a few thousand cubits of where the prince's party was
camped at the base of Mount Nibo—but even as fast as he flew,
morning had still dawned behind the heavy clouds by the time
he reached the site. Prince Ahmad and his companions were
already awake and packing their gear upon their horses for
the day's traveling—but instead of moving at the magical
speed allowed by Kharouf's spell, they were proceeding slowly
up a rocky path toward a city that lay nestled against the mountain itself.

Zarfun set his passengers down gently on the ground behind some rocks where Prince Ahmad's group could not see
them, and vanished without further word. The rimahniya were
once again alone with nought but their own skills to fulfill their
vows—but with their quarry well within range, that would
only be a matter of a short time.

Not wanting the sound of their horses' hooves to give
them away, Abdel ibn Zaid and his people left their steeds at
the base of the mountain and proceeded up the path on foot
after the prince's party. They moved so quietly that their
quarry did not hear them, and they passed through the gate
their prey had so conveniently left ajar for them. In such manner did the rimahniya enter the city of the apes.

Using the stealth for which they were justly famous, the
rimahniya crept through the silent city behind their prey, hiding in the spaces between the houses and taking care to be
neither seen nor heard. The cold drizzle that had begun to fall
helped conceal their movements. Moving from house to house
they followed the mounted party up the main street of the city
until they saw them reach a dead end facing the cliff wall. With
Prince Ahmad and his friends boxed in and having no chance

to escape, and with the rimahniya outnumbering their opponents so dramatically, this seemed the perfect time to attack.

At the same instant the apes appeared in the rocks around the city and the rain became torrential, Abdel ibn Zaid signaled his people to charge. The assassins leaped from their places of concealment and ran toward Prince Ahmad's party with their swords at the ready, confident of victory. So intent were they upon their mission that at first they scarcely even noticed the clamor and confusion caused by the apes; and even when they did, they did not slow their charge. They were determined to kill Prince Ahmad no matter what else was happening around them.

The apes swarmed down from the rocks, shrieking their ear-piercing ululations through the battering raindrops. They made no distinctions between the two groups of humans. All they saw was intruders within their city, and they were determined to protect their property at all costs. Assassin or prince, it made no difference to them; they would kill democratically.

As the vast numbers of apes closed in upon the people, they filled the gap between the prince's party and the rimahniya, preventing the assassins from getting nearer the prince. Using only their natural weapons of claws and teeth, they snarled and spat and ripped at the offending humans. The rimahniya as well as Prince Ahmad's group swung their swords furiously at their beastly attackers, but for each animal they killed there were four more eager to take its place.

Jafar al-Sharif was dazed by the abrupt change in their situation, one moment peaceful and the next a chaotic slaughterhouse. The rain clouded his vision as he swung his sword inexpertly with as much strength as he could manage, but an ape got through and bit savagely into his left leg. Cari killed the beast instantly, but even she was so beset she could do little to protect her master from all possible dangers.

The pain from the wound made everything seem as though seen through a filmy curtain. Jafar's sword arm moved by reflex to swing at the oncoming apes, and it was a major effort to lift it after each blow to prepare for the next. Selima was screaming something at him, but he couldn't hear a thing above the shrieking of the apes. He tried to force his mind away from fear, back into thinking; fighting with a sword was not his greatest talent, and he was at his best when figuring alternate solutions to a problem.

He remembered Ali Maimun's journal mentioning some phrase that, when called aloud, would make the apes subservient to the speaker's wishes. If it had been spoken to him he could have remembered it instantly, for he had excellent recall of anything he heard. Having only read the phrase silently, however, he had some trouble bringing it to mind, and the chaos about him did nothing to help his powers of recollection.

After a few moments, however, the phrase came back to him. Hoping he was pronouncing it properly, he yelled out as loudly as he could, "Sallah koda bin jemahl!"

Some of the nearer apes heard what he said and stopped abruptly in their attack to stare at him dumbfounded. He had to repeat himself several times, however, before the message reached the rest of the beasts. Then suddenly the scene in the rain was transformed as the creatures collectively stopped their attack and bowed to the ground in the direction of Jafar al-Sharif.

For a few moments the tableau was frozen with Jafar and his friends mounted on their horses, the rimahniya standing with their swords ready to strike, and the shaggy apes prostrate on the ground in obeisance to Jafar and his words of command. The rain stormed down, soaking everyone equally, and the only sound was the harsh panting of the horses and the beating of the raindrops on their bodies and on the ground.

Then the rimahniya, realizing they'd been given a reprieve from the apes, leaped forward toward their original goal of Prince Ahmad. Giving a hoarse battle cry, Abdel ibn Zaid charged once more at the prince's steed and was followed by the rest of his assassins. The clang of steel on steel was heard as Prince Ahmad and Umar tried to fend off the blows directed against them.

According to Ali Maimun's journal, the words he had spoken were supposed to give Jafar al-Sharif mastery over the apes, to make him their king. It was time to test his powers. "Apes, arise!" he called out. Then, pointing at the rimahniya, he shouted, "Spare my friends, but kill those people at once!"

As though of one body, the apes rose quickly to their feet and converged exclusively on the rimahniya. The assassins, realizing they would be killed before they could achieve their goal, decided retreat would be the better alternative for now. Turning back toward the front gate, the rimahniya slashed their way through the apes who swarmed around them in an angry mob. The assassins fought like demons as they cut a path through the hairy bodies that closed in on them from all sides, and such was their skill and daring that some of the assassins actually made it through.

They began running for the gate. Three of them slipped on the wet paving stones of the street, and the apes gave them no time to recover. The beasts were upon them in an instant, tearing at them with claws and teeth and killing them in a painful, bloody fashion that made Zarfun seem merciful. Several of the other rimahniya were too slow, and the pursuing apes caught up with them. Leaping on their backs, the apes knocked the assassins to the ground, where they killed them in an equally gruesome manner.

Of the original contingent, only Abdel ibn Zaid and four of his companions escaped the city alive, racing out the gate and down the precipitous road to the plain below. The apes pursued them only a short distance beyond the city walls, then turned back frustrated. Apparently they either could not or would not stray far from their city walls, even to obey the commands of their new king.

With the threat from the assassins now ended, the apes converged on the travelers once more. There was awe rather than anger in their manner this time as they crowded around Jafar al-Sharif and his horse. The rust-colored, long-haired apes peered out from heavy folds of skin around their faces. These "old men of the forest," as they sometimes were called by the few who ever saw them, were hideous primarily because of their resemblance to slovenly, jowly men. Some of the apes reached out hesitantly to touch Jafar, then shrank back at their own daring, as though he were some god who had descended into their midst. The other members of Jafar's party were all but ignored as the creatures concentrated their attention on Jafar al-Sharif.

"I don't know what you said to them," Leila commented, "but I wish I could find four words that'd work that well on people."

Jafar was too woozy from the pain of the bite in his left leg to respond in a joking manner. He nearly fell from his saddle as he called, "Cari!"

"At your side, O master."

"Can . . . can you heal my wounds?"

"Hearkening and obedience." Cari performed the spell she'd used before, and suddenly the wounds were healed as though they'd never been. Jafar felt as healthy as he had before the battle began and he thanked Cari, then asked if anyone else needed healing. Fortunately, though it had seemed to last an eternity, the battle had ended before any of the other members in the group had been wounded, so no one else required Cari's services.

With that problem attended to, Jafar looked over the crowd of apes who were now thronging around him and staring at him with adoring, obedient eyes. Never in all his life had Jafar been the object of such mass adoration, and he was unsure how to handle it. "What do I do with them now?" he asked Prince Ahmad.

The prince was smiling broadly. "It looks as though you've found your kingdom before I find mine, O wizard."

"It's not funny, Your Highness," Jafar growled. "I've never commanded a large number of subjects before. What do I tell them to do?"

The prince's grin narrowed but a little. "Well, we can't just sit here like this forever. We're tired and hungry, and our horses need care. Why not attend to first things first?"

Accordingly, Jafar al-Sharif commanded the apes to lead the travelers to a place where their horses could be cared for and where the people could eat and rest. They were guided to a large house off the main street. The horses were taken aside and, once their initial nervousness around the apes was overcome, were given water and such grains and forage as were available. The people were taken inside the house, out of the driving rain.

The building's interior was dark and dingy, but at least it was dry. A crude wooden table and some pallets of grass for sleeping were the only furnishings. There was no fireplace nor any facilities for cooking food; the apes apparently had not mastered the secrets of fire. They did clean up litter and soil, so the place was tolerably clean.

The food they brought the travelers was largely an assortment of fruit and nuts, with some raw meat from birds the apes had killed. Rather than light a fire indoors and smoke up the house's interior, the humans ate the fruit and nuts and supplemented it with some bread and dried meat from their own saddle pouches.

After the meal the three men left the house to look more closely at the bodies of the people who had attacked them. The apes had collected the bodies in one pile, apparently awaiting their new king's orders for disposing of them.

"Why should they attack us?" Jafar wondered as they approached the pile of bodies. "We've made some enemies along the way, it's true, but Kharouf is dead and this is awfully far from Punjar for King Zargov to send anyone after us."

"They might be brigands, seeing us as easy pickings," the prince commented.

But Umar bin Ibrahim was shaking his head. "They certainly didn't fight like ordinary brigands," he said, "and our small group doesn't look rich enough to attract such attention. Brigands prefer to attack the large caravans where there's a greater chance of reward in money and merchandise. These people were fighting to kill, not to rob."

They reached the pile of corpses sitting out in the rain, and knelt beside them to examine them more closely. The bodies were maimed and cut up from the apes' teeth and claws, making the men even more reluctant to touch them than they would normally be. They stared at the bodies for a few minutes, trying to deduce some clues from the nondescript clothing of the attackers.

Finally Umar spotted a detail that interested him—a medallion around the neck of one corpse. Pulling the chain gingerly over the body's head, he examined the design carefully in the fading afternoon light. The silver medallion was engraved on one side with an image of the fierce dragon daeva Azhi Dahaka, and on the other with mystic symbols and the phrase, "Great is the name of Rimahn, the source of power on earth."

Umar's hand clenched into a fist around the medallion as he read those words. "The rimahniya," he whispered. "They're after us."

Even though his voice had been soft, still his words reached Prince Ahmad and Jafar al-Sharif. The two younger men knew a moment of cold fear as they heard Umar mention the tribe of assassins. The rimahniya were legendary throughout Parsina, and many were the horrifying stories of their cold-blooded murders.

Prince Ahmad recovered his tongue first. "Why would the rimahniya want to kill us?" he asked.

"There can be only one reason, and its name is Shammara," Umar said with a shake of his head. "She must have learned you didn't die in the ambush as she'd planned, and she fears you may threaten her reign in Ravan. This isn't the first time she's tried such a thing."

"It isn't?" Prince Ahmad looked startled.

Umar bin Ibrahim looked at the young man sadly. "Forgive me, Your Highness, but there seemed no point in alarming you at the time. After your father's death, while you were being taught in the madrasa, the rimahniya made several attempts against you—all, we suspect, at Shammara's behest. Only our careful security within the Temple of the Faith saved you on those occasions, and several noble priests died on your behalf. When the recent theft of the urn of Aeshma occurred, my first thought was it might be another assassination attempt—but when the intruder went nowhere near your chambers I realized it was just an ordinary thief."

Prince Ahmad's face was stern. "This is the second time you've withheld information from me," he said coldly. "First the prophecy about my reign, and now this. Is there anything more I didn't know that I should?"

Umar bin Ibrahim looked abashedly at his feet. "I believe not, Your Highness."

"Good. Such surprises do little to improve my disposition on a day when my life has barely been spared." He stared at the bodies in the rain for a moment, then continued, "What is to be done about the rimahniya who escaped? Should we seek them out rather than wait for them to strike at us again?"

His advisor shrugged. "The rimahniya are renowned for their stealth and their ability to hide. Trying to hunt them down would be nearly impossible with our resources. I'm afraid there's little we can do, Your Highness, except remain alert at all times. Our mission is too important to stop now. We may try to hide our tracks a little better, though I doubt that'll have much effect. Better to go on as we've been doing, and hope that the difficulty of our journey will prove equally deterring to our enemies. They'll have to face the same hazards we do."

"I'll tell Cari to keep watch for them," Jafar said. "She's very sharp-sighted; now that she knows what to look for, she can probably give us advance warning of their attack." Although Prince Ahmad didn't like these answers, he could think of no alternatives and accepted them for the moment as the only practical solution.

At Umar's suggestion, Jafar had the apes place the bodies of the dead rimahniya high on one of the rock piles that towered over the city. It was not an official dahkma, but it served much the same purpose. The vultures and ravens were gathering even in the storm; the bodies would be picked clean of flesh within a few days. In view of the rimahniya's religious convictions, Umar did not feel a funeral service was called for. Their souls would assuredly be damned to the Pits of Torment, there to wait in agony until the final rehabilitation.

With the gathering of night, the men returned to the house they had been given and explained the situation to the others. Since there was no fire to make light within the building, there was nothing for them to do at night but sleep—and after the stresses of the day, that was all they were capable of, anyway. They were cold and soaked through to the skin, but they curled up on the crude pallets and fell into a fitful sleep marred by dreams of apes and assassins with long knives and evil leers.

Jafar al-Sharif awoke early in the morning to find himself surrounded by an assemblage of the apes, all staring intently at him with unreadable expressions on their faces. He raised himself up on his elbows and returned their stare, and this sudden motion startled them, causing them to back away slightly. Beside Jafar, Leila also stirred at his movements, then gasped as she came awake and saw the apes gathered around her. Then, remembering the events of the previous day, she relaxed once more.

As the rest of the party woke up slowly, the apes brought more food for their morning meal. When the people were done eating, the apes beckoned excitedly for Jafar al-Sharif to come outside the house. Curious, the storyteller followed them.

The rain had stopped sometime during the night. Though the sky was still heavy with thick, gray clouds, the morning sun found its way through and shone brightly on the scene in the street. But the scene itself stunned Jafar's mind and left even his glib tongue momentarily speechless.

Facing the doorway, crowded into every conceivable open space, were thousands upon thousands of the apes, more even than there'd been yesterday during the battle. They stood silently transfixed, watching the house where their new king was staying, and Jafar felt suddenly burdened with the collective weight of their stares. They were looking at him as though they expected something of great import to happen at any moment.

Feeling a speech of some sort was called for, Jafar cleared his throat and said, "The peace of Oromasd be upon you, O my . . . subjects. You've shown me and my companions great kindness and hospitality yesterday and today, and we're most grateful. I shall always treasure this memory."

The apes continued staring at him, a sea of furry faces unmoved and unmoving. Jafar al-Sharif began to feel distinctly uncomfortable, as though something specific was expected of him and he knew not what it was. "You certainly have a fine city here," he continued. "I can say without question it's the finest city built by apes I've ever seen in my life. You should be very proud of yourselves."

Again he was met by the solemn stares of the multitude. Jafar was running out of polite chatter; he had little in common with the apes and knew not what would interest them. In desperation he was about to begin a story, the fable of the monkey and the tiger, when one of the apes at the front of the assembly stepped forward and held out to him an object. Jafar saw to his surprise that it was a crown—crudely forged and asymmetrical, to be sure, but solid gold with a large ruby in the front.

Jafar's eyes went wide and he swallowed a gulp. "You flatter me," he said aloud, "but I cannot accept such a gift. I'm unworthy of your treasure. The kindness and the help you've given me are sufficient unto my needs."

This answer did not please the crowd, however. There were some angry glances and a few shrieks and snarls from the back of the assembly. From behind Jafar, Umar said, "They seem to be insulted. I suggest you take the crown to appease them. We're in no position to anger them."

Reluctantly, Jafar stepped forward toward the ape holding the crown. "Unworthy as I am, however, I shall accept your gracious offer until you find someone more noble and suitable for reigning over you."

He knelt on one knee and the leading ape stepped forward to stand in front of him. Gently the creature placed the crown on Jafar's head, and as he did so the throng of apes went wild with celebration. There were cheers and shrieks and claps, so loud that they echoed through the valley as though the mountains themselves were applauding the coronation.

When the ape who had crowned him stepped back once more, Jafar stood up and bowed to his subjects. "I will try to be the best king I can be," he promised, "for as long as my reign should last." It was his every intention to have the shortest reign in history.

Now that the ceremony was over, the crowd of apes began slowly to disperse. Jafar al-Sharif returned to the house and consulted with his companions. "Have you any ideas what we should do now?" he asked.

"Perhaps Your Majesty should set up court, appoint his wazirs, and take a queen from among his people," Leila laughed.

"And what apish consort could serve me better than thee?" Jafar retorted. "But I speak seriously. I never meant to be king of these apes. I only spoke those words to foil the rimahniya who would otherwise have killed us. I don't want to mislead these poor creatures into thinking I'll stay here forever as their king."

"The best thing we can do is be on our way as quickly as possible," Umar said. "Ask one of your subjects if he knows a way to reach the summit of Mount Nibo."

Jafar al-Sharif went outside the house. The few apes who were waiting in attendance for him bowed deeply in a parody of a salaam. When Jafar asked them about a way to reach the top of Mount Nibo, however, they became very agitated, shrieking and howling at the top of their voices and attracting the attention of others, who added to the cacophony.

Jafar retreated into the house. "Mount Nibo seems to be a sore subject with them," he told the others. "I don't think they're likely to help us."

"I know Ali Maimun's journal said we must go through this city to reach the peak," Prince Ahmad said, "but this appears to be a dead end. I think we'll have to leave the city and find another way around to the top. There must be more than one path up there."

They all agreed there was no other choice, so they made their preparations for leaving, gathered up their gear, and went outside to load up their horses once more. The apes in attendance watched them closely, but made no move to interfere. As the party mounted and began riding down the street toward the gate, however, these apes followed them, chattering after Jafar in a tongue no one could understand. More and more of their brethren joined them, until the procession became a parade of hundreds of apes, all following their newfound king. Jafar kept turning around to look at the growing numbers behind him. He chewed nervously on his lip, but said nothing.

As the travelers approached the gate, they could see a similar army of apes standing before them, blocking their path out of the city. Prince Ahmad, who was in the lead, pulled his horse Churash to within a few cubits of the mob, but they would not part for him and some of the apes began snarling in defiance. The prince stopped and looked back at Jafar. "I think you'd best come up here, O king, and have a word with your subjects."

Jafar rode to the front of the procession and affected his most imperious manner. "Clear a path for your sovereign, that I may go out the gate," he said.

The apes in front of him merely bared their teeth and snarled. A few of the ones in the back waved their claws in the air in threatening gestures.

"Maybe they're afraid I'm trying to steal their crown," Jafar said quietly to Prince Ahmad. "Maybe they'll let us go if I give it back to them."

He started to remove the crown from his head, but the prince grabbed his arm and stopped him before he could do so. "Removing that crown could be the final affront to them," he whispered harshly to Jafar. "Don't take it off, or we may all die on the spot."

"Ali Maimun's journal said the apes were fiercely protective of their property," Leila said. "Maybe that means their king, too. They don't want to let you go."

Jafar looked out at the sea of apish faces staring at him and decided on a course of prudence. "Let's go back to the house and discuss this further," he told his companions.

Turning his horse around, he announced to the crowd, "I was just testing you. I didn't really want to leave, after all. We're going back to the house you gave us, now. Please clear a path for me."

And this time the apes obeyed, moving out of the street leading back the way they had come so the horses could travel unimpeded. The travelers returned to the house they had slept in overnight, where they unpacked their horses again and went inside for a conference.

"I now see what Ali Maimun meant when he said that uttering those words would bring trouble of its own," Jafar said with a sigh. "The apes are determined to keep me here. I suppose it's flattering to be wanted so badly, but it's an honor I'd rather do without."

"There must be some way out," Selima said. "Can't Cari fly us to safety?"

"I could carry you out of here one at a time, O mistress," Cari said, "but I'm not strong enough to carry the horses. Wherever I set you down, you'd have to go on foot from there. Our journey is taking long enough already; I don't think the additional delay would be good for us."

"Not to mention we'd be easier prey for the rimahniya," Leila pointed out.

"Cari could set us down near a town where we could buy more horses," Umar said, "but that still wouldn't get us to the top of Mount Nibo or to Varyu's castle." He shook his head. "I think we must use that idea only as a final alternative. Let's try to think of something else instead."

"Why don't we sneak out the gate the same way we sneaked in?" Jafar suggested.

"They're alert to our plans," Prince Ahmad said. "They'll keep a guard posted at the gate to sound the alarm if we try anything. They're obviously very determined creatures."

"Then let me try," said Leila. "Since I'm not their king, they might not care if I leave. We can all go one at a time, leaving Jafar back here. Then when the rest of us are safely away, Cari can fly him over the walls to join us."

"Ali Maimun's journal said there was a way through this city," Selima spoke up. "We haven't really tried to find it yet. Even if we did sneak out the front gate, we'd still be without a path to the top of Mount Nibo. We're safe enough here for now. Let's at least spend some time looking for the answer Ali Maimun promised before we decide on some other way."

"She's right," Jafar said, supporting his daughter's position. "Oromasd has guided our steps this far and made sure the proper answer always appeared to us when it was needed. Let's have a little more faith in him. The apes don't threaten us unless we approach the gates and try to leave; maybe that's a sign from Oromasd that we're not supposed to go. I don't think the apes will stop us from exploring their city. Let's see what we can find here before we talk more of leaving."

The others agreed to this as the best plan under the circumstances, and so for the next two days the travelers split up into groups and set about exploring the city of the apes. For the most part they found the village depressingly uniform: crude, unpainted stone houses with low doorways and little if any furniture inside. For apes, this was a staggering achievement, but the humans still felt it was rather poor as a city.

The humans, as friends of the king, were allowed to wander through the settlement as they pleased, so long as they didn't go too close to the main gate. The apes ignored them, for the most part, but the travelers could find nothing in all this city that would help them in their quest to escape and reach Mount Nibo.

On the second day of their search, however, Prince Ahmad and Umar came to a high stone wall erected around an area that abutted the cliff face at the rear of the city. "Another wall," Umar mused aloud. "Aside from the one around the town itself, this is the only wall we've seen here. The apes don't generally fence things in. I wonder if it could be important."

There was a wide wooden gate in the wall, and Umar and the prince stepped toward it to investigate more closely. Suddenly, from behind buildings and around corners, four apes appeared, snarling at the men not to approach further. Umar and Prince Ahmad backed away respectfully, and the apes did not chase them—but the wall was the center of their thoughts on the way home.

"That's the only place other than the front gate where we've been forbidden to go," Prince Ahmad said. "There must be some significance to that."

Excited by the possibilities, they returned to the house that served as their headquarters. When their companions returned from their own explorations, the two men described what they had discovered. All agreed this was the most promising avenue of speculation they'd yet found, and that more investigation was needed.

Because of her ability to become invisible and intangible, Cari was chosen to make a surreptitious examination of the area and report back her findings. The young Jann was gone for half an hour, but when she returned she was beaming with good news.

"Behind the wall lies a large garden," she told the others. "It looks as though it was once well tended, but it hasn't been kept up lately; the trees are unpruned and the vines have gone wild. Weeds are everywhere. I flew through the garden, but found nothing exceptional until I came to the back wall, which is the face of the unscalable cliff. In this wall I found a wide iron door, and inscribed in the stone above it in plain Parsine was the legend, 'He who would reach Mount Nibo must open this door and walk the path beyond.' The writing of the inscription matches the hand of Ali Maimun in the journal. I passed beyond the solid door and found a dark tunnel leading through the mountain and upward. The tunnel is high enough and broad enough for people on horseback to pass along its length. I flew rapidly through the tunnel and came out at the far side, on a ledge that stands near the top of this mountain. There's no place else to go from there, but the journal did say you had to stand there and summon the Afrits of the air to take you to the castle of the king of the winds."

"It sounds like we've found our escape, then," Prince Ahmad said enthusiastically.

"But what about the apes standing guard?" Leila asked. "Cari could pass through because they couldn't see her; the rest of us, with our horses, make a formidable caravan. The alarm will spread quickly and they'll mass to stop us just as they did at the front gate."

"We'll have to plan a diversion for them," the prince admitted. "But with Jafar as their king, that shouldn't be hard. When we have them busy elsewhere, we can slip through this secret doorway and up the tunnel to Mount Nibo, where we rendezvous with the Afrits."

Jafar al-Sharif was silent. While the idea of escaping this city appealed to him, this particular method of doing so did not. The path beyond this hidden door led to a dead end. They would not be able to return to the city of the apes, or the beasts would surely kill them whether he was their king or not.

That meant he would be called upon to summon the Afrits of the air and order them to do his bidding. Remembering those tall, malicious spirits and the way they had treated him, Jafar al-Sharif grew frightened. This time it certainly appeared as though Oromasd had planted an obstacle in his path that he couldn't overcome.

5

The Prophet's Doom

The day Abdel ibn Zaid and his rimahniya followers left the oasis at Sarafiq, the prophet Muhmad gathered his most senior acolytes together in his private-audience chamber. All the men wore face cloths over their noses and mouths so their breath would not accidentally pollute the Adaran fire that burned steadily behind the prophet. The frail old man who was Muhmad looked out upon a sea of white: white marble walls and floor, and white robed priests with white turbans and white face cloths. He looked into the eyes of these five men who had served him so faithfully over the years—and even though he knew that what he did was according to Oromasd's great plan, still he regretted having to tell them what they must now hear.

"The time has come," he said aloud, "for Sarafiq to die."

It was now that the proof of his training showed. Even though this news must have shocked the acolytes before him, they betrayed no expressions of surprise, and Muhmad was proud of them.

"We who have been its keepers and its servants," Muhmad continued, "must now preside over its dissolution, to ensure Sarafiq a dignified end as befits so holy a place. Our love and the love of Oromasd will reign here forever, long after the buildings and the walls are destroyed."

The acolytes knew better than to challenge Muhmad's authority. If he said a thing must be done, then it would be done. But still there were questions, and it was left to the youngest of the men—only in his early forties—to ask the major one.

He made a formal salaam to his master and said, "May a humble learner ask the cause of this action, that he might better understand the plan of Oromasd?"

"The springs that feed this oasis are drying up," Muhmad said, giving but the superficial reason. "Soon this place will be

62

as dead as the desert around it. I will direct you to a spot in the desert that is just coming into bloom, a spot that will serve as a nurturing oasis for many ages to come. There shall the emigrants from Sarafiq flourish even better than they've done here."

"Must we also abandon this shrine, this holy place?" the acolyte persisted.

"Without the life of the oasis around it, the shrine would be a mockery," Muhmad explained gently. "As Oromasd is the symbol and sustainer of life, so his shrines must be in the center of life. We shall deconsecrate this old shrine and in the new oasis you will build a new one, even more splendid than this. And when it is completed, a great mage will come to consecrate it for you—though I doubt he'll stay very long."

"Will you not come with us, O master?" another acolyte asked sadly, already guessing the answer.

"It is fitting that I should die with Sarafiq," replied Muhmad. "Now go and tell this news to the others. Tell it as a cause for rejoicing, not for tears. There are many preparations to be made, and I will give you a list later this afternoon."

And the acolytes left with the proper salaam and reverence, though in their hearts they were sad for they knew they were witnessing the passing of an era.

Muhmad, meanwhile, sat alone and contemplated the dancing flames of the Adaran fire. His life had been long and full, and each day brought with it new pains and new fatigues. But there was yet one more important duty he must perform for his lord Oromasd, one last vision he must impart. Once that was done, Muhmad could rest in peace, knowing that the great plan was proceeding exactly as Oromasd had intended it.

When the duel in the desert between Aeshma and Akar ended so abruptly, sending Aeshma and Hakem Rafi fleeing southward into Fricaz to begin their new plans of conquest, the blind sorcerer Akar had existed in the form of a tower of black flame standing amid the burning ruins of Hakem Rafi's palatial home. Though the wizard's manifestation was glowing brightly, his strength and power were almost spent. The battle with the king of the daevas had so drained his energies that there was little enough left to keep him alive. Though he would never have admitted it, Akar was grateful to Hakem Rafi for calling off the fight when he did and fleeing the scene of the battle.

When he could no longer feel Aeshma's presence nearby, the wizard from the north transformed himself once more, this time into the shape of a tiny black beetle, a form so small it would conserve what feeble energies he had left to him. As the blazing inferno raged around him, he dug into the sand of the courtyard and there lay safely buried while the fire consumed every brick, stone, and structure of the palace, obliterating once and for all the last monument to the greatness of the one-time emperor Rashwenath.

For three weeks Akar lay buried beneath the earth. He did not eat or drink, he barely even breathed. All his feeble energy and all his attention were concentrated on restoring his power so he could move again. Simple survival required the full effort of his mind and body.

After three weeks in the sand Akar felt recovered enough to stir from his hiding place. He was hungry and thirsty, but part of his training as a wizard had required extensive fasting to control his body, and he was quite used to the sensation. Burrowing up to the surface of the ground once more, he transformed himself back into his normal shape.

Where once had been a magnificent palace the size of several cities, now was nothing but level ground leading naturally to the base of the nearby mountains. For parasangs around, the earth was covered by a layer of fine gray ash, all that remained of the once-mighty structure. Akar the wizard stood amid this desolation, weak from the loss of energy needed for even this simple transformation. After several minutes he summoned what little strength he had left and spoke a spell of power, and soon the shape of the mighty eagle who had originally borne him here came flying through the distant sky to land at his feet and carry him back to Shahdur Castle.

Akar mounted the eagle and together they flew northeast toward the Himali Mountains. The wizard brooded silently on his near-fatal encounter with Aeshma for the many hours of the flight. His dark trance made the aerial journey a piece of no time bracketed by his near defeat and his return home.

Once back in his mountaintop retreat, however, his spirits picked up enormously. His servants fed him and rubbed magical salves into his body, and he slept in his regular bed and recharged the energies his battle had so badly drained. After two days of recuperation he felt like his old self again, and was prepared to analyze more fully what had gone wrong with his carefully laid plans.

Simply stated, he had overestimated his own abilities. If he could have captured Aeshma before the daeva had been released from his imprisonment, he would have had no trouble controlling even so powerful a spirit. The spells upon the urn, added to his own arcane knowledge, would have seen to that.

But now the only thing holding Aeshma in check was his vow to that fool, Hakem Rafi—and Akar had scant hope that would last very long. Aeshma, even after all these centuries of imprisonment, was still more powerful than anything Akar had ever beheld. Extraordinary situations would call for extraordinary remedies.

For four weeks Akar remained secluded within his vast library, emerging only occasionally to eat or sleep. Hour upon hour would his magical servants read to him from the exhaustive collection of tomes he had spent a lifetime accumulating, as Akar searched for some spell, some key to power, that would enable him to conquer the daeva.

But all was for nought. Aeshma was the ultimate power of Rimahn upon the earth, and his abilities were limitless. Such unbridled power was unthinkable. There must be *some* way to control him, or he could never have been put inside that urn in the first place, much less held there—but how could it be done? That answer eluded Akar's most devious schemes.

At last, driven to the point of desperation, Akar realized he had only one place left to turn, a place he hated to contemplate: the shrine of Sarafiq. It was there, many years ago, that he had studied with the prophet Muhmad—and even in those days Muhmad was considered the wisest man in Parsina. It was also from there, these many years ago, that Akar had fled in anger and disgust, vowing he would never return. And all the while the gently smiling face of Muhmad had troubled his dreams over the intervening decades. Had the prophet known, even then, that Akar would return one day seeking the answer to this, the ultimate question of his life?

It took Akar two days to steel up his nerve to make the long and emotionally trying journey to Sarafiq. Finally, when he knew beyond question there was no other choice and he dared postpone the trip no longer, he summoned a team of Marids, four hideous djinni, and had them carry him through the air to the Kholaj Desert wherein lay the oasis of Sarafiq.

Out of some long-forgotten superstition or respect, he had the Marids set him down outside the white walls of the oasis and bid them wait for him there. On foot, as he had left it many years ago, the blind wizard approached the gates of Sarafiq, which lay open and inviting.

Akar could well remember how beautiful the shrine had looked in his youth, with its white alabaster walls rising pristine from the desolation of the Kholaj around it, with its well-tended gardens and its bustling bazaar filled with merchants and stopover caravans. There was always a bustle about the place that filled it with life and energy. Even after all his bitter disagreements with Muhmad, that still remained one of the fonder memories of his early years.

But now, sightless though he was, he could tell the shrine wasn't what it once had been. There was no groaning of camels, no hawking from merchants in the bazaars, no children running and playing—none of the sounds every important oasis spawned. There were, in fact, no sounds at all save the buzzing of a few stubborn insects. The once fragrant gardens were still there, but the scents were frail and dying as though untended for some time. There was no smell of people and sweat, merely the hot, dry air of the desert assailing his nostrils.

Using a stick to help find his way, Akar strode slowly through the open gates and down the main path into the sahn of the shrine. As long as Sarafiq had existed, there were students here to study and serve, and he kept expecting to be greeted by one of the acolytes who attended the prophet. He himself had once worked in that capacity, waiting on Muhmad and on the strangers who came here to seek the prophet's visions.

But no acolytes came to him, and the silence of the desert was the only greeting he received. He walked to the center of the sahn, his bewilderment growing with each step he took. When he reached the fauwara, he stopped and extended his senses, trying to solve the unexpected puzzle he'd been dealt in this holy place.

Then he felt it, a familiar presence not far away: the strong, unmistakable aura of his former master Muhmad. Even after all these years, the power and the light had not dimmed. If anything they seemed brighter than he remembered, and this annoyed Akar without his even realizing why.

Holding his stick proudly and determined to show no signs of weakness, Akar the wizard walked around the fauwara toward the spot where Muhmad was seated. He stopped a few cubits away from his mentor and waited. There was no sound of splashing water in the fountain. Had the fauwara been stopped along with all the other activity in this oasis?

Irritated at finding things so out of order, Akar gave but a brusque salaam as he said, "Greetings, O Muhmad."

"The peace of Oromasd be upon you, O Akar," replied the prophet. "As you can tell, I've been awaiting your arrival."

Still more annoyed at the old man's smugness, Akar said, "Why is Sarafiq so deserted? Have oases become so common in the Kholaj that people can abandon one at will?"

"I sent the people away," Muhmad explained quietly. "This spot will soon be worthless, but I guided the people to a new location where they'll prosper even more than they did here. The major caravans and Badawi tribes have all been informed of the move."

"But what of the shrine, of the religious power invested here?" Akar asked.

"Shrines are but buildings, and the power is within the believer, not in some stone walls. My power comes from Oromasd, and he can find me wherever I am."

"That was always the difference between us," Akar said. "I make my own power."

But the prophet shook his head, a gesture Akar couldn't see. "You only borrow your power, and from sources less honest than mine. You've yet to learn there are only two sources of power in the world, Oromasd and Rimahn, equally balanced. All power comes from one or the other, or—since they're brothers split from the same parent—from some combination of the two. You create nothing that was not ultimately derived from them."

Akar's anger flared as he remembered how Muhmad had always belittled his accomplishments. But for now he decided not to argue the philosophical point; knowing his old teacher, they could have debated for weeks with no clear resolution of the matter. "Wherever the power comes from, I control it, bend it to my will, use it to establish a system of order. That's certainly better than letting it flow through you and disappear for no good reason, as you do."

"Yet with all your control, you come to me for advice," the prophet said with no little irony.

Akar was reminded anew of why he'd left the shrine so angrily, vowing never to return. Muhmad was always so infuriatingly right that it made the sorcerer tremble with rage. "You must know Aeshma's been freed from his imprisonment," he said. "As a devoted follower of Oromasd, this must worry you."

"Only in the short term. I know that Oromasd will ultimately defeat Rimahn and proclaim a new age for men."

"But in the meantime, many will suffer and die if Aeshma's fury isn't held in check."

When the prophet did not reply, Akar pressed his point home. "I've investigated this matter, and it seems Aeshma is being controlled by a petty thief named Hakem Rafi, who has bound the daeva to him by oath. That state of affairs can't last much longer, and then Aeshma will be free to ravage Parsina."

"The daevas cannot be destroyed until the end of the world, at the Final Battle. Neither you nor I can change that."

"But Aeshma may be controlled for the good of mankind. He was controlled before, when he was placed in his urn. If we could discover some way of harnessing his power, we could turn a force of evil into good."

Muhmad shifted slightly in his seated position, and there was an amused tone to his voice when he spoke. "And how would you use this unheard of power? What would you do with it?"

Is he so caught up in his own importance that he fails to see how someone else could help the world? "You think I'd use it for my own selfish ends, don't you? But that's not the case. In my own way, which you never could tolerate, I care as much for justice and for the good of mankind as you do. I would use the power of Aeshma to establish the rule of order upon the earth. I would eliminate oppression, eliminate poverty, eliminate crime and war and destruction. No man would suffer except by his own actions. The world would live under one rule of perfect order, perfect justice, perfect peace."

"And that one rule would be your own, of course," the prophet said.

Is he afraid I'll become more powerful than he is? "I seek not power for the sake of power, but only for what it can do to help mankind," Akar insisted. "As I am the one who'd be controlling Aeshma, I naturally would be the one to administer the regime.

"But beyond that, I'm the perfect one to wield such power because I'm incorruptible. I've long since renounced the world of the flesh, so its temptations can't interest me. I've devoted my life to the pursuit and practical application of knowledge, free of emotional entanglements. I would be the impartial administrator, devoid of passion and prejudice—the perfect judge dispensing perfect justice."

"You would bring to the world order and rigor and discipline," Muhmad suggested.

"Exactly," Akar said. "You should agree with that, since Oromasd stands for the eternal order against Rimahn, the spirit of chaos. In that way I'd fulfill Oromasd's plan for the world. You must support me."

"I would, if men were the perfect beings Oromasd originally created," the prophet said. "But since men came to earth and were corrupted, they are as imperfect as anything else in the mortal world.

"I agree you could dispense law in perfect fairness—but imperfect people can't live under a perfect system, or they'll go mad. And justice goes far beyond a mere balance sheet of facts. Flawed people must be ruled more by compassion than by logic, more by intuition than by intellect. The wise king is not always the most impartial, but the most understanding of the ways and needs of his people.

"In your intellectual pursuit of knowledge you've abandoned the qualities of compassion, intuition, and understanding. The qualities that would make you the king you hope to be are the very ones you discarded years ago. Even with the best of intentions, you'd become a tyrant worse than the world has ever witnessed—and after your death, the world would fall into chaos once more. For that reason, I'll not give you the secret of how to control Aeshma—though you'd fail to understand it even if I did."

"Then there *is* a way," Akar said. That bit of knowledge alone made this entire trip worthwhile, even if the frustration of dealing with Muhmad enraged him time after time.

"Of course there is," the prophet chided him. "Do you think a beneficent god would give us a problem with no solution? The secret of controlling Aeshma lies along the same path it did before—through the Crystal of Oromasd."

"The Crystal of Oromasd!" Akar exclaimed, dismayed by his own shortsightedness. "Of course. I should have thought of that myself."

"Perhaps you would have, if Oromasd had been more in your thoughts," Muhmad commented gently. It saddened him that his brightest student should have fallen so far short of his potential—but he reminded himself that even failures were part of Oromasd's great plan.

Akar paid no attention to the old man's gibe. "The Crystal was broken into four pieces by Ali Maimun," he muttered, beginning his new set of schemes. "I must find where those pieces are and gather them together for my use, before it's too late to stop Aeshma."

"Another man is already about that task, a mage known as Jafar al-Sharif. It is he, not you, who will collect the four pieces."

Akar stopped his plotting at the mention of Jafar's name. Merely thinking of the storyteller who'd outwitted him set him shaking with anger. "You call him a mage? Did he fool you too, then? The man's an arrant fraud, and a dangerous one. He lies and steals and skulks about in shadows with no respect for any man's property. He's as evil as any of Rimahn's minions. His clever tongue speaks nothing but deceit, and his mind has no purpose but to betray the hospitality of his host. He has no power of his own, just what he can steal from others. He could never control something as powerful as the Crystal of Oromasd."

"That is true," Muhmad said agreeably. "But he is none-theless the one who will gather the four pieces."

"Then I must take them from him," said Akar decisively. "I am the greatest wizard of our age, just as Ali Maimun was the greatest of his. Only I can harness the power of the Crystal of Oromasd."

"You cannot."

More rage exploded in Akar at this simple statement of defiance. "What do you mean? You're senile, old man. You're old and feeble and impotent, and you think everyone must be as impotent as you. But I'm just reaching the peak of my powers. With my knowledge, my strength, and the proper tools, there's nothing in Parsina I can't accomplish. I *will* control the Crystal of Oromasd, I *will* control Aeshma, and I *will* rule the world with my kingdom of order and justice."

Akar's tirade was met by silence for a moment. There were tears in the prophet's eyes, unseen by the blind wizard, at the tragedy of how badly Akar had perverted and misunderstood all Muhmad had taught him.

Then Muhmad spoke. The prophet's voice was soft and measured, a sharp contrast to the wizard's ranting—yet in the silence of the desert oasis each word rang with the clarity of a bell in the night.

"Though you asked not for my vision like most other men who come here, even so will I share that vision with you. Listen then, O Akar, to the vision Oromasd has granted me.

"All your dreams will end in despair and your empire will end in dust if you take the Crystal of Oromasd for your own purposes. Your wisdom and your strength won't aid you; in fact, your very knowledge and power will cause your destruction. Only the ignorant and well-meaning fraud Jafar al-Sharif can succeed where the vaunted intellectual Akar has failed. Such is the kismet Oromasd has decreed."

Akar's outrage flared at this final insult. How dare the old man presume to stand between Akar and Akar's appointed destiny? Muhmad must not succeed. He must be stopped forever from interfering in the affairs of his betters.

All the years of frustrated hatred for his teacher built within him, then directed itself outward toward the defenseless figure of the prophet sitting by the still fauwara. There were no visible manifestations of this power, but so piercing was it that Muhmad never spoke another word. The poison of Akar's hatred flew through him like a hard-thrown knife. The prophet gave a small sigh and fell over dead. But that was not enough revenge, and the power of Akar poured into the lifeless body until, at last, the corpse exploded into a shower of dust that rained onto the arid ground.

And still Akar's fury raged. Large cracks split the walls of the shrine, and they collapsed like a child's mud castle along the riverside. "Enter here, O Marids," he called to his servants waiting beyond the oasis's walls. "Enter and raze this place to the ground. Let nothing remain to show the world where a foolish old man defied the greatest wizard of his age!"

And because Muhmad had already deconsecrated the shrine and extinguished the holy fires that burned there, the Marids could enter through the gates and carry out the destruction their master had decreed. Stone, tile, and alabaster were smashed to dust. Trees and flowers were uprooted and buried beneath piles of sand. The djinni obliterated Sarafiq from the face of Parsina as though it had never existed.

While his minions worked, Akar stood in contemplation. The cold fury of his anger was fading, now, but he felt no triumph in the destruction of his former mentor. Muhmad had known he would die and the shrine would be destroyed; why else would he have sent all the others away? Once again, even in death, he had flaunted his superiority at his student by making Akar behave in the way he'd prophesied.

But things would be different from now on. Akar was no man's puppet. He controlled his own destiny. Muhmad was but an old man who'd long outlived his time. He had given Akar the key to conquering Aeshma, but beyond that he'd been useless, spouting rubbish that made no sense to anyone who knew how the world really worked. Knowledge always prevailed over ignorance, just as Akar would certainly prevail over Aeshma and over that clever fraud, Jafar al-Sharif.

With the shrine of Sarafiq totally obliterated, Akar ordered the Marids to bear him up into the air. He would return now to Shahdur Castle high in the Himali Mountains, where he would plot his future efforts to gain the Crystal of Oromasd for himself. Then *he* would control the power of Aeshma, thus dominating the world with his perfect and just regime.

6

The Afrits of the Air

In the city of the apes, it was agreed among the travelers that they would attempt their escape through the hidden doorway the next morning, since the apes appeared most active at night and should be less willing to pursue them in daylight. A strategy was devised whereby the apes would be diverted and would not notice the travelers' escape until it was too late. Then the people retired to their beds to sleep as best they could before their ordeal in the morning.

Jafar al-Sharif, however, had a troubled night. When he was certain the others were asleep he summoned Cari the Jann to him and talked to her in whispered tones about his doubts and fears.

"I'm facing a predicament I can't talk my way out of," he admitted. "Once we go up that tunnel we can never return this way, or the apes will kill us. But the tunnel itself leads to a dead end. If I can't summon the Afrits of the air to carry us further, we'll be stranded on top of the mountain—and I don't know how to summon the Afrits. I couldn't find anything in either Ali Maimun's journal or in Kharouf's grimoire about them."

"You know how to summon me," Cari pointed out. "I'm a relative of the Afrits, though a distant one and less powerful."

"But for you I have the ring," Jafar said. "You *have* to come. How can I summon the Afrits?"

"The same way you work any magic—by using the strength of your will to control the forces you want to command."

As Jafar snorted doubtfully, the Jann continued. "I grant you it won't be easy. In my case, the wizard Akar put the power of his will permanently into a tool, that ring, and he inscribed it with my name. I'm bound to that ring, and simply by wearing it you can command me to your will.

"With the Afrits of the air, you'll have to go through the original effort Akar used to get me. Not knowing specific names for any of the Afrits will make it harder yet—but not impossible. You must draw up the feeling of power as you've done before and put out a general call. If you're commanding enough, the Afrits will come—if only to see who's impudent enough to call them."

Jafar found that thought less than comforting. "Are there spells or incantations I should use?"

"Spells and incantations are but tools to help you focus your attention," Cari told him. "A hammer is useful, but if you don't have one, you can find some other object to serve its purpose. A spell is handy, but you can improvise something that will do the same job if you have to. Do you think wizards waste their time memorizing millions of spells? They learn primarily how to control their will, and use that to control the forces of the magical realm."

"All right, even assuming I can summon the Afrits, how can I possibly make them do what I tell them?" Jafar moaned. "I can't improvise that. You saw how powerful they are, and how scornful they were of me when we rode on the carpet. I don't know which scares me worse—the thought that they won't come when I summon them, or the chance that they will!"

Cari thought quietly for some time before replying. "You must do what you'd do to make anyone obey you," she said at last. "Since you can't offer them a reward for their obedience, you must promise to punish them for their disobedience. You must make them fear the consequences of *not* obeying you more than they dislike the thought of obeying you."

"What could *I* ever do to punish them?"

"You have Achmet's staff of lightning that we found in the sand djinn's cave, and you know how to use it. In this region and at this time of year we're blessed with plenty of clouds to draw the lightning from. Afrits, as all djinni, are mortal. I don't suppose they'd relish the thought of being blasted by lightning; I know I wouldn't."

Jafar al-Sharif shook his head. "This is all very chancy, Cari. We're risking so much on something I know so little about."

"Did you know more about wizardry when you lied to me in the dungeons of Ravan, or when you bluffed my former master Akar? You have no choice now, just as you had none then.

You are on a mission of Oromasd; you must trust to his divine guidance to see you through the crisis."

"I suppose you're right," sighed Jafar. "But my faith would come much easier if I really knew what I was doing."

That night as he slept, Jafar woke Leila several times with his thrashing and moaning. She didn't need her gift of truth-seeing to know his fears, or the courage with which he'd face them. She was proud of loving this man; she hoped he'd be around to love far into the future.

In the morning, Jafar al-Sharif dressed in his cloak of invisibility, but did not say the magic word that would make him vanish. Instead, after wishing good luck to his companions, he stepped outside the house and called to his subjects. "I am going to make an important speech to all of you," he told them. "Follow me, and spread the word that all other residents of this fair community—everyone, from the youngest babe to the oldest ape who can still walk—are to come along."

With that, he started walking down the street away from the house where his friends were awaiting the results of his actions. As they had hoped, the apes who'd been guarding the house followed their king, leaving the people free to assemble their belongings and pack everything onto their horses. Then, with Cari acting as scout to make sure the pathway was clear, the group led their horses quietly down the crude, twisting lanes of the city of the apes.

They halted some distance from the entrance to the garden while Cari checked ahead of them. As they had feared, a pair of apes still stood guard there; they feared the travelers' escape more than they feared the displeasure of their new king. Making herself invisible, Cari flew to the two apes and hit them on the head with rocks, knocking them unconscious. With that barrier gone, the rest of the party quickly led their horses through the gate and into the tangled garden beyond the wall.

Cari's description of the garden had been generous. Weeds as tall as a man had sprouted up everywhere, all but obliterating the beautiful plants that had once flourished here. The tree branches overhead interlaced so densely it was impossible to see the sky through them. The ground was so overgrown with vines and covered with dead leaves it was close to impossible to pick a path through the brush. The air smelled of damp earth and moldering vegetation.

Carefully, following Cari's lead, the travelers pushed their way through the overgrowth until they reached the secret door that led to the mountain passage. Here, though, they encountered an unexpected problem. Cari, on her initial exploration, had simply passed through the solid steel of the door—but the others couldn't do that. There was no handle on the door, no latch, nothing by which the door could be pulled outward. Prince Ahmad and Umar bin Ibrahim tried pushing it inward, but it would not budge. Working from the other side, Cari used all her strength to push it outward, but again there were no results.

"The inscription makes it clear the door is supposed to be opened," Umar said, "but it doesn't say how to do it."

"If Jafar were here, he'd find the spell to do it," said the prince.

"We must have the door open *before* he gets here," Umar insisted. "The apes will be angry and frustrated when he vanishes, and this is bound to be one of the places they'll check. If we're trapped here, they'll kill us easily. We must find a way to open this door ourselves."

Leila was staring at the door thoughtfully. "The legend is inscribed in plain Parsine. The inscriber obviously thought there was no danger of the apes reading it, yet it's clear to any literate human. In a similar way, the door must be impossible for the apes to open, yet simple for people. What can people do that the apes can't?"

"We can make fire," Selima suggested.

"I don't see how fire could open a door," Prince Ahmad said. "This one's solid steel; we couldn't even burn it down."

"We must remember who set this door here," said Umar. "Ali Maimun was the greatest mage of his time. There must be some magical spell that will open the door for us. It must be simple enough for us to discover on our own, yet too complex for the apes to use."

"If we need a spell, why not simply talk to the door?" Leila asked.

"Talk to it?" Prince Ahmad was perplexed at this answer.

"Yes," Leila replied. "The apes understand what we say to them, but they can't speak themselves. They could never talk to the door or command it to open, yet it would be simple for any person with a tongue. Just asking the door to open would be easy for people, yet impossible for apes."

Deciding it was worth a try, Umar bin Ibrahim stood in front of the door. In his deepest voice, the one he normally reserved for religious services, he said, "In the name of blessed Oromasd, creator of the world and lord of all that is light and good, I command thee, O door, to open for us now."

For an instant, nothing happened. Then the ground shook slightly and, with a loud grating sound, the door swung outward on unseen hinges. Leila beamed proudly and Umar nodded to acknowledge the contribution she'd made. He and Ahmad were becoming more used to having her around, and more willing to admit she was a valued member of their party instead of just a piece of useless baggage they'd picked up in Punjar.

They guided the horses inside the entrance. Cari had spent part of the night gathering dry, resinous branches to use as torches, and had set them beside the doorway. She now used a simple spell she knew to light the torches quickly and provide them with light in the long, dark tunnel. When all was in readiness for their departure, Umar told the Jann, "Fly back now and bring your master to us so we can be free of this place." Cari nodded and flew off in search of Jafar al-Sharif.

The storyteller had led his subjects far away from both the house where the people had been staying and the garden through which they hoped to escape. As long as he did not go near the main gate, the apes were content to follow him placidly, and the throng grew as word spread that their king wished to speak to all of them at once. Jafar dared not look back over his shoulder for fear of how many hairy bodies he'd see trailing after him.

At last he came to a square area where four streets intersected, and decided this would be a good place to hold the crowd. He stood still here, and the apes gathered all around him, looking up at him expectantly with large, brown eyes and furry faces. In all four streets surrounding the intersection they gathered, a crowd so huge they blocked out all sight of the ground and extended to the limits of his sight. Never had Jafar al-Sharif spoken to so large an audience, but his enthusiasm was tempered by the knowledge that these were apes rather than people, and if he did anything wrong, they were just as likely to tear him limb from limb as applaud.

He cleared his throat and held up his hands for silence. Instantly the crowd obeyed, and the sea of apes became so still

Jafar could hear his own heartbeat. He had no idea what he was going to say to these creatures; he only knew he had to stall them long enough for his friends to escape through the secret door in the garden.

He decided, naturally enough, to tell them some stories. He started simply with the tale of Khardan the mountain lad and the three ladies of the forest. From there he progressed to the saga of al-Araq, and his voice picked up enthusiasm as the tale moved to its climax. As always in his storytelling he used his hands to gesticulate in broad gestures, emphasizing his dramatic points. The apes listened, enrapt. Jafar wondered whether it was his wonderful storytelling ability, or whether they were just politely sitting through what was to them some meaningless speech merely because their king requested it.

Jafar al-Sharif became so engrossed in his storytelling he almost forgot the real purpose of his being here. Storytelling was his life, his avocation, and it gave him the greatest joy in the world to be performing his tales, even before an audience of apes. As he spoke, the feeling of power built up inside him, bringing force to his voice and strength to his soul. The magic was part of him once again, the knowledge that he could make great things happen through the power of his craft.

He had just finished with al-Araq and started on the cycle of the hero Argun when he grew aware of Cari's invisible presence beside him. "We're ready now, O master," she whispered in his ear.

The interruption was like a physical jolt, sending a shiver through his entire body. The feeling of magic tried to flee him in an instant, but he grabbed tightly onto it and held it within his mind, knowing he would need it soon enough to summon and control the Afrits of the air. Raising his arms slightly so Cari could grab him easily, he uttered the magic word "Decibah," and vanished from the apes' sight. At the same time, Cari lifted him up into the air with her and flew him quickly back to the garden where the others were waiting beyond the threshold of the hidden door.

The apes at first were left blinking at their king's sudden disappearance. After a moment some of them snorted, and a few of the braver ones in the front rows moved forward to examine the spot where Jafar al-Sharif had but lately stood. When they could find no trace of him they started a keening wail that was picked up by more and more of their fellows, until soon the air in this mountain town reverberated with the unearthly cries of the forsaken apes.

Jafar al-Sharif could hear the wails even as Cari set him down at the entrance to the escape tunnel, and to him it was not so much a lament as a warning that he'd better be away from this place as fast as possible. He could see his friends mounted on their horses awaiting him, and he removed his cloak of invisibility so they could see he had arrived beside them. Taking the apes' crown from atop his head, he laid it gently on a tree branch just outside the garden door, for he did not want it said that he stole the treasure of the apes. Then he quickly mounted his own horse and Umar bin Ibrahim commanded the door to swing shut behind them, sealing them off forever from the city of the apes. From now on, for better or worse, their destiny was committed to the path ahead of them.

As Cari had said, the tunnel was high enough and broad enough for the travelers to ride single file on their mounts. The walls had been roughly carved from the native stone of the mountain, here and there glistening with condensed moisture. The light of the party's torches was muted in this tunnel, but after a while it seemed sufficient to illuminate the narrow world around them.

Prince Ahmad, riding Churash, took the lead, holding the reins of Selima's horse following behind him. Next came Umar bin Ibrahim, then Leila, and finally Jafar al-Sharif bringing up the rear.

"It seems I escaped one land of tunnels only to reach another," Leila commented, but no one answered her. Everyone was too aware of the dangers that lay ahead, and the group seemed content to ride in silence, with only the sound of the horses' hooves clopping on the stone floor to break the stillness of this age-old passage.

Jafar al-Sharif spent the time with his stomach tightening in knots as he anticipated the ordeal to come. The prince, Umar, and Leila had no idea what sort of beings they would soon be facing; he did. It was sheer lunacy to believe an untutored wizard could control such powerful forces—but then, it was lunacy to believe he could even have carried his impersonation this far with such success.

If lunacy was required, Jafar al-Sharif would howl with the wildest madman. He had just indulged in the delicate art of storytelling, and the feeling of *that* magic was still upon him.

He hadn't quite reached the ultimate fever pitch with the apes, perhaps because they were a different kind of audience and he couldn't read the cues of their body language—but he'd worked himself up close to the frenzy he would need to summon and command the Afrits.

Telling Cari to guide his horse for him, Jafar closed his eyes and looked inward, into his soul. He took the sand djinn's magical staff and clutched it so tightly his knuckles were white with the effort. He fed on the feeling within himself, letting it build like a desert dust storm, starting with some eddy currents and pulling in more and more wind until it eventually became a funnel cloud that darkened the entire sky. Jafar's spirit became the cloud, guiding its direction and speed, shaping its dimensions, nurturing it while nourishing himself from it at the same time.

The others in the group, seeing Jafar so intent on his meditations, said nothing to interrupt his thoughts. They knew how dependent they would be on him when they reached the end of the tunnel, and they allowed him his solitude.

Selima, too, was quiet and withdrawn as they rode. Although she had nothing physical to fear from the Afrits, she well remembered their power and disdain, and worried about the future of their expedition if her father couldn't perform this latest miracle.

Prince Ahmad would look back at her every now and then with a concerned look on his face. It was hard for him even to see her in the smoky torchlight, but her brooding melancholy was almost tangible. She had perplexed him greatly the last week or so, ever since they left Astaburya. The closeness that had been growing between the two of them along the trail seemed to have suddenly vanished, and he was at a loss to understand why. He wanted to ask her what the matter was, but he didn't even know how to describe the problem. He concentrated, instead, on leading the group forward and ignoring other problems for now.

The tunnel moved constantly upward, but at a gradual enough slope that it was no strain on the horses. It seemed to go straight for its entire length, yet they knew that was impossible, for the mountain was not wide enough that they could travel so long in a single direction and not emerge on the other side. Perhaps the path they followed was actually a very gentle spiral leading upwards within the mountain, or perhaps the mage Ali Maimun had blessed this passage with some magical qualities that made it appear straight. Whatever the cause, they rode for hour upon hour straight ahead and slightly upward, trusting blindly in the words of the ages-dead Ali Maimun to guide them to their destination.

Their eyes had become so used to the light from the torches that at first they failed even to notice the intrusion of daylight into the tunnel ahead of them. Eventually Prince Ahmad held up a hand to call them to a halt. He peered ahead, then dismounted, handed his torch back to Umar, and walked forward into the darkness. He was back a moment later with the news that they were reaching the end of their trek through the mountain, and the group continued on with new enthusiasm.

Within just a few minutes the encroaching light from the end of the tunnel was strong enough that they could see it even through the torchlight, and soon they could extinguish their smoky torches altogether and proceed by the daylight that filtered in. The tunnel broadened at this point, too, so they could even ride two abreast toward the opening.

At last the tunnel made a slight bend to the left and they came abruptly to the end. They found themselves in a wide-mouthed cavern high up the side of Mount Nibo. A chill wind gusted by them, freezing them even through their heavy garments. Looking out of the cavern, they could see only a dense fog that swirled through the air. Prince Ahmad dismounted again and walked to the lip of the opening, but looking down, he could see only the side of the mountain disappearing into the mists below him. Perhaps it was well he couldn't see all the way to the ground, for he had never been so high in all his life and the sight might have unnerved even as stalwart a young man as he.

For the first time in these many hours of riding, Jafar al-Sharif opened his eyes, but it was as though he were seeing another world quite different from the one the others were in. The power of his particular magic was swirling in him at a strength he'd never felt before, and even though he was frightened unto death at the prospect ahead of him, he knew what had to be done. Without a word to the others in the group, the storyteller dismounted and walked forward to the very lip of the cave opening, facing out into the late afternoon sun and the gathering clouds overhead.

Taking the massive wooden staff in his right hand, he held it up with his arms spread wide and began to chant to the open

skies. He knew not where the words came from; he only knew
they sounded correct.

> Come to me, O djinni.
> Come to me, O spirits of the air.
> Hear my voice, O Afrits,
> O you who dwell in the wind and weather.
> Hear the summons of Jafar al-Sharif.
> Hear the call of the southern mage.
> Gather round my mountain cavern,
> Gather round Mount Nibo's peak.
> Gather in your numbers beyond counting,
> Gather and hear the commands I speak.
> Through the air, I summon you.
> Through the sky, I summon you.
> Through the clouds, I summon you.
> Through the wind, I summon you.
> Gather now and hear the words
> Of Oromasd's mage who will command you.

He paused when he finished, but nothing appeared to
have happened. Undaunted, he repeated his incantation a second, and then a third time. With each repetition his voice grew
surer, the tone of command grew stronger and more au-
thoritative. Jafar's fear was gone, now, lost in the tones of the
spell he had invented. He was no longer just a storyteller; he
was no longer even just a man. He was Jafar al-Sharif, and he
was the magic personified. In that moment he became greater
than he was, and his power surged forth to bring the djinni to
him. He was Jafar al-Sharif, and his summons would not be
denied.

Slowly at first the gray mists outside the cave mouth began swirling in a more definitive pattern than they'd done before. Little pockets of fog and cloud coalesced and danced in
the air, separating themselves from the random pattern and
taking new shape, new substance. Except for Jafar al-Sharif,
who was too busy focusing his power to pay attention to such
trivial details, the travelers stared in wonder at the forms that
slowly appeared in the air before them.

The figures took shapes that might generously be called
manlike, but with bizarre distortions and odd angles that made
them look misshapen and deformed. Their bodies were composed all of sharp angles and corners, yet they had no distinct

edges to them; instead they blurred off into one another and into the general cloudy background. The figures ranged in height from a dozen cubits to well over a hundred, and were in constant motion, dancing in and out among each other so their numbers could never be easily estimated. There may have been twenty, there may have been fifty, there may even have been as many as a hundred of the djinni dancing in midair impatiently before the cave entrance.

One of the Afrits floated near the lip of the ledge where Jafar stood with his staff upraised. The djinn's eyes glowed like balls of red lightning set within the elongated parody of a human face. "Who dares to summon the Afrits of the air?" he roared in a voice like rolling thunder. His breath was an icy wind that threatened to blow the travelers right off their precarious perch.

But Jafar stood his ground. "It is I, Jafar al-Sharif, mage of the southern regions, who summons thee to my purpose."

"I know not the name of Jafar," said the Afrit, "but your features are familiar, O man."

"Whether you know my name is of little consequence," Jafar told him. "You will know it henceforth, and you will obey my wishes."

Another Afrit, one of the largest, swirled in front of the first. "The Afrits of the air bow to no man."

"Even Afrits must bow before the power of Oromasd," Jafar said calmly, "and it is he, the beneficent lord of all goodness and light, that commands your obedience."

"Now I recognize you," said the first Afrit, his voice howling like a windstorm in the desert. "You're the insignificant mortal who dared fly through our sky on that silly carpet. I remember you shaking and quivering in fear before us, and how easily you fell from your perch. Think you then that powerful Afrits will heed your commands when your only power is to make your knees knock together in dread?"

"When you saw me before I was weak, just recovering from a duel of sorcery with my enemy Akar," said the storyteller, refusing to yield in the battle of wills. "You see me now in greater strength, prepared to enforce my commands upon you."

Still the Afrits were not impressed. "Try thy best, O thou self-professed mage," sneered the second. "See thee how strong are the Afrits of the air, and how puny are human efforts to contain them."

Jafar al-Sharif did not speak a reply, but instead lifted his
magical staff even higher, now directly above his head. Silently
he focused his will through the finely carved wood, drawing on
the power inherent in the staff to work its magical effects. He
gazed at the clouds that filled the sky around Mount Nibo and,
through his rod, pulled the lightning from them as a physician
might extract a tooth.

Twin forks of lightning crackled through the mountain air,
striking the defiant Afrits who floated before the cave. There
was a blinding explosion and a peal of thunder that shook
Mount Nibo to its base. The very air crackled all around them,
and the travelers had to shut their eyes at the brightness of the
effect. When again they dared open them, the two defiant
djinni were gone, vanished as though they had never existed.

"So will it be for all who defy me, for I am the wizard Jafar
and no mere Afrit can disobey my will," Jafar bellowed in his
most powerful voice. "Hearken unto me now, O Afrits, and
heed my words carefully."

But the Afrits, terrified by this unexpected display of
power, did not want to listen. They wanted to escape. With a
speed that brought winds racing past the mountaintop, they
fled through the air away from the summit of Mount Nibo and
the sorcerer who would try to control them.

Jafar al-Sharif raised his staff once more. "In the name of
Oromasd," he intoned, "none who flee my service will survive
to torment others."

And the lightning forked out of the skies again, a dozen
streaks at a time. Now the bolts were all far away from the
cavern, striking down the most distant of the fleeing djinni.
The clouds rumbled so loudly with thunder that Jafar's voice
was drowned out in the general roar, as were the anguished
wails of the Afrits who realized they were trapped by the
power of this previously unknown wizard.

The remaining Afrits stopped their panicked flight and
quivered in the air before Mount Nibo, uncertain what they
should do. As more lightning forked around them, they slowly
retreated to the cavern and, with great reluctance, offered a
salaam to Jafar al-Sharif.

"Speak your wish, O wizard," said one of the Afrits in the
front, "and if it is within our power we shall grant it."

"You will carry me and my party and our horses and all our
gear to the castle of Varyu, king of the winds, where we shall
converse with him on a matter of utmost urgency."

"But the king of the winds does not deal with humans," one Afrit protested from the back row.

Jafar al-Sharif raised his staff once more and lightning again flashed through the skies as a warning, though none touched any of the remaining djinni.

"It's not your concern whether he'll deal with us," Jafar told the Afrits. "You shall merely take us to his castle. We'll handle matters from there. Now, will you obey my commands or must I use more persuasion?"

The Afrits of the air had had quite enough of Jafar's persuasion. Obediently they swooped down toward the mouth of the cavern, their large arms spread wide to envelop their passengers. Before Jafar or any of his companions could utter another word, they were taken by the Afrits from the lip of the cavern and spun out into the air with a drop of thousands of cubits below them.

7

The King of the Winds

The travelers were startled by the suddenness with which the Afrits obeyed Jafar's command. The spirits of the air grabbed them in arms that seemed little more than wisps of cloud and carried them off the ledge into open air. The instinctive fear of falling gripped all of them, even Jafar who'd thought he had the situation well under control. Selima could be carried because she was still seated on her horse; it whinnied in fright and tried to rear, as did the other horses, but it could gain no purchase on its hind legs—which only made it more frightened.

Though the Afrits were huge, they looked too insubstantial to carry the weight of a man, let alone a horse. They turned out to be soft and billowy, like being surrounded by cold, wet pillows. The group felt as though they were floating on a raft in the ocean of the sky, bobbing up and down on the waves of air currents as the djinni carried people and horses effortlessly toward their destination. As they drew away from Mount Nibo, the clouds around them parted and they could see down to the ground. Prince Ahmad, Umar, and Leila had never looked down from such a height, and were predictably nervous; Jafar, Selima, and Cari, who had all flown before, took the situation much more in stride.

The fact that the clouds had dissipated meant Jafar could no longer use his lightning if any of the Afrits changed their minds and became obstreperous again; if that happened, the powerful djinni would simply drop the people to ignominious death on the ground far below. Jafar was hoping his demonstration had been spectacular enough that the Afrits wouldn't question his authority further—at least not until they had delivered the travelers safely to Varyu's castle.

Further north and slightly to the west they flew, beyond the regions inhabited by men. The few farms and other signs of

habitation below them gradually disappeared, to be replaced
by large sheets of ice and snow covering the ground like a
chilly blanket. The upper air became quite frigid, and the travelers were shivering even inside the warm furs they had pur-
chased along their northwesterly trek.

Cari was not being carried by the Afrits, but rather flew
along with them under her own power. As they flew, she took
the time to edge toward Jafar and whisper in his ear so the
Afrits could not hear her. "I'm proud of you, O my master," she
said. "You handled the magic expertly, as though you'd been
born to it."

"Kismet is being kind to me," Jafar replied just as softly.
"It usually does that just before playing another nasty trick."

Off in the distance, their destination slowly came into
view. At first it appeared a mere speck in the otherwise clear
sky ahead, but as they neared it they could see it was a solid
structure floating unsupported in the open air, higher than the
top of any mountain known to man. Yet it was so strange a
structure that few mortal eyes had ever beheld its like.

The red rays of the sun low on the western horizon spar-
kled on the side of its crystalline walls, which took the light
and refracted it in many directions and colors. The walls all
stood together and yet did not appear connected, as though
joined just by a wish and a prayer. The entire edifice appeared
to be made of the same crystal material and looked as though it
should be transparent, but no one could see through. There
were towers upon towers, and turrets, and minarets, reaching
so tall that a man standing at its base would have to bend over
backward to see its very top. On the one hand it gave the appearance of a sturdy fortress; on the other, it appeared as flimsy
and ill constructed as a house made of playing cards.

It was to this remarkable fortress that the Afrits flew carrying their human and equine cargo. When they reached the
front doors, they descended to a patch of cloud that looked less
substantial than a fluffy ball of cotton—yet when the humans
and their horses were set upon it, the cloud felt spongy but
firm under their feet.

"We have brought you and your party here as you requested, O mighty wizard," said the Afrit who had carried
Jafar, as he made a salaam to the storyteller.

"You've performed your task commendably," said Jafar al-
Sharif. "You may now return to your fellows with my thanks
and my blessings."

The Afrits began spinning as though in one giant whirlwind, dancing around and around with one another so fast that
their individual features became a blur of gray clouds and
wisps of mist. This frenzied cyclone of activity whirled off to
the east, gradually disappearing from view and leaving the
travelers alone on another kind of ledge.

With the departure of the Afrits, the trance of power that
had held Jafar al-Sharif was broken. His body, which had been
erect and dignified, went suddenly limp, and he began coughing and gasping for breath. His mind was dizzy and he would
have collapsed onto the surface of the cloud had not Cari
quickly steadied him. The others, seeing his sudden change,
asked if they could help, but Jafar waved them off.

"It's but the aftereffect of a major spell," he said weakly.
"It sapped my strength, but I'll be all right soon."

Turning their attention back to the fortress, the group
faced a set of enormous doors the height of three tall men. The
material was of unknown origin; it was as smooth as the finest
crystal or glass, yet it had the fire of bright opal that changed
color with the light and the mood of the observer. As with the
hidden door in the city of the apes, there were no knobs or
latches on these doors, no way to open them from the outside.

The travelers stood for a moment, awed by the lofty structure before them and unsure what to do next. Finally Prince
Ahmad walked up to the huge doors and pounded on them
with his fist.

For a moment there was no response, and the people at
the doors could hear the echo of the prince's pounding spread
through the distant interior of the castle like a set of far-off
bells. The prince stopped his pounding and waited for the
echoes to die off. He was just about to try a second time when
the answer finally came.

A wind arose out of nowhere, rattling the walls of the castle until the entire structure trembled like a set of wind
chimes. Out of the chiming sound came a deceptively soft,
high-pitched voice saying, "Who dares disturb the peace in the
castle of Varyu, king of the winds?"

"I am Prince Ahmad of the Holy City of Ravan. With me
are the high priest Umar bin Ibrahim and Jafar al-Sharif, mage
of the southern regions," answered the prince in official tones
that would have done his heralds proud.

"Varyu knows you not," replied the soft wind-voice. "What
business have you before him?"

Umar bin Ibrahim dismounted and came to stand beside his prince. "We come on the highest business," he said. "We come on the business of the great lord Oromasd, creator of the world, before whom all must bow and pay reverence. As you would honor the name of Oromasd, so must you open your doors to us."

"Varyu does his reverence by performing the tasks Oromasd ordained for him," the wind-voice flowed evenly around them. "That does not include talking to mortals or welcoming them into his castle."

Emboldened by his recent success, Jafar al-Sharif gathered what little strength he had left and stepped forward toward the door, raising his staff upright over his head. "We ask politely but once. If you refuse us then, in Oromasd's name, we will take what we need."

At that the walls of the castle began to shake again, so strongly that the travelers thought surely the structure would collapse upon them. The shaking was not from fear, however, but from a deep, rumbling laughter that rolled through the clouds beneath them like a wave rolling to the shore. Little gusts of wind blew in all directions around the castle as the lord of this realm roared in merriment.

"Varyu bids you enter," whispered the wind-voice suddenly as the doors opened slowly inward. "Your beasts, however, must remain outside."

Wondering what new treacheries might lie in store for them, the travelers left their horses to stand on the solid cloud outside, and together they walked through the giant portals into the castle of the king of the winds.

Inside, the castle seemed to stretch forever upwards into the sky, with no ceiling in sight. The main entrance hall branched into dozens of diverging corridors, and all the walls were lined with mirrors that distorted shapes and perspectives. Breezes blew constantly up and down the hallways, bringing with them a myriad of conflicting scents: now the perfume of orangeblossoms, now the stink of pigs' urine, now the fragrance of freshly fried fish. The gusts blew at Cari's and Leila's hair, sending it billowing around their heads; Selima's hair was unaffected by the winds and remained as it had been, hanging straight down her back.

A deep bass voice enveloped them, billowing against the walls like the breezes themselves. "Do you think to frighten me with threats of lightning, O wizard?" roared the wind, so

loud the travelers had to cup their hands to their ears to avoid
being deafened by its sound. "Who do you think creates the
lightning you threw around so casually? It is I, Varyu, king of
the winds and master of the ruddy lights. You cannot touch me
with your threats, for I am a yazata and responsible only to
Oromasd."

"It is precisely for Oromasd's sake that we come," Umar
bin Ibrahim began, but he was not allowed to complete this
sentence.

"You who would call yourselves Oromasd's servants must
learn his true humility," bellowed the wind. "I have been appointed your teacher."

And suddenly a gale arose within the castle, a wind so
strong that no man could stand against it. It blew so fiercely it
lifted each of the travelers off the ground and carried them
down separate corridors, apart from one another. Then the
wind died again as abruptly as it had come, leaving only Selima
standing alone and unaffected in the front entry hall.

"You had no right to do that," she scolded the wind angrily. "We're honest and humble creatures serving Oromasd as
you yourself claim to do. You don't act like I expected a yazata
to behave."

"Yazatas don't live by human expectations," rumbled the
wind. "Oromasd made us all according to our separate natures,
and yazatas differ in their ways from men just as men differ
from fish. Do men live the way fish think they should?"

"A servant of Oromasd should be kind and generous,"
Selima insisted.

"The wind can be kind and generous," Varyu said. "It can
also be cruel and treacherous, as any sailor can tell you."

"But you were created by Oromasd to further his plan for
the world and the elimination of Rimahn. How can the god of
ultimate benevolence allow such harsh behavior?"

"Mankind is the primary tool of Oromasd in his battle with
Rimahn, yet cannot men be cruel and treacherous? Consis-
tency can't be maintained in an imperfect world, even by the
best of our lord's creations; everything becomes twisted by the
warp of Rimahn's hatred. Still, Oromasd has taken all of this
into account in his masterful plan, which is subtle beyond
human conception. Few mortals have seen even a glimpse of
its design, and no one but Oromasd himself knows its totality.
If at times I appear cruel and callous, rest assured it is all
within our lord's guidelines."

"But my father and the others . . ."

"If, as you insist, they are 'honest and humble creatures,' they will be unharmed by what befalls them. If not, however, we had best know it now. Along their path they will yet meet greater trials than I can devise, and they must be hardened like steel if they're to survive the tests—just as you must be by your own trial. Nothing can change that fact. It is kismet."

"You all talk so lightly of kismet, but it's poor people like me who get caught in its grip."

"It's best to talk lightly of the unavoidable, since to take it seriously is to go mad. Still, you have courage for one so small to speak to me thus, and I admire that. Don't stand in my entry chiding me like a village scold. Come into the heart of my castle and we can talk further of such important matters."

A doorway opened in the wall before her, where she had not even thought a door existed. From beyond, she could see a golden glow of light that dazzled her eyes with its soft radiance. Hesitantly Selima walked forward, knowing the wind couldn't harm her but still worried about the fate of her father and her friends.

When the wild wind that carried him down the castle corridors finally stopped, it deposited Jafar al-Sharif on the floor of a darkened room. Jafar lay still on the black floor, so weak from the aftereffects of his magic and the buffeting of the wind that he could barely move. After several minutes, with great effort, he pulled himself first to his knees and then unsteadily to his feet. There was light coming from somewhere, for he could look down and see his body quite plainly—but the source of that light was a mystery. About him was utter blackness; the ceiling, walls, and floor absorbed all light that reached them, reflecting nothing back to a human's eye. Brushing himself off and straightening his turban, Jafar wondered what trick fate and the wind would play on him next.

"Varyu!" he called, but there was no answer, and the walls around him deadened the sound of his voice as effectively as they deadened the light. In the distance he heard the faint tinkling of chimes blowing in the breeze—normally a comforting sound, but now the chimes mocked him from afar as though daring him to leave this eerie place.

With everything black around him he had no way to judge perspective or distance. He took tentative steps with his arms out before him like a blind beggar. After three steps he

touched something, and as he did so the room about him
changed dramatically.

He was standing at the head of a long banquet cloth whose
top was laden with succulent dishes: baked quail, curried
lamb, a whole roasted pig, mountains of pilau, dishes heaped
with steamed vegetables, sweet salads of cucumbers and oranges, bowls of flaky baklava and plates arrayed with fresh
fruits—enough food to feed an army. Around the edge of the
carpet sat people dressed in the richest of robes, wearing
enough jewels to make even King Zargov of Punjar jealous. In
the background a band of musicians played sweet, gentle music and a fountain splashed its cooling water in the durqa. The
air was rich with the smell of cooked food and exotic spices.

The people around the edge of the carpet looked up toward Jafar, but their faces were hidden in shadows. They beckoned him to join them, calling for him with cries of, "Come, O
Jafar al-Sharif. Come to us, O prince of storytellers. Liven our
meal and soothe our spirits with thy wondrous tales. Join our
number and share our food, and we shall ever be thine audience."

Jafar knew he could talk for days before these people and
never once lose their interest. They would feed him and honor
him and hang on his every syllable. Each story he told them
would be fresh to their ears. He could make them laugh and
cry at his choosing with the power of his tales. There need be
no more traveling, no more danger, no more desperately pretending to be something he wasn't. These people wanted *him*,
Jafar the storyteller, not some mock-mage with the answers to
all problems.

As though in a dream Jafar took a single step forward—
and as he did so the light changed and the shadows moved
from the faces of the banqueters. In this new light, Jafar could
see these were not men but daevas, hideous minions of the
dark lord Rimahn. Some had scaly skin, others were leprous,
others pallid and wormlike. Some had red eyes like glowing
embers, some had black eyes like wrinkled prunes, and others
had no eyes at all. Their noses were twisted and bent, their
mouths were lopsided, their teeth jagged and protruding.
Their beckoning hands were sharp, rending talons. There was
not a one that hadn't escaped from a madman's nightmare, and
they sat cross-legged on the floor before him, calling his name
and beckoning him on.

Jafar al-Sharif tried to step back, to turn and run from these monsters, but his legs were paralyzed. And still the daevas summoned him to join their hellish feast; but when Jafar looked back at the spread, he could see his initial impressions of the food were mistaken. The dishes were filled with living snakes and spiders, scorpions and beetles, writhing on the plates and trying to devour one another before the diners could devour them in turn. What at first looked like a whole roasted pig was now a dead human child that had been turned over a spit until the skin was burnt and crackling.

"Jafar al-Sharif, O greatest storyteller of the ages, come regale us with thy wit," the daevas insisted.

The paralysis broke all at once and Jafar al-Sharif stepped back from the banquet into the darkness once more, stumbling and falling to the floor in his eagerness to be away. The banquet vanished, and Jafar found himself confronting yet another strange sight.

His small, dark world was suddenly lined with mirrors, and he faced a legion of his own reflections lying alone on a black floor. Ten, fifteen, twenty images stared back into his face; it was impossible to tell how many there were, for when he turned to count them, he lost track of which was his starting point. An army of Jafars stared in confusion, wondering what to do and where to go to escape this madhouse.

Then, even as he watched, some of the images began to shimmer like reflections in a rippling pond. As they rippled, they became distorted; the features elongated or broadened, the eyes changed their shape, the ears sprouted out of the head, teeth protruded beyond the lips, the nose flattened against the face. Though the images would not hold still to be seen distinctly, they looked like demons in a parody of Jafar's body. These hideous, slavering creatures had a life of their own, for they moved in their mirrors whether Jafar moved or not. Slowly their arms raised and beckoned Jafar toward them. At the same time a gentle breeze wafted to his ears, bringing a sweet lilt of music and enticing him toward the images.

And yet it was not to these that Jafar looked, but to the other mirrors that were not rippling like a windblown lake— for they were showing scenes of even greater horror. There were visions of Jafar as he truly looked, but he was performing acts he had never before performed. In one mirror he stood gleefully torturing Aswad, the former dungeon master of

Ravan, in much the same way Aswad had tortured him; the Jafar in the mirror was grinning with undisguised delight at the other man's pain. In another mirror, Jafar was telling stories before a banquet of Durkhashi nobles while his late wife Amineh lay starving to death on a pallet in the background. Still another mirror showed Jafar making love to Leila, unconcerned, while behind him poor Selima burst into flames and screamed in pain. The mirrors showed the demon within him, the worst he could possibly be, and Jafar al-Sharif howled to witness the evil that was ever part of his soul.

Slowly Jafar's hand reached for the hizam at his waist and closed around the hilt of his khanjar. As in a dream he pulled it from its sheath and flung it with all his depleted strength at one of the mocking mirrors.

The mirror shattered as the blade hit it, exploding into a thousand pieces with an echoing blast that reverberated through the room. Beyond the shattered mirror was more blackness, a corridor as inky as the room had been when Jafar had first arrived.

Around him the demonic Jafars were laughing in ridicule, but Jafar paid them no heed. Stopping only to pick up his knife from the shards of the broken mirror on the black floor, he strode out of the mirrored room and into the corridor ahead.

Umar bin Ibrahim, meanwhile, found himself beside the altar in a golden temple, a temple so huge it dwarfed even the Temple of the Faith in Ravan. Behind him burned the Bahram fire of Oromasd and before him knelt a host of supplicants in ardent worship. Even as his priestly mind told him so many people could not approach the Bahram fire for fear of polluting it, the worshipers were chanting their earnest devotion.

"Lead us in prayer, O Umar," they cried. "Guide our souls and teach us from thy bounteous wisdom, and we will venerate thee as high priest of the greatest temple in all Parsina. Renew our faith, that we shall live forever in thy blessing."

Umar smiled and held up his hands in benediction. The worshipers before him moaned in ecstasy and swayed back and forth as the tide of their feelings swelled and caught them at its peak. A new chant began in an unfamiliar rhythm, the words low and indistinct, but its power built as the faith of the supplicants grew ever mightier. Umar bin Ibrahim leaned forward, trying to hear the words of this strange prayer.

As the chanting grew louder, Umar finally understood what the people were saying. "Renounce Oromasd, O blessed

Umar, and let us worship thee as our god. Thou art good and wise and righteous, and we will do thee homage as our lord and protector. We will obey thy commands and honor thy name, and thou shalt be a wonder unto our children. Become our god and all manner of earthly praise shall be thine."

And the people in the front row arose. Three of them came forward with a crown to place on Umar's head, while the others walked behind him and started pissing on the Bahram fire to extinguish it forever. And more people entered the temple bearing a sacrifice for the altar, a young calf that looked up at Umar with Ahmad's eyes. One of the congregation came forward, extending the handle of a silver knife for Umar to perform the sacrifice and bless their new worship.

In panic Umar turned and fled this blasphemous congregation to face a series of mirrors even as Jafar had done. He saw himself physically transformed into a horrible monster in some, while in others he witnessed his own capacity for monstrous behavior. In one mirror he saw himself conspiring with Shammara to betray Prince Ahmad; in another mirror he saw himself ignoring the pleas of the hungry and the dying so he could build a new and fancier temple; in yet another mirror he saw himself renouncing the priesthood altogether in exchange for a wealth of temporal luxuries.

Umar screwed his eyes shut and began to pray. "O blessed Oromasd, creator of light and all that is good, help me now to overcome the weaknesses in my soul. I know I am prone to weakness and capable of great evil because I am a creation of the physical world. But as I am also a creation of yours, I know there is the seed of good within me as well, and I may yet be saved if I nourish it and help it to blossom. Grant me the wisdom to nurture the divine goodness within my soul and turn my mind against the evil inside it." And his words echoed hollowly in the stillness of that mirrored room.

Prince Ahmad found himself on the pinnacle of a mountain at dawn, the glorious sun rising behind him amid high, silvery clouds. Below him were untold millions of people eagerly awaiting his coronation and the chance to proclaim themselves his loyal subjects. Upon his shoulders was a heavy cloth-of-silver cloak lined with silk and embroidered with pearls, while in his arms he cradled a silver scepter with a fist-sized diamond in its head. Up the mountainside, paced by solemn chanting, came a procession of priests, wazirs, and nobles, carrying lamps or swinging censers in time to their dignified gait. In the center of the procession was a beautiful young girl, no more than ten, carrying on a velvet cushion the crown that would symbolize his reign.

The procession stopped in front of him and the girl knelt at his feet. "Accept this crown, O mighty Ahmad, that forever after thou shalt be known as the greatest king of the greatest age of mankind."

Two priests took the crown from its pillow and Ahmad knelt so they could place it on his head.

But before they could do so, two figures were brought before him dressed in rags and weighed down with heavy iron chains. Ahmad looked into their faces and knew them to be Umar bin Ibrahim and Jafar al-Sharif. Though they did not open their mouths, the men's souls cried out to him through their eyes.

"Kill the traitors!" the crowd shouted up to him. "Kill these men who would lead you to your death, and by that act make yourself our immortal king."

Jafar and Umar were made to kneel before Ahmad, and a gleaming sword was placed in the prince's hand. The men waited, necks stretched, for the blow that would end their lives and begin Ahmad's reign.

Ahmad dropped the sword and fled this scene, as his friends had done, only to find himself facing the deadly mirrors. As the demon Ahmads grinned wickedly at him, he looked in other mirrors and saw himself commiting acts that shocked and horrified him. He saw himself taking the saddle pouch filled with treasure and stealing off in the night while his companions slept, leaving them to fend for themselves as best they could. He saw himself leading an army of brigands against unarmed villages, slaughtering the helpless men for their food and possessions, and carrying off the women for rape. He saw himself forming an alliance with Shammara, becoming her lover while he condemned his half-brother Haroun to the same grotesque tortures Haroun used on his slave girls.

"No," he whispered to himself. "These are impossible. I could never do these things."

And he thought he heard Umar's voice saying in his ear, "You are capable of these and worse, O my prince. Human beings are not *made* good; they must *choose* good for themselves. In that choice is your salvation."

Prince Ahmad Khaled bin Shunnar el-Ravani straightened his shoulders and looked forthrightly at the images before him.

"I refuse you," he said boldly. "I refuse you and all your implications. I am a prince ordained by Oromasd, not a traitor to forswear him." And as he spoke these words with regal conviction, the mirrors before him vanished, to be replaced by the black corridor leading away from this chamber of horrors.

Because Leila could discern the difference between truth and illusion, she was not as deeply affected as her companions were by the visions she saw when she reached her place of trial. She almost laughed out loud at the first vision, of herself as a queen with a harem of demon lovers, all competing with one another for the honor of pleasing her. Her mood became more somber, however, as she watched the dark side of her nature come to the fore—visions of her stealing Kharouf's grimoire and becoming a mighty sorceress to torment King Zargov with the myriad tortures she had devised for him over the past ten years; of her marrying Jafar but making him a laughingstock by sleeping with lecherous princes to further her own ambitions; of her aborting her own child to make a spell that would give her eternal beauty. Seeing past these illusions, she walked toward the exit and started down the twisting corridor.

But there were more illusions here, illusions that played on private fears. She saw visions of King Zargov's minions finding her and dragging her back to Punjar in chains; of herself being wounded in a rimahniya attack and being so badly disfigured that no man, especially Jafar, would find her desirable; of Selima dying and Jafar being so overwrought with grief that he blamed her and sent her away forever.

Although Leila was not deluded by these visions, they told her things about herself she would have preferred not to know. She didn't like having her fears and temptations displayed so openly; she hated even admitting she had any. She walked very slowly through the maze with a thoughtful look on her face and a worried mood within her soul.

When Umar bin Ibrahim opened his eyes again after his determined prayer, the mirrors that had reflected the demonic side of his soul were gone, and he faced instead a long corridor of blackness. But as he walked its twisted length, more mirrors appeared with scenes that were harder to ignore. There was his beloved Alhena bewailing his death, and killing herself out of grief just moments before the Khmeri priest arrived with Umar's letter. In another mirror he saw Shammara's minions burst into his house and drag Alhena to a dungeon call, where she was stripped naked, raped, and brutally tortured by the bestial guards. And in yet another mirror—the cruelest of all—he saw Alhena laughing at the news of her husband's death and cheerfully marrying his successor, Yusef bin Nard.

"I shall trust in the goodness of Oromasd," Umar bin Ibrahim repeated under his breath as he walked the corridors in Varyu's castle. "Whatever destiny is decreed, it is according to his divine plan for the salvation of the world. He shall calm my fears and be balm to my troubled mind, and he shall give me strength to continue in the face of hardship and adversity."

And by repeating his pledge of faith in the goodness of Oromasd, Umar bin Ibrahim found the courage to walk by these worst of his fears and emerge in a room in the center of Varyu's castle. A golden glow filled the air all about him, making him blink at its brightness, and Selima was there to welcome him joyously back to her company.

As Prince Ahmad walked the tortuous path through the maze of blackness and illusion, new mirrors lined his way and reflected his private fears and doubts. He saw himself in the cave of yet another sand Jinn, but this time he stumbled and the djinn was upon him, rending him limb from limb while Selima looked on in horror and disgust. He saw the great upcoming battle that Muhmad had foretold, with himself at the head of the united armies of mankind against the daevas—and he watched as the phantom Prince Ahmad made all the wrong decisions, leading his followers into the most disastrous route ever recorded in history, thus giving victory to Rimahn and the powers that dwelt in the darkness. And he saw himself standing helplessly by as poor, beautiful Selima faded into nothingness, a cry of anguish dying on her vanished lips.

Prince Ahmad grew angry as he witnessed these scenes— angry at the mirrors and at Varyu for showing them, and even angrier at himself for feeling these fears. He was a prince, a leader of men; if he gave in to fear and despair, then all who followed him were also lost. He had responsibilities. He couldn't let that happen. Each step he took became more forceful and made him more determined to overcome these obstacles until, unexpectedly, he turned a corner and marched into the brightness of the room with the golden glow, and suddenly had to shield his eyes from its beautiful glare.

As Jafar al-Sharif stepped into the black corridor beyond the mirrored room, still more mirrors awaited him—some showing true reflections, others showing false scenes with more demons. There were scenes of Jafar the storyteller being ridiculed by an audience that pelted him with stones and over-ripe fruit. There were scenes of Jafar the father standing help-lessly as his daughter Selima vanished into nothingness. There were scenes of Jafar the would-be wizard holding all four pieces of the Crystal of Oromasd and being unable to work their magic. Jafar trembled at these visions and took a shaky breath, wondering what he should do and frightened to take another step.

Then, remembering the story of Shiratz and the maze of Corniz, Jafar gazed down at his feet and followed the path of the black floor, rather than looking at the reflections about him. The path wound at jagged angles through the mirrored maze, doubling back on itself more often than it went straight—but it was a way to follow, and any direction, at this point, was better than standing still.

As he came around one sharp corner he saw another pair of feet standing on the path before him. Looking up, he saw Leila smiling at him. "I was wondering how long it would take you to get here," she said.

Jafar sighed with relief. "Was it as nightmarish for you as it was for me?" he asked.

Leila shook her head. "Remember, I can see when things are not what they appear. The mirrors amused me, nothing more. Here, let me show you the way out." She offered her hand and Jafar automatically reached out to take it.

The instant he gripped it, though, he knew something was wrong. Leila's skin felt as cold as a corpse, and there was a slimy texture to it that raised gooseflesh on his arm. He tried to pull his hand away, but Leila merely smiled and gripped his wrist so tightly he could not escape. As she pulled him toward her with a strength far beyond a woman's scope, her features began to change—just as had his own features in those de-monic mirrors. Fangs sprouted from her upper jaw, and long claws extended from her hands. Her body grew taller until she towered over Jafar, looking at him with hungry cat's eyes. A stray breeze brought the smell of carrion to Jafar's nostrils.

Reaching awkwardly with his free left hand, Jafar grabbed the hilt of his saif and pulled it from its scabbard. With an ungainly stroke he swung it at the false Leila who held him in her grip. The sword swished harmlessly through the creature as though it weren't there—but at the same time Jafar felt the grip on his right wrist suddenly dissolve. The creature turned to smoke, becoming as insubstantial even as Selima. The wisps of smoke lingered for a minute in the hallway before finally vanishing, leaving Jafar alone once more with the images around him.

Jafar al-Sharif stared ahead at the spot where the demon had stood, fear banging in his heart. He looked slowly down at the sword he still held clumsily in his left hand, as though not believing what had happened. Then, his paralysis breaking all at once, he ran down the path swinging his sword wildly before him with his left hand, uncaring who or what might stand in his way.

The corridor ended directly in front of him with another mirror, this one reflecting a wild-eyed Jafar waving a sword menacingly as it ran at him. Jafar paid it no heed, but plunged straight at the mirror with the sword crashing down at its twin reflection.

This mirror shattered like the other one, and Jafar al-Sharif was suddenly blinded by the golden glow that enveloped him. The light was like a physical blow after the blackness in those jagged corridors, and Jafar staggered for a moment before falling to his knees on the silvered floor of this brightly lit room.

"Father!" came a cry, and Jafar squinted through the light to see Selima rushing toward him. Fearing another false demon, he raised his arm and swung the heavy saif through the space where Selima stood. Fortunately at this moment she was her insubstantial self and the blade passed harmlessly through her, but she looked at her father in horror that he could do such a thing.

Jafar knelt on the floor, his mind too confused for a moment to realize what he'd done. Then, as the reality of his act sank in, his eyes widened in horror. He dropped the sword to the floor with a clatter and opened his arms to embrace his daughter, a futile gesture since he could not touch her.

"Selima!" he cried in anguish. "What have I done? Would that Oromasd pluck out my eyes rather than I should strike at thee."

After her initial shock, Selima realized her father must have undergone a great ordeal and had momentarily lost his mind. To comfort him she replied softly, "You've done no harm, Father. I'm still as far from the world of the living as I was before we came here." The true Leila, Umar, and Prince Ahmad also came over to comfort the anguished storyteller.

But Jafar al-Sharif was not to be so easily assuaged. He fell prostrate on the ground before Selima and rolled around in agony, moaning over and over again in words that were barely comprehensible. "O mighty lord Oromasd, ever beneficent and compassionate, forgive thy servant his trespasses against the natural laws of parental affection. Had my daughter been of flesh and blood at this moment I'd have killed her, and her murder would be on my head to be judged at the Bridge of Shinvar."

The booming laughter of Varyu filled the glowing room. "Is this the proud Jafar who threatened to take from me what I would not give him? Has he been sufficiently humbled to know the proper deference due a yazata?"

Slowly, his body still shaking, Jafar al-Sharif drew himself up onto his knees and made a deep salaam. "My most sincere and humble apologies, O king of the winds, O powerful yazata. It was my love for my daughter, and my desire to rid her of her hated curse, that made me so bold, and now it is my love for her that has humbled me again."

"Arise then, O Jafar, and regain thy human dignity. Thy sin was not so great and thy penance is genuine. Thou mayest yet achieve the House of Song."

In some ways Cari was the least affected of all by Varyu's trials, while in other ways she suffered deeply. As a creature of magic herself, even if not totally skilled, she could recognize the scent of sorcery and knew that, while the visions she saw might disturb her, they would cause her no physical harm. Still she could sense, by her link with the ring on Jafar's finger, that her master was in trouble and she should rush to his aid—yet the magic of Varyu came between them and prevented her from performing her bounden duty.

She didn't need the mirrors to envision all the horrible things that could happen to her master while she stood powerless to help him. Akar the wizard could materialize, his fearsome temper unchecked, determined to wreak vengeance upon the smooth-tongued rascal who had cheated him of his treasures. An army of rimahniya could descend upon the castle, slicing Jafar to ribbons with their razor-edged swords. Aeshma and his legion of the daevas could rise up and grab Jafar al-Sharif, casting the storyteller down into the Pits of Torment without even giving Rashti the chance to judge him at the Bridge of Shinvar. Cari stood and wept as these images and worse flashed before her and she could do nothing to stop them.

Then suddenly the paralysis left her and she was free to fly to her master's side once more. She flew with a great burst of speed, not even stopping first to wipe her tears, until she was in front of him once more in the hall of the golden glow. Kneeling before the man who wore her name-ring, she stared down at the ground by his feet and pleaded, "Forgive my failure, O master. I know my duty was to be with you and protect you, but Varyu's magic held me powerless. My failure is inexcusable, and my shame is as deep as my happiness at seeing you still alive and well."

Jafar al-Sharif held her chin in his right hand and tilted her head up so he could look straight into her eyes. His eyes were still red from his own tears. "Your sins are far less than mine, for mine were of my own causing. Yet Varyu has seen fit to forgive my trespasses; can I be any less generous than he? You've done nothing to be ashamed of, O Cari, and much to take pride in. Hold your head up and rejoice that we're still alive and still in Oromasd's service."

The travelers stood now in this room of light, chastened by what they had just seen but nonetheless determined to pursue their mission. By implicit mutual consent, the ordeals they'd undergone remained personal and private; none could bring himself to share such depths with his friends. Finally, after a long awkward silence, Jafar looked upward and said, "You have tested us severely, O mighty yazata, and I hope not found us lacking. We stand humbled in your presence, but still ardent in our devotion to Oromasd. Will you help us perform our mission in his name?"

"Explain this mission to me," Varyu said, his voice less hostile but still wary.

Despite his recent frights, and despite the weakness that was still upon him from performing his magic, Jafar al-Sharif gave a slight smile and launched into his full storytelling style. In flowing words and broad gestures he related their adventures to this date and explained that they needed the piece of the Crystal of Oromasd given to Varyu centuries ago by the great mage Ali Maimun.

The king of the winds was silent for some time after Jafar had finished his tale. Then, to the accompaniment of a slow breeze, Varyu said, "How may I know the truth of your story?"

"After what we've just endured, would we lie to you and test your wrath yet again?" Jafar asked.

"That you believe in your mission, I do not doubt," Varyu said. "The question remains whether that mission is indeed in Oromasd's plan."

"You may ask the prophet Muhmad," suggested Prince Ahmad.

"The prophet has passed the Bridge of Shinvar and is beyond casual conversation," Varyu announced.

This news shocked the travelers, even though they had known Muhmad was an old man. He had seemed so full of life when Jafar and Ahmad talked to him and received his visions for them that the thought of his death was alien to their minds.

When Jafar overcame his surprise, he said, "May he be sitting beside Oromasd in the House of Song even as we speak, and may his memory last among men until the end of time. But we have other proof we could offer you, O Varyu. The prophet Muhmad gave me the journal of Ali Maimun to help me on this quest, and I already have the first piece of the Crystal in my saddle pouch. I can get them and bring them for you to see, if you'd like."

"There's no need," Varyu replied. "I already know it's there. I merely wonder whether you are indeed the one destined to use it, and whether yon prince is the man to properly unite the armies of mankind and face the threat that is to come."

"The prophet Muhmad thought so," Leila said.

"But do *you* think so?" Varyu persisted. "Do you know the force against which you so casually align yourselves?"

The air above the people's heads began to swirl with fog, and in the mist another vision appeared. The travelers saw the continent of Fricaz, saw villages leveled to the ground and black-skinned people dying of famine and disease. And as the visions changed rapidly, they saw an army of men, stretching from horizon to horizon, marching in unison at the order of their lord. And as this vision faded, another took its place, the features of a bitter and hateful man. For the first time the travelers looked directly into the face of the enemy, Hakem Rafi.

"And this is but the army he has today," Varyu said. "By next spring, when your battle comes, he will have legions beyond counting, brave men who will fight with all their strength because they know the horrors that await them if they disobey.

"Nor is that all," the yazata continued, "for if the armies show signs of faltering, Aeshma will draw upon his subjects, the daevas, to defend the cause of Rimahn and destroy mankind. Know you the power they contain within their number?"

More visions swirled in the mists, and the travelers gasped in horror as they saw for the first time the incarnations of the daevas. There was Akah Manah smiling his gap-toothed grin, his eyes burning with maniacal fervor and his long, tapering claws eager to clasp some protesting enemy. There was bloated Saura, a heavy menace with sweating, warty skin and a cruel, sadistic laugh. There was the skeletal Pairimaiti, his twisted body a gross parody of the human form, his jaws slavering with unsated appetite for flesh. There was Nasu, a study in decomposition with her pale skin and her flaking hair and her breath blowing the stench of death. There was Jahi, the great harlot, with pointed tongue and painted face, and nails like an eagle's talons. And there was Aeshma himself, his evil, black face twisted with its eternal hatred for mankind, the creation of Oromasd.

And swarming around these figures were a host of lesser creatures—minor demons, djinni, spirits of all sizes, shapes, and colors who existed to torment mankind. All would rally to Aeshma's side, all would fight to destroy men and wipe Oromasd's creation from the face of Parsina.

As the travelers watched this scene in shocked horror, Varyu spoke again. "And this is what you challenge, this is what you so casually wish to fight. Can you look upon these visions and say you can triumph, with no fears or doubts to cloud your minds?"

There was a long silence, as none of the people dared answer immediately. Finally Jafar screwed up his courage to say, "We have fears and doubts, O yazata. That's part of being human. But I love my daughter, and must do what I can to save her. I also love Oromasd, and must do what I can to aid his great plan. We take our doubts and fears and conquer them, tame them to our needs. That's the divine spark that Oromasd placed within our souls, and that's why Oromasd's plan will ultimately defeat Rimahn. The lord of darkness can only create doubt and fear; man, with Oromasd's help, can overcome it."

"Well spoken," Varyu said. "If words alone could defeat Rimahn, I'd have no doubts of my own. You have not the look of heroes, except for Prince Ahmad and in him it glows but faintly. Still, this has been a lackluster age and you may well be the appropriate symbols of its end and a new beginning."

Down from the sky, a sky so bright that no ceiling could be seen, floated a glowing shape that could only be Varyu's piece of the Crystal of Oromasd. It wafted gently into Jafar's outstretched hands, and he clutched it firmly to his breast.

"I thank you, O beneficent Varyu, for trusting me with this object of power. I vow before you and Oromasd and all the Bounteous Immortals that I will never betray your trust."

"That's not my worry," said Varyu, "for should you even try you would be punished by a force much greater than my own."

And at this moment Cari's uncle Suleim sensed the momentous change on the magical web of the world as Jafar took possession of the second piece of the Crystal. True to the plan developed by him and the shaykh of the Righteous Jann, he commanded the army of these magical beings to place themselves between Varyu's castle and Fricaz and to perform their chaotic dance once more, so when Aeshma sensed the vibrations on the magical web and looked to find its source, he would see just the Righteous Jann and take no notice of greater activities beyond them.

Thus it was that Jafar al-Sharif acquired the second piece of the Crystal of Oromasd and the travelers completed the first half of their perilous mission. Though the visions Varyu had shown them filled them with fear, they nonetheless forced themselves to feel new hope—and in their future lay new challenges before their destinies could be fulfilled.

8

The Sea Invasion

Emperor Hakem Rafi—for so he had styled himself—now controlled the largest dominion ever assembled on the face of Parsina. From the northern seacoast of Fricaz almost to its southernmost tip, the fragmented tribes and nations were subservient to his wishes. In terms of land area it was the most far-reaching empire; in terms of subjects governed, it was the most populous; in terms of potential wealth within its borders, it was the richest; and in terms of time, it was the fastest empire ever conquered. Many men would have been content with owning a continent all to themselves.

But still, it was only Fricaz. And Hakem Rafi chafed.

He stalked restlessly through the corridors of the Tropil palace that formerly belonged to the Libayyan king. It was a magnificent structure of airy colonnades, beautiful gardens, splashing fountains, alabaster walls and polished marble floors—but after having lived in the palace of Rashwenath, Hakem Rafi found it tawdry and confining. He wanted Aeshma to build him a new palace even grander than the old one had been—assuming he could put it someplace where people could see it and appreciate both its splendor and the fact that it belonged to him alone.

"When are we going to capture some *real* land?" he asked Aeshma as servants kept the desert heat from him with long fans of peacock feathers. "I have all these barbarian villages and nothing to show for it except millions of black-skinned people who aren't good for anything but slaves in civilized countries. Libayy and Sudarr at least I've heard of—but when does the rest of the world get to hear of *me*?"

"Already the word is spreading," Aeshma tried to assure him. "Ships have fled from Tropil carrying word of Hakem Rafi the conqueror to other ports where people will marvel at the news of a sorcerer who conquered all of Fricaz."

"It's not the same thing," Hakem Rafi whined. "People must fear me and obey me. They must acknowledge me as their emperor and pay me taxes. How can they do that if I'm stuck way down here in Fricaz?"

"Plans are already under way, O my master. You have the largest army ever assembled since the time of Rashwenath himself. You have a solid base that no one can take from you, and now you can expand from here. Within a week your army will launch itself across the Central Sea and begin the invasion of Jibral."

"Jibral—another place at the end of nowhere. Why can't we conquer Nikhrash or Bann, or someplace important?"

Calling upon dwindling reserves of patience, Aeshma explained once again to his master the reasons for his conservative strategy. "While you remain in Fricaz, you are merely a curiosity. The instant your armies set foot in more civilized countries, you become a threat. If we go east around the border of the Central Sea and then north, we will divide Parsina down the middle. In one sense this might be good because it keeps everyone else from uniting against us—but for the most part it is bad, because then our enemies will come at us from all directions and we will have to fight on two fronts simultaneously. This way, instead, we can sweep quickly up the shore of the Western Sea all the way to Norgeland with little opposition, then press our way rapidly eastward, presenting always a solid front against our enemies."

"But you promised to make me master of the world, and it's taking so long."

"My powers, great as they are, are still limited. Take solace in your position. You are well fed, well housed, well cared for. You command the largest army in the world. Even now, no one can stand against you. Soon, when your armies have swept across the face of the world, no one will even dare. For now, you must gather your strength for the next conquests."

And as Aeshma spoke those last words, he snapped his fingers. Out of the perfume of the blossom-scented fountain, a trio of maidens began to form. Golden-skinned, they were, with hair of ivory hue flowing to their hips and slanted eyes the color of young leaves. One bore a basin of oils for massage; one carried a crystal vase of hashish blended with opium; the third bore Hakem Rafi's favorite pipe. Clad only in their floating hair, they walked out of the fountain toward their master.

"Go then, Aeshma, and see to the preparations," said the thief. "But first, fasten my silk ropes to the pillars of my bed."

"I hear and I obey," said the daeva king, and only a trace of his evil laughter was heard as he finished.

Lost in his lust, Hakem Rafi never heard it at all.

And even as Aeshma had said, the invasion plans were being implemented. A fleet of ships, the largest armada the world had ever seen—all built by Aeshma—lay in Tropil harbor. A thousand ships of differing sizes, but each holding between fifty and a hundred soldiers, plus their gear, horses, and supplies in addition to the normal ship's crew. So closely were the vessels crowded that a man could walk from one deck to the next all the way across the mouth of the harbor with hardly a fear of slipping into the water. The ships flew sails of many colors, turning the bay into a waving rainbow of brightly colored cloth, but they all flew the same flag—the flag bearing the personal symbol of their new emperor, Hakem Rafi.

Never in all the varied and colorful history of Tropil was there a day such as the one, eight days later, on which Hakem Rafi's armada was finally launched. From the first faint light of dawn until the tide went out shortly before sunset, men swarmed over the harbor like ants over a dead pigeon. There were endless streams of them in mass confusion, shouting orders, grunting at their burdens, cursing the stubborn animals—and, when they thought no one could overhear them, cursing their new emperor as well. The din was so monstrous it could be heard as far as a parasang inland, and the citizens of Tropil who would be staying behind could only marvel at the immensity of this undertaking. Those who spent any time thinking of such things could only shake their heads in despair at the future of mankind.

The armada, Hakem Rafi's fabled fleet of a thousand ships, sailed with the outgoing tide. No effort of this magnitude had ever been undertaken before—in large part because no one before in history could have afforded so many military vessels, and in part because it was hard to find that many skilled seamen who would serve in any king's navy. Many of the people in Hakem Rafi's own fleet, in fact, had little if any practical seafaring experience. But in this case, it did not matter. Aeshma would see to the ships' welfare. Aeshma would make certain the vessels arrived safely at their goal.

As the ships rode out of the harbor, Aeshma prepared himself for battle with the unpredictable king of the winds. As Oromasd's minion, the yazata Varyu could be expected to oppose this enterprise in a variety of methods both direct and subtle. Aeshma was prepared to cope with gales, hurricanes, waterspouts, treacherous cross breezes, or any of the hundreds of other tricks the wind has played on mariners since the beginning of time. The king of the daevas had an answer for each one of them, violence of his own to combat the violence of the wind.

Instead, he found the fleet becalmed in preternatural stillness. No breezes blew, no sails billowed, no flags flapped overhead. The air lay dead and muggy, and the breathing of both men and beasts was labored. The oppressive atmosphere weighed even more heavily on the spirits of the grumbling soldiers who didn't really want to be on this expedition in the first place.

Realizing this stillness was just another, if unexpected, form of resistance, Aeshma fought back against it. Diving under the water, he caused the ocean to rise up and form a giant tidal wave, which caught the fleet on its crest and carried it northward toward Jibral. The sudden surge created its own wind, startling sailors and steeds alike with its rapid motion. Aeshma did not care whether the passengers liked the journey. They were men, after all, the creations of Oromasd, and anything he could do to confound them was part of his ordained mission.

The armada, then, swept northward and west, riding the demonic tidal wave's crest, for three nights and three days, and yet another night, till on the fourth day Jibral's coast came in sight. The soldiers of Hakem Rafi's army were much heartened by the sight of land, even though it meant they would have to fight and possibly die, because at least it brought an end to their unearthly voyage atop the mammoth waves that could have sent them crashing and drowning at any moment. They preferred to face death on solid ground if they had to face it at all.

Jibral was a thriving seaport that lay at the southernmost tip of the long Espani Peninsula separating the Western and Central Seas. It owed much of its success to the fact that it was the closest point to Fricaz for the western portion of the civilized world, and as such it had become a major center of trade. Ships going between the Western and Central Seas also routinely stopped there—both for supplies, and because the Jibrali kings were known to attack and sink ships that passed within their jurisdiction without paying tribute.

Jibral was thus a pearl of high price, well worth the taking, and many wars had been fought over possession of this strategic point of land. Even more wars would have been fought there were it not for the freak fact of geography that let the fortified city of Jibral perch atop unscalable cliffs rising more than a hundred cubits above the narrow beach at their feet. Paths had been cut into the cliffs so there could be commerce between the town at the top and the docks at the bottom, but no invading army had ever successfully stormed up those paths to conquer the town. The only way to attack Jibral was to come over land down from the north, and the Jibrali kept that perimeter well guarded indeed.

Even on this morning, with the approach of an enormous tidal wave and a fleet of unparalleled proportions, the Jibrali did not panic. The army was called to duty to defend the cliffs, and a large contingent was set to guarding the northern walls in case some foolhardy invaders tried to sneak around that end. The common citizens gossiped and speculated, wondering at the nature of this armada that had appeared from nowhere.

Rumors had been coming out of Fricaz for weeks about this new conqueror and his supposed magical powers, and preparations had been made for just such an invasion. Supplies had been stored in case of a siege. Priests and wizards had both been consulted, and both had placed their particular protections on the town. Jibral was ringed with holy benedictions and mystical spells, making it as impervious to the minions of Rimahn as mortal beings could reasonably contrive. And as for their human foes, the Jibrali were content to rely on the defenses that had served them well for centuries.

The vast flotilla lay peacefully off the coast of Jibral for a day and a night without making any attempt at communication, without showing any gestures of hostility. All attempts the Jibrali made to signal them were ignored, and the Jibrali admirals were not so foolish as to attack a fleet that so vastly outnumbered their own. That first day was a war of nerves, a war easily won by the forces of Hakem Rafi and Aeshma.

On the second morning of the siege, Aeshma flew Hakem Rafi, who had been unwilling to risk his precious body to the rigors of a sea voyage, from the palace in Tropil to the coast of Jibral. There, the king of daevas made an image of his master thirty cubits tall so Hakem Rafi could confront his enemies directly. This giant image strode through the shallow waters just off the beach and stopped at the base of the cliffs. The army of Jibral rained rocks and boiling water down upon the image, but they bounced harmlessly away. Then the apparition spoke, in a voice that boomed clearly through the air to the people massed at the top of the cliffs.

"I am the Emperor Hakem Rafi, master of Fricaz and future king of all Parsina. Those who value their lives must bow to me and acknowledge my dominion over them. I am generous to all who accept me peacefully, but I annihilate all who oppose my destined rule. Let your king come forward and swear his allegiance to me, that Jibral may take its rightful place within my empire."

And the king of Jibral, adorned in sanctified robes and wearing powerful talismans about his neck, spoke bravely to the man who would usurp his kingdom. "The people of Jibral fear no upstart from Fricaz. We always have been and always will be free of foreign domination. Take your fleet and sail back to Fricaz, O monstrous pretender, for you'll find no conquest or glory here."

"This day will the people of Jibral curse your name forever," said Hakem Rafi, "for by your folly you lead them to slavery and death." And the magnified image of the black-hearted thief vanished from the view of men.

For five hours, nothing further happened. The people of Jibral grew more nervous by the minute, wondering what magical powers this wizard from Fricaz would bring to bear against their land. Many who had heretofore thought their town invincible began to doubt, and even those who still had faith questioned the wisdom of their king in defying the enemy so vehemently.

Then, as the sun sank midway between the zenith and the western horizon, the waters off the coast rose up as of their own accord in the form of a giant monster with salty eyes and fangs of foam. The monster lashed out with a mighty fist and pounded against the cliffs, so hard that buildings shook in the town of Jibral. Then the monster swung against the cliffs with its other fist, and more buildings shook. First with one hand, then with the other, the sea monster battered at the high cliffs of Jibral. The soldiers used catapults to hurl boulders at the creature, but the mightiest stones had no more effect on it than pebbles dropped into a pond. The Jibrali archers fired their arrows, which splashed into the water and then were seen no more. All the military might of this wealthy city was of no avail against the creature of the ocean that pounded mercilessly against the bluffs.

Slowly the cliffs began to crumble. First it was just a few rocks that fell here and there, but soon the pounding took a deeper toll. Tiny cracks appeared, then grew larger, then developed into fissures running the length of the cliffs. And still the ocean pounded relentlessly, the monster doing eons of damage in almost as many minutes. Hour upon hour the sea pounded and the ground shook, and the citizens of Jibral held their ears against the noise and prayed to Oromasd for relief from this oppression.

When no heavenly help appeared, the people of the high city, not wishing to see their cliffs reduced to rubble, took matters into their own hands. They stood trembling at the edge of the cliffs and offered as homage to Hakem Rafi the head of their now-deceased king. With this sacrifice, the pounding ceased, the surf subsided, and all became tranquil once more. At Aeshma's urging, a gentle tide swept the invading boats into the docks, where their crews quickly moored them and the soldiers clambered ashore, eternally grateful to have reached solid land again.

Hakem Rafi, in robes of the finest silk and dripping with gems of incomparable beauty, rode through the streets of Jibral in a gilded palanquin borne by four husky servants. The cheering of the people as they beheld their new emperor for the first time was unequaled in the history of Jibral—though many, perhaps, were merely cheering the fact that their lives and their city had been spared, rather than any change in temporal administration.

Hakem Rafi spent but a single day in Jibral, for he was anxious to renew his campaign of conquest. His troops gained little respite from their voyage before being asked to march outward from their new base to fight again in the name of their emperor. They grumbled about this fate, as troops have done since the invention of the army, but the rumblings of discontent were never so loud as to reach the ears of their commander, for they all knew how short was his temper and how severe were his punishments.

Joined by conscripts from the newly conquered army of Jibral, Hakem Rafi's forces marched northward up the Espani Peninsula, sweeping all before them with minimal resistance.

At first they encountered only small villages, where word of Jibral's fall had set the natives into panic. As was the case in Fricaz, these defenseless towns chose not to test the powers of the wizard who marched against them, but quickly surrendered and were absorbed into Hakem Rafi's rapidly growing empire. Their able-bodied men were taken into the army, swelling its ranks still further. It was an army that seldom fought, because it seldom had to; its sheer size intimidated opponents into surrender.

Progress became a little slower as they moved into the northern lands, because the nations there were more accustomed to wars and sieges. People took refuge within walled cities, and prayed fervently along with their priests for Oromasd's intervention against this evil invader.

But Oromasd's power was not infinite, and Rimahn's influence in the immediate region—personified by Aeshma—was stronger. Even magical blessings upon the walls of these cities did little good. With the help of the hairy demons, Aeshma blackened the land outside the walls to such a degree that the natives feared it might never be habitable again. When the catapults of Hakem Rafi's army began raining destruction within the walls as well, the townspeople reluctantly capitulated and opened their gates to the hideous conqueror from the south.

In such a manner, then, did Hakem Rafi's forces sweep north along the shores of the Western Sea, swallowing up all of Espani, Porghal, Bellandy, Faranza, and the frigid plains of Norgeland. With each new conquest, Hakem Rafi's army grew, his wealth and power increased, and his reputation spread. And at last, with his forces arrayed along the entire western rim of the world, Hakem Rafi turned his eyes eastward.

Hakem Rafi felt fully alive, the ultimate thief. He had stolen, not merely jewels or money, but whole cities and nations. Soon, as Aeshma had promised, his unbeaten and unbeatable forces would strike eastward into the very heart of Parsina, and all the world would tremble at the mere mention of his name.

9

The Wizard's Plan

As the two Marids flew the wizard Akar back from Sarafiq to his mountaintop castle, their blind passenger was lost in thought. With the anger against his former mentor now so lethally vented, he could concentrate more fully on the problem before him—and the more he thought, the more simple his solution appeared to be.

Aeshma could be controlled only through the Crystal of Oromasd; once Muhmad had mentioned it, that truth was obvious. The great mage Ali Maimun had broken the Crystal into four pieces and hidden them around the world; that much was well-known from the ancient legends. But nowhere in his vast library had Akar come across any reference to where the pieces had been hidden. Ali Maimun had done his job well in concealing the pieces from envious mortals; Akar could spend years combing the world without finding them. And in those years, Aeshma's power could grow so vast that nothing—not even the Crystal itself—could stem the tide of evil.

But Muhmad had been very specific in his pronouncement: Jafar al-Sharif would gather the pieces of the Crystal. Not merely that Jafar al-Sharif was *looking* for the pieces, but that he actually would get them. For all his scorn of the old man's conservatism, Akar respected his ex-master's ability to determine the true course within the misty patterns of the future. Somewhere—probably from Muhmad himself—Jafar the fraudulent must have gained secret knowledge of the pieces' whereabouts, and was even now on his way to collect them. Muhmad's certainty about Jafar's success was a knife the wizard could still feel twisting in his soul.

As the Marids flew him northwards into the chilly wastes, Akar carefully replayed the conversation in his mind, listening to each word and inflection, slighting only the prophet's final vision—which Akar was certain was based solely on spite, any-

114

way. He knew how precise his teacher had always been about his phraseology. In that conversation would be clues Akar could use to his advantage.

Twice in that talk, Muhmad had said it would be Jafar al-Sharif, rather than Akar, who would gather the pieces of the Crystal. But never had Muhmad said that Jafar would ultimately *use* the pieces. Quite the opposite—he had agreed with Akar that Jafar could never control the Crystal of Oromasd.

Putting the pieces of the puzzle together, then, was simplicity itself. Muhmad had spoken confidently that the Crystal of Oromasd would be used to control Aeshma. Jafar al-Sharif could not control the Crystal, even though he would be the one to gather the pieces. Since Akar knew there was no one stronger than he in the magical arts, this could only mean that *he* was the man destined to wield the Crystal in the war against Aeshma and the powers of Rimahn.

Even as he reached this conclusion, his Marids set him lightly down upon the roof of Shahdur Castle. Without a word of gratitude, Akar dismissed them and descended into his citadel to contemplate his future actions.

In darkness did the wizard sit, his mind awash with possibilities that warmed the darkness of his soul. Plan succeeded plan, each with its own advantages and pitfalls, but Akar was determined not to take rash action again as he had done against Aeshma. This time there could be no mistakes.

As he considered his moves, he felt a disturbance on the magical web of the world—and, as he had done before, he retired to his room of meditation to discover its cause. From his vantage point, he could see the righteous Jann swirling about in chaotic confusion; he puzzled at this, but continued to probe for the truth. The Jann had interposed themselves between Aeshma and Jafar, but they were not concealing events from Akar, who could see truthfully that Varyu had given a piece of the Crystal to Jafar—and Akar could see that this was already the second piece Jafar had accumulated. The fraud was already halfway on his road to success.

I must move quickly, Akar thought. *I dare not let Jafar and his party out of my sight. Wherever they go, whatever they do, I must be able to act at a moment's notice. Now that I know where they are, I must not let them get away from me until I decide what final action to take.*

Once again he summoned the two Marids who had carried him to Sarafiq, and once again he gave them commands. "The impostor named Jafar al-Sharif is currently in Varyu's castle. You dare not enter there, but the fraud will not stay there for long. Disguise yourselves and, when he leaves, follow after him. Keep me apprised of all that he does and all that befalls him, but take no action except to defend yourselves unless I so command it."

And as the Marids flew off on their mission, Akar allowed himself to feel satisfied for the first time in many weeks. *At last, Jafar,* he gloated. *At last, you will pay me back for the cruel hoax you played on me when first we met. Had it not been for your trickery, I would have found the urn first and bent Aeshma to my will long before this. But you shall rectify the situation yourself. You shall gather the four pieces of the Crystal of Oromasd for me. You shall face the perils, you shall do the work. And when you've done, I will steal the Crystal from you, just as you stole my treasures from me. In such ways is the balance of the universe maintained.*

Thus did the wizard Akar, in his evil mind, twist his ambition to an illusion of Oromasd's plan that fooled only him—but fooled him completely.

As opposed to Shahdur Castle, a place of perpetual darkness, Varyu's castle was a place of perpetual light. The wind needed windows even less than did the blind wizard, and so the rising and setting of the sun on the earth far below had no bearing on the occupants of this heavenly abode. The light was as constant as the smells that continually wafted through the corridors, and the lack of a reference made time difficult to measure.

The travelers were resolved not to linger in this bizarre and uncomfortable place, and the yazata Varyu—never an adherent of human etiquette—was not offended by their desire for a rapid departure after they had obtained his piece of the Crystal. After promising to serve Oromasd's cause—though never saying in what ways he intended to do it—Varyu summoned the Afrits of the air once more to carry the travelers and their horses and gear down to the surface of the world once more.

The group flew in silence in the billowy arms of the huge Afrits, who were as docile as lambs. Not only did the djinni of the air well remember Jafar's powers, but they also knew how foolish it would be for them to ignore the orders of the king of the winds, the yazata who held ultimate dominion over the realm in which they lived.

After a short, uneventful flight, the Afrits set the travelers upon level ground and, before the humans could question them, flew off into the sky, glad to be rid of their unwanted charges. It was early in the morning; the air was brisk and hung with dew, and the small breeze there sufficed to chill them thoroughly. A chain of mountains rose to one side of them. The rest of the landscape was frozen grassland as far as they could see.

For the first time since they entered the tunnel into Mount Nibo, the humans felt as though a spell of tension was broken and they were free to talk once more with the same ease they'd always had on the trail. Looking around at the unfamiliar landscape, Selima voiced the question in all their minds. "Where are we?"

"Those appear to be the Altai Mountains," Umar said, pointing to the east where the sun was rising from behind the hills. "Varyu has kindly deposited us on the other side so we don't have to negotiate the difficult mountain passes."

"If that's so," Leila said thoughtfully, "then we must be in or near Tatarry."

Prince Ahmad looked at her. "If it's true we're in your homeland, I must pay a call at the court to ask the king to join us in the battle to come. I know you don't want to return there—"

"I don't want to *live* there," Leila corrected him. "I don't mind visiting. It will be nice to see some of my old friends and relatives again. Meanwhile, I'm famished."

Leila's words reminded them all of how hungry they were. They had not eaten in Varyu's castle, nor had they felt the need—but now that they were again in human territory, their stomachs were bemoaning their emptiness. Their last meal had been breakfast in the city of the apes—and even in that city, for several days, they had been unable to make fires and had to settle for raw food. Their palates as well as their stomachs cried out for nourishment.

Even though it would cut into their precious traveling time, they all agreed food was the highest priority, so they took a while to build a fire and cook their first real meal in longer than they cared to think. Cari, who would eat later, kept an aerial watch on the land around them; the rimahniya, after all, might track them down and attack them on this exposed plain.

It was late morning by the time they had finished and cleaned up after themselves. Cari had spotted a small village several hours' ride away, and the prince decided they should not feed their horses the magic powder today, but instead should ride to the village and get their bearings. Cari flew on ahead and found no hostile force awaiting them there, so they rode boldly into the town as simple travelers wishing to replenish their supplies. To avoid unwanted attention, Cari rode on the same horse as Selima and kept a heavy robe wrapped around the two of them—but Leila's statuesque build, long blond hair, and unabashedly naked face still caused talk among the provincial villagers.

They learned from talking to the locals that, as they had surmised, they were now on the northern reaches of Tatarry. Leila didn't reveal her identity as a minor princess, but she did astonish the befurred peasants with her knowledge of local geography, dialects, and stories. Their native reserve was still evident, but they did show more hospitality than they would have done with ordinary strangers.

The travelers were stunned to learn, however, that their calendar was a week off. Although it had only seemed like a matter of hours, six days had elapsed since they had left the city of the apes for the tunnel through Mount Nibo. Six precious days were gone from their journey, and now they would have to cover more ground even faster than before. Prince Ahmad, in particular, was shaken by this news, and withdrew into himself so completely that he hardly spoke the rest of the day.

Leila's charm gained them a vacant room for the night in one villager's hut, for which they paid despite their host's protests. With the first light of morning they ate a simple peasant breakfast, mounted their steeds, and rode a short distance outside the village before feeding the horses the daily allotment of magical powder and beginning to ride in earnest.

During the ride, Leila would occasionally turn in her saddle to look at something behind them. After the third time this happened, Prince Ahmad signaled for the group to stop, and broke his moody silence to ask Leila what the matter was.

"Do you see those two crows up there?" she said.

"Yes."

"They're not crows. I don't know what they are, but they're not the simple birds they appear to be. And they've been following us all day, no matter how fast we ride."

The prince called Jafar over to confer with him on this development. "Perhaps Cari can explain this riddle," Jafar said after hearing Leila's warning. Summoning the Jann, he told her, "Investigate those two crows as closely as you can without endangering yourself."

"Hearkening and obedience, O master."

Cari flew upwards toward the crows, but as she neared them they spread their black wings in a threatening posture, with talons spread and sharp beaks at the ready. The air filled with their deafening caws, and Cari, startled, returned to her master's side.

"They are djinni," she said. "There can be no mistaking that. I don't know what race they are, though by the power they radiate they could be Marids or even Shaitans. They do not want me checking any closer than I did, and they threatened great harm if I ventured nearer. I don't want to seem cowardly, but your orders did say—"

"I know, and I think none the less of you," Jafar soothed. "I won't ask you to fight Marids or Shaitans without knowing more about them and having a trick or two in reserve."

"Why are they here, following us?" asked Umar bin Ibrahim.

"That, O priest, they would not tell me," Cari replied.

"Perhaps they're minions of Aeshma," Selima suggested. "He wouldn't want us succeeding in our quest."

"But why would Aeshma send spies?" Jafar wondered. "Wouldn't he deal with us personally? Without the completed Crystal we certainly couldn't stand before his power."

"Perhaps the rimahniya sent them," Selima suggested. "They want to track us just as badly as Aeshma."

"The rimahniya have been known to employ yatus," Umar agreed. "But the rimahniya also prefer stealth and nighttime, and would scarcely act so blatantly during the day. The birds don't seem to care that we know they are there."

"They may have been sent by a wizard," Jafar said. "Akar hates me so much that anyone he sent would have attacked us on sight, but perhaps some other sorcerer is curious about the magical energy that surrounds us now that we have two pieces of the Crystal of Oromasd."

"So far, they've been content just to watch us," Leila pointed out. "They could have attacked us, and we'd have had a hard time fighting them off. But they just follow and watch."

"Then we must watch, too," Prince Ahmad decided. There was a harsh edge to his voice that the others hadn't heard before. "We can't challenge them right now, but we *can* keep our eyes open. If they change their methods, we'll reconsider what we must do—but knowing they're around gives us some warning, at least. In the meantime, we'll do what we must do—ride." He would say no more, and lapsed back into his moody silence.

The further south they went, the more familiar the land looked to Leila, whose first husband had let her accompany him on some of his sport hunting expeditions. After three days of riding across the frigid plain at magical speeds—and of frequently glancing over her shoulder to see the crows still following them—Leila pointed to the horizon and showed them the walls of her home city, Tarass. Tomorrow they would ride at normal speed and reach the gate by late afternoon.

That night, alone with Jafar in their tent, Leila's cool reserve broke down. "I'm worried about tomorrow," she confessed.

"Why should you worry? You're coming home."

Leila shook her head. "Tarass is not my home. A pampered princess lived there, and a spoiled young wife. Neither of them is me."

"But you have family and friends—"

"They'll remember my name, and they may remember my face, but they won't know who I am. They'll know the young girl I was, and they probably won't even remember *her* accurately. Everything I say, everything I do, will be measured against old standards that don't apply any more. I'll be a stranger wearing their old, cast-off clothes, and no one will be comfortable."

She sighed deeply. "I made the right decision not to return here to live. The sooner I am away, the better we'll all feel."

And Jafar made love to her, and held her through the night, so that in the morning she could face the new day and her old life.

The djinni-crows were still in the air, circling, as the travelers broke camp and rode at normal speed toward the Tatarry city of Tarass. By midafternoon they were within the shadows of the walls, which were built of heavy stone blocks that gave the city a solid, rooted-to-the-earth appearance. The outer wall was not high, barely taller than a one-story house; the second wall, ten cubits inside the first, was only two stories high, and the minaret, with its perpetual flame of Oromasd, was barely four stories tall. A large army could have stormed the city and breached the walls—but large armies seldom attacked Tatarry.

The Tatarriya were descendants of nomads similar to the Badawi—but while the Badawi traveled through the deserts and wastes of the world, the Tatarriya had wandered the plains and grasslands. Though most of the time they had traveled peacefully, tending their herds and flocks, some of their more zealous leaders had taken them on rampages against their neighboring tribes. So ruthless were they as fighters that they earned a reputation for ferocity and aggression that swept before them wherever they roamed.

Some of the tribes still preferred the nomadic life and refused to take up sedentary ways, though most of the Tatarriya, under command of their greatest ruler, Ghenjik, finally settled in the land that was given their name. They built the city of Tarass and the lesser villages in the land, and made a home for themselves that few, because of the Tatarriya reputation, dared to challenge. Though an occasional king of Tatarry would make inroads into adjoining lands, they lived in relative peace with their neighbors because they had sufficient resources for themselves and no one wanted their land badly enough to fight them for it.

Indeed, the Tatarry reputation was maintained even to the present day. Their men were excellent horsemen and experienced swordsmen with the thin-bladed, razor-sharp scimitars that were their trademark. Tatarri mercenaries served with distinction in armies throughout Parsina, though they were usually so intense of manner that few outsiders could make friends with them.

Though Cari flew invisibly beside them, the travelers rode with some mild concern up to the heavy wooden gate of Tarass, for they all knew stories of Tatarriya ferocity and were counting heavily on Leila's connections to make their entry easier. Leila had worries of her own, but entry into Tarass was not among them.

Two stern-faced, armored guards challenged them as they approached the gate. Unlike Ravan, a city that relied on commerce for its livelihood, Tarass did not have a steady stream of visitors coming and going all day long. Farmers came in the morning to sell their wares at the bazaars, and left in late afternoon when the bazaars closed; any other pattern merited suspicion.

For once it was Leila, rather than Prince Ahmad, who rode to the front of the group and addressed the guards. "I am Princess Leila, niece to His Sovereign Majesty, King Rasbul. I am on urgent business of His Majesty. Let me and my retinue pass."

The younger of the guards did not recognize her name, but the older one thought for a second before a flicker of recognition lit up his face. "I remember a Princess Leila," he said slowly. "But she died many years ago in a far-off land."

"A common misunderstanding. But I assure you, if you keep me from seeing my uncle, the king, your own death may not be far away. As I recall, my uncle is an unpleasant man when angered."

The older guard waved his hand. "You may pass."

The younger guard had, perhaps, more of a flair for officiousness, for he started to protest. "But we don't know who they are."

"If she's as she says, she deserves to enter," the older man reasoned. "If she isn't, they're no threat to Tarass, anyway. Let the palace guards deal with them."

With that ambivalent welcome, the travelers passed through the large gate and entered the city of Tarass. While it was not as poor a city as Astaburya, the streets were narrow and few people traveled them. The houses they passed were small but well kept, built solidly of stone with roofs of hide and bone to defy the cold northern winters. Men and women alike dressed in furs, or in heavy fur felt garments trimmed with fur. The men had long, thin mustaches and crudely shorn goatees; they did not wear turbans, but instead had pointed caps with weasel or other fur edges, and most had on heavily embroidered coats over woolen trousers and thick leather boots. The few women about on the street were warmly dressed in plain clothing, and with covered heads. They stared in wonder at Leila and the ghost-girl Selima going so brazenly bareheaded in public. Leila pointedly ignored the stares, keeping her eyes front as she led her companions through the streets toward the palace.

Tarass was a quiet city. There were no street vendors hawking their wares, no camels bawling their complaints— even the few children they saw playing in the streets played more quietly than chidren from the southern lands. As the walls and the buildings, so the very atmosphere of Tarass seemed heavy and solemn. The citizens were under no threat, as they were in Astaburya; Tarass was just naturally a somber place.

Leila pulled to a halt before the doors of the palace, dismounted, and walked up the stone steps to knock on the brass doors. An aged retainer with a wrinkled face and skin as tough as leather stuck his head out and looked them over. He was obviously aghast at seeing strangers, but Leila didn't give him time to voice his indignation.

"Hello, Aral," she said blithely. "Are you pleased to see me again?"

The old man squinted uncertainly.

"It's been many years since you saw me," she said, "but—"

"Leila?" His voice was high and shaky. "But . . . but . . . you're dead."

"I was dead for quite a while," Leila agreed with a nod. "I was buried underground like old sewage. But these kind people rescued me and brought me up to the air and light once more, praise be to Oromasd. So now I've come back, at least to visit. But I must see my uncle, quickly. We are on a matter of utmost urgency for the entire world."

The old man could only stand, gaping, and point at her, so after a moment Leila pushed gently past him into the palace. Afraid of losing their native guide, the others in the party did likewise.

The palace was large, but close. The halls bent at many sudden right angles, with tapestries or burnished nail-studded hide curtains to block the violent, ice-filled winter winds and retain the coolness in summer. The colors were rich, earthen tones—in simple designs, for the most part, though here and there were rugs and hangings from all corners of the world.

The party had to follow quickly behind Leila so they wouldn't lose her in this unexpected maze. They heard voices behind several hide doorways, but since Leila didn't pause, they were forced to ignore the happy sounds of family life and walk steadily behind her.

Leila strode regally down the long, empty passages toward the dining hall. Years of being a queen—even an involuntary queen—in Punjar lent majesty to her step and imperiousness to her demeanor. She was not to be stopped on her mission, and no one could have detained her.

She fairly flew through the doorway into the dining room where the king, his advisers, and some of the court were seated at dinner. There were guards at the door, but so quickly did Leila move that they scarcely had time to draw their swords before she approached King Rasbul and made a deep salaam before him.

"Forgive me, O my uncle, for appearing thus immodestly before you," she said, keeping her head bowed and her eyes on the floor. "The harsh years have removed from me all sense of shame. But they could not rob me of my affection for you."

King Rasbul was a man in his early sixties—a large man of great bulk, but no flabbiness about his person. His dark eyes scanned this stranger while his ears analyzed her voice and her words, and suddenly his face lit up with surprise. "Leila! I am astonished. I had not thought to see you again outside the House of Song."

"I got tired of being a corpse," Leila said. "There's no future in it." She looked up just enough to give him a smile, and she could see that he looked pleased.

"Leila?" said another man from across the room. Leila looked up at hearing that familiar voice, and stared across at the face of her father, much older than she remembered him. The prince looked across at his daughter, then at his older brother, the king. "Your Majesty, may I rise in your presence and—?"

"You would be no father if you did otherwise," said the king.

With this royal permission, Leila's father stood up from his place and started around the table. Leila also rose and ran around to meet him halfway. Father and daughter embraced, and kissed, and wept, with such obvious love that all in the room felt moved.

"Where is Mother?" Leila asked when she could speak again.

Her father's face fell. "Dead these last three years," he admitted. "It was one of her consolations that she would be joining you in the House of Song."

"Oh." Leila cast her eyes sadly downward. "I'm only slightly sorry I've disappointed her—but time passes quickly in the House of Song, so I'm told, and our reunion will come soon enough for her. In the meantime, I must give you the love I've saved up for the both of you." And she hugged her father even tighter.

When at last the depths of their emotion had been plumbed, the king chose to interrupt. "May I inquire, O shameless niece, about these strangers you seem to have brought with you?"

Leila looked up at her companions standing in the doorway, and saw them as though for the first time. "Your Majesty, may I present my friends and rescuers, the people who saved me from enslavement within the very bowels of the earth? I am especially honored to present Prince Ahmad of Ravan, who must speak to you on a matter of great urgency."

King Rasbul's eyes went wide. "Is today the end of the world, then? Have all the dead risen to face the final Rehabilitation? I have heard word from Ravan about your death at the hands of brigands—"

"Greatly exaggerated," Prince Ahmad said, and his voice was so filled with fatigue and resignation that it startled his companions. Dealing with other royalty, convincing them to join in this holy crusade, had always excited him most about this mission. The prince could be counted upon to deliver a vigorous, forceful argument and sway a righteous king to his side. Yet, ever since their return from Varyu's castle, Ahmad had been moody and withdrawn, scarcely speaking to any of them.

The travelers could all see that the prince, for whatever reason, was in no condition to deliver the speech they needed now. They knew not the reason for his strange behavior, but they could not afford to falter before the powerful king of Tatarry.

Ever prepared to fill an awkward silence, Jafar al-Sharif stepped forward and addressed King Rasbul. "Your Majesty, may you live forever, I fear His Highness is worn out from our long day's journey, and so he has appointed me to tell his story for him. I am called Jafar al-Sharif, wizard of the southern provinces, and it is a grand honor to stand before such a magnificent gathering this evening and relate the wondrous tale of our adventures. While it is true that Prince Ahmad's wedding

party was attacked by brigands, there was a miracle that occurred in the woods. . . ."

And Jafar al-Sharif went on, with many gesticulations and
flowery turns of speech, to relate the story of how they all had
met, where they had traveled, and what they had done. He
emphasized Muhmad's dire prophecy, and how the other kings
they had met had promised them aid in the battle to come.
Then Leila spoke up, telling her own story of imprisonment in
the pits of Punjar and the mutual rescuing she had engaged in
with this band of travelers.

And all the while they spoke, Prince Ahmad stood staring
blankly ahead, not even seeming to care what King Rasbul's
response would be. Umar looked concerned, at first, and then
understanding came to his eyes. Selima, though, looked in
sheer perplexity at the handsome young man she'd been traveling with, wondering whether he was ill and whether she
could do anything to help him.

When Jafar had finished spinning his tale, King Rasbul
looked at the group thoughtfully. "There is no doubt that
Tatarry wants to fight on the side of Oromasd," he said. "But
rumors have reached us about an army marching eastward
across the face of Parsina, the vanguard of an invincible conqueror. If these forces come against us, our soldiers must stay
here and fight to defend our land."

"This may indeed be the army of Rimahn," Umar bin
Ibrahim spoke up. "The yazata Varyu vouchsafed us a glimpse
of their might, and they are strong indeed. I know the reputation of Tatarry's warriors, and I know that they are unmatched
in skill and daring—but even they will never be able to stand
against the overwhelming numbers and the potent evil magic
Rimahn will hurl against them. They will have a better chance
if they retreat from their homeland and join the armies of mankind on the Leewahr Plain."

"Abandon our people?" The idea was clearly unpalatable
to the king. "I fear you do not understand the Tatarriya mind.
But for now, let us put aside such discussions. I can see you
eyeing our meal with covetous eyes. Though this is but simple
fare, it must appear a banquet after so many meals of trail
rations. Join us, please, and enjoy our hospitality at least for
this night before you must depart once more upon your destined path."

And the travelers sat around the royal banquet and ate of
the peppered cured ox meat and chelo, and other delights.

And when the meal was over, King Rasbul assigned them to suitable rooms within the palace where they could sleep in comfort before venturing out on the trail again.

Although the quarters assigned to her were pleasant, Selima could not sleep. In her mind she kept seeing the image of Prince Ahmad standing sullenly and silently while her father told their tale for him. She saw him sitting at dinner, barely picking at the food before him while the others ate so heartily. And she saw him as he'd been for the last few days, lost and drifting in some private fog. He needed help, and he was too proud to ask for it. She was frightened of giving it, but she was even more frightened of not doing so.

She left her room quietly, so that none in the palace knew she was about. Her insubstantial feet made no noise on the hard stone floor as she wound through the passageways to the room where the prince was staying. She might have had a hard time navigating through a larger palace, but the simplicity of King Rasbul's family quarters helped her reach her destination with a minimum of confusion. There were but four sleeping rooms for unmarried men and women, and she had heard Ahmad's voice go past her door as he was guided to his chamber.

The door was closed, but she could see under the crack that a light was still burning in the room. She could neither knock nor open the door by herself, so she called in a harsh whisper, "Your Highness, this is Selima."

There was a short silence, then, "Yes, I know your voice after all this time."

"Will you let me in?"

"No. It wouldn't be proper."

"Nothing indecent can happen between us. I just want to talk to you."

"After all the silence you've given me on the trail since Buryan, this is a fine day for you to want to talk. Go away."

"I want to help you."

"Thank you, but you can't. Nothing you can do will help. Go away."

The fire of anger was kindled in Selima's soul. "If you won't open this door," she said, "I will start screaming at the top of my voice until everyone in the palace is awake. Then you'll have to explain to our host, the king, why you didn't want to talk to me."

After a minute of silence, the door opened and Prince Ahmad stood in the doorway looking both angry and confused. "Why would you do such a thing?"

Selima dashed into the room before he could change his mind. "If I can't sleep, why should anyone else?" she explained.

"That doesn't make sense. Why can't you sleep?"

"Because I'm worried about you." Looking around, she could see that the prince had been given less than regal accommodations by Ravani standards: a sparsely furnished room with a few pillows on the floor and an unrolled mat in one corner—obviously a quickly converted anteroom. The bare stone walls had a few niches in which small statuettes had been placed, but they were the only concession to ornamentation. A pair of oil lamps provided faint illumination that left her all but invisible; a tiny brazier burning rosewood incense could not entirely mask the smells of sweat and sheep. Yet, to have the space all alone was honor indeed.

"You have no cause to worry," Prince Ahmad said. "I'm fine."

"We've been on the trail together for months. I've seen you when you're fine. This is not it."

"It would do no good to explain it to you," the prince said. "There's absolutely nothing you can do about it."

"A problem shared is a problem halved," Selima quoted.

"An old wives' saying. Maybe it works for old wives. Princes are different."

"How are they different? Did not Oromasd make us all?"

"A prince is a leader. He has responsibilities. It's wrong for him to have personal feelings. He cannot show weakness."

"Right now, I see the weakness of pride. Can it be so wrong for even a prince to tell his troubles to trusted friends?"

Prince Ahmad paced the room, not answering, not even daring to look at her. Finally he stopped and, with a deep sigh, stood by the arched window and stared out at the stars, pointedly avoiding so much as a glance at her beautiful, caring face. "Today is my eighteenth birthday," he said at last.

Selima had been prepared to hear a tale of heartrending tragedy or serious personal conflict. She took a long moment to consider what the prince had said, not understanding why it should have this effect on him. "I know how it feels to have milestones ignored," she said. "I passed my fifteenth birthday almost two months ago, and no one, not even my father, made note of it. We're not under normal conditions now, but once this journey is over—"

"You don't understand," the prince said. "I knew you wouldn't."

Selima's temper flared. "I'm sure Her Highness, Princess Rida, would understand it perfectly, but perhaps if you explained it to a poor, ignorant nobody like me instead of sighing and making vague pronouncements—"

"What does Princess Rida have to do with this?" Ahmad asked, turning at last to face her.

"What *doesn't* she have to do with it?"

The prince shook his head. "I don't understand."

"Then that makes us even. Will you explain your problem so a mere commoner's child can understand it?"

Prince Ahmad turned back to stare out the window. "Today is not just a birthday," he said. "Today I attain my legal majority. Today ambassadors from all over Parsina would have flocked to Ravan, and all the nobles of the city would have gathered in the sahn of the Royal Temple. Today I would have been anointed with holy oils and worn the robe of my father. Today I would have climbed to the minbar before the holy flame of Oromasd and sworn my holiest oaths to protect the people of the city. Today Umar would have placed my ancestors' crown upon my head, and today I would have been proclaimed king of Ravan."

Whatever anger was left in Selima died instantly in her heart. Whatever hot words she might have spoken melted in her throat. She looked at the young man silhouetted against the window and remembered anew that he was not merely a pleasant, if sometimes overearnest, traveling companion, but a prince of royal blood, a man born to rule, a figure of power and majesty. Ahmad should this evening be seated upon the golden throne of Ravan, issuing proclamations, dictating commands, and being adored by the populace of the world's most holy and revered city. He should have slaves to serve his smallest whim, wazirs to answer his every question, wives and concubines to . . . to . . .

She put that thought from her mind. Prince Ahmad was not mooning over lost wives and concubines, but instead over the lost power and respect that were his due by birth. Today, more than any other, was his loss most keenly felt, and today his grief was an open sore on his soul.

"You have lost much," she agreed quietly.

"'Much'? I have lost my land, my followers, my birth-right, even my name, which I dare not speak carelessly lest it be overheard by assassins. Everything I was raised to has been cast into the dust and mashed under Shammara's dainty foot. What am I offered in return? Arduous journeying, a battle against hopeless odds and fearsome forces, and the promised loss of my kingdom no matter what the outcome."

Selima looked at him, perplexed. "I hadn't heard that part of the prophecy."

"Muhmad told me I would lose what I desired most to gain. He also—" Ahmad stopped abruptly, turned, and looked at Selima, and changed what he was going to say. "He also told me I would gain more than I ever dreamed possible," he finished weakly.

"Well, then, is that to be so terrible? To be promised great gains is a wonderful thing. I would that Muhmad had said such things to my father."

The prince turned abruptly away from her and stared out the window into the night once more. "The future offers scant consolation tonight," he said bitterly. "Tomorrow I may think of it again with some eagerness, but today . . . today was to be the greatest moment of my life, the moment I was groomed for, like a prize horse for a great race. And instead it all goes to my idiot brother, Haroun. For him will be the throne and the throngs in a month's time, while I am still circling Parsina on the prophet's errand."

He paused and lowered his head. "I'm glad old Umar can't see me at this moment. He thinks of me as his prince—indeed, his king in fact, ruler of Oromasd's holiest city. He would be broken to see me as I am tonight, a bitter man losing his faith, cursing the supposed plan of Oromasd that has cast me out from all that is rightfully mine. Tonight would I give my heart and soul to Rimahn in return for my kingdom."

He whirled to face her again. "Now you know the blackness that engulfs my soul. Now you will shun me, as I deserve to be shunned."

"I will do no such thing," Selima said. For a moment, instinct overcame reason and she rushed toward him to give a comforting embrace. As her arms closed about him, however, they passed through his body with no effect, and both were forcibly reminded of the unbridgeable gap between them. This time, it was Selima who turned away, embarrassed by the effrontery of her action.

The two young people both stood in silence for a long moment before Prince Ahmad spoke again. "Here I stand, bawling like a babe, bewailing my losses, when I still possess Oromasd's greatest gift, life—something you have lost, and yet bear with such grace and nobility. Compared to you I am rich beyond measure, and I selfishly wish for more. You teach me the meaning of courage every day. No wonder Oromasd has cast me from my throne, and why Varyu questioned my integrity. I am not fit to govern decent people. My only regret is that I couldn't yield the throne to a brave, sensible, compassionate person like you.

"Come. We have wallowed in misery too much this evening. Let us sit and converse as we did so many nights upon the trail."

And Prince Ahmad and Selima sat upon the pillows on his floor, and the prince read to her from his books of poetry until the late hours of the morning, when they finally fell asleep together, exhausted.

10

The Poison

The next morning, Prince Ahmad was more his normal self as he came before King Rasbul to plead the case for uniting with the other armies of humanity to stop Aeshma's advance. He spoke with great eloquence on Oromasd's behalf, but his words could not dent the armor of King Rasbul's first loyalty to his people and their lands.

"To do as you suggest," their host argued, "would leave my kingdom defenseless when the invaders come through—and they must sweep through Tatarry on their way to the Leewahr Plains. Would you have the men of Tatarry desert their wives and daughters to the mercies of Rimahn's army? We must stand and make our fight here to defend our homeland."

"The valor and skill of Tatarriya warriors is undisputed," Prince Ahmad rebutted. "But no single army, no matter how brave, no matter how fierce, can hope to stop the oncoming foe. Only by uniting with all the other nations, as in the days of good King Shahriyan, can we hope to defeat this implacable enemy and further Oromasd's great plan. The other kings I've spoken to—"

"—Are all to the east of here," King Rasbul interrupted. "They will not be leaving their homes and their women empty-handed to face this heartless conqueror. They will place themselves, their honor, their lives between this invader and their lands. We, on the other hand, would be fleeing in cowardly fear in the face of Rimahn's legions."

"But the prophet Muhmad said—"

"The prophet Muhmad did not have wives and children to protect, as we do. It's easy to make pronouncements seated on a satin pillow in a comfortable oasis. The choices are not so easy when you sit on a throne and rule the lives of your subjects, as Your Highness ought to know by now."

Perhaps pretending to wizardry for so long had gone to Jafar's head, for from some unknown depths he found the courage to interpose himself in this argument between two such illustrious personages. "O noble King Rasbul, may you live forever, may a humble wizard seek to find a solution where two such eminent royal philosophers have failed?"

Rasbul looked wary of this interruption, but before he could speak, Prince Ahmad said, "Your wisdom ever guides us, O Jafar, as the prophet Muhmad knew it would."

Well, Muhmad was a little distracted that day, Jafar thought, but plunged ahead anyway. "O mighty king, your illustrious niece has spent many hours along the trail telling me the history of your fine land and its brave people. I have heard other stories as well about their nomadic background. The Tatarriya, so the stories would tell us, once carried all their belongings on their backs and on their horses, and drove their livestock before them across the vast plains of Parsina."

"So the storytellers would have it," growled the king. "I've never personally found them to be a dependable lot."

Jafar al-Sharif prudently decided this was not the occasion to take umbrage on behalf of his profession. "Could not they do so again?" he asked. "If you worry about deserting your women and children, why leave them behind? Why could not the Tatarriya move as a tribe, together, southward to the Leewahr Plains, as their ancestors did so many ages ago?"

King Rasbul was stunned. "What you propose is insanity—"

Jafar bowed his head humbly. "Perhaps Your Majesty is right. It would be foolish to compare the present stock of Tatarriya to their rugged nomadic ancestors. So many years of domestication—"

"The Tatarriya are no less than they ever were," roared the king.

"I suppose not," Jafar conceded. "Perhaps they suffer only in comparison to the Badawi, who—"

"The Tatarriya compare to no one," the king insisted.

"Then your people would not suffer," Jafar concluded. "Let them leave their homes behind; houses are only buildings. Let them leave their furniture behind; the invader does not care about cupboards and tables. Let them take their horses and flocks and herds. Let them take what treasures they can carry with them. And let them all go together to join the noblest army since the time of King Shahriyan. Join us on the Leewahr Plains to combat the legions of Rimahn and honor the name of our lord Oromasd."

King Rasbul was silent for several minutes. "Your wizard is clever," he finally said to Prince Ahmad. "He has found the weakness of the Tatarriya, our pride, and he plays on it, forgetting it will not be easy—"

"It never is," said Umar bin Ibrahim. "To do the easy thing is to fall into Rimahn's snares. The easy thing is to sit safely in your city and welcome the invaders when they come. To be on the side of Oromasd is to be constantly vigilant, constantly fighting against the temptations Rimahn puts in our path to lead us away from the honest road. I hope Your Majesty can see the difference."

"Indeed I can," said the king. "You argue well, all three of you; Oromasd has found an effective triumvirate. Come the first floods of spring, our armies will assemble with yours on the Leewahr Plains, and then you will see what true fighting is. No horsemen can fight better on open land than the Tatarriya, and we fear no one, mortal or immortal, except our benevolent lord Oromasd and his Bounteous Immortals. Our women and our children will be there, too, to cheer us on to victory. And when the invader comes to Tarass, he will find nothing to satisfy his greed but a city of ghosts."

With this assurance, all that was left was for Leila to once again bid farewell to her father and her other relatives she had seen during the one-night visit. In theory she would see them again in just a few months at the great battle on the Leewahr Plains, but they all knew they could not count on that. Leila's path was fraught with danger, and her family's path would be harsh. There was a good chance they would never see one another again—and for all Leila's cynicism about her estrangement from her family, they were still the people she'd grown up and shared the early part of her life with. She had said these farewells before, when she and her first husband set off for the courts of far Sinjin, and it had been heartbreaking then. This parting was more bittersweet, more tearful, because the chances of reunion were so much less.

But finally, after fighting off the pleas of her father to stay with him, Leila rejoined her traveling companions. Her eyes were reddened, her cheeks were stained with tears, and the kohl about her eyes was smudged, but she insisted she was ready to travel. The others did not need to ask how the farewells had gone.

Before they left Tarass, Umar bin Ibrahim insisted they all stop in the city's main temple for a purification and rededication. They had, after all, touched the dead bodies of the rimahniya, however carefully, back in the city of the apes, and they needed a ritual cleansing of this contamination before he could feel totally comfortable again. The travelers drank the haoma the local priest gave them, confessed to him the tiny sins they dared not tell to one another, and received both his absolution and his blessing on their holy endeavor.

Umar also had a talk with his ward, and gave him what comfort he could over the passing of his eighteenth birthday. After the conversation, Prince Ahmad seemed much more at ease with himself and his role in Oromasd's great plan— though occasionally he would get a wistful gleam in his eye when anyone referred to him as "Your Highness."

Thus fortified, the travelers rode forth from Tarass once more and headed south toward the Central Sea.

They rode for four days across the wintry plains south of Tatarry. The weather grew slightly milder as they approached the Central Sea, for this region of Parsina was noted for its mild winters. Nevertheless, the winds created by their rapid riding still chilled their bodies, and they continued to wear the fur cloaks they had bought in the northern reaches of the world. The two djinni-crows, who had disappeared during their stay in Tarass, were also back following them, no matter how quickly they rode. The travelers became so used to their presence that they seldom paid the crows more than perfunctory attention.

On the afternoon of the fourth day they approached the gates of Damasc, and Prince Ahmad called a halt to their ride so they could discuss how they wanted to proceed.

"Up to this point," said Umar bin Ibrahim, "we have been fairly safe marching together into the cities we visit, because the places were far from Ravan and you were largely unknown there. That certainly is not the case in Damasc, which has much commerce with Ravan. Shammara may have made a treaty with King Kasem to have you killed if you ever showed up here. You may also be at risk from the rimahniya, who have been known to operate here."

"My good captain, Nurredin al-Damasci, was to precede us here and smooth the path for us," Ahmad said.

"Assuming his head isn't already on a pike," Leila commented acidly.

"Perhaps we could do as we did in Khmeria," Jafar suggested. "Surely you must have some trustworthy contacts among the priesthood of Damasc, O Umar."

"I believe I do," said the high priest with a nod. "But even so, I would not like to risk His Highness's being spotted within the city until we know he'll be safe there. I propose to enter the city alone and talk to my brothers in service about the political climate. If they can assure me of Ahmad's safety, I will ride back to the rest of you and we can enter Damasc together."

"But if King Kasem has been corrupted by Shammara," Prince Ahmad argued, "your life may be equally at risk simply for being my ally."

"I'm an old man, and if kismet decrees I shall die in Damasc, I cannot deny it," Umar said. "This is my duty to serve you, O my prince, and I will not shirk it."

Jafar al-Sharif was about to argue that he could travel into Damasc, invisibly if necessary, when he saw the look of fixed purpose in the priest's eyes. Umar bin Ibrahim was feeling more and more pushed into the background and relegated to a secondary role in this mission. Jafar could tell he wanted to do something to reaffirm his importance, and this task was ideally suited to him. Besides, Umar's connections within the priesthood would give them faster, more reliable information than Jafar could gather from any other sources.

He made no objections, and Umar bin Ibrahim set out toward Damasc. After the priest was gone, however, Jafar summoned Cari and told her, "Follow Umar invisibly into the city. Don't let him know you're there, but keep him safe from harm."

"Hearkening and obedience, O my master," said Cari.

The rest of the party waited a parasang from the gates as the afternoon shadows lengthened. Just as they were about to set up camp for the night, they saw the figure of a lone horseman riding toward them through the deepening gloom of dusk. They cheered as the man approached and they could see it was Umar returning alive and well.

"King Kasem died two months ago, apparently of natural causes," Umar informed them after the greetings were done.

"His son, King Hamal, now sits on the throne. According to my contacts, who I believe are honorable, Hamal is an able and honest monarch. We are welcomed to enter the city. Special provision was made to keep the gates open for us at night, so let us not tarry here."

"He is not under any coercion, and speaks the truth," Cari whispered in Jafar's ear to confirm what the priest had said.

Thus assured of safe passage, the travelers rode to the gates of Damasc, where a party of Damascine guards waited with torches blazing to escort them directly into the palace. Jafar al-Sharif was distinctly nervous about this armed escort, and kept his cloak of invisibility wrapped tightly about him under his fur cloak, just in case a quick exit was in order.

The group was ushered directly into the royal presence. Damasc's young king was holding an improvised diwan for their benefit, in a throne room of brown marble with ruby fixtures and braziers burning cinnamon incense. Hamal was but a few years older than Prince Ahmad, with dark, curly hair, a meticulously trimmed beard, and sharp eyes that scrutinized them intensely. There was no smile, no friendship on his face, but no animosity, either. This king would listen critically, but he would make his own decisions.

As was their custom, Prince Ahmad explained their position in strong, eloquent terms. King Hamal listened silently, his expression never changing, his gaze never wavering. When the prince was done, Hamal sat stonily for several minutes, considering all the ramifications of what had happened and what was to come.

"This is the first I've heard of these matters," he said at last. "Your man Nurredin did not arrive at my court, or he would have been listened to with respect, for I have heard his name mentioned favorably by my own officers. If he arrived during the last days of my father's reign, there is a chance he would have been killed; my father was indeed the sort of man who would have made a pact with Shammara. Had you arrived two months ago, your welcome would not have been this cordial.

"But we are of an age, you and I. We share perspectives that our fathers and our older wazirs do not understand. I sympathize on the loss of your kingdom, although you catch me in an awkward moment, for I am in the process of forming a party to travel to Ravan to attend your brother's coronation in a few weeks' time. Whatever my sympathies for you, reasons of state compel me to attend that event."

"I understand," Prince Ahmad said with a nod.

"I will be honest with you, as honest as one king can ever be with another. I don't know whether I can join you in your holy crusade. There are many factors entering into the problem, not the least of which is this invader coming out of the west. I, too, have heard reports of his invincible army, and Damasc also stands between him and the Leewahr Plains. The Damasci are not nomadic people like the Tatarriya, and there are far more of us. We cannot abandon our city to the enemy as you have convinced them to do. There is too much that would be irreparably lost."

"It will be lost anyway," Ahmad argued. "No one nation can stand alone against the power of Rimahn. Only by uniting, by standing together, can we defeat these forces. If you hold out, you will be swallowed by the empire of evil and your own soldiers will be forced to fight in the cause of Rimahn. Would you cause them to risk their souls, to risk eons in the Pits of Torment, rather than make a temporary retreat in order to gain strength for the battle to come?"

"I haven't said no," Hamal retorted. "I just haven't said yes. Perhaps older kings, with eyes dimmed by age, can see such issues in pure black and white. I still see things in colors and shadings, and decisions are seldom clear. I am not fleeing the decision; I am merely trying not to panic, and waiting until more facts are known. In time I will decide what I and my people must do—and if the only way to stop this pestilence is to retreat, my army and I will join you on the Leewahr Plains to take a stand against Rimahn's legions."

He paused and looked straight into Ahmad's eyes. "I will make you another kind of offer, an alliance of kings. As I said, I must travel to Ravan in several weeks to attend your brother's coronation. I will be taking a retinue with me. If you would wish to return to your city in disguise, I could offer you a position in my guard. Once there, you might have the chance to assassinate your brother and Shammara and reclaim the throne for yourself. Beyond helping you through the gates, I would take no action—but I and my men would support you if you were successful."

Prince Ahmad's eyes glazed over, and his friends looked at him with some alarm. Selima, in particular, knew how much the throne of Ravan mattered to him. Ahmad had never gone back for fear of being recognized and killed at the gates—but if he could get safe passage inside with King Hamal's entourage, would he take the chance to regain his lost kingdom?

But after a moment, the look faded from his face. "I am most grateful for your offer, Your Majesty," he said, "but on many grounds I cannot accept. For one thing, I cannot allow you to entangle yourself in acts of war against Ravan; it would not be in your people's best interests, were your role in that deception discovered. For another, and more important, reason, I am no longer merely a deposed prince looking for a country to rule. The prophet Muhmad has given me a mission for Oromasd, and all my personal desires must be postponed until that is done. I have begun this undertaking, and I cannot now desert my friends and companions. Besides, what good would it do me to reclaim my throne if, in another month or so, Ravan were swallowed up by the festering evil Rimahn has spawned upon the world? I will stay to the path the prophet outlined for me and trust to Oromasd's beneficence to provide my reward."

"I think the prophet has chosen wisely," King Hamal said. "Were it me and my kingdom . . . well, I thank Oromasd it is not. I'm sorry I cannot give you a more definite answer right now, but at least accept my hospitality for the night before you continue on your journey. And as a lover of our lord Oromasd, I will wish you the greatest success upon your mission."

"I am most worried about the fate of Nurredin al-Damasci," said Prince Ahmad as the travelers mounted their horses the next day to leave Damasc. "He was the best of my officers, one that all the men admired. Intelligent, loyal, strong, brave—all the qualities a warrior should have. I hate to think of him perishing at the hands of the corrupt King Kasem."

"Perhaps he just hasn't reached here yet," Selima suggested.

"His route was far more direct than ours," Umar said with a sad shake of his head. "The roads are not always safe for a single traveler. Much evil could have befallen him."

"Let's not be so pessimistic," Jafar said. "Perhaps he merely encountered others along the road to whom he could tell the story of the prince's mission, and thus enlisted them in our struggle. Perhaps he took a long detour through Durkhash, or even Bann, and is winning us allies even as we ride.

Mayhap we'll arrive at the Leewahr Plains and find him awaiting us with an army of fifty thousand soldiers ready for battle."

"Perhaps," said Prince Ahmad, but his voice was far from
joyful as he considered the many glum possibilities Fate may
have dealt to his teacher and friend.

They rode south for three more days, with the djinni-
crows still following patiently after them, watching but not interfering. Now that they were back in civilized country again,
they found caravanserais along the road, spaced one normal
day's journey apart from one another. At the magical rate of
speed their horses could run, they passed several caravanserais
each day, but they always stopped at one near nightfall. Thus
were they spared more nights in their tiny tents with nothing
but trail rations to eat, and they survived in some degree of
comfort after all the hardships they had so far endured.

Each morning and evening, Jafar and Selima continued
their reading lessons, and by now were reading satisfactorily
on their own, much to Cari's delight. Jafar was even becoming
a tutor in his turn, teaching what he had learned to a willing
Leila.

Each day, too, Jafar would take out the leather-bound journal of Ali Maimun and attempt to open it to a new section, to
learn where they were bound and what the ancient mage had
to tell him about the sunken city of Atluri. But the book stubbornly refused to yield more than he already knew, and he
continued railing against the so-called holy man who would
tantalize a true believer in such cruel ways.

The character of the land began to change along with the
weather. Now there were more hills rather than plains, and
sometimes steep bluffs towering over the valleys through
which they rode. There were groves of olive trees and small
oranges, and flocks of sheep grazed on the hillsides. There
were also many shepherds to gaze at them in awe as their
horses ran through the countryside at speeds no one could
dare imagine. Some of the witnesses told their compatriots
what they'd seen, and were judged mad. Others kept quiet, for
fear of the same judgment.

This was the land of Nikhrash, of which they'd all heard—
a land supposedly filled with swamps and marshes. The fabled
wetlands, though, were well to the east of the road Prince
Ahmad and his party traveled, and though they looked hard,
they could not spy any marshes. While they were disappointed
at not seeing these noted features, they were just as relieved

not to have to travel through the swamps where, so legend had it, the mosquitoes were as large as hummingbirds.

On the third day of their travels south of Damasc they came to the gates of the city of Pastar, capital of Nikhrash. This was a larger city than they were used to seeing of late, far larger than Tarass or Astaburya or the city of the apes—larger even than Damasc, one of the major cities on the western trade routes from Ravan. Pastar was a city to rival Ravan in size, if not in splendor, and it was an important hub of the area's commerce. Most trade being sent down to be shipped through this portion of the Central Sea had to travel through Pastar because of the mountain passes that made other routes difficult and expensive. Pastar thrived on that trade.

The travelers pulled to a halt outside the gates. "The same problem faces us as it did in Damasc," Umar said. "We have no way of knowing whether the king of Nikhrash, whose name I don't even know, has made some bargain with Shammara. Worse even than that, I have no personal contacts within the Pastari priesthood, so I have no way to vouch for the king's integrity. I do know that the Nikhrashi have a reputation for treachery, even under the best of circumstances. I hate to judge an entire people by idle stories, but in our exposed condition we want to minimize our risks as much as possible."

"Perhaps we should skip Nikhrash altogether," Jafar suggested. "There are plenty of other kings willing to help us. The few Nikhrashi I've known personally have all been devious sorts—and 'idle stories' usually don't circulate for long if there's no truth behind them."

But Prince Ahmad shook his head as he counterargued, "I was charged by the prophet Muhmad to gather the forces of mankind as I traveled through Parsina on our quest. We will certainly need all the allies we can get in the battle against Rimahn. The Nikhrashi would make strong allies, if we can convince them to join us. I feel we must at least try, provided they have not already allied themselves with our enemies."

"But how can we ascertain that?" Umar asked.

"May I make a suggestion, O wise and venerable priest?" Leila said. "This is winter, and the night falls quickly here. The city gates will soon shut until morning, and I'd rather not camp just outside the walls—it tends to make the soldiers nervous. Why don't we enter the city as commoners, find a comfortable caravanserai in which to spend the night, and *then* discuss how to determine this king's trustworthiness?"

The others could not fault Leila's reasoning, so they rode to the gate just in time to get through before the city closed up for the night. Prince Ahmad pulled the hood of his fur-lined cape up around his head, but if any people this far from Ravan recognized him, they gave no indication. The guards at the gate recommended, for a small consideration, a caravanserai not far from the entrance where the travelers could find decent accommodations for the evening.

Once safely ensconced in their rooms, with their bodies warm and their bellies full, the group resumed their deliberations. As the arguments went around and around, Leila began emitting a series of deep sighs. Finally she could stay silent no longer. "Is it necessary to tell the Nikhrashi king that Ahmad is the deposed prince of Ravan? Why can't he be simply a warrior of noble birth, as he claimed in Buryan? That way the king would be far less tempted to kill him."

"But would a powerful king be willing to withdraw his forces from his city, leaving it defenseless in the path of the invader, to ally himself with a simple warrior?" Jafar asked. "Prince Ahmad's title has always been a strong convincing argument before."

"We shall invoke the name of Oromasd," Umar said.

"I don't wish to sound sacrilegious," Jafar replied, "but there are many monarchs to whom that is not quite enough of a reference. Any fool can claim to be acting in Oromasd's name; many do, in fact. Whatever traits this Nikhrashi king may have, I doubt that a trusting nature will be one of them."

"If he cannot see the truth of our cause—particularly in the face of what he must know about these invaders from the west—then he is no fit ally to fight in Oromasd's army," Umar declared with an air of decision. And with that, the discussion ended for the evening.

When they talked some more in the morning, the men decided that Leila and Selima should stay safely back in the caravanserai, lest any trouble occur; the prince, Umar, and Jafar—with Cari accompanying him invisibly, as usual—would visit the palace and seek an audience with the king of Nikhrash.

The three guards at the palace door tried to prevent their entry, saying that the king was not holding a diwan today, and that he was conferring with his wazirs on state business. Since Prince Ahmad did not have his royal title to fall back on, they had no official leverage; Jafar decided, instead, to use a little "magic."

"No man may obstruct the path of Jafar al-Sharif, wizard of the southern provinces," he said with grandiloquent dignity, then raised his arms to the heavens and intoned:

"Spirits that hearken to my plea,
Support, sustain, and succor me;
Spirits of air and spirits of grass,
Disarm these men and let us pass."

Ever quick to pick up her cue, Cari swept into action. The nearest of the three guards had his scimitar yanked from its sheath and thrown with a clang to the ground some cubits away. The other two guards reached for their own swords, but had the blades yanked from their grasp and thrown similarly to the ground.

The men stared at Jafar, confused and frightened—but now that he had made his point, Jafar tried to be conciliatory. "Had I been an enemy, your heads would have been removed by your own swords. But my companions and I bear no ill will to you or to your king or to Nikhrash. We merely wish to speak to your sovereign on a matter of utmost urgency. Please be so kind as to escort us to His Majesty's presence at once, and you will each receive a golden dinar for your trouble."

With the request phrased in such a manner, the guards cooperated fully. They led the strangers down marble halls with rows of tall columns on either side, until at last they came to the council chamber where King Machenos sat in conference with his advisers.

King Machenos was a tall man with a hard, leathery face and a scowl permanently etched upon his features. He might at one time have been called handsome, but his scowl and the scar running down his face from his right eye to the corner of his mouth gave him a sinister appearance. The scar he had gained in battle and could not help—but the scowl he had developed for many years on his own, and could blame on no one but himself.

"Explain this intrusion on my council of state!" he bellowed when he saw the strangers enter. "No one may interrupt the king and his advisers."

"Your Majesty, were it not so desperate a situation, we would not have chosen to do so," Prince Ahmad said, stepping forward. "Only the current emergency made us prevail so upon your guards."

King Machenos snorted. "My *former* guards, you mean."

"Be not angry with them, O mighty and exalted king, for they were bewitched into helping us by the power of my wizard, Jafar al-Sharif."

The king's eyes narrowed—an ugly gesture, considering his scar and his scowl. With a wave of his hand he dismissed the errant guards, then continued looking at Prince Ahmad. "You still have given no explanation for your presence or your behavior, nor for this 'emergency' you claim as rationale."

Prince Ahmad bowed low and introduced himself simply as Ahmad Khaled, a noble warrior, then introduced his companions by their full names. King Machenos ignored the priest and turned his gaze to Jafar al-Sharif. "A wizard, eh. Perhaps you know *my* court magician, Appolinar Dektros." He gestured to an older man sitting calmly cross-legged on a cushion beside the throne.

Jafar's stomach turned itself into knots, but he refused to let his nervousness show. After all, hadn't he already fooled one wizard and killed another? "I have not had the honor of meeting Appolinar Dektros before today," he said with a slight bow.

"Nor I you, O Jafar," said the wizard in a high voice. His head gave the slightest of nods in Jafar's direction, but the rest of his body remained completely undisturbed upon his cushion.

Prince Ahmad spoke again, returning everyone's attention to him. "We come before you, O great king, on a matter of dire urgency for the entire world." And then he explained, yet again, the situation as told to him by Muhmad, including his mission to unite mankind into a single army to oppose Rimahn.

"You have no doubt heard about the growing army driving eastward from the Western Sea," he concluded. "This can only be the forces of Aeshma marching to crush mankind. Our only hope is to face this force together and, with Oromasd's help, defeat the powers of evil as King Shahriyan did so many ages ago."

King Machenos listened stonily to the prince's recitation, giving no indication of what thoughts were hiding behind that scowling mask. Finally, when the younger man was done, King Machenos spoke again. "You tell a disturbing story, O warrior. If it is true, it requires much thought. I must speak privately with my wazirs and gain the wisdom of their advice. Please wait outside."

"Of course, Your Majesty," said Prince Ahmad as he and his companions turned to go.

As soon as the three strangers had left the room, the wizard Appolinar Dektros waved his right hand through the air in a mystical gesture. "I have surrounded us with an invisible wall of silence, Your Majesty," he said. "No one outside, not even that wizard, can overhear us without my knowing of it."

"Good." The king nodded. "Now, what do you men make of this matter?"

"There *are* rumors coming out of the west and Fricaz about a demonic sorcerer and his invincible army," one adviser said. "That much of the story, at least, holds true."

The king turned to Appolinar Dektros. "What do you make of this young man's story?"

"Improbable, but not impossible. The mage Muhmad is known for his eccentricities. He may indeed have sent these people on such a mission—though if he did, it's doomed to failure."

"Why do you say that?"

"Because the Crystal of Oromasd has only been used once, by the great mage Ali Maimun. No lesser man could dare handle it—and this Jafar al-Sharif has not the power of that mage of yore."

"You can tell that just by looking at him?"

"I did more than look, Your Majesty. I tested him. While the young man was speaking, I silently crafted invisible spells and hurled them against this foreign wizard. An ordinary man would have withered and died, yet my spells had no effect on him."

King Machenos looked puzzled. "That would seem to indicate he has some strong power."

"Some power, yes. But a powerful wizard would have realized what I was doing and thrown spells back at me to test my own defenses. This Jafar did no such thing. In fact, he acted as though he didn't even know I was doing anything. He cannot have the strength needed to wield the Crystal of Oromasd."

"Or perhaps," the king suggested, "he's so strong he doesn't have to bother about the likes of you."

Appolinar Dektros smiled. "I'll take my chances on that. I know what I know."

"Assuming that what you say is true, that this Jafar al-Sharif does not have the power needed to use the Crystal of Oromasd, then the army being gathered by this Ahmad Khaled will be easily defeated; no mortals could stand unaided against the power of Aeshma and Rimahn. He doesn't even *claim* to have any heroes on his side like Argun or Shiratz. His battle will be lost—and we will be, too, if we side with him."

"Quite so, Your Majesty," spoke up a fawning wazir.

"On the other hand," the king continued, "there is a chance we can bargain with this invader out of the west, form an alliance that will be to our mutual advantage."

Appolinar Dektros frowned. "The rumors I've heard say that this conqueror does not bargain, that he simply takes what he wants and murders all who oppose him."

"You'd better hope he bargains, O worker of magic, for the rumors also say he kills all wizards he finds within his realm. But I think we may be in a position to offer him something he'd like to have."

"What is that?"

"Conclusive proof that his ordained enemy, the man who was to lead the armies of mankind against him, no longer exists—the head of Ahmad Khaled. Even if this young man has delusions of grandeur and is not the ordained one, the mere fact that we disposed of a troublemaker may sit well with this new emperor. If we show that we can cooperate with him, he may be favorably inclined toward us."

He looked around at the riches of his palace. "I shall miss being king of Pastar—but there may be some advantages to being a high satrap in so vast an empire."

"How do you propose to kill these strangers?" Appolinar Dektros asked. "The wizard has shown some proficiency at dealing with swords, and he appears immune to my magical spells."

"Directness sometimes has its virtues, but there are other methods equally tried and equally true. Let us experiment. Perhaps a subtler means will be more effective at achieving our ends."

And thus it was that King Machenos invited the three travelers to dine with him at his midday meal and discuss further the nature of the crisis that threatened Parsina. They ate of shish kebob and hummus, and grape leaves stuffed with spiced meats, and nan-e lavash. And it was during this meal that the three travelers drank of poisoned wine and collapsed, one after another, on the floor of the king's dining chamber.

And two mice who had been watching this procedure— who had until recently worn the shapes of crows—vanished immediately from their hiding place to report to their master, many thousands of parasangs away in Shahdur Castle.

11

The Reunion

The weeks that followed her marriage to Prince Haroun were trying ones for Princess Oma. In her father's kingdom, there had been diversions galore: tutors to instruct her, musicians to play for her, her sisters and the other women of the harem to talk with, and a whole cadre of servants carefully cultivated over the years to fill her in on all the political machinations within the palace. Princess Oma was an intelligent woman with a restless spirit, and she could not be content relegated to enforced idleness.

Here in Ravan she felt isolated from all that interested her. There were no tutors, no sources of intellectual stimulation. When she asked for books, she received blank stares; she wasn't sure whether Shammara had deliberately cut her off from any enlightenment, or whether the thought of a woman, a princess, reading was just totally alien to the eunuchs who attended her. No musicians played specifically to entertain her. She had brought a few of her favorite servants with her, but the other women in the harem shunned her; perhaps they felt that becoming too friendly with this foreign princess might incur Shammara's displeasure. And as for political intrigues, that was a dangerous field to explore—Shammara's sense of territoriality was finely tuned, and she looked unfavorably on trespassers.

At first, Oma contented herself with exploring the delights of the royal gardens, which numbered among the wonders of the world. Such were their beauty that a person could spend hours enrapt by the brilliant colors of the blossoms, the scents both subtle and strong, the songs of the many birds who nested here year round, the taste of the many fruits ripe for the picking, and the caress of the gentle breezes that wafted through the arbor. So large and varied were the gardens that she spent several whole days happily exploring their many twisting avenues and discovering both their beauties and their mysteries. These peaceful days allowed her to postpone temporarily her worries about the dismal prospects for her future as Haroun's all-but-ignored queen.

She indulged in intimacies with her handmaidens with a fervor just short of religious, but the excitement of this paled quickly. And then there was nothing left for her to do. She roamed the corridors of the women's section of the palace like a hungry spirit eagerly seeking amusement to quench the fires of her soul. Hers was a life that Leila, had she known of it, would have commiserated with.

As autumn merged slowly into winter, Oma took to bribing the palace servants to learn any interesting tidbits of gossip about the goings-on in the city. The servants took her coins and gave her innocuous information, then—as befit prudent people—they told Shammara exactly what was going on. The older woman kept a close watch on Princess Oma and thought deeply about her situation.

"I'd have preferred a daughter-in-law with the brain of a cow," Shammara told the wali of police during one of their periodic meetings. "One who did as she was told and lounged around the harem, eating rahat lakhoum and staring idly at the walls, and occasionally servicing my son as a wife ought to do. This Oma is entirely too smart, both for her sake and for mine. She'll cause trouble if we don't do something about her quickly."

"She's served the purpose we had of her," the wali pointed out. "Now that she's legitimized Haroun's claim to Marakh, she can be eliminated with little bother and no one would care."

But Shammara shook her head. "*I* would care. You're always too quick to try the ultimate solution, which keeps you from reaching the top rungs on the ladder of power. Subtlety is every bit as important as ruthlessness.

"For all her contrariness, this headstrong princess is a resource we dare not squander. If she were a little less smart, I would take her as my apprentice and guide her political career; she could be the daughter I never had. But I can't trust her that far. Her restless energy could become a flame that consumes all of us.

"At the same time, there may come a day when we need someone with her qualities of intellect and drive. She may need to become Haroun's queen in fact as well as in name. We don't need to eliminate her, merely to channel her energies in a beneficial way, much as a farmer diverts a stream to irrigate his field. Given the proper inducements, she will cease to be a threat and yet remain intact for our future use. And I think I have some idea of what those inducements might be."

And thus it was that one day, several weeks later, as Princess Oma was sitting in her room and wondering which of the multitudinous and, for all practical purposes, identical corridors she would prowl, she heard a woman's voice say, "Good morning, Your Highness. I hope a humble concubine may still find favor within your eyes."

Oma leaped up from her cushion before even turning her head to confirm what her ears had told her. "Rabah!" she exclaimed. "Rabah, you have come to me!"

And, ignoring all her royal dignity, she raced to the side of her old friend and confidant. The two women embraced, and kissed, and wept, and kissed some more, and for the next several hours were so lost in one another's presence that no words were necessary. Only after physical exhaustion set in did Princess Oma lie back upon her mattress and say, "Oh, Rabah, I'm so happy to see you. But how come you to be here in Ravan?"

"I am a concubine to the king of Marakh. When your father died, I became concubine to the new king, your husband, Prince Haroun. Forgive me, but I find it hard to call him king—he's still just a little boy, and an ugly one at that."

"*You* haven't had to belly with him."

"Not yet, at least," Rabah said with a shudder. "With luck, I may never have to."

"May Oromasd so bless us both," the princess echoed.

"Anyway, most of the harem was dispersed," Rabah continued her story. "Your father's wives were retired into comfortable widowhood, and most of the concubines were sold. Since I was Haroun's property anyway, I entreated Raoul, the harem master, to transfer me to Haroun's harem here in Ravan. Knowing the great affection you have for me, Raoul acceded for only a modest bribe. I was sent with an accommodating caravan, and here I am. But tell me, O my doe-eyed princess, how do you fare in the world's most fabulous city?"

And because her heart was aching, the dam of Oma's reserve broke and her story gushed out: the horrible trip from Marakh, her chilling encounter with Shammara, the beautiful if ominous wedding ceremony, the horrors of her wedding night, and the weight of the tedium upon her shoulders since that date. Rabah listened and stroked her princess tenderly, making cooing sounds and shaking her head in sympathy.

When the tale had completely unfolded, Rabah held Oma's head tenderly to her breast and said, "Such sorrows ill befit such an illustrious lady as yourself. Had I known all that awaited you here in Ravan, I would not have urged you so eagerly to uphold your royal duties. But I do hope that the experience of your wedding night will not prejudice you forever against the enjoyment of men."

"Haroun shall not touch me again," Oma said between clenched teeth. "On that matter I have sworn to Oromasd my mightiest oaths."

"Not Haroun," Rabah agreed. "No, never Haroun."

"What else is there? I'm surrounded by eunuchs and other women."

Rabah was silent for a moment, then spoke slowly. "I spent some time in this harem as an attendant before being given to your father as a concubine. This palace is old, and I know many of its secrets. There are unused corridors, hidden doors, secret chambers that women of courage and imagination can use to their advantage."

Oma's eyes lit up at the prospect of adventure. "Are you suggesting I slip away from the palace?"

Rabah was even more hesitant. "Well, not at first, Your Highness. There are many dangers outside palace walls that you've never faced, and you would make a rich prize for some thief or murderer. And, if your absence should be discovered, the penalty would be harsh for both of us."

"No one even knows or cares if I'm here or not," Oma muttered.

"What I am saying," Rabah stressed, "is that there are other avenues open to you. Your maidenhead, which you so rightly cherished before, is now no longer an issue. There is a new world that, with caution, you may sample to your heart's content."

Even with her head resting on Rabah's bosom, Princess Oma felt uneasy. "I don't know. It sounds exciting . . . but after Haroun—"

"Haroun is not typical of anything. He is a walking pustule that Oromasd, perhaps as a jest upon the world, elevated to king. Other men can be handsome and gentle and kind and good. There is an almost infinite diversity, and much of it is worth tasting. Would you swear off all fruit because you bit into one bitter orange?"

"I don't even know where to begin—"

"Let me be your guide on this adventure. Let me find a man worthy to be your first real love, and let me bring him to you secretly within the palace. I will stay with you as you explore the richness of his body, to ensure the success of your experiment."

"Well, perhaps," Oma said. "As long as you stay with me."

"Ever at your side, O my princess. Just put yourself in my hands."

"Don't I always?" Oma giggled.

And three days later, Rabah brought into the palace, via secret tunnels, a young man so breathtakingly handsome that even Oma gasped when first she beheld him. Frightened, she clung to Rabah, who gently awoke her desire until it overcame her fear. Then Oma turned, finally, to the exquisite man the concubine had brought. The young man held her with a gentle firmness, and kissed her and caressed her, and made love to her with such passion that the princess was carried with him on the waves of rapture. Thus, with Rabah's skillful help, did Princess Oma discover her new calling—and the city of Ravan was never to be the same.

In a different way, the weeks following his marriage and his sudden accession to the throne of Marakh were as confusing and frustrating for Prince Haroun as they were for Oma. There was his anger over the fiasco on his wedding night, only partially soothed by the swarms of new slave girls his mother obligingly bought for him. Then, when he was declared king of Marakh in his own right, with no regent appointed over him, he had thought he'd finally come into the power his mother had promised him all along.

But no, it was not to be. His mother still made the decisions. She told him what to say. Every speech he gave in public, every pronouncement he made, he could feel her standing over his shoulder, checking his every word to make sure it was as she intended it to be. On those few occasions when he tried to improvise something on his own, she slashed at him verbally when they were alone in his apartment, reducing him to tears and then holding him afterwards to assure him that she still loved him, that everything was still all right. His moments of defiance became rarer and rarer, and his devotion to his mother increased ever deeper—but the slave girls were being used up at an alarming rate.

In one rare burst of initiative, he asked his mother if he could travel to Marakh, so that he could rule more directly there while she herself ruled Ravan. Her refusal was fast and firm. She insisted that the roads were unsafe, and reminded him of what had happened to his half brother. Marakh was a peaceful kingdom that could be ruled just as easily from afar. She sent her own handpicked emissaries to administer Haroun's justice just as she would have done—but Haroun himself was to stay by her side because, as she said, she loved him so much she didn't dare be parted from him for even a single day.

Haroun pouted. What fun was it to rule a country he'd never even seen? He felt he might as well be talking to the clouds, for all the impact he had on life.

Haroun had never been the student that his brother Ahmad had been. After learning the rudiments of reading and writing, the priests of the Royal Temple had dismissed him from the madrasa as a waste of their time, and his. He had turned to gambling, women, and drinking as a way to pass the heavy time of his neglected youth while his brother received all the accolades. Now that he was suddenly in the forefront, he scorned the priests and held himself deliberately apart from them. He attended the regent's diwan, even though his mother made him stay to the side and keep silent.

He quickly grew bored with the old regent, Kateb bin Salih, and his senile ways. Even on those rare days when the regent had some semblance of his faculties about him, Haroun chafed at the direction the so-called justice was taking. Kateb bin Salih seemed to think there was some objective notion known as "fair," and was trying to mete out his justice according to impartial standards. To Haroun's mind, this was pure silliness. Oromasd had obviously established a system of rank, with Haroun at the top, and it was sacrilege to suggest anything else. Certain people were better than others by virtue of birth and wealth, and they naturally deserved the benefit of any doubts or ambiguities in the law.

Well, Haroun would straighten that out soon enough. His eighteenth birthday was rapidly approaching. Then he would ascend his real throne, the throne of Ravan, and no one, not even his mother, could tell him what to do then.

* * *

All the while she thought her husband was dead, Alhena had refrained from the pleasantries of daily life. What right had she to partake of living, she thought, when her husband had been so cruelly denied these same pleasures? She went through the motions of living, but already she had resigned herself to the dahkma.

The note brought by the Khmeri priest changed all that. Umar was alive, and life was again worth living. *Oromasd has plans for my husband*, she thought, *so he might have plans for me, too. Who am I to thwart his will? I must be ready to answer his call, when it comes.*

She could not let the rest of Ravan know that Umar was still alive, so she had to keep up with the social proprieties of dress and manner. But the rest of her widowhood was cast aside like an old rag. She delighted once again in the taste and aroma of her food. She cleaned her house so that it was sparkling, in case Umar arrived tomorrow to reclaim it. She weeded her garden and planted new winter seeds, and cleared dirt from the fountain so it would flow freely again. She wore the clothes of mourning, but her heart sang a song of hope.

And finally, after a prudent period, she visited the hammam. She undressed gracefully in the camekan, took a towel, and walked into the soguluk, where the attendant oiled her skin and rubbed away the tensions of the day. Alhena spent only a short time in the heat of the sicakluk, then returned to the middle room to sit and watch and listen.

At first glance, nothing seemed to have changed from those happier days before Umar had left the city. The women still laughed and chatted and gossiped, comparing stories of their husbands and of the different merchants in the bazaars. Only after a long time of listening was a subtle difference made apparent: people no longer commented about their taxes, or about the justice that was being dispensed, or about any of the political affairs of the city. True, such talk had always been rare among women, but now it was totally nonexistent. People were frightened, and so buried themselves in the trivialities of life instead of the larger issues.

Alhena was about to leave when she saw an old friend, Barakah, enter the room. Barakah was the wife of Kalem bin Ali, a minor nobleman and a friend of Umar's. Bin Ali had always donated generously to the temple, and Umar had said of him on many occasions that he was an honest and righteous man.

Barakah saw Alhena at almost the same instant, and came over to speak with her. "My heart yearns to comfort you in this time of your sorrow, O noble Alhena," she said. "Your husband's death was a loss to us all. I know how deeply you loved him, and how keenly you must feel his loss."

"It was a heavy blow," Alhena admitted, "though with each passing day the pain diminishes. Umar and I shared so much good in our lives—how can I allow the bad to outweigh that?"

"I know Umar would have been proud of you for bearing up this way. And as tragic as his loss was to you, so was the loss of Prince Ahmad to all of Ravan. He was—"

She stopped abruptly as she realized what she was doing. Her life and her husband's were probably hostage to her silence. She let the thought go uncompleted, and switched the topic instead to the management of the temple and the job that Yusef bin Nard was doing in Umar's place. From there, the topic drifted to the quality and price of winter vegetables.

Finally, unable to endure the trivia any longer, Alhena excused herself, citing pressing matters at home. As she got up to leave, Barakah grabbed her by the elbow. Alhena looked down and saw a look of desperation in the other woman's eyes.

"I will see you again, won't I?" Barakah asked. "We can meet again here in the hammam."

"Sometime, I'm sure."

"I'm here every week. Every week, this same day, this same time."

"Next week, then, if it be Oromasd's will," Alhena promised.

Normally she left the hammam feeling relaxed and refreshed, but today was different. She left feeling as though a heavy weight had just been dropped onto her back, and she had no idea what it was or how to get rid of it.

12

The Sea Captain

When his Marid spies brought him word of the poisoning of Jafar al-Sharif, the wizard Akar was torn between conflicting desires. Jafar al-Sharif was his sworn enemy, a man he himself had striven to kill with the mightiest curse at his disposal. His heart welcomed the news of Jafar's imminent death, even as he cursed its timing.

If this fraud dies now, before he gathers the pieces of the Crystal, I could lose much time, he thought. *Jafar al-Sharif already has the first two pieces, which I would have to regain. Then I would have to discover the hiding places of the remaining two pieces, which he obviously already knows. Having to interfere on his behalf is galling—the fool cannot detect even the most simple of poisons!—but Aeshma must be brought to heel quickly, before he gains full mastery of himself and the world. This mountebank has half the weapon to do that, and can find the rest. However annoying it is, the eventual power is worth the temporary displeasure. My revenge shall be sweeter for the delay.*

Whatever action he took would have to be quick—even he could not reverse death once it occurred. He wondered whether he should do anything to save Jafar's companions as well. Muhmad had said nothing about them, and they probably had no bearing on the matter of the Crystal. Still, since Jafar al-Sharif had so few talents of his own, he would need the help of others in his quest. It would be just as easy to save the whole party together—and perhaps he could find some use for these people after he had gained what he wanted.

"Return immediately to Pastar," he ordered the Marids. "Rid the accursed Jafar and his companions of the poison that they swallowed, and help them escape the clutches of this King Machenos. Do not let yourselves be seen, and do as little as possible, but all that it necessary. Quickly now, before the poison's effects are irreversible!"

As the djinni sped off on their mission, Akar sat down cross-legged to contemplate his future course of action. He was already interfering once on behalf of his enemy, and that left a bitter feeling on his tongue. Furthermore, his action would be blatant, far more obvious than the subtle maneuvering he preferred. Only the immediacy of the problem caused him to act so rashly; had he more time, he would have chosen a method far less obvious. He would not have tolerated an apprentice who behaved in so coarse a manner, even if he could have tolerated any apprentice at all. This was inexcusable within himself.

But short of being on the spot personally, there was little else he could do—and that was a journey he would not take. There were too many preliminary details to be made within Shahdur Castle to prepare for the arrival of the Crystal of Oromasd. The castle itself had to be purified, a special room had to be readied. Akar's presence could not be spared—nor could he keep wasting time watching over every little crisis that occurred to Jafar al-Sharif. This long-distance interference was too costly in terms of time and energy.

Somehow, a new solution would have to be found.

When Cari saw her master and the others fall, she immediately knew foul play had occurred. The bonds of the ring Jafar wore would have made her move to his rescue, even if the cries of her own spirit hadn't already pushed her in that direction.

She first flew to his side, noting that his breathing was ragged and his eyes were glassy. She felt for his pulse and found it uneven, growing rapidly weaker. She had no knowledge of poisons, and could think of no way to counteract what the Nikhrashi king and his wizard had done to her master.

In a blinding rage she flew at the villains who sat at the other end of the table, smiling at the results of their handiwork. The Jann's thoughts were far from righteous as she contemplated the revenge she would wreak upon their fragile human bodies. Let the priests of the temples counsel patience; she would have bloody retribution upon those who would murder her master.

Perhaps for the good of her soul, she was stopped short of her intentions by the magical charms Appolinar Dektros had

routinely placed around himself and the king to protect them
from counterattack by Jafar al-Sharif. Rail though she might,
she could not approach the two men and perform the mayhem
her heart so craved.

But as her heart cried out, so did her voice—a keening
wail that echoed through King Machenos's palace with its anguished anger. Many who heard it fell prostrate in fear, and to
their dying day swore the palace of Pastar was haunted by the
wrathful spirit of the wizard Jafar al-Sharif. Many were the
prayers to Oromasd that afternoon from men who normally
only went to temple at the turning of the seasons, and many
were the people who counted themselves blessed that they
survived the experience.

Frustrated by her inability to save her master or destroy
his murderers, Cari exacted her toll on the rest of the room.
The king's fine silver plates flew off the sofreh and clattered
alarmingly against the marble walls, flung there with the su-
perhuman strength of an enraged Jann. Invisible hands shattered glass goblets and pitchers. Thick tapestries on the walls
were ripped in two; heavy wooden doors were smashed by the
rampaging Cari.

But the wizard Appolinar Dektros was not about to allow
the palace to be terrorized in this manner. Even as Cari raged,
the yatu was calmly making mystic gestures and reciting a spell
beneath his breath. As he finished his final words and gestures,
Cari found herself bound by invisible ropes and threads—
much as she had felt on that accursed day when the wizard
Akar had chained her soul to the brass ring. Struggle though
she might, she could not break free of these bonds. She took
slim comfort in the knowledge that she was still invisible to
human eyes—but if Appolinar Dektros knew the proper
spells, he might compel her to become visible, and then her
life could be extinguished as abruptly as her master's.

But the Nikhrashi sorcerer either did not know those
spells or chose not to use them. Instead, she felt an oppressive
darkness closing in on her mind, and soon there were no
thoughts. Cari's consciousness fled to a formless place beyond
even the dreams of djinni.

The wailing stopped, the destruction stopped, and
Appolinar Dektros began congratulating himself on winning
yet another battle with the forces of the magical world. Just as
he was sure of his success, however, events took a new turn,
one that even his powers could never handle.

The two Marids, working at top speed, entered in turn the bodies of Jafar al-Sharif, Prince Ahmad, and Umar bin Ibrahim. As they passed through the bodies, they absorbed into themselves all traces of the poison King Machenos had used, so that the toxins no longer worked their evils upon the three unconscious men. Within minutes they all started blinking, and then Prince Ahmad opened his eyes. Jafar and Umar quickly joined him in consciousness, and they sat up, wondering at the change in the world around them and almost oblivious to the goggle-eyed stare of the king and his wazirs.

Even though he didn't know the reason, King Machenos could see that his plot was unraveling. Abandoning all subtlety, he called for his personal guards to kill the strangers who still sat, dazed, on the ground. The highly trained soldiers, handpicked by King Machenos as the best in his realm, strode forward with swords drawn, ready to obey despite the curious happenings in the hall these past few minutes.

But they never made it to their quarries. With a fierce howl, the Marids became a whirlwind springing up from the floor of the dining room, reaching to the very ceiling, and this whirlwind did suck into it each of the guards who had drawn a sword. Each soldier screamed briefly as he was pulled off his feet into the eye of this cyclone, and then was heard of no more. When they saw what was happening, the rest of the bystanders turned and fled the chamber, leaving the king and his wizard alone with the eerie phenomena.

Appolinar Dektros began a new spell to counter the magic that was obviously at work against him. These Marids, however, were not lost in rage as Cari had been; they could clearly sense the magical forces being directed toward them, and they would not allow themselves to fall prey to any second-rate human conjurer. Only someone as strong as Akar could hope to command them, and no lesser sorcerer could defend against them if they were determined to attack.

The spells used by Appolinar Dektros were sufficient to protect him from minor djinni, and even other wizards with abilities similar to his own. These Marids, however, were each nearly two thousand years old, and filled with the pride and power of their race.

The Marids took his spell as a challenge, and struck against the wizard's shield with the full power of their fury. Although nothing physical happened, the wizard felt their assault as a knife to his innards, and he doubled up in pain. This,

in turn, reduced his ability to focus his will on the protection
spells, which weakened them still further. Encouraged by this
success, the Marids battered repeatedly against the wizard's
defenses until at last they overwhelmed his shields and all barriers crumbled. Then they raced in upon him and devoured
him alive. To the few spectators left in the room, it seemed as
though his flesh were simply disappearing into nothingness
leaving but a skeleton behind, and his screams of anguish
chilled the blood.

Jafar, Ahmad, and Umar did not know precisely what was
happening, but their wits were quick enough to piece together
most of the story. There could be no safety for them within this
palace—or indeed, within this city. Escape was their highest
priority; getting an explanation of the events was at best a dim
second.

Rising unsteadily to their feet, they staggered toward the
door through which they had entered. With each step their
legs became steadier and their strength returned still more,
until by the time they left the dining room they were only
slightly wobbly. No one blocked their exit, so captured was the
spectators' attention by the wizard's grisly fate.

Once the Marids finished devouring Appolinar Dektros
and the three travelers had left the room, they ceased their
havoc within the palace. Belatedly they remembered Akar's
command to be as inconspicuous as possible, and to use minimal force on Jafar's behalf. The storyteller and his companions
had been rescued from the worst of the fate King Machenos
had held in store for them; the Marids would do nothing further unless imminent death again loomed for their charge.

Jafar and his comrades ran into the hallway, to be confronted by a milling mob of the king's men. The soldiers were
in disarray after the catastrophe in the dining room, but they
knew their king would be displeased if these strangers escaped
from the palace. The braver among them drew their swords,
prepared to block the travelers' exit.

Prince Ahmad drew his own sword and braced himself for
another fight against impossible odds. But before he could advance against the foe, Jafar al-Sharif stepped forward and
raised his arms above his head. "Begone!" the would-be wizard
bellowed. "He who interferes with us in any way will suffer a
worse fate than the king's wizard."

Jafar had no idea whether Cari was still with him, or
whether she had been responsible for the mayhem he'd wit-

nessed in the other room. He had no idea how he could back up his threat if any of the guards defied him—but fortunately, none of them was that foolhardy. Their king couldn't single out any one person for punishment—and in any case, they would rather face his wrath than the supernatural menace Jafar al-Sharif had used against the royal sorcerer.

A path cleared before the travelers, who hesitated no longer, but ran as fast as they could out of the palace. King Machenos and his people were confused for now, but there was no telling how quickly they could recover their wits and re-group their forces. Before that happened, the travelers wanted to be as far from this city as possible, beyond the king's clutches.

As the trio stopped on one street corner to catch their breath, Jafar called for Cari, but received no reply. Worried, he rubbed the ring on the middle finger of his left hand and in-voked the spell that brought her to him.

With Appolinar Dektros now dead, the spells he had placed upon Cari were dissolving. The power of Jafar's ring reasserted itself upon her, and she materialized before him, still a little groggy, in a cloud of pink smoke scented of ylang-ylang. "I come at your command, O my master," she said as she made the ritual salaam. Then, as she remembered she'd last seen him poisoned and lying near death on the palace floor, she smiled and said, "I am pleased to see you made it safely out of the treacherous king's clutches."

"Thanks to your quick work," Jafar said, misinterpreting what had happened.

"Mine? But master—"

"There's no time to discuss it now. Fly on ahead of us to the caravanserai. Help Leila pack up the horses. Tell her and Selima to be ready to leave the instant we get there. We must be far from this city before King Machenos reorganizes his forces and comes after us."

"Hearkening and obedience," Cari said, and sped off on her task. The men, meanwhile, ran through the crowded streets of the city at their own fastest pace, pushing people aside in their haste to escape from the Nikhrashi king.

After half an hour they arrived back at the caravanserai. True to Jafar's instructions, the women were prepared for im-minent departure. The men mounted their horses and, though they could not ride at their usual magical speed through these twisting, crowded streets, they did reach the gates in short order—only to find a party of soldiers waiting for them.

King Machenos, once he had recovered from the horror of seeing his wizard killed and his plans demolished, became more determined than ever not to let these strangers escape. He sent his fastest runner to the gates, ordering the guards to stop this wizard and his group from leaving the city—although, prudently, the king himself would not be there to help them. He had been spared from the last burst of magical mayhem, and did not want to tickle kismet any further.

The city gate had been locked shut in midday, and a squad of ten mounted men, all armed with swords, stood directly in the fugitives' path. Once again a fight would be impossible; Jafar sighed as he realized another bluff was needed here.

"Another diversion, O Cari," he whispered. "Something to unhorse our opposition."

Aloud, he cried out, "I call upon the magical forces at my command to clear the path so my companions and I can leave this city in peace, as indeed we entered it."

And as he raised his arms in a broad gesture, Cari flew invisibly behind the back legs of the enemy horses, hitting their knees as she went by. Some of the mounts stumbled and fell; others reared in panic and tossed their riders to the ground. There was now a clear path to the closed gate ahead of the travelers.

Jafar al-Sharif made another series of what he hoped looked like mystic gestures. "May the great gate of Pastar open for us, that we may leave the city," he intoned.

Cari found the giant wheel that controlled the gate, and began turning it as the gatekeeper looked on, startled. Other people who had gathered in the streets nearby, seeing this further manifestation of Jafar's magical powers, fled in panic. The area around them was soon barren of anyone but themselves.

In such manner are stories born, Jafar thought with mild amazement. *Years from now, these people will tell their children about the day when the mighty wizard visited Pastar and rained death and destruction upon their city. They'll say the sky was full of comets, and that I razed buildings to the ground and uprooted trees with the wiggle of a finger. I wonder—are the stories I tell, with all their grand deeds and fabulous events, based on as little as this? Were the heroes of old as fraudulent as I am?*

But Jafar al-Sharif had little inclination and less time to ponder this question, so basic to his chosen vocation, as the travelers took advantage of the opening in front of them. They rode out the gate and into the countryside, where they stopped briefly to feed their horses some of the mystical powder. Then, with no further impediments in their way, they raced southward and west at magical speed, so fast that none from the palace could follow them. By the end of the day they had so outdistanced any possible pursuit that they no longer worried about any threat from Pastar.

That evening they did not stop at a caravanserai, but camped instead in the open fields. The incident in Pastar had left a bad taste in everyone's mouth, and the less they had to do with other people tonight, the better they would feel. The weather at least cooperated with them; the sky was clear and the air was not too cold, considering the time of year.

Winter was coming hard upon them, which worried Prince Ahmad. He had an appointment to lead the united armies of mankind on the Leewahr Plains at the first thaws of spring; it was almost winter, and they had only half the pieces of the Crystal they needed. Jafar, too, was worried. His daughter was fading rapidly, and he was afraid he would get the Crystal's pieces too late to save her.

As they sat around their campfire, Jafar told Leila and Selima the story of what had happened to them at King Machenos's palace up until the point where he and his companions had passed out from the wine. "I'm not sure what happened during the next few minutes," he admitted.

"You were poisoned, O master," Cari spoke up. "I raced to your side, as is my duty, but I know nothing of poisons and could not help you. Then I tried to attack the king and his wizard, but could not do anything against them, either, because of the wizard's spells."

"Then how *did* you save us?" Jafar asked.

Cari felt torn. On the one hand, it was flattering to have those powerful acts attributed to her, and her master's respect for her would rise enormously if she could claim credit for them. On the other hand, Cari was of the righteous Jann, and had grown up knowing that a lie, no matter how small, could endanger her very fragile soul.

In the end, honesty won out. "To tell the truth, O master, I do not know. The wizard Appolinar Dektros bound me in a spell, and from that point I remember nothing until you summoned me to you on the street outside the palace."

Jafar al-Sharif described what he had seen as he was waking up from the poison stupor, and said, "Are you sure you did none of those things?"

"I remember none of it."

"I have talked to many warriors," Umar said. "Sometimes they have been known to go into a trance as they fight, a trance as deep as any temple mystic's. They can fight for hours, with great passion and amazing strength, and not remember a moment of it later."

"I know how that can be," Prince Ahmad said. "In the forest against the brigands, and then again on the plain against Kharouf's evil army, I myself felt almost that way. Nothing existed for me but the fighting, and I can recall very little of that."

"But these things . . . I am of the *righteous* Jann. I may not kill anyone except in the immediate defense of myself or my master. I cannot have done what you said."

"Perhaps you're a little less pure than you think you are," Leila said caustically.

Cari shot her a vicious glance, but before she could speak further, Umar stepped into the conversation. "The cause of whatever happened may be a major mystery to us, but I think there can be little doubt that Oromasd is looking after us upon our journey."

"He's never interfered this directly before," Leila said.

"It's never been needed before, either," said Prince Ahmad. "I think there's one more thing we can have little doubt about: We can no longer count on enlisting any kings to our cause. Even those who are righteous will be reluctant to leave their kingdoms unguarded in the face of the invader— and who can blame them? Were I such a king, I know how hard the decision would be for me. And for those kings who are not righteous—well, we can't afford more delays due to treachery. Oromasd may lose patience with our foolishness and not interfere next time."

Owing to the magical speed at which their horses could run, they made it all the way to the coastal city of Attan by nightfall of the next day. They had chosen Attan carefully when they were initially setting up their route, for it was among the largest seaports along the eastern half of the Central Sea. Here, as well as anywhere, they would find a ship's captain willing to take them on a voyage into the unknown—and if they couldn't find one here, there were still a number of lesser ports to the south where they might run across an adventurous captain willing to take their money.

As with much of Nikhrash, the land around Attan was mountainous, and Attan itself was built on a group of hills that made its twisting streets and alleys difficult to navigate. There was no wall around the town; as part of the kingdom of Nikhrash, it had no enemies immediately around it and relied on the Nikhrashi army for protection from a land invasion. Attan was much more vulnerable to invasion by sea, and so had invested most of its defenses in a large navy that patrolled the waters off its shore.

In the Fourth Cycle of the world, in the Age of Heroes, Attan had been justly famous—not for its heroics, but as a center of culture theretofore unequaled in human history. Here it was that great thinkers came to debate matters of philosophy. The world's greatest poets lived here then, and storytellers. Here it was, too, that the theater was born, and great dramas were enacted on Attani stages. The city was alive with intellectual excitement, and all the world spoke of Attan's brilliance.

But with the changing of worldly Cycles and the creation of Ravan, Attan sank into a decline from which it never recovered. All the great thinkers now went to the madrasa at Ravan, or studied with the prophets of Sarafiq, or attended one of the other half dozen new centers that sprang up in this age of peace. Attan's name slipped from currency, and its people gradually lost the spark that had made them great. Attan today was little more than a sleepy harbor town, with only its ghosts to attest to its former greatness.

As the travelers rode through the streets, they were most impressed by the amount of marble they saw in the buildings; that stone, apparently, was as plentiful for construction as wood. The architectural style was regular and rectangular; many of the larger, more important-looking buildings had rows of columns along their facades. Marble statues abounded, too, in public squares, with their surfaces painted in bright and lifelike colors. The universal garb was togas, in many exotic hues. The men here wore no turbans or other headgear; the women did not wear veils and often traveled unescorted in the

streets, so Leila's and Selima's bare faces caused no com-
ment—though those who looked closely at Selima in the
gathering gloom of night were still startled by her insubstantial
nature.

The travelers found a room at a local caravanserai, and
after they had their dinner, Umar asked directions of the landlord to find the Sea Temple. Having received the directions,
Umar went off to the temple, leaving his companions behind.

This was another reason they had chosen Attan as their
destination. One of Umar's prize pupils at the madrasa in
Ravan, a man named Arianos, had returned to this, his native
city, after receiving his ordination in the priesthood. He had
written frequently to his old instructor, informing him of his
progress, and Umar felt that, in all of Nikhrash, Arianos was
the one man he could trust to give him good advice.

Graduates of Ravan's madrasa were considered among the
world's best priests, and Arianos had been offered positions in
Attan's fanciest temples when he returned home. He turned
down all those offers, though, in favor of a position at a poorer
temple near the docks.

"My father was a sailor," he explained in one of his letters
to Umar several years earlier. "These people risk their lives on
the sea for the world's commerce. They are not wealthy, they
are not polished, but they need Oromasd's blessing every bit as
much as the merchant who keeps his shop and makes regular
donations to the temple. Many of these sailors go out upon the
sea, never knowing whether they will return; they need the
comfort of knowing that Oromasd travels with them and will
guide their souls if they give themselves into his hands. My
calling, as I've known ever since I was a boy, is to minister to
these people and serve them as a priest must—with truth,
with affection, with courage, and with compassion. It is the
Sea Temple to which I will devote my life."

Many of Umar's pupils had gone on to important positions
in respected temples. Some had even attained the rank of high
priest in other cities. But when Umar received that letter, he
knew he had achieved his greatest success as a teacher and
that, even if he accomplished nothing further, his life would
not have been spent in vain.

It was to Arianos and the Sea Temple that Umar now
went, leaving his companions behind to relax in the caravanserai. In his room with Selima, Leila, and Cari, Jafar al-Sharif
took the journal of Ali Maimun from the saddle pouch he'd

brought up with him, and held it tightly, as he'd done almost every night since they'd left Varyu's castle.

"O Ali Maimun, thou incorrigible prankster," he said, looking at the leather-bound volume, "know that we are about to embark on our voyage to Atluri to seek the third piece of Oromasd's Crystal. It would be greatly to our advantage—and Oromasd's—if we could tell our captain where we are supposed to sail. Please open to the next section so we don't have to look like bumbling lunatics when we tell him where we have to go."

He pried at the leaves of the book carefully and, much to his own amazement, the journal did indeed open to a section he'd never seen before. As a prospector looking upon new-found treasure, Jafar stared for a moment, eyes wide, and then brought the book down to eye level so he could read Ali Maimun's words with his own eyes.

"The third piece of the Crystal of Oromasd did I take to hide beneath the waters of the Western Sea in the sunken city of Atluri. First, though, I had to travel to the island known as the Isle of Illusions, on the thirty-seventh parallel of latitude, three days hard sail north northwest of the island of Korluf; only wizards dare visit it because the creatures of that island have the power to fool the senses of normal men and lure them to their deaths. On this island, in the very center, I found the tree named Raffiliz, the tree which lives as does a man, and I did bribe it with one of my magical implements to obtain a piece of its bark. This piece of bark, when swallowed, allows a man to live and breathe underwater for up to two days. It was this aid that enabled me to visit my undersea destination.

"The city of Atluri, which sank beneath the Western Sea many ages ago, is located on the thirty-fifth parallel of latitude, five days' hard sail west southwest of Jibral. Its approximate location can be spotted because it is a favorite playing ground for dolphins, and because the sea birds are constantly circling to feed on the leavings floating up from the city.

"The inhabitants of that underwater city, part fish and part human, are known for their sportive nature, and agreed to hold their portion of the Crystal as part of some grand game in the cosmic scheme. The man who would deal with them must keep his wits about him at all times and refuse to lose himself in their carefree pastimes."

There the account ended, and the book refused to open further. Jafar al-Sharif rubbed at his temples with his long, slender fingers, wondering what new tribulations lay in store for him.

"The Isle of Illusions," Leila said with a smile. "I think I could help you there."

"It says only wizards dare go there," Jafar said, worried but, at the same time, proud he could read the passage all the way through with no problem. "I think we're all in deep trouble."

Umar bin Ibrahim did not return to the caravanserai until the early hours of the morning, so excited was he by his reunion with his prize pupil. When he did return, all the others had gone to sleep, and he fell into a restless nap himself until the sunrise woke them all.

Jafar al-Sharif opened his eyes as sunlight streamed through his window. Leila lay beside him, still asleep, and Selima was curled up in her own corner, as contentedly as though she were not under imminent sentence of death. His eyes still misted every time he thought about her fate, and he redoubled his resolve to do everything within his power—and quite a few things beyond his power—to save her.

He did not see Cari. She might be invisibly here in the room with him, or she might be out patrolling the caravanserai in case the rimahniya or King Machenos's men came after them. It did not matter in either case. The ring that controlled her felt warm and comfortable on his finger, and he knew she could be here at an instant's notice if he needed her.

He stood up, stretched, and looked out the window—and immediately a chill ran up his spine. On the rooftop across the way, staring directly at him, was a large brown monkey. It had a tail and was of a different kind and color than the apes who had made him their king, only slightly more than half their size with a face that was much more muzzled, much less human looking. But still, after that experience, any ape or monkey looked suspicious to him—particularly a monkey that stared straight at him as though it knew his name, his father's name, and his whole lineage all the way back to Gayomar.

Jafar stood for an eternal instant, his gaze locked with that of the monkey. Then suddenly the spell broke, and he turned and called aloud for Cari, who was at his side in seconds.

"What is your wish, O master?"

Jafar turned back to the window, but the creature was gone. "There was something out there, a monkey. I saw it on the rooftop."

Cari looked. "There is nothing there now. Perhaps your shout frightened it away."

"Perhaps," Jafar agreed, his heart still pounding furiously.

The women, meanwhile, were waking up and wondering what all the commotion was about. Jafar explained as best he could about the mysterious creature and the eerie feeling it gave him.

"You certainly do attract apes," Leila commented. "I think you must secretly have enjoyed being their king."

"Let's go to breakfast," Jafar said testily, ignoring the remark. "Perhaps Umar has returned from the Sea Temple and is willing to tell us what's happening."

Umar was indeed awake, already dining with Prince Ahmad. He was more than eager to tell them about the visit with his student. "Arianos has agreed to help us. He is a righteous man, and staunch in Oromasd's cause. He agrees that King Machenos is no ally of ours; whether he knows it yet or not, the king threw in his lot with Rimahn many years ago. Arianos does what he can to hold Oromasd's flame high in his little corner of Nikhrash, but it's a difficult struggle.

"As for helping us find a ship, Arianos says he will try his best—but these are bad days for sea commerce. All around the harbor boats are anchoring, afraid to sail forth to the regions of the west. Aeshma's empire controls that region, and any ship entering those waters is subject to seizure and having its crew impressed into the enemy's forces. What little shipping being done from here goes up and down the eastern shore, basically between here and Bann—and there's not enough business in that direction to keep all these ships moving."

"Then that's good for us," Jafar exclaimed. "There'll be many captains who feel the pinch and will be more willing to take us where we need to go."

"Perhaps," Umar said. "But it will take a captain who is either desperate, or foolhardy, or both. We venture not only into Aeshma's territory, but also into unknown, magical lands that few dare visit. When they hear our destination, I cannot believe many men will accept, no matter how bad their situation is here."

"Then let's not tell them," Leila said.

"No," Prince Ahmad insisted. "Our captain must know sometime—and better at the beginning, when we can gauge what sort of man he is by the reaction he makes to our demands. If we withhold the information until we put to sea, he may rightly assume we tried to trick him, and he may have his crew toss us overboard or strand us in some desolate place. If he knows in advance, he can at least reject us honestly."

"Arianos is considering our needs right now," Umar went on. "He knows most of the men and ships along the docks, and he will evaluate them based on our requirements. He knows we need a brave captain and crew who are deep believers in Oromasd and are willing to risk their lives to save the world. He will send prospective candidates to our caravanserai, so we may interview them and perhaps find one who meets our needs."

Indeed, the candidates started arriving within the hour. Each talked with Umar, Ahmad, and Jafar for several minutes, but the result each time was the same. Most men simply refused to sail into the western half of the Central Sea, let alone into the Western Sea, because of the powerful new empire arising in the west. Of those who would go that far, none would venture to seek the sunken city of Atluri. It was a myth, a story told to children, they said—but if it did exist, they certainly didn't want to go near it.

Seventeen captains were offered the commission, and seventeen captains refused outright, no matter how much gold Prince Ahmad offered them. The travelers were becoming discouraged. How could they fulfill Muhmad's quest if they could find no one willing to take them where they needed to go?

In midafternoon, shortly after the seventeenth rejection, the priest Arianos himself dropped by to ask how they were faring in their search for a captain. Arianos was a handsome, but relatively short, man in the white toga of a priest, with curly black hair and a close-cut beard. He was swarthy complexioned, and he accentuated his speech with gestures even broader than Jafar's. He was as discouraged as the others to learn that everyone he'd sent had turned down their offer.

"I'd thought at least one of them would accept—if not for their own sake, then for Oromasd's. All of them claim to be pious men, and I honestly believe some of them are. But piety need not lead one into suicide, and I'm afraid that's how they view this project."

"Are there no other captains in the harbor you could recommend?" Umar asked. "I saw far more than seventeen ships out there."

"Many of those ships aren't big enough to make the voyage you require. And of those that are, some of the captains are men I wouldn't trust with a cargo of rice, let alone a mission of such importance to Oromasd."

Arianos paused. "There is yet one man. He's not pious, or reliable, or even honest—but he is, I believe, honorable. He has never come to the temple to pray, but he often sends generous gifts for seamen's widows. He's coarse and crude, and I believe him to be at least a part-time smuggler—not the man I would choose to do the work of Oromasd—"

"Oromasd must choose his own representatives," Umar said softly.

"And sometimes his choices are strange, indeed," Jafar agreed.

"I will send him around, then, to see you," said Arianos. "Do not be put off by his appearance or manner, for I believe he honors the laws of Oromasd, if not always the laws of men. He is called simply El-Hadar." And Arianos bade them farewell and went to the docks to seek out this new captain.

A little more than an hour later, a man entered the caravanserai. He was an enormous black man, tall of build and broad of shoulders and chest. He wore no Sadre, but just a yellow cotton shirt, open down the front almost to the waist, and white sirwaal trousers, and simple niaal on his feet. His white turban was wrapped casually about his head in the manner often affected by seamen. His eyes surveyed the dining room almost scornfully, and then he caught sight of Umar's white robes. Having been told he would deal with a priest— and since there was almost no one else in the dining room right now—he walked directly over to them with a swagger characteristic of men who sailed the waters.

He confronted Umar, Jafar, Prince Ahmad, and Leila, who sat on benches around a table in a dark corner; Selima had been left up in the sleeping room to avoid undue attention, and Cari was, as usual, hovering invisibly near her master. "Are you those who would speak with El-Hadar?" he asked. He probably did not mean to bellow, but El-Hadar was one of those men whose voices are even bigger than they are. His was a deep, rich voice that rumbled through a room like thunder, a voice used to command, a voice of power and authority.

"Only if this El-Hadar has a ship for our hire," Prince Ahmad said, refusing to be intimidated.

El-Hadar smiled, displaying an impressive set of white teeth. "Such matters can always be arranged if the conditions are right. Whom does El-Hadar have the honor of addressing?"

"I am Ahmad Khaled, and these are my companions, Umar bin Ibrahim, Jafar al-Sharif, and Leila. May the blessings of Oromasd be upon you, El-Hadar, in all your voyages."

The niceties of social negotiation would have had them trading blessings and inquiries about health and prosperity for several minutes before getting on with their business, but El-Hadar was obviously a man who was impatient with life. He brushed aside the prince's benediction with a casual wave of his hand, pulled another bench over to the table, and sat down facing the group. "Thank you, and upon yourselves as well. What is this important commission priest Arianos said you have?" He said "priest" as though it was a word that seldom came to his tongue with favor. "What cargo would you have Hauvarta's Shield carry?"

"No cargo," said Prince Ahmad. "Just passengers. The four of us plus Jafar's daughter and servant, and our horses and gear. That is all."

El-Hadar glanced at Leila with some distaste. "Women do not do well on sailing vessels," he said. "Best to keep them locked safely back home where they can get into little mischief."

"Are you afraid, then, of a woman's mischief?" Leila asked sardonically.

"El-Hadar fears little else, O yellow-haired temptress," the captain said. "Was it not Jahi who seduced Gayomar and brought about the destruction of paradise?"

"And of the seven Bounteous Immortals, are not Ashath and Armaith and Hauvarta and Amerta all female?"

Prince Ahmad interrupted before the argument could go any further. "This discussion is beside the point. We cannot leave the women behind, because we will not be returning to this place; therefore, the ship that accepts our commission must accept our women as well. This is not a matter for negotiation."

"All things are a matter of negotiation," said El-Hadar, the smile returning to his lips. "If not on one side of the equation, then certainly on the other. But pray, tell this humble sea captain where you wish his ship to take you."

"To the Isle of Illusion, then to the sunken land of Atluri in the Western Sea, and from there back to the shores of Sudarr near the mouth of the Nilot River."

Even El-Hadar's mountain of self-assurance was shaken by this news. "By Anahil's tits, you ask too much of any man."

This scurrilous reference to the yazata of the waters, to the tall, beautiful, and pure Anahil, left the others in silence for a moment; even the normally unshockable Leila looked uncomfortably away. Nonetheless, it was she who first recovered her tongue. "Forgive us for wasting your time then, O seaman. We were told this El-Hadar of legendary repute was no coward."

"El-Hadar is no coward, O lady of the acid tongue, nor is any man of his crew," bellowed the captain. "But El-Hadar is also a businessman, and there are certain risks it is not profitable to take."

"And yet, if we were prepared to offer you a profit . . . ?" Umar suggested.

El-Hadar paused and looked the group over again critically. Then he shook his head again. "The four of you together couldn't carry enough gold to make the venture profitable."

"We have horses to carry our gold," Jafar said. "How much would you require?"

"Well, the voyage would be a month, probably longer. El-Hadar would have to forgo all the other profitable cargoes he could have shipped in the meantime. Then there is that new accursed empire spreading throughout the west, attacking ships and seizing their cargoes and crews. Then there is this mysterious Isle of Illusion—of which El-Hadar has never heard—and the equally accursed Atluri. And if we survive that, we must return through the empire's realm once more to the north shore of Fricaz, where this emperor, so they say, has his greatest strength. Then, after dropping you off, the ship must return safely to a civilized port where this money can be spent."

His eyes narrowed as he studied this group, noting the rich fabrics and the style of their clothes. "El-Hadar could not consider such a voyage profitable for anything less than five hundred dinars."

Prince Ahmad did not even blink at this outlandish sum. He was tired of this delay in Attan, and wanted to get on with his mission as quickly as possible. "Done," he said, slamming his right palm down on the tabletop.

El-Hadar was taken slightly aback by this intense youngster who refused even to haggle, but he was equal to the occasion. "That much gold would pay for the ship," he said, "but there is also the crew to consider. They must get their regular pay, of course, plus a bonus for all the dangers they will encounter on such a voyage. These wages are easily another five hundred dinars in sum."

"Done."

"Then there is the matter of your horses. *Hauvarta's Shield* does not regularly carry horses, and special gear will be needed for their safety and comfort. That would take yet another two hundred dinars."

"Done."

"Then there are supplies and provisions, not just for the regular crew, but for the passengers and the horses, for a month or more—"

"How much?" Prince Ahmad asked impatiently.

"Another three hundred dinars."

"Done."

"And then—"

The prince's hand was a fist this time as it crashed on the table. "My patience, O mammoth sea captain, is not limitless. I have just agreed, with good grace, to pay you the sum of fifteen hundred dinars, for which many captains would sell me their ships three times over. It is not customary to experience piracy *before* leaving the land, and I will suffer no more of it. Either you will accept our bargain now, or I'll be forced to look elsewhere."

El-Hadar gave a laugh that shook the walls of the caravanserai. "A bargain made and struck, then, O young man of the bottomless purse, though I fear no good can come of this voyage."

"Then why do you laugh?"

"A man of the sea must laugh at calamity, or else he goes mad. With the changing of the winds and tides, with the storms and monsters, with all the treachery Rimahn's creatures throw at us, we either laugh or we cry. El-Hadar and his crew have sailed to lands unknown on any charts, fought monsters so hideous Rimahn himself would wince to look upon them, seen wonders so bizarre it would fill a storyteller's sack. You will find us all a very merry crew."

He stood up. "So give El-Hadar half his money in advance, and he will start the preparations for your voyage."

"If I give you that much money in advance, you may well start a voyage without us. I will give you three hundred, enough to arrange accommodations for our horses and to buy some supplies. And in return, you will swear by your holiest oath to fulfill our mission and take us safely where we want to go."

El-Hadar looked into the prince's eyes for a moment, then into the eyes of each of the others around the table. "El-Hadar swears by his ship, by the honor of his crew, and by Hauvarta herself that he will fulfill your charge and take you safely where you wish, subject only to the usual hazards of the sea. It will take a day to provision the ship and get it ready for your horses. The tide leaves tomorrow at four hours past noon. *Hauvarta's Shield* will be ready then to await your departure at dock number twenty-seven on the north side of the harbor."

The big man turned and, with no other word of farewell, strode with giant steps out the door of the caravanserai. The travelers waited until they were sure he was gone, then looked at one another in varying degrees of disbelief.

"Arianos will never be a storyteller," Jafar finally said. "He did not capture that man by half."

"I mistrust any man who speaks of himself in the third person," Umar added.

"He was lying quite blatantly, of course, about his figures," Leila said. "But when he gave his vow, there was no deceit in him. I believe Arianos was right, that he is an honorable man. I don't think he and I will get along very well, but I trust him to do right by us."

"In any event," said Prince Ahmad, "we have very little choice. We must sail soon, and his ship was our last hope in Attan. We have no guarantee of faring any better at the next port, so we must take our chances on him."

"And may the blessed Hauvarta indeed shield us from harm," Leila muttered under her breath.

But it was to Sraoshar that Leila should have directed her prayer, for it was out of the night, and on land, that their next threat was to come.

13

The Monkey

Abdel ibn Zaid and four of his rimahniya companions escaped with their lives from the debacle in the city of the apes, but that was tantamount to failure in their minds. The rimahniya prided themselves on their dedication and their abilities; having their purpose thwarted by circumstances so completely beyond their control fired their frustrations almost past human endurance. The fact that other members of their cult had also failed to kill Prince Ahmad on previous occasions only lent more fuel to their rage, and made them rededicate themselves to the performance of their sacred mission.

There would be no purpose served by returning to the city of the apes. Either the apes had already killed the prince in their lust for blood, or else Ahmad would find some way of getting past them to his objective. If the former, ibn Zaid would eventually need some proof of the prince's death to show Shammara—but that could be obtained later, in a safer manner. If the latter, the rimahniya would have to track him down at some later point in his journey—and best to start now on that.

Again, with the prince able to ride so quickly, there was little hope of simply following him—and ibn Zaid was less than satisfied with their previous method of catching up. He did not have anyone he could spare, now, as sacrifice to some djinn. Even though the rimahniya maintained temples in most major cities and ibn Zaid could have gone to any of them for reinforcements, excessive pride still made him feel his original group of zealots should be able to handle the job.

The best way to find Prince Ahmad, then, would be to anticipate his movements and lie in ambush for him somewhere along his projected route. According to that fool Muhmad, the prince would be visiting Varyu's castle—wherever that was—and then the sunken city of Atluri. Ibn Zaid knew only that Atluri was reported to lie somewhere beneath the Western Sea. In order to reach that land, the prince would have to hire a ship.

Ibn Zaid studied his maps, pondering the problem long and hard. One option would be for the prince to ride due west until he reached the shore of the Western Sea itself, possibly in Faranza or Norgeland. But ibn Zaid also knew that the prince was gathering the armies of mankind for a war against Aeshma this coming spring, and the armies of those lands were simply too far away. Even if they mobilized immediately, they could probably not reach the Leewahr Plains in time to do any good.

If, on the other hand, the prince turned his path southward, he could talk to such possible allies as Tatarry, Damasc, and Nikhrash on his way to the Central Sea; he could even venture as far south as Bann before finding a ship—although that was unlikely, since it would take him nearly a thousand parasangs out of his way. He would probably find that an unconscionable delay.

Nikhrash, then, looked like the best possibility—and in Nikhrash, there was no better port than Attan for finding the ship Ahmad needed. Ibn Zaid knew there was a chance he had guessed wrong, but once in Attan he could spread word to other rimahniya temples to be on the lookout for the prince. If Ahmad slipped through his grasp here, there was still Mount Denavan. But somehow, Abdel ibn Zaid knew he was not wrong. Rimahn would lead him to his target. It was inevitable; it was kismet.

The five assassins rode hard, and even though they could not travel at magical speeds, they also did not suffer the delays that the prince's party met. They arrived in Attan the day before Prince Ahmad began interviewing captains.

The rimahniya prowled the docks, and one of them heard the rumor of some people seeking a ship for a peculiar mission to the west. He followed a prospective captain to the caravanserai and spotted Prince Ahmad and his companions at a table. He immediately returned to ibn Zaid to report this good news.

"Rimahn has delivered the enemy into our hands, as I knew he would," ibn Zaid proclaimed. "The rest falls upon our shoulders. We cannot let the prince escape again. Whatever ship he takes will not leave before tomorrow's tide, so tonight is our night of opportunity. Prince Ahmad must die before leaving Attan. We must take steps to create our own confusion, that this time the advantage is on *our* side."

He paused to consider the tactics of the situation. "The prince and his group are staying at the Grape Arbor caravan-serai. We can set fires around the building, burn it to the ground. If the prince and his people die in the flames, our work is done for us. If Ahmad and his companions race out into the street for safety, they will be so confused and helpless they will be easy prey for our blades. Either way, the flames of Oromasd will help us kill his appointed champion."

After dinner that evening, as he was preparing for sleep, Jafar al-Sharif looked out the window of his room and saw the monkey once again. It was staring at him from the roof across the way, its large brown eyes blinking slowly in the dim moon-light, its gaze never wavering from him, apparently reading every line of his soul as would the righteous Rashti himself when Jafar reached the Bridge of Shinvar. But somehow Jafar could not believe this monkey was quite so blessed or quite so impartial.

"Cari! Leila! Selima! Come look!" he called, only this time he did not take his eyes from the beast across the way.

At the sound of his voice, the monkey darted across the rooftop at a speed Jafar would have thought impossible for any mortal creature. By the time the women made it over to the window, the monkey was gone again, into the shadows of the night. "Did you see it?" Jafar asked them.

"I saw something," Leila said, "but in the darkness I couldn't tell what it was."

"It was the monkey again."

"Twice in one day is unusual," Selima said. "I wonder what it wants."

"Perhaps its cousins, the apes, sent it to scout for their former king," Leila suggested—but behind the light banter, Jafar could see that she, too, was disturbed. With a mission as critical as theirs, no incident was insignificant. Everything had a meaning somewhere, somehow.

"Should I go out and search for it, O master?" Cari asked.

"No, no, don't," Jafar said. He continued staring into the darkness, at the now-empty roof across the way. The gap be-tween that building and his window was only a couple of cubits. He could probably leap across it himself, given a run-ning start; he was sure it would be no impediment to an agile monkey. Even if Jafar shuttered the window, the monkey looked strong enough to tear through quickly. Or it could even leap into the caravanserai through some other window and come at him via the hallway.

"I want you to stay here in the room with me tonight," he continued to the Jann. "I don't feel very secure with that creature running loose, and I'd like to have you nearby for protection."

"Hearkening and obedience, O master."

Despite Cari's presence, Jafar al-Sharif was slow to fall asleep, his mind haunted by images of that simian face staring at him through the darkness. When he did fall asleep, it was a fitful slumber filled with formless dreams and nameless dreads—and monkeys swinging through the trees, staring at him, mocking him.

He was awakened by a hand shaking his shoulder, the smell of smoke, and Cari's voice in his ear, "Master, there is a fire!"

He lay still for a moment, comprehension seeping but slowly into his sleep-soaked mind. Then, as the reality of the situation finally reached his brain, he sat up. "Selima! Selima!"

His daughter sat up slowly, still waking up. "Yes, Father?"

"The building is on fire. I know it can't hurt you, so you can warn the others. Stand outside and scream the alarm until everyone in the building is awakened. Cari, open the door for her, quickly."

As the two rushed to obey, Jafar shook Leila awake as well. Through the open door, Jafar could see the flames spreading along the ground floor of the caravanserai, though they hadn't yet reached the second floor where the guests were sleeping. There was still time to save themselves, if they acted quickly.

Leila sat up, blinking, a question on her lips. Jafar merely had to point out of the open door, and Leila understood instantly. She was on her feet before he was, slipping on her thawb and racing for the door.

Jafar tried to think clearly. Their first priority was to save themselves. Next came the saddle pouches with the two pieces of the Crystal of Oromasd, the journal of Ali Maimun and Kharouf's grimoire, his other magical implements—and his magical staff of lightning. Then the pouches with the gold they'd need to pay El-Hadar, then their clothes and other belongings, then, if possible, their horses.

"Cari," he said, "gather up all our belongings you can carry, especially the magical ones and the gold, and take them to safety. The rest of us will try to escape on our own."

"Hearkening and obedience."

Outside on the balcony, Selima was doing a proper job of screaming loudly enough to rouse the dead. Even though she was fading ever faster from the world these days, her voice still carried well over the roar of the flames. Next door, Jafar could hear Umar and the prince bestirring themselves, and he could see other doors opening around the central courtyard as the caravanserai's other guests woke up and realized what was happening.

Jafar was barefoot, wearing just a kaftan, but he did not stop for anything else. Cari had already gathered the rest of his things; only he and Leila were left in the room, and they departed hurriedly.

The center of the building was an inferno, flames shooting up from the ground and licking all about them with soul-searing heat. Prince Ahmad and Umar were standing outside their room as Jafar and Leila ran toward them, both wearing just their night robes. They all conferred quickly, with Umar saying that Cari had come in and taken their belongings. "Let's get the horses, then," Jafar said, and the others nodded.

It took all the self-control they had to walk down the stairs, into the teeth of the flames. With each downward step, the heat seemed to double, and the black smoke that roiled upward made them cough and cover their faces with their arms. Jafar could feel the hair of his eyebrows being singed off by the heat, and he had to fight the fear that his beard would soon catch fire and burn his face. He was drenched in sweat, and his lungs were burning as though he'd been locked inside a madman's sicakluk. Beside him, coughing just as badly, was Leila, while behind him he could see from the corner of his eye that Selima had joined the prince and Umar.

The courtyard of the caravanserai could easily have been the Pits of Torment themselves. People were running about and screaming, but their voices could scarcely be heard over the roar of the flames. Someone had already been to the stables and opened the doors, but the horses were frightened and would not come out into the flames. A man would have to go in and lead the creatures to safety, trying not to get trampled by their hooves as they reared in panic.

Prince Ahmad turned to the others. "Umar, you take Leila to safety. Jafar and I will try to save the horses."

Umar thought about protesting, then realized it would be pride talking in place of reason. Ahmad was right; Umar was neither young enough nor strong enough to battle panicked horses as well as the heat and smoke. His task was to save himself and Leila, and let the others handle what they could. With a nod, he took Leila's hand and led her toward the doorway to the street.

The prince and Jafar raced into the stables, into the face of the billowing clouds of black smoke. Churash and Umar's horse had been housed near the back of the building, while their other mounts were stabled toward the front, so by unspoken agreement Prince Ahmad went deeper into the building while Jafar tended to the nearer horses.

As Prince Ahmad ran to the back of the stable, he heard the frenzied whinnies around him. Even a noble steed like Churash, trained to remain calm in the heat of battle, was frightened near out of his wits by the flames, the heat, the smoke, and the confusion all about him. Ahmad approached him slowly, speaking calmly, trying to exert a steadying influence.

Suddenly from behind him, a shape loomed up, a human shape. Ahmad whirled to see a man with a sword standing behind him, a man in black robes coming at him with death in his eyes. His hand reached for the saif that was normally tied at his waist—but it was among the possessions Cari had taken to safety, and it was not there now. Unarmed, the prince faced the assassin who advanced on him with naked steel.

Suddenly Selima darted between the two men. The assassin, seeing this new threat coming from the corner of his eye, reacted instinctively and swung his sword at her. The steel blade swept right through the place where she should have been, and the assassin, realizing he had been tricked, turned his attention back to Prince Ahmad.

But this diversion, as brief as it was, gave the prince a chance to recover from his surprise. He had no sword, but a quick glance around showed a coil of rope at his feet and a pitchfork leaning against a nearby wall. He bent, picked up the rope, and threw it at the black-clad assassin. The man ducked, but this gave Ahmad time to grab the pitchfork and hold it up to block the downward stroke of the other man's sword. The assassin still advanced, but more cautiously, until Ahmad found himself backed against an as yet unburnt section of wall.

Jafar, too, had moved toward the nearer stalls, only to find a black-robed assassin popping up nearby. Jafar was no fighter, and could not react with Ahmad's trained reflexes. He froze, not knowing what to do, and saw the glint of the fire on the sword blade as it came flashing through the superheated air toward his neck.

And then a dark form came hurtling through the air, landing on the assassin and knocking him sideways. At first, Jafar thought it must be Cari, coming to his rescue yet again—but then he realized the form was much too small to be her. As the assassin struggled on the ground with his attacker, the flickering flames finally lit their bodies at the proper angle, and Jafar could see that it was the monkey who had saved him—the same monkey he'd seen twice already watching him from the rooftops.

The monkey was tearing at the assassin with the fury of a demon, scratching at his eyes with its sharp little claws, tearing at his throat with its long, sharp teeth. The contest was totally uneven, and within seconds it was over. The assassin lay dead on the ground and the monkey bounded up. Without so much as a glance at the man whose life it had saved, it leaped deeper into the flames, toward Prince Ahmad.

The rimahniya assassin who had cornered the prince swung again with his sword. Ahmad again parried the blow, but it had been a feint. The assassin let the momentum of his sword carry both it and the pitchfork away from their two bodies. Meanwhile he had reached to his belt with his left hand, drawn a dagger, and lunged at the prince. Ahmad turned quickly sideways and the blade of the knife barely missed scratching him as it passed through the space he'd just left.

Then, from out of the smoke and flames, the form of the monkey bounded onto the assassin's back, shrieking its fury as it ripped and tore at the would-be killer. The assassin in black was knocked to the ground, but even as he fell, he was slashing wildly at his attacker with his knife. The monkey was a blur of motion and he never quite connected, but this delay gave Prince Ahmad the chance to recover his balance. Holding his pitchfork tightly, he stabbed its tines with all his might into the body of the man who would have killed him. The assassin's body shuddered in a few rapid convulsions, then lay still, impaled against the wooden floor.

The prince paused only a few seconds to regain his breath, realized Selima was by his side and smiled at her, then turned back to his original task of rescuing the horses. A crackling sound overhead meant that the beams were about to give way, but he did not hurry, did not panic. He stroked Churash's muzzle for a few seconds while Selima made soothing sounds; then they led the steeds by their tether ropes out of the stables—passing Jafar, who had just recovered from his own shock enough to start rescuing his own horses. The two men and Selima forced themselves to walk at a deliberate pace, despite their urges to run and escape the inferno that threatened to devour them, and eventually made it to the street, where yet another tragic sight awaited them.

Eleven bodies lay sprawled on the ground. Two of them wore the same black robes as the assassins in the stables; their bloody bodies were covered with scratches and bites that could have been delivered only by the mysterious monkey. One of the bodies was the landlord of the caravanserai and another was his wife; five more had been guests staying at the caravanserai. All of these had been stabbed by the assassins as they raced out of the burning building.

The other two on the ground were Umar and Leila. They had been helping the others get out first, and the assassins had attacked them only just before the monkey came on the scene. Umar had been stabbed in the side, while Leila had a long gash down her right arm. Neither wound was necessarily fatal, but both victims were lying on the ground and writhing in pain.

Around them, the caravanserai's neighbors had already formed a fire brigade, passing buckets of water along the line to throw on the blaze and keep it from spreading farther. The caravanserai was already being given up as lost; the main concern now was to contain the fire and keep it from spreading to the adjacent buildings. There was much bustle and scurrying about, but all Ahmad, Jafar, and Selima could look at was their two dear companions moaning on the cold ground.

"Cari!" Jafar called, his voice a plaintive wail like a lone wolf in the forest night.

"I come, O master," said a voice in his ear. "I just . . ." Her voice died abruptly as she suddenly saw what had happened.

"You just what?"

"I just buried your articles safely until you need them. No human can take them. What happened here?"

"Rimahniya, I suspect. Can you cure their wounds and make it look as though I'm doing it?"

"Hearkening and obedience."

And as he'd done on the Buryani battlefield after the war with Kharouf's army of the dead, Jafar knelt beside first Umar, then Leila, and made mystical passes in the air, muttering strange spells under his breath, while Cari did her magical healing and closed up the sword wounds. Jafar checked on the rimahniya's other victims, but they were beyond anyone's help but Sraoshar's.

Umar climbed shakily to his feet, still looking a little woozy. Jafar took Leila's arm and helped her stand. "I still feel very light-headed," she admitted. "I've never been stabbed before." This perplexed Jafar, since on the occasions when Cari cured him, he had always felt perfectly fine immediately afterward. Perhaps the spell worked differently on women than on men—but no, that couldn't be, either; Umar also was looking very shaky. Jafar resolved to ask the Jann about this at his earliest opportunity.

Prince Ahmad, meanwhile, had knelt beside the two people in black, touching the dead bodies gingerly for fear of spiritual contamination. About their necks were necklaces similar to the ones he'd seen on the bodies in the city of the apes. He stood up again and walked over to Jafar's side.

"Rimahniya," he said quietly, so the general bystanders wouldn't overhear him. "They must have waited outside the gate, killing everyone who came out in order to get at us. We are indirectly responsible for the deaths of these innocent people."

"No," said Umar firmly as he came over to join the conference. "The rimahniya are fully responsible. They and their victims will meet their respective judgments three days from now at the Bridge of Shinvar—and I can't imagine Rashti will judge the killers lightly."

"They probably started the fire themselves," Jafar said.

Umar nodded solemnly. "That's why we must get word of this to Arianos. This site must be purified immediately."

The others knew what he meant. In some respects, arson was a more heinous crime than murder, for it took the flame that was the sacred symbol of Oromasd and perverted it, used it for purposes of destruction. Arson coupled with murder was a sin so abominable that decent people shuddered at the thought. It took someone thoroughly committed to the path of Rimahn to contemplate this unspeakable act so coldly.

"We will get word to Arianos quickly—if indeed, someone hasn't notified the temples already," Ahmad told Umar. He then turned to look for Selima, who was hard to see in the darkness, but eventually he spotted her standing silently behind her father.

"O shrewd Selima, even though you are insubstantial, this is the second time your quick-witted intervention has saved my life. I don't have enough words of gratitude and my worldly wealth is too limited to properly thank you for what you have done."

Selima studiously examined her feet and refused to meet his gaze. "What need have I for words or treasure, Your Highness? The only thing I need is what even so great a man as yourself cannot give me—my life. Whether I personally am saved or not, I must accept winning Oromasd's battle as my ultimate reward."

Jafar, meanwhile, had been looking around them at what was happening in the neighborhood. The local townspeople had continued their frantic efforts to control the blaze, and for the most part they were successful. The buildings adjacent to the caravanserai had not caught fire, and the danger to them was diminishing with each passing minute. The caravanserai itself was still burning, but even Jafar could see that the fire was dying slowly as it consumed the building and ran out of fuel. The fire might burn for several more hours and would require constant vigilance, but the worst of the danger had been passed.

Then Jafar's sharp eyes noticed something off to the left, well out of the way of people running wildly back and forth. It was the small silhouette of the monkey that had saved their lives by killing the rimahniya who had laid such a clever trap for them.

"Make no sudden movements," he told his friends quietly, "but look over to our left."

"It's the monkey!" Selima exclaimed softly.

"It's not a monkey," Leila said. Though her voice sounded weak and tired, there was conviction behind her words.

The others looked at her. "What do you mean?" asked Prince Ahmad.

"What it is, I know not—but I do know it bears only the outward form of a monkey. It is not as it appears."

Jafar felt a sudden chill down his back, despite the intense heat from the burning building. "Cari, what do you make of this?" he asked quietly, so that the noise from the fire would not let Umar or the prince overhear this conversation.

"There is much magic involved with this creature, O master, but beyond that I can say nothing."

"Is it a djinn?"

"I don't know."

"I thought you told me all djinni were visible to all others."

"Indeed it is so, but this—this is different." She struggled to find the words to explain it. "This creature is surrounded by a glow of magic that even my eye can't penetrate. Think, O master, if you met a creature completely encased in a suit of mirrors that reflected all light back at you. You would know that something was inside it because of the way it behaved, but you couldn't tell whether it was a man or woman, peri or djinn, because you couldn't see beyond the surface. That is the problem I have now. The magic that surrounds this creature prevents me from seeing what it is."

"Is this creature disguising itself, then?"

"My ignorance betrays me, O master, but—I do not believe this magic is self-controlled. It feels more like a spell or a curse placed upon this creature by some outside force, much like the curse that was placed upon your daughter."

Jafar shivered again at the reminder of that horrible curse. If this monkey were under some similar constraint, he could almost sympathize with it.

The monkey stood still some fifteen cubits away, watching them watching it. It made no movement either to run away or to come closer. It was waiting for them to do something.

Prince Ahmad leaned over toward Jafar. "What do you make of this creature, O wizard?"

"There is some strange magic about it that I cannot fathom, Your Highness," Jafar replied, repeating Cari's analogies. "I only know that we owe our lives, all of us, to the creature's timely help."

"Since that is so," Umar added, his voice thin and frail, "this monkey must have some part in Oromasd's great plan."

Prince Ahmad stood and considered for a moment, then took a few slow steps toward the creature with his arms outstretched. It was true that the monkey had saved their lives, but he could not forget the image of the little creature biting and scratching fiercely at the assassin. He did not want that to happen to him.

He approached to within three cubits of the monkey and stopped. The creature still showed no indication whether it

would stand or flee. "You saved us all from the rimahniya,"
Ahmad said. It was half statement, half question.

The monkey nodded, wide eyes blinking at him.

"You can understand me?" Ahmad said with some as-
tonishment.

The monkey nodded again.

"My wizard tells me you're under some enchantment or
curse. Is this true?"

A very vigorous nod.

"What sort of creature are you really?" Ahmad knew the
question was poorly phrased, that the monkey could not answer easily, but he was at a loss to know exactly what to say in
this peculiar circumstance.

The monkey scratched its head for a moment, then looked
around. Seeing a broken clay pot among the ruins of the building, it pawed through the shards until it found a piece of the lip
with a smooth, curved arc on one side and a jagged edge on the
other. It placed this shard upon its head as a crown, then stared
serenely back at Prince Ahmad.

"A king?" Ahmad asked, amazed.

The monkey shook its head slowly.

"A prince, then?"

This time the monkey nodded.

"A prince under an enchantment," Ahmad said. "This is
hard indeed to countenance."

"It would make a great story, though," Jafar muttered
quietly.

"Why did you save us?" Ahmad asked, continuing his interrogation. "We're grateful, of course, but of what importance
are we to you?"

Again the monkey scratched its head, searching for a way
to express such abstract concepts. Finally it pointed at itself,
then at Prince Ahmad, then made a sweeping gesture with its
arm, pointing off into the distance. It repeated this performance twice more before Selima cried, "It wants to come with
us."

"Why would it want to do that?" Ahmad asked.

"Maybe it needs its own curse lifted, just as I do," Selima
said.

The monkey nodded furiously.

Ahmad stared at the creature, as though with a new light.
"Do you know what we seek? Do you know the hardships we
must endure?"

And yet again, the monkey nodded.

"Apparently he thinks it's worth it," Selima said. "In that respect, is he so much different from us?"

Umar was looking strained, even in the harsh light of the fire, but he kept his voice level as he said, "Again, I must urge caution, Your Highness. We know nothing whatsoever about this creature—"

"Except that it saved our lives," Ahmad pointed out.

"Its motives may not be the same as ours. It may have saved us merely to deal us a more horrible fate. We know nothing about it except what it tells us, and it could easily be lying for reasons of its own. We do know it's a creature with magic about it, and most magic—begging your pardon, O noble Jafar—is rooted in the treachery and deceit of Rimahn."

"I would never deny that," Jafar agreed.

"And even if this creature is indeed a prince, even if he is noble and kind and as good a prince as you are, the fact remains that he is still under an enchantment. The enchantment may affect him, and us, in ways even he does not understand, and may seriously jeopardize our mission. At this point, we cannot afford the risk."

"Can we deny him what he asks after the way he risked his life to save us? Doesn't Oromasd require us to repay kindness with kindness? Doesn't he tell us to treat strangers with respect and hospitality?"

"But we have no way of knowing—"

Jafar al-Sharif cleared his throat. "May I say a few words?" When he had the attention of the other two men, he continued. "The point of contention is that we don't know whether we can trust this monkey's word. I, too, feel grateful to it, and would like to offer it my trust. If there was some way of guaranteeing what it claims, O Umar, would you accept it?"

Umar looked too feeble to argue. "I suppose so. But how—"

"Cari, fetch me the cap of truth from where you've hidden it."

"Hearkening and obedience, O master." Since she'd been invisible, Jafar had no way of knowing whether she'd actually departed, but in another minute she appeared before him, made a deep salaam, and presented him with the cap he'd taken from Estanash's cave.

Holding the cap loosely in his hands, he approached the monkey as slowly as Ahmad had done. He passed the prince and came even closer, until he was standing directly before the creature. His heart was banging heavily in his chest as the monkey warily watched his every movement.

"This is a cap of truth," Jafar explained slowly. "It will not hurt you, but when I place it on your head you must answer three questions truthfully. Since you can't speak, we will accept a nod or a shake of the head as yes or no respectively. This is the only way we can decide whether we can trust you or not, so if you want to come with us, you must agree to the test. Do you understand?"

The monkey nodded.

Jafar reached out and placed the cap over the monkey's head. The cap was too large, and came down so far it almost covered the creature's eyes—but it would not be on for long, and stylishness was not its purpose. Jafar took a deep breath and answered his first question.

"Are you truly, as you claimed, a prince under a magical enchantment?"

The monkey nodded yes.

"Will aiding our quest help you rid yourself of the spell that surrounds you and makes you appear as a monkey?"

Again, the monkey nodded.

Jafar paused, giving much thought to his final question. It had to be phrased properly so the monkey could give them a definitive yes-or-no answer. "If we agree to let you come with us, do you swear by your most sacred vow that you will help us in our quest for the pieces of the Crystal of Oromasd, that you will work with us toward that goal, that you will fight to protect us from our enemies at all times during our quest, and that you will never work to do us harm, either alone or in collaboration with anyone else?"

The monkey nodded with slow deliberation.

Jafar removed the helmet from the creature's head and turned back to face Umar. "Does that satisfy your objections?" he asked.

This time it was the priest who nodded. "It seems adequate. But I still find it hard to trust the creature, even though it saved all our lives. There is something most unnerving about it."

Prince Ahmad approached the creature and knelt before it, so he could face it eye to eye. "Have you a name, O monkey, so we may address you honorably?"

The monkey simply stared back at him, blinking its large eyes. "Since monkeys can neither speak nor write," said Leila, "his communication seems slightly handicapped."

"I'll give him a name," Selima said. "I'll call him Verethran, because he came to us as a strong wind, the first incarnation of the yazata Verethran, and because he'll help bring victory to us. Does this name please you, O monkey?"

The monkey gave her a dignified salaam, as a man might give to a queen. Selima laughed and instinctively reached out to pet him, drawing back only at the last moment as she realized how hopeless that would be. The others pretended not to notice her gesture.

Priests from the local temples had been arriving at the scene of the fire for the past several minutes, and now Arianos had arrived. Spotting Umar and his friends to one side, he came over to inquire after them and find out what had happened. Umar told him in detail about the treachery of the rimahniya, the arson, and the murders of innocent victims. Arianos was as shocked as they had been to contemplate such blasphemy.

"Fear not, O beloved teacher," he told Umar. "Tomorrow will I and my colleagues come to this spot and pray our strongest prayers, and sprinkle ashes from the Bahram fire to mingle with the common ashes and purify the site from the blasphemous taint of the rimahni fire. We will wash away the stain those people have made upon the good city of Attan so our neighborhood will belong to us again, and not to Rimahn."

"We will give you money, too," Prince Ahmad pledged. "Some of it is to go to the families of the murder victims, if you can trace them down. The bulk is to rebuild the caravanserai, and to give to the family of the landlord, if any remain alive; if not, it is to be run for the poor people of Attan."

"It shall be as you say," Arianos promised. "But for now, you must all be exhausted after such an ordeal. Let me take you to my temple and offer you our humble hospitality for the night, so that you may board your ship freshly rested on the morrow. You will need rest, I believe, to deal with El-Hadar."

And as he led them off, a lurker watched from the shadows beside the still-burning building. Abdel ibn Zaid glowered with a fire in his eyes hotter than the blaze that had razed the caravanserai. His people were all killed, and he alone survived to carry on his mission.

But within his blackened soul burned a renewed sense of purpose as his hatred for Prince Ahmad consumed him. *You travel now beyond my reach*, he thought. *But soon you must return—return to Mount Denavan. There will I have you, there in the land of my own master, Rimahn, where Oromasd himself cannot save you. There will your life be mine and my vow be fulfilled, and there will Rimahn's triumph become complete!*

14

The Summoning

Prince Ahmad and his party spent the night at the Sea Temple as guests of Arianos and the other local priests, all of whom were thrilled to meet the Umar bin Ibrahim their colleague had spoken so glowingly about. Umar, however, was in no condition to be the center of adulation, and so he went straight to bed, as did the others.

Because they had been through so much excitement the night before, the priests let them sleep late the next morning. It was several hours past sunrise when they finally awoke and performed their morning ablutions. Umar and Leila in particular looked pale and complained that they could not eat even the wholesome fare the priests placed before them. The monkey, Verethran, picked the food off their plates and ate it himself, pretending to the priests to be merely a clever pet of Ahmad's.

Arianos reiterated his promise of the night before to purify the scene of the fire from the taint of evil the rimahniya arson had brought to it. He and the other priests were also worried about Prince Ahmad's contention that Aeshma's expanding empire would sweep through Nikhrash before it could be stopped.

"There are many righteous people in Attan," Arianos said. "How can we save them from servitude to Rimahn?"

"You can try to persuade them to leave their homes," Ahmad told him. "I will give you some gold to hire these ships that are sitting idle. The ships can take them to Bann, which should be safe from the invaders. If any of these people wish to join the armies meeting on the Leewahr Plains to combat Aeshma, they will be welcomed in Oromasd's name."

"I and my fellows shall do as you suggest. But meanwhile, we should not tarry. The tides won't wait for you no matter how holy your mission, and you must get to your ship before El-Hadar changes his mind—which has been known to happen."

Umar and Leila were both so weak they needed help walking to the docks, leaning on the prince and Jafar, respectively. Cari materialized and marched behind the others, leading the horses, on which she had loaded the gear she'd saved from the fire. Arianos personally led the party to dock twenty-seven on the north side of the harbor, and there it was that the travelers first caught sight of the ship that was to carry them on their hazardous voyage.

Hauvarta's Shield was a sewn ship, some sixty cubits long, with two masts—one foresail and one mainsail—and a much smaller sail in the stern. The tough, fibrous hull—which appeared to be made of bark—was sewn together with coconut rope, while the sails were of cotton canvas. There was but a single, open top deck, its wooden surface cluttered with ropes and pulleys, and a large brazier near the bow for cooking the crew's food. The large, wooden rudder was bound on the aft of the vessel by rope and leather lashes.

Though he had been busy supervising his crew, El-Hadar came over to greet his passengers personally when they arrived. "By Rapthwen's beard, it is good to see you all here—particularly after the news about the tragic fire that swept your lodgings last night. Rumors fly with amazing speed in a port like Attan, and one hears stories one almost dare not repeat—stories of black-robed assassins who killed everyone in the caravanserai."

"It was almost true," Ahmad said.

"Indeed, some members of your party do not look as though they fared very well—him and her," he indicated Umar and Leila, "and especially her." He pointed to the transparent, nearly invisible Selima.

"The first two were injured in the melee last night and lost a lot of blood," Ahmad explained. "As for Jafar's daughter, it is partly to cure her condition that we make this journey."

"Most understandable," the captain nodded. "She is a delicate looking flower indeed. El-Hadar sees, too, that you have acquired a pet." He looked with some distaste at Verethran, whom he obviously pictured scampering up and down the rigging and causing havoc among his crew.

"He is a clever beast who will give you no trouble. That I assure you."

"Your assurances are as blessings from Oromasd. El-Hadar is delighted to see you all survived the calamity, and hopes that your belongings and possessions likewise remained unharmed."

"If you mean our gold, never fear," Ahmad said cynically. "You will be paid your fee."

"Another assurance. El-Hadar is indeed blessed this day. Though with so many priests involved in this matter, how could it be otherwise? Still, this crew is not as sophisticated as their captain, and can understand only the simple clink of coinage to ease the worries of their minds."

"When we get our gear stowed away below, then I will count out your money. It will all be done before we sail."

"Of course, O gracious patron." The large black man made a bow that stopped just short of being a salaam. "All shall be as you wish. *Hauvarta's Shield* shall be at your complete disposal. Some of the crew will help you arrange things in the hold."

El-Hadar assigned two of his men to get the travelers' belongings squared away, and two more to deal with the horses. Then he put his passengers out of his mind and concentrated on overseeing his crew and getting his ship ready to sail with the afternoon tide.

The interior of the ship was dingy, lit only by a series of lamps in their own special compartments so that even in the heaviest storm they would not spill their oil and set the rest of the ship on fire. A set of carved planks had been placed inside the hull to provide level flooring, though some of them could be lifted for crewmen to swab the inside of the hull periodically with vegetable oil to preserve the stitches and keep the hull watertight. Normally the hold was one large, open area, with the crew sleeping on one side and any cargo being stored on the other. For this voyage, though, different accommodations had to be made.

A set of ropes and flimsy wooden partitions had been hastily crafted to stable the horses in the stern of the ship, and the lamps had been removed from that side to prevent the horses from accidentally kicking them over and causing a fire. This made the hold even dingier than usual. In the bow, a series of faded old carpets had been strung up from port to starboard, providing an area of privacy for the women. It was in this area, away from the crew's prying eyes, that the prince and Jafar decided to store the bulk of their gear, including their rapidly dwindling supply of money.

The people adjusted easily enough to shipboard, but the horses were another matter. They balked at walking on the planks from the pier onto the top deck, and then there was no easy way to get them into the hold. They had to be wrapped in blankets and lowered with winches and pulleys, protesting every bit of the way—and once they were down in the holds, they were so upset that they were hard to lead to their positions. The sailors swore profusely, sparing neither horses nor passengers their glowering looks. Prince Ahmad wondered again at the need to take the steeds with them, but knew that there was little chance of finding new ones once they reached the northern shores of Fricaz for the final leg of their journey. Better to put up with all the trouble now than to go in need of the creatures later.

While the rest of the prince's group watched the loading of the horses, Umar bin Ibrahim took Arianos aside and had a long, private talk with him. Arianos clearly was not pleased by what he heard and tried to argue with Umar about it, but Umar, though weak, was adamant. Finally Arianos walked away from the discussion and went up to El-Hadar.

"Treat well these passengers of yours for as long as you have them," he told the captain. "The fate of the world rests with them. And if that isn't enough incentive for you, I swear by Oromasd and all the Bounteous Immortals that if you fail them, you will never find a welcome port no matter how far you sail."

"El-Hadar needs no threats," the black man bellowed. "El-Hadar has given his word, and that word is currency all around the Central Sea."

Arianos made an indeterminate noise and turned to Prince Ahmad. "I leave you, then, in the hands of El-Hadar. I wish I could have done better, but Oromasd willed otherwise. I will say special prayers for you every day until the battle of the Leewahr Plains is fought. After that, one way or the other, you won't need them." He embraced the prince, nodded his farewell to the others, and left the ship to return to his temple.

Prince Ahmad and El-Hadar went into the hold to count out the money the prince had promised, but Ahmad held back five hundred dinars until their safe landing in Fricaz. The captain grumbled a bit about how insulted he was that his word was thus disputed, but he did not seem seriously upset by the prince's behavior.

The next few hours were ones of frenetic activity as the fourteen-man crew bustled about preparing *Hauvarta's Shield* for sea. They ignored the jealous jibes from sailors on nearby ships as they carefully checked all seven hundred square cubits of the mainsail for tears, scraped the hull to remove barnacles and checked for marine worms, recounted the provisions they had brought aboard, and applied another layer of vegetable oil to the coconut rope that held the hull stitched in place. Prince Ahmad and his companions, realizing they could not help, tried as best they could to stay out of the men's way, but they were constantly moving as the crew seemingly needed to be everywhere at once.

Finally, with all in readiness, the crew prepared to cast off. The anchor was lifted and the forward spar was tilted so the foresail would catch the breeze. The crewmen grabbed the ropes and began chanting as they lifted the mainsail up the mast, pulling to the beat of one crewman's drum. El-Hadar went up and down their line, shouting obscene encouragements at them and keeping a careful eye on how the ship was handling. The men grunted and sweated as their labors paid off and *Hauvarta's Shield* moved slowly out into the harbor.

By nightfall, the ship was well under way, sailing southward paralleling the Nikhrashi coast. The cook lit the coals in the brazier and prepared the simple meal of the evening. He baked a flatbread on a hot pan, and cooked some dried fish and rice with dates on the side. It was a simple meal, as simple as the trail rations the travelers were becoming thoroughly sick of—but it was a different simple meal, so they welcomed it as a wonderful change.

But even as simple as the fare was, Leila and Umar could not eat it. The mere smell of it made Leila crawl to the rail and retch over the side, even though there was little in her stomach to lose, while Umar lay back and moaned softly. Both people were pale and starting to become feverish.

"Many landsmen's stomachs cannot adapt to the rolling of the sea," El-Hadar clucked with at least a modicum of sympathy.

"It can't be that," Prince Ahmad said. "Umar has told me he's sailed on the Zaind River many times with no ill effects."

"The sea is different from the river."

"Just as what I feel is different from seasickness," Umar spoke up. "My worst fears are being confirmed."

"And what are they?" Prince Ahmad asked, turning with great concern to face his friend and teacher.

"The rimahniya have been known, on occasion, to coat their blades with a slow-acting poison. It kills the victim in four or five days, even if the initial wound was not fatal. There is no known cure."

A stunned silence greeted this news. The people stared unabashedly at Umar—and at Leila who lay sprawled by the rail. Leila gazed back at her friends, a frenzied look in her eyes. She wanted to deny that it was so, that she was not about to die. She wanted to shout out that Umar was a liar—but her own gift for the truth betrayed her. When she looked at him, she could see that he spoke the truth—at least as far as he knew it. More importantly, she could feel death creeping slowly over her own body. She could not eat, she could not drink so much as a sip of water no matter how hot she felt, no matter how parched her mouth was. The poison was spreading through her system. The rimahniya had won this round.

Prince Ahmad's fists were shaking with rage. "No," he said firmly. "I can't permit it. *Oromasd* can't permit it. He'll intervene and remove the poison, just as he intervened in Pastar."

"He won't act to save me alone, or even Leila, lovely and bright as she is. We are not the major part of his plan. I had an argument with Arianos just before he left the ship. He wanted me to come with him, to have the local doctors help me. But I knew I was beyond help, and that would only delay you, for you would not have left without me."

"But Muhmad's prophecy—" Jafar began.

"His prophecy was for you and Ahmad," Umar said gently. "You are necessary. I am not. I invited myself along on this dangerous mission, an old man full of foolish pride. Leila, too, invited herself where she did not belong. We tried to persuade you—" He looked regretfully at the tall blond woman.

"At least I'm not dying of boredom," Leila said, and coughed. "At least I'm out of those cursed tunnels."

"I won't hear of this," Prince Ahmad insisted. "Perhaps the doctors and the priests know of no cure, but that doesn't mean there isn't one. What say you, O mighty Jafar?"

Jafar felt a cold feeling spread from the pit of his stomach. In the few weeks he'd known her, he had come to feel deeply for Leila. He couldn't bring himself to call it love, yet—love, after all, was what he had felt for Amineh—but he knew she

had touched his soul more deeply than any other human being
alive except Selima. And now he had to listen to her death
sentence, to resolve himself to the fact that he must lose her
once more.

And now to be badgered by this boy to produce another
miracle from thin air—this was too much!

"I don't know, Your Highness," Jafar snapped. "There are
limits to what even wizards can do. I've never encountered this
before, and I doubt I can cure it. Sometimes that happens. I'm
sorry."

Prince Ahmad was taken aback by this hostility, and he
stared at Jafar al-Sharif as though he were a stranger. But El-
Hadar stared at both of them with wide-eyed wonder.

"You call him a wizard. He calls you 'Your Highness.'
What kind of passengers does *Hauvarta's Shield* carry? El-
Hadar must know."

Prince Ahmad turned to him, irked at the interruption. "I
am Prince Ahmad Khaled bin Shunnar el-Ravani, who might
have been king of the Holy City. That is Umar bin Ibrahim,
high priest of the Royal Temple. And that is Jafar al-Sharif,
wizard of the southern provinces."

"Such honored guests," said El-Hadar. "*Hauvarta's Shield*
is humbled before you."

"Don't worry," Leila said, fatigue heavy in her voice.
"There'll be two less of us before long."

Prince Ahmad turned back to Jafar. "I did not mean to
annoy you, O wizard—but surely I think there must be some
sorcery you can do to right this terrible injustice. These two
people should not be dying. The poison was meant for me."

"Those other people at the caravanserai shouldn't have
died, either," Jafar said. "It makes no difference to Oromasd. I
have often felt he plays cruel and bizarre tricks; now I'm sure of
it." He paused and gave a deep sigh. "Very well, I'll study the
matter. But I doubt the answer will be much different."

As soon as he could break away, Jafar went into the hold
below to confer privately with Cari and Selima. "I don't suppose you know anything about poisons?" he asked the Jann.

"Alas, no, O my master. I can cure simple cuts and
damage to the outer skin, but little within the body itself."

"And I know even less," he admitted. "It's hopeless. There
is nothing we can do to save either of them."

"Is this the father who told me the story of Goha and King Firkush's ass?" Selima said angrily. "Is this the father who fooled a wizard and made Afrits cower? My condition is even more hopeless than theirs, yet you told me not to despair, that you would find the solution. Will you now give up without even trying?"

This is what I get for following, however innocently, the path of Rimahn, thought Jafar. *I have become such an accomplished liar that even those I love, who should know me best, believe the lies I tell to and about myself, and expect them to become the truth. Subtle indeed is your punishment for liars, O Oromasd, to trap them so thoroughly within their own lies.*

"You are right to chide me," he said wearily. "But facing death one more time, in so sudden and unexpected a fashion, has warped my feeble and aged mind. My wit has deserted me, O daughter. I am at a loss for what to do."

"Was not Ali Maimun the greatest mage who ever lived? Might not his journal give some remedy for this poison?"

Almost, Jafar laughed. "The only thing that book does is tantalize and tease. For each answer it gives, it extracts a thousand questions as payment. I am already so in debt to it I fear I may become an intellectual bankrupt." He sighed. "But you're right, I should at least see whether it will help us."

He went to his saddle pouch and took out the leather-bound volume. "O Ali Maimun, my venerable predecessor," he intoned, "vast indeed was your wisdom and knowledge. I seek now your advice on the matter of life and death, not for my own benefit, but for the sakes of two good people doomed to travel prematurely to the Bridge of Shinvar, which you have already crossed. For the good of our mission, in Oromasd's name, I ask that we not be deprived of their valuable insights and assistance. Give me the key that I may save them from the evil that ravages their bodies."

But despite his entreaty, the book refused to open to any pages he had not already seen.

"It's as I thought," Jafar said wearily. "Either there's nothing in the book about such poisons, or else it simply doesn't care. As Umar himself said, he and Leila aren't crucial to the mission. Muhmad's vision was not for them, so the book will not help us."

Selima paused. "What, then, of Kharouf's grimoire? Even though he was our enemy, his spell has helped us speed our horses and cover vast distances we otherwise could never have traveled. Perhaps an evil man such as he knew more about the evils of poison than a holy man like Ali Maimun."

"Perhaps," Jafar said, "although his book is unhelpful in other ways. At least with Ali Maimun's journal, when it feels there's something I need, it opens directly to that place. From what I've seen of Kharouf's grimoire, there's no sense to it, no organization. It must be searched from cover to cover for any scrap of information. Perhaps Kharouf knew where everything in it was, but that wisdom died with him."

Cari spoke up for the first time in this discussion. "If you request it, O master, I will read through the book for you and see whether there is anything in it that might help us."

Jafar looked at her for a second, blinking. He knew she disapproved of Leila, and her feelings of Umar were neutral at best. Yet she was volunteering for this task.

"I will not ask that of you," he said. "As you told me so long ago in the Kholaj Desert, I must learn to do these things for myself. I know I'm not as fast a reader as you, and Kharouf's handwriting is hard for even an expert to read, but if I dedicate myself to this, I believe I can do it. If there is anything in Kharouf's grimoire at all that will help us, I will dig it out."

And thus did Jafar al-Sharif begin his journey through the twisted ways of sorcery, as practiced by Kharouf the yatu. He read by piecing out the words, bit by little bit, sitting by himself in a corner of the top deck, and no one there was who dared disturb him, not even El-Hadar himself. He read of many things, some of which fascinated him, some of which disgusted him. Some of Kharouf's spells and formulas had no conceivable bearing on anything that was likely to touch Jafar's life; those he looked at briefly, then skipped onward. Others, he could see, might be useful to him at some later time, even though they did not apply to this particular problem; those he read in some detail to at least familiarize himself with what could be done. Most of them called for exotic ingredients, or for powers he did not have, but a few looked as though even he might be able to make them work.

But he still read with a sense of urgency, for he could feel the lives of his two companions slipping rapidly away. Neither could take any food or water. Umar, being the older, was the worse off. By the middle of their first full day at sea, he was in the grips of a high fever, moaning and writhing on his pallet, talking deliriously to his absent wife Alhena, or to students long graduated from the madrasa, or to people no one could recognize. After a while he stopped making any sense at all.

Leila, younger and stronger, was still conscious part of the time, but that was at best a dubious blessing, for she could feel the pain the poison was bringing to her system. She would lie on her pallet, too weak to move, with awareness in her eyes—a sad awareness of the fire in her belly, the dryness of her mouth, and the cracking of her lips. If she could have spoken, she would have begged for a quick death; if she could have moved, she would have tried to end her life herself. But all she could do was lie still and wait for the poison to do its evil work upon her.

At last, Jafar found something in Kharouf's grimoire that brought a sudden excitement to his pulse. He read the passage over a second, then a third time to make sure he had interpreted it correctly, and when he knew he was right, he called Cari to show it to her and ask her opinion.

Cari read it over with a solemn expression on her face. "I am but a poor, unschooled Jann," she said, "but in my humble view, O master, you should not attempt this thing."

"Why not? It's just summoning up a single Afrit, and I've called dozens of them—and this Axabara knows all about poisons and their cures, according to Kharouf. This should be perfect."

"It is not at all the same. For one thing, you summoned the Afrits of the air. According to this book, Axabara is of a different clan, an Afrit of the earth; they are far less . . . flighty than their cousins. You'll find him much harder to deal with and control than the others."

"All I have to do is trap him inside the circles with the right signs and sigils. They're all drawn here—"

"And every single one of them will have to be done perfectly, or Axabara will escape and kill you, and possibly even sink the ship in his anger before he returns to his home."

"You can check them for me, can't you? Wouldn't you know whether they're secure or not?"

"I probably could, but—" She sighed with exasperation. "O master, you've never dealt with a djinn under these circumstances. The ring gives you the power to order me about as you wish. At the summit of Mount Nibo you used lightning to control the Afrits of the air, and you made no concessions to them. It will be different with Axabara. You will have to bargain with him, to offer him a price for his services—a terrible price."

Jafar looked at Kharouf's grimoire again. "It's not so bad—it's just one drop of my blood. Surely I can spare that to save Umar and Leila."

"You still don't understand. It's much more than a single drop of fluid from your body. Magically, that drop of blood represents a piece of your soul. Not a very large piece, as these things go, but you will nonetheless be tainted for life. A part of your soul will have been offered freely to a servant of Rimahn. In this life, you could never again expect to pass the walls of Ravan without being vaporized by the spells of Ali Maimun."

"Small loss. I wasn't all that happy with Ravan, anyway," Jafar muttered.

"You will forever be changed," Cari continued. "When the righteous Rashti comes to judge you at the Bridge of Shinvar, such a sin will count heavily against you. This taint may even be enough to prevent you from using the Crystal of Oromasd; our lord and creator may deem you unworthy of such a tool if you have demeaned yourself in this way.

"Please think seriously about this. Umar is old and has led an exemplary life; if he dies now, he will assuredly go to the House of Song. Leila—well, she is a riskier proposition, but her help on this quest will surely count in her favor at the Bridge of Shinvar. But weighing against them you have your own soul, the success of our mission, and your daughter's life. You ordered me, on our first night together, to advise you if I felt you were making a mistake. I am doing so now, O master. I beg you to let Umar and Leila die, if you must, rather than summon the Afrit Axabara."

Jafar paused for a long moment and looked at her. "Your eloquent and passionate plea is noted, O Cari, and your reasoning is sound. I hadn't realized how serious a matter a little drop of blood could be—yet allowing my friends to die for lack of it seems far more evil. Whether I ultimately heed your advice or reject it, I thank you for offering it in so straightforward, honest, and caring a manner. You are better than any mere servant, Cari; you are a friend."

Had Cari been a real woman, she would have blushed at that remark. Djinni, however, were not affected in such ways. Jafar's words did touch her deeply, and she turned quickly away rather than let her face betray any emotions.

Jafar al-Sharif had much to think about for the next two hours. Cari's words made eminent sense. Oromasd certainly frowned on people who trafficked with creatures of Rimahn, and Jafar could well be condemning himself to the Pits of Torment for ages until the final rehabilitation. He could also be jeopardizing his ability to use the Crystal of Oromasd, and thus risking the fate of both the world and Selima. That would be, as Cari had said, a terrible price to pay.

On the other hand, did the priests not say that sacrificing one's own comfort for the good of others was a noble gesture? What could be a greater sacrifice than to risk his own soul so that others might live? Was not the trading of one soul for two a worthwhile bargain?

He wished Umar were available to talk with. The old priest was sometimes a little straitlaced, but he did have the uncanny ability to see into the heart of moral dilemmas and untangle them so clearly even Jafar could understand them. Umar would have been able to tell him which road was the better one.

But Umar was not available. The whole point of the ritual was to make him available once more. For better or for worse, Jafar al-Sharif would have to make this decision on his own, and live with the consequences of his choice.

Finally he went over to where Umar and Leila lay on their pallets. Standing over their feverish, sweating bodies, he looked down at them and thought, *If I gave part of my soul away to Rimahn for selfish gain, I would deserve Oromasd's condemnation. But here I do it to save the lives of two friends, causing hurt to no one but myself, with no personal gain but the pleasure of sharing my time with them. Surely Oromasd will not hold that offensive; surely it can be at most a minor sin. And if he would condemn me for such an act—why, then, he is not the compassionate, forgiving god the priests tell me about, and thus he is no god of mine . . . and he can use his own damned Crystal if it means that much to him. But my friends mean that much to me, and I will do what is in my power to save them.*

"I am sorry to ignore thy wise advice, O friend Cari," he said aloud, "but lives are lives—and my soul was probably lost long ago, anyway."

Jafar instructed Cari to fly back to a city on the mainland and purchase some white paint and four thick white candles. She was back in less than an hour, during which time he had given instructions to Prince Ahmad and El-Hadar.

"While I am working my spell," he said, "let no one venture into the hold if he values his life. The night is mild and clear; stay up on deck and enjoy the weather. Ignore any noises you hear coming from below—and pray your finest prayers, that Oromasd may smile on us this night."

When Cari returned, she and Jafar went down into the hold and began painting the mystic symbols on the floor in accordance with the instructions in Kharouf's grimoire. First they painted a small inner circle and, within its perimeter, they painted sigils representing bears, lions, wolves, tigers, jackals, boars, and other ferocious beasts. Then they painted a much larger concentric outer circle, and around its border was a series of strange letters from a language unspoken by men for millennia. They dragged the unconscious bodies of Leila and Umar into the region between the inner and outer circle and tried to make them as comfortable as possible. They placed the four white candles at the cardinal points around the outer circle and lit them; Cari promised to keep an eye on them from the outside while the spell was being performed, to make sure the rocking of the boat did not tip them over and start a fire.

Finally came the moment for the crucial ingredient. Jafar al-Sharif took a pin and jabbed its point into the tip of the little finger on his left hand. When he squeezed, a drop of red blood oozed from the wound, which he touched to the surface of a small dish. He took the dish and set it down gently inside the inner circle. Looking up, he could see Cari watching him with an expression of great sadness on her face. She looked away quickly, but he knew that she genuinely grieved for him and for what he must do.

Finally, all was in readiness. As Jafar was about to step inside the outer circle, Cari found the boldness to grab his arm. "Please remember, O master, that the circles and the sigils are merely there as aids to concentration, and have little meaning by themselves. It is the strength of your will, and that alone, which makes the power of the circle, which summons Axabara, and which compels him to bargain with you. The circles and the signs are as close to perfect as we can make them—but if your will should falter, the spell will fail and we may all be doomed. I pray Oromasd will give you the strength you need—although asking Oromasd for strength to barter with Rimahn is an odd idea indeed."

Jafar thanked her for her kind wishes and stepped inside the outer circle. He closed his eyes to concentrate, to arouse within himself the feeling of power he had drawn on before. He knew this would be the hardest magic he'd done yet, and he would need every iota of his faculties to work the spell and save his friends.

He started with the simplest part first—raising the protection of the outer circle. He had long since memorized the incantations that Kharouf's grimoire said he would need:

> Candles of the north and south,
> Shine your benign light on my endeavors.
> Candles of the east and west,
> Guard your stations from evil's breach.
> May all the holy yazatas protect this room
> From Rimahn's expanding influence.
> May this outer circle be the wall,
> The bastion that contains all evil within,
> Preserving all of Oromasd's creation,
> All that is good and pure, from evil's taint.
> By Afda, I will it.
> By Basda, I will it.
> By Gimmal, I will it.
> By Dalith, I will it.
> So, then, it is.

As Jafar spoke, as the power resonated from within him, he saw the line of the outer circle begin to glow, while the candles outside the circle continued to shine—but now they shone with a dark light, as though somehow they were radiating blackness. With each line he spoke, the circle grew brighter, the outside world dimmer. As he named the letters of the archaic alphabet, each one blazed in its turn, and as he uttered the final line, the circle sprang up around him like a wall of light, cutting him off from the rest of the universe. Nothing existed beyond that boundary, but its glow was bright enough for him to see by.

Already Jafar felt tired, as though he'd done a hard day's work—and the spell had barely begun. Determined, he pushed on.

The next step was to work on the blood in the dish, to turn it from a simple drop of fluid into a trap for a powerful Afrit.

This blood of my body, freely given,
I do offer as a sacrifice to the powers that come.
In trade do I yield up this, my life's essence,
So that he who partakes of my bounty
Will, in return, give of his own power.
A favor given, a favor returned,
So the balance of the universe is ever maintained.

The fatigue doubled, and there was still so much left to do. The next step was to build up the inner circle as a cage to hold Axabara. Jafar rubbed at his eyes and forced them to focus as he chanted:

A wall I build to contain evil.
A wall I build to contain anger.
A wall I build to contain sorcery.
Let the beasts of the field stand their guard.
Let the beasts of the forests stand their guard.
Let no creature escape from this imprisonment.
In Oromasd's name I encompass thee.
In Oromasd's name I bind thee.
In Oromasd's name I control thee.

The inner circle began glowing, too, with a softer but firmer light. The images representing the animals lit up with bright fire, and seemed to snarl their rage at anything that would dare step beyond the boundaries they delineated. As Jafar finished this incantation, the second wall went up, like a sheet made both of glass and fire.

Jafar al-Sharif was sweating, and he felt as though the weight of the world had been placed on his shoulders. He had told many tales of wizards, and had spoken of them waving their hands and producing miracles—but never had it seemed such exhaustive labor until now. He could understand why great wizards spent so many years developing their craft—it would take that long to build up the discipline and the stamina to make this sort of effort as routine as Akar made it appear.

Jafar nodded slightly with fatigue, and the glowing walls around him flickered ominously. He quickly straightened up and shook his head vigorously to renew his concentration. He dared not lose control now. This was the hardest part, and to slip now would be disastrous.

I call now the name of the being I summon;
I call now the name of Axabara the Afrit.
Axabara, my words shall call you.
Axabara, my voice shall summon you.
Axabara, my will shall bind you.
Be you on land, you will fly to me.
Be you in the sea, you will fly to me.
Be you in the air, you will fly to me.
Axabara, I pen you within my prison.
Axabara, I snare you within my cage.
Axabara, I bind you within my circle.
Axabara, come you to me now!

Suddenly the inner circle was filled with flame and smoke, and the air within the outer circle stank heavily of smoldering leaves and rotting fruit. Jafar al-Sharif began coughing as the stench overwhelmed him, and the fumes brought tears to his eyes as well. When next he could see, there was *something* moving about within the inner circle.

Axabara was large, so big he had little room to move within the circle. His head and torso were those of a jackal, with pointed snout and ears, sharp teeth, and sly, conniving eyes. The ends of his paws, though, were as agile as any human fingers. The bottom half of his body was that of an enormous scorpion with stinger raised and menacing, and he moved about on six multijointed legs. The combination of the terrible stench, overwhelming fatigue, and just plain fear nearly made Jafar pass out, but he clung tenaciously to consciousness with the knowledge that all his friends were depending on him for their very lives at this moment.

Axabara raged against the walls of his tiny cell, and each time he battered against the rim of the circle, it was like a physical blow to Jafar. Time and again Axabara battered, and each time the walls held. With each blow Jafar's strength ebbed that much lower, and he prayed fervently to Oromasd that he could hold on long enough to do what must be done.

But the blows took their toll on Axabara, too, and after what seemed like days—but was probably only minutes—he ceased trying to escape. Then he spied the dish with Jafar's blood at his feet, and he pounced on it, devouring blood *and* dish in a single swallow.

Then fire lanced through Jafar's body, as though all his veins and arteries were suddenly carrying white-hot molten

metal instead of blood. *This* was what Cari had tried to warn
him about, and he regretted now not having listened to her. In
the face of such pain, he could not stand, could not even cry
out. He sank to his knees, hugged his arms around his chest,
and screwed his eyes tightly shut. Again he nearly fainted, and
perhaps the only thing that saved him was the knowledge that
if he lost consciousness the protection of the circles would vanish, and Axabara would escape his prison to inflict his venom
on the entire boat.

The pain vanished again almost as abruptly as it came, but
its aftermath still left Jafar's body shaking. Jafar luxuriated for a
moment in the lack-of-pain sensation, then opened his eyes—
and found himself staring straight into the jackal eyes of
Axabara.

The Afrit's face was flaming with anger, his white teeth
gleaming, his jaws dripping saliva at the thought of snatching
Jafar up and devouring him at a single bite. Only Jafar's will,
manifested as the wall of the inner circle, prevented him—and
that will was growing weaker all the time. Jafar knew he'd have
to hurry through the rest of this ritual, or he would not hold
out to complete it.

From some unknown depths he found the strength to continue. Through teeth clenched against the fatigue and pain, he
said, "Now, Axabara, thou art mine!"

"Axabara belongs to no man!" growled the Afrit, snapping
his jaws shut harshly to emphasize his point.

"Thou accepted my sacrifice, and art bound to do my bidding."

"Your bidding, O weakling? You can't even bid your feet to
support your weight."

Slowly, with every muscle of his body trembling, Jafar al-
Sharif lifted his right knee so the foot was flat on the floor;
then, steadying himself with his left arm, he pushed up and
rose until he stood erect. He was wobbly and his eyes had
trouble focusing, but he was standing on his two feet as a man
should as he faced the monster in the inner circle.

"Hear now my commands, O thou piece of filth, thou
pond scum, thou bastard spawn of Rimahn. Thou art to use thy
knowledge to rid my two friends of the poisons that wrack their
bodies, and to heal them and return them to full health. Not
until thou hast done that will I discharge thee from thy duty
and dismiss thee from my presence."

Axabara railed again, and pounded against the walls—but now that he knew he had the upper hand, Jafar found new strength flowing into him and he stood firm against the abuse. Finally, realizing he was trapped, Axabara stopped his raging and looked again into Jafar's face.

"Know you that I cannot cure them from within this circle," he said. "To remove the poison, I must touch them. I must be out of this confinement and in there with them and you."

Kharouf's grimoire had warned of such a contingency. "Then I shall command thee to give thy oath, that if I release thee from thy prison thou wilt do no harm to me or any living being within this circle, but will promptly perform thy services as I have bidden."

"And if I do not so swear?"

"Then I will leave thee in that circle until the end of eternity, until Oromasd has won the final victory and has cast Rimahn forever into the darkness from which he was spawned."

Axabara glowered, a particularly unnerving sight considering his features. "Very well. To rid myself of this loathsome burden as quickly as possible, I do swear in the name of Rimahn the destroyer, Rimahn the father of the lie, that I will do your bidding and do all within my power to cure these people of the poisons within them, and that I will harm no living being within your circle."

Thus assured, Jafar raised both his arms, even though each one felt as heavy as a stone obelisk. He looked at the inner circle and tried to make both eyes focus at once as he intoned:

A wall I destroy to release evil-turned-to-good.
A wall I destroy to release anger-turned-to-aid.
A wall I destroy to release sorcery-turned-to-medicine.
Let the beasts of the field relax their guard.
Let the beasts of the forests relax their guard.
Let a humbled creature escape this imprisonment.
In Oromasd's name I loose thee.
In Oromasd's name I release thee.
In Oromasd's name I free thee.

The inner wall of light dissolved, and Jafar instinctively stepped back, away from the hideous creature he had released.

He had done what the book said was necessary, but that did not leave him feeling very comfortable in the presence of so frightening a monster. He'd hoped to regain some of his strength, now that his will was no longer needed to maintain the inner circle, but the magic did not work that way. He felt as tired as ever.

Axabara stretched his muscles after the tight confines of his prison. The sight of those strong upper arms and that long, deadly tail stretching to their limits sent chills through Jafar's body. If he'd made even the slightest mistake, Axabara would be upon him before he could even blink—and then he'd devour Umar and Leila for dessert. Then Prince Ahmad, and El-Hadar, and the rest of the crew . . .

The outer circle flickered briefly, and Jafar al-Sharif ruthlessly quashed those thoughts. Now was not the time for doubts; now was the time for certainty, whether the situation warranted it or not. Axabara would not harm them. Axabara would cure Leila and Umar. There could be no other way.

"Do not delay, thou lazy djinn. Cure them at once."

Axabara glowered at him once more, but said nothing. Instead, he scuttled over to Umar and knelt beside him. Suddenly his stinger tail lashed out and pierced the old priest's skin. Rather than injecting poison, as a scorpion would, Axabara's tail sucked all the fluid from Umar's body until the skin shriveled and collapsed, leaving Umar looking like one of the dessicated mummies found in the caves of Bellandy. Jafar's eyes widened in horror at what the Afrit had done to his companion.

But before he could yell his protest, Axabara quickly turned around and put his long-jackal snout to Umar's mouth. The Afrit blew his magical breath down the priest's throat, and like an inflatable bladder Umar's body filled out once more. The unnatural wrinkles vanished, the skin became smooth, the complexion became healthier. Axabara pressed his hands against Umar's chest, and a belch of air, glowing like blue fire, escaped the priest's mouth.

Axabara moved to perform the same process on Leila, and Jafar turned quickly away. He did not want to watch this woman with whom he made love turn into a mummy, did not want to see her body shrivel and her skin wrinkle into a bag of worthless flesh, did not want that image to haunt his dreams and stand between them when he took her in his arms. Only when he heard her belch, as Umar had, did Jafar turn back to observe the scene.

"It is done," Axabara announced.

"Why do they still lie there unconscious? Why are they not back to health?"

"I have removed the poison from their bodies, but it did much damage while it was in them. I breathed curatives back into them, but the rebuilding will take at least as much time as the poison did, if not longer. It will all depend on their own strength and their own will. If kismet decrees they will survive, they will—but I can do no more.

"In the meantime, I have done your bidding. Release me from this odious bond, that I may go upon my business."

Jafar nodded. "I certify that thou hast fulfilled our compact, and I discharge thee from thy duty and dismiss thee from this circle. Depart to whence thou camest, and stop not to molest any aboard this ship. Go with the peace of Oromasd, if his peace be what thou wishest."

The Afrit vanished, so abruptly that Jafar could almost believe he'd never been there at all.

The storyteller stood unsteadily on his feet, swaying as he looked back and forth at Umar and Leila. They looked little different, but at least they lay still and did not moan as they had done before. Jafar hoped the ritual had worked; he knew he couldn't do anything like this again in the near future.

More than anything in the world, he wanted to lie down beside Leila and join her in sleep for the next seven years or so—but he had one task left to do. Slowly, meticulously, straining at every word, he spoke the spell that dissolved the wall of the outer circle so he could rejoin the real world once more.

The wall of light vanished, to be replaced by the much darker interior of the ship, lit only by the four white candles and the scattered lamps. Cari stood just on the other side of the line, concern etched into her lovely features. She stared at Jafar almost as though she didn't recognize him—and as though she'd feared it would be the Afrit, not him, who emerged from the circle.

"O master, I—"

Jafar heard no more. He slumped forward into her arms, and she caught him with her gentle strength and lowered him slowly to the ground.

Cari looked over to Umar and Leila, who were both breathing normally for the first time in two days. Then she looked back down at Jafar, his beard slightly grayer than she remembered it, his face a little more lined, but no less handsome. She started to worry for his health. And then he began snoring.

Cari took a cushion and placed it beneath his head. "Sleep the blessed sleep," she whispered. "Tonight, O master, thou art in truth become a wizard."

15

The Daevas

Hakem Rafi the thief was pleased, at first, with the way his new campaign was succeeding. Starting from the shore of the Western Sea, his army swept eastward across the face of Parsina like a grass fire in the heat of summer. With Aeshma smoothing the path, none could stand against him. On land, city after city, kingdom after kingdom surrendered to his absolute authority. In the Central Sea, his ships controlled the traffic throughout the western half. Those merchants who refused to pay a 50 percent tax on their wares had their ships looted and everything confiscated in the name of Hakem Rafi, their new emperor. Sometimes, if the merchants were quick enough to swear allegiance, Hakem Rafi allowed them to live—provided they paid outrageous sums for licenses and agreed to his taxes on their future trade.

In every land they conquered, at Aeshma's suggestion, the king of the daevas searched out the wizards, the yatus, the sorcerers, even the lowliest practitioners of magic. Those who were too powerful, who represented a threat to Hakem Rafi—and thus to Aeshma—were killed outright. Those who were no serious threat to the emperor's reign merely had their equipment destroyed, their grimoires burned, and were forced to swear allegiance to Hakem Rafi. Each of these also had one of the hairy demons assigned to watch him constantly, to ensure that he caused no trouble to the new regime.

As word of this policy quickly spread among the craftsmen who practiced the magical arts, there grew a vast eastward migration of the more talented individuals. These magicians were hoping some power would arise to stop the advance of this inexorable conqueror—and in the meantime, they planned to stay ahead of his expansion and well out of his way. Even the yatus who had devoted themselves and their magic to the benefit of Rimahn could not feel safe, for their brethren, too, were being destroyed in the indiscriminate wave of killing. Mere devotion to Aeshma's master did not spare anyone from Hakem Rafi's vengeance.

The other immediate victims of Hakem Rafi's rule were the priests and the temples. Hakem Rafi had never liked priests anyway, because they always had sided with the law against him. They always claimed to help the common man, but never once had they helped *him*. The temples were centers for hypocrisy and enslavement of the masses, institutions that supported the kings and the nobles. They were an annoyance Hakem Rafi had always envied and disdained.

To Aeshma, the priests were anathema. They were the enemy, and the temples were their fortresses. Left intact, they would sow the seeds of dissension within this new empire he was forging in Hakem Rafi's name, by preaching the word of Oromasd and opposing the rule of Rimahn. That could not be permitted. Such pockets of resistance were to be destroyed before they could spread their political cancers among the citizens of the realm.

Consequently, Hakem Rafi's soldiers ransacked the temples in every city and town they conquered. All priests, even simple novitiates, were put to death; the flames of Oromasd were extinguished; religious relics and works of art that hadn't been hidden before the conqueror arrived were smashed or defaced; the treasures of the temples were confiscated for Hakem Rafi's coffers; and the buildings themselves were often razed to the ground.

Many of the local citizens were horrified by this profane treatment of all they considered holy. But Hakem Rafi was so strong that no one dared challenge his authority, and so people resigned themselves to whispering in corners and hating the man who commanded their bodies, but not their hearts, who had their fear, but not their love.

The priests—at least, the good ones—did not flee in the face of Hakem Rafi's advancing armies, as did the magicians. As devoted followers of Oromasd, they remained where they were to help guide the people who needed their solace. Some doffed their white priestly robes out of cowardice, and thus survived the purges. Others doffed their robes in order to survive and help their people through the spiritual trials that were sure to come. Some did not forsake their robes at all, but stayed to their posts in an attempt to ward off the oncoming menace.

But no amount of their prayers and blessings could halt Hakem Rafi's advance. It was as inexorable as the tides, and just as predictable. The line of Hakem Rafi's empire swept eastward across the face of Parsina, changing ages-old political boundaries forever afterward.

But finally the empire met a challenge it could not easily defeat. In the land of Hugheri, refugees from the west gathered in an effort to make a stand against the oncoming hordes. Magicians, priests, and local rulers from several kingdoms around formed a strong, if uneasy, alliance against the threat from this conqueror. And it was this alliance that caused Hakem Rafi and Aeshma to rethink their strategies.

Hugheri was a land rich in tradition and strong in its religious faith. Here it was, in the dark forests to the south, that the hero Argun was born and grew to manhood. Here, too, it was that the renowned priest, Faral al-Hugheri, deceived the mighty Shaitan Dalebhan and retrieved the Cup of Wisdom, which remained even to that day enshrined in the Paskegaran Temple in the center of the city. In times past, the people of Hugheri had never failed to stand against the evil of Rimahn, and the present king—in consultation with his neighbors—agreed that another stand must be made against a force that was so clearly rooted in evil.

The priests conferred with the magician-refugees who streamed into the city from the west, and they conceived a plan to protect the region from Hakem Rafi's army. The priests took the holiest relics from the temples and scattered them around the perimeter of the land to be protected. The wizards, in a rare display of cooperation, pooled their knowledge and their powers to create their strongest spells. The defensive spells, it was hoped, would keep the invader's forces from penetrating the boundaries of the kingdom. The offensive spells would protect the Hugheri army and enable them to strike back at the enemy with some chance of success—something no one else had ever accomplished.

The army of Hakem Rafi had grown overconfident from their many easy victories. With Aeshma leading the way for them, and with their growing reputation for invincibility, they had seldom had to fight. Most cities simply surrendered when they came in sight, and even the contentious ones had been so battered by Aeshma's powers that they had little resistance left in them by the time the army appeared on the scene. Hakem Rafi's soldiers suffered few injuries and even fewer casualties.

Their worst physical threat was sore feet from marching too far too quickly.

Neither Aeshma nor Hakem Rafi were with them as they approached the borders of Hugheri. With such an extended front line of advance, and with a vast empire already to administer, their time could not be spared for every campaign. They had placed trusted officers in charge of this division, men who were thoroughly willing to carry out Hakem Rafi's cruel orders in exchange for a taste of power for themselves.

The invaders rode toward Hugheri, and suddenly found themselves crashing into an invisible wall around the land. Their horses could not ride through the shield, and the men could not walk through it. After half a day of trying stubbornly to broach this unexpected obstacle, the officers in charge called a halt and set up a camp while they tried to decide what to do next.

While they were thus occupied, the Hugheri army came out to attack them, riding with impunity through the invisible wall that Hakem Rafi's men could not pass. The thief's forces, caught by surprise, had difficulty fighting back. Even those who reached their weapons found they could not penetrate the Hugheri shields. Their blows could not touch the local defenders, while the Hugheri swords repeatedly found their marks.

The result was a disaster for Hakem Rafi's army. A division with almost a thousand men was virtually wiped out, leaving only a handful of survivors who had acted quickly and fled the scene. The Hugheri forces suffered no injuries, no casualties—and when the camp was decimated, they rode back within their shield where no enemy could touch them.

The celebrations in Hugheri that night were beyond description. The invincible army had been stopped dead in its tracks; the would-be emperor had been repelled. The Hugheri had accomplished something no one else in the world had been able to. The shadow of inevitable death that had cast its pall over the land was suddenly lifted, to be replaced by that brightest of commodities, hope. Messengers were quickly dispatched eastward to other kingdoms, urging them to join the Hugheri alliance to halt this horrible threat from the west and restore the righteous rule of Oromasd to the world once more. Hugheri would stand like a beacon of light and freedom at the edge of Hakem Rafi's dark empire.

Word also spread eastward quickly through the network of information relays established by Aeshma, until it reached the emperor's headquarters. When Hakem Rafi heard that his troops had been routed by a small band of local militia, his anger raged supreme.

"Crush them, O Aeshma," he said coldly. "Leave not a stone of their city standing. Let them learn the penalty for defying Hakem Rafi, the master of all Parsina."

"I hear and I obey, O master," said Aeshma, who was himself quite disturbed at this development. Things had been going very smoothly according to his plan, and he was not about to tolerate any delays at this point.

The king of the daevas flew personally to the site of the debacle, and found the invisible magical wall still standing. Though he struck against it with all the considerable strength at his disposal, still he could not breach its surface or enter into the defended land. The more he tried, the angrier he grew— but finally, as he realized the barrier would not yield to him, another plan hatched in his diabolical mind. There could yet be a way to solve the puzzle of this wall, and further his ultimate cause at the same time.

He returned to face Hakem Rafi with abject humility. "Alas, O master, that barrier is too strong for me. Even my fiercest blows were as an idle gust of wind against an oak tree."

Hakem Rafi raged still hotter. "You promised me I would rule Parsina. You claimed to be the most powerful being in the world. And one little city defies us with impunity."

"I *am* the most powerful being in the world," Aeshma replied. "But I am not the only being with any power. If enough others band together against me, as they've obviously done here, they can combine their own puny powers to match mine."

"That gives me small comfort," Hakem Rafi railed. "When word of this spreads, other lands will join in alliance with Hugheri. They will combine their 'puny powers' still further, and overwhelm us. They will unite to push us back, and we'll lose everything we've conquered."

"Fear not, O master. Before that happens, I can destroy Hugheri for you in such a dramatic way that no city will dare oppose you again."

"How?"

"You know I am king of the daevas, but thus far you have not allowed me to contact my subjects other than the hairy demons. If you would but let me travel to Mount Denavan and draw on the power of the other daevas, we would make an irresistible force that would sweep all before us."

Hakem Rafi was silent. He had deliberately forbidden Aeshma from contacting the rest of the daevas because he feared the daeva king would then become too strong. He knew how slender was his hold on this powerful creature, and isolation seemed the best way to keep him from gaining the upper hand.

"What if we just bypass Hugheri for now?" he asked. "We could go around them and then come back to deal with them once we've conquered everything else."

"That would leave them as a thorn in your side, behind your front lines," Aeshma argued. "They could emerge from their protective wall and strike at you at will, perhaps even liberating some of the cities you've taken. Their influence will expand like a cancer within the body of your empire, and the energy I would have to use to deal with them would be taken away from other wars on the front. Most importantly, they will stand as an example to the rest of the world that you can be defied with impunity, and other nations will band together as they did to thwart your will. They must be defeated now, at once, or I cannot guarantee the success of your cause."

But Hakem Rafi still resisted the idea. "What if we pull in the rest of our army and surround them, lay siege to their land? We have so many men they can't attack us all. We could pen them in until they're forced to surrender—"

"The boundaries of their circle extend for many parasangs. Within their protection are rivers, fields, forests, wells, whole cities. They could survive for months, perhaps years, without contact from the outside. You cannot just waste your men by letting them sit around watching the enemy. The men will rot away, and so will your empire. Not only that, Hugheri will again stand as a symbol of resistance, a rallying point for the other nations. You cannot allow that to happen. You must take decisive action."

Hakem Rafi stood up and paced about his room. "The point is, I do not trust you, O Aeshma."

"You have said that before, O wise master. And yet, have I ever done anything to betray your trust?"

"Do you want a list? You've lied to me consistently about your powers. It nearly got us destroyed by that wizard Akar, and now it's stalled my conquest of the world. How do I know you won't combine with the other daevas to destroy me?"

"I am bound by my oath to protect you, and to not encourage anyone else to harm you. How can I then betray you?"

"You're looking for some way, I know it."

"Why should I, O master, when your path of conquest already serves the needs of Rimahn, so well?"

Hakem Rafi had no ready answer for that. He was silent for several minutes before speaking again. "If I let you contact the other daevas, it must be with the understanding that I will accompany you. I must be privy to all communication between you and them, so I can see for myself that there is no conspiracy against me."

Aeshma hesitated. "O master, were I to take you with me, I would fear for your safety."

"You mean you cannot protect me?"

"I would certainly try. But you remember the cavern of the hairy demons, and how frightening an experience that was for you. I can promise you that that would seem as a stroll in a garden compared to the journey I now contemplate. The daevas are infinitely more powerful than my simple offspring; they are immortal creatures of Rimahn, just as I am. Few are the men who have gazed upon even one of them and lived, and you are asking to meet several at once. Are you sure you want to risk such a venture?"

Hakem Rafi paused. He still had nightmares about the cavern of the hairy demons—but he had even worse dreads about Aeshma slipping loose from the constraints the thief had placed on him. "If, as you say, the only way to deal with this Hugheri defiance is to enlist the aid of other daevas, then you must go to them—and if you must go to them, then I must go with you to monitor your contact. Just remember—you must do all within your power to protect me from any dangers that might threaten."

Aeshma sighed. "I hear and I obey, O my master."

And before Hakem Rafi had a chance to change his mind, Aeshma swept him up in one monstrous claw and flew off through an open window into the air, changing again into the form of a rukh as he did so. They flew to the southeast, over farms and forests and mountains, and finally over the vast Central Sea. Hakem Rafi had by now become quite used to having Aeshma fly him to various places, and actually enjoyed the feeling of exhilaration as he looked down upon the world and watched the scenery slide by. The Central Sea, though, was nothing but water as far as the horizon, and one section of it looked much like any other. Hakem Rafi quickly grew bored looking at it and concentrated, instead, on not showing any fear when he finally faced the rest of the daevas.

At last they reached land again, crossing the southern shore of the Central Sea and heading inland. They passed over the broad Nilot River that, at this latitude, marked the eastern boundary of Hakem Rafi's domain. The land they flew over was mostly wasteland, with small settlements here and there, but at last a mountain appeared ahead of them on the southern horizon.

Mount Denavan stood imposingly by itself, like an ugly pimple on the otherwise smooth face of the earth. Smoke could occasionally be seen drifting from the cone of this almost-dormant volcano, as though the mountain could never quite decide whether or not to blow off its tremendous energy and spew molten rock and ash over the surrounding countryside. There was no sign of human habitation for more than two days' travel around the mountain, for it was widely known that this place, more than any other in Parsina, was dedicated to Rimahn—and therefore hostile to man. Here, it was said, there were more scorpions, spiders, snakes, flies, and other noxious creatures of Rimahn, than in any similar area elsewhere. No one came to this region by choice, and no one stayed longer than he absolutely had to.

Aeshma flew with his passenger straight at the mountain's cone and dived inside with the familiar feeling of coming home after a long absence. For Hakem Rafi, though, the sight was anything but cheering. Ahead of them were vast beds of open lava, red-hot pools of molten rock that seethed and steamed the air, making everything waver and become indistinct. There was also the stench of sulfur that made the thief gag, barely containing his morning meal.

Hakem Rafi was afraid Aeshma would dive straight into the molten lava, as he'd dived into the solid earth to reach the cavern of the hairy demons, but Aeshma did not do that. He skimmed low over the bed of lava, so that the heat became almost overwhelming, then zipped through a series of tunnels and caverns carved into the interior of the mountain. The tunnels wove sinuously through the rock, leading gradually downward into the bowels of the earth to the land where the daevas dwelt.

As they passed one point, an eerie sound of screaming and moaning reached Hakem Rafi's ears, so loud he had to clap his hands to his head to block out the worst of the noise. "What is that?" he asked his guide.

"That is the wailing of the souls condemned to the Pits of Torment," Aeshma said very matter-of-factly. "Would you like to see them? Their tortures are far worse than those you devise for your own enemies. You might get some interesting ideas."

Despite the heat, Hakem Rafi felt a chill go up his spine. Almost—*almost*—he was tempted to reform and give up his wicked ways, rather than be condemned to the anguish he'd heard. But he knew he could never do enough good to make up for all the sins he'd committed in his life, so what was the point? He was condemned here, anyway, so he might as well take what life had to offer him. Besides, he controlled Aeshma, who was satrap of the demons of the Pits of Torment. He would not suffer as badly as those other poor fools who had no protector to watch over them.

Hakem Rafi put these thoughts quickly out of his mind. "No," he said simply. There were other, more important matters to be dealt with today. The Pits of Torment could wait.

Aeshma flew him down and around, around and down, until at last they reached the cavern where dwelt the daevas of Rimahn. Unlike the home of the hairy demons, this place was so dim and smoky that Hakem Rafi could barely make out the most indistinct of shapes. The smell had grown a thousand times worse, a combination of every rotten odor the world could produce. Hakem Rafi started retching so badly that he asked Aeshma to banish the smells from the area. Unable to do that, Aeshma produced a pomander that Hakem Rafi could hold under his nose, so only the fresh scent of cinnamon and spices entered his nostrils.

"I can't see what's happening around me," the thief complained.

"Consider yourself fortunate," Aeshma told him as he resumed his normal shape. "Men's hearts have been known to fail at the direct sight of but a single daeva. I have taken care to soften my appearance for your sake; my companions will not be so compassionate."

Hakem Rafi accordingly let the subject drop, and simply concentrated on making out what he could through the red-hued gloom of the cavern.

A tall creature approached, a scaled creature with a lizard-like beak, rows of small but pointed teeth, and saucerlike, yellow eyes. His body was coated with a glistening, shiny substance like mucus that made Hakem Rafi want to shrink away.

"So, Aeshma, thou hast returned to us, lo these many months after you were freed from your imprisonment. Were we then not worthy of your consideration?"

"I have been busy, Az, serving the human who released me from my urn."

Another daeva approached. He had an enormous, burly body, splotchy orange, with a head that was three sizes too small for it that seemed to disappear into the muscles arching over his shoulders. A grin displaying gaps in its teeth seemed permanently affixed to its features. He had arms that reached below his knees and long, tapering fingers that were constantly in motion, one hand always fondling one or the other of his penises. "And hast thou then abandoned service to our lord Rimahn?"

"Akah Manah, thou knowest it not to be the case. This human, *under my protection*, is Hakem Rafi, and he serves the cause of Rimahn as steadfastly as do any of us. To do his bidding is to do Rimahn's."

"We have noticed his empire spreading, with thy assistance," said Az. "It has some possibilities."

"It will bring about the ultimate victory of Rimahn, if we act in concert," Aeshma proclaimed. "Without my presence here to unify you, you have fought and argued amongst yourselves, ignoring the greater goals our lord had set for you. Now I am returned, and I shall give you direction once more."

An enormous, bloated figure approached, its skin of mottled brown and green and covered with ugly warts and pustules. Its thick arms were like clubs, swinging ominously back and forth as it walked. It had no genitals at all, and its voice was as high as a eunuch's as it said, "Dost thou doubt our devotion to Rimahn, or our efforts on his behalf while thou wert away?"

"No, Saura, I do not. But effective action requires a leader, it requires coordination, and you had none of either. If you had, Mankind would not have survived to this day, for, given the lack of heroes in the world, your combined talents would have rid the world of Oromasd's ally long before now."

"But who is to say that thou shouldst be that leader?" said Akah Manah. "Thou wert before, and led us into disarray from which we are only now recovering. Thou art right, we do need a leader—but perhaps it should be one of us, and perhaps thou shouldst obey *our* commands."

Hakem Rafi felt distinctly uncomfortable. He was held securely in Aeshma's right hand, while Aeshma himself was surrounded by three ugly, powerful daevas. At any moment they could attack, and Aeshma could not completely defend himself from them one-handed. In hindsight, Hakem Rafi realized just how right Aeshma had been in asking him not to come along on this journey.

But Aeshma did not wait to defend himself. Faster than the eye could see, his left arm reached out and grabbed Az by the throat. Even though the daevas could not die, Hakem Rafi imagined that grip could not have felt pleasant.

"Thou wouldst challenge me for command, then?" he bellowed. "Art thou grown so great in thine own eyes? Has our lord Rimahn whispered in thine ear, acknowledging thee his favorite?"

Another daeva approached, this one in the shape of an enormous woman with pallid skin and paint exaggerating the features of her face. Her pointed tongue, long enough to reach her waist, darted in and out continually like a snake's, and her long, curved fingernails were as sharp as an eagle's talons. Hakem Rafi did not need any introduction to know that this was Jahi, the great harlot, who seduced and killed Gayomar, the first man.

"Perhaps our comrades wish to reconsider their hasty arguments," Jahi said in oily tones.

"Possibly we were hasty," Akah Manah admitted.

"Certainly we were never more unified than when under Aeshma's leadership," Saura said.

Az was still struggling for breath, his throat tightly in Aeshma's grasp. Even so, his lizard mouth choked out a sound that was vaguely conciliatory.

Aeshma picked Az up by the throat and threw him across the cavern. The lizard daeva fell in an undignified heap, more humiliated than hurt, and scrambled to his feet, glowering silently at Aeshma but rebelling no longer.

"Now," said Aeshma, "what do you all know about Hugheri?"

"They've built a wall to keep thee and thy army out," said Saura, "but it does no good against us. We've all visited there on our regular rounds for centuries. We know the ways to get in."

"It is as I suspected," Aeshma said. "Now I will tell you what you all must do to assist my lord Hakem Rafi and me in our march to conquest."

And so it was that, while the priests and the magicians in Hugheri concentrated their efforts against Aeshma, other daevas slipped past their guard to work Rimahn's mischief in their own particular ways, thus to sap the strength of the defenders.

Many were the celebrations throughout Hugheri at their stunning victory over the oppressor. Such was fertile ground for Saura's wiles, and the daeva slipped deviously into the haunts of men to encourage drunkenness. As the soldiers drank, they deserted their posts and insulted their superiors, bringing disorder and anarchy to the ranks of the army. The discipline and sense of purpose that enabled them to stand against Hakem Rafi's forces began to disintegrate. Within two days, this once-proud army was reduced to a handful of loyal officers trying vainly to maintain control and discipline.

Among the priests and magicians, it was Akah Manah who worked his will. The priests felt it was chiefly their prayers that had repelled the invaders, while the magicians knew it was their spells—and within their ranks, each was convinced it was his own particular bit of skill that had provided the crucial ingredient. As they met in council and discussed what should be done next, they fell into violent discord about who was responsible for what. The rare unity that had enabled them to become so effective was now shattered—and with that disunity, the wall around the land began to dissolve as well.

Jahi appeared to the men of Hugheri in the guise of their neighbors' wives, seducing them with reckless abandon and causing quarrels where none should exist. Pairimaiti spoke in the ear of the weak-willed, encouraging them to take what they wanted from their neighbors, since their victory meant wealth was certain to come to all. A wave of rioting, raping, and looting swept through Hugheri the likes of which had not been seen in many ages.

And with chaos now prevailing within Hugheri, Hakem Rafi's forces marched virtually unopposed into the city to begin their own cycle of destruction. All the inhabitants were ruthlessly slaughtered, even down to the infants. The weaker priests were made to gather up the holy relics that the daevas, for all their power, couldn't touch. The priests were then taken, each with his own sacred object, to the edge of a great swamp. There the priests' bellies were slit open, their entrails spilled on the ground, and the relics placed in their bodies. The skin magically closed over them, and each was cast into the quagmire. It is said their screams and prayers can be heard echoing through the swamp to this very day.

The city of Hugheri was put to the torch, and some areas burned for days. When the town was reduced to a lifeless pile of rubble, Aeshma himself strode through it, smashing the ruins into the ground and leveling the area until nothing remained upright to remind people that once a civilization had flourished here. All physical traces of Hugheri were obliterated from the land—but not even Aeshma and all his daevas could obliterate Hugheri, its proud history, and its noble stand, from the minds of men.

And when the daevas were finished with Hugheri, Aeshma looked ahead to the possibility of future conquests in the name of Hakem Rafi. No kingdom could mount the power to defy them now, no land could stand against them, no city's walls could hold them out. No city, that is, but one, the city where Aeshma and his daevas were forbidden to enter, where their power and authority were all but nullified. This city alone stood in Aeshma's path toward complete world domination.

And so Aeshma began carefully laying his plans to deal with this sole obstacle to his total success—the holy city of Ravan.

16

The Legend of Atluri

Jafar al-Sharif slept for two full days following his ritual to save the lives of Umar and Leila. He was unwakable during that interval, the only signs of life being his regular breathing and occasional snores. During this time he was attended constantly by the Jann Cari, who sat beside him and bathed his forehead with a wet cloth. Selima also spent much time by her father's side; although she was of little physical help, she and Cari both agreed that her presence could not help but improve Jafar's spiritual well-being.

When Jafar finally did open his eyes, it was nighttime down in the hold, and all was dark except for the lamps that were kept constantly burning. Through half-opened lids he looked up and saw Cari's face gazing down at him, and her gentle scent of ylang-ylang filtered into his nostrils. When she saw his eyes were opened, she placed one hand gently behind his head and raised it up slightly, then lifted a cup of water to his dry lips and let him drink slowly.

Jafar's mouth felt like the Kholaj Desert itself, and the water helped only slightly to ease the dryness. He tried to speak several times, but his voice cracked so much he could not make himself intelligible.

Selima, seeing this activity, came to sit within his line of sight. "Are you well, Father?" she asked.

Jafar nodded, then pointed to his throat.

"I understand," Selima said. "Cari tells me you'll probably be weak for another day or two, yet."

"How are they?" Jafar croaked, his words barely comprehensible.

"Take a look for yourself," Cari said. She helped pull her master into a sitting position, leaning his back against her, and pointed at Umar and Leila a few cubits away.

226

The two victims of rimahniya poisoning were lying still on their pallets, the only signs of life being shallow breathing. They were no longer moaning and writhing in agony, as they had been doing, but they were far from recovered from the aftereffects of the poison.

"Their fevers broke shortly after you finished the spell," Cari said. "They've been lying quiet and relaxed for two days ever since. I believe they will recover. You did it, O master. You conjured up the Afrit and forced him to cure them."

As weary as he was, Jafar could feel no triumph at his accomplishment, merely relief that his mammoth effort had not been wasted. His whole body felt stiff and sore after so long a period of inactivity, and he suddenly felt the urge to exercise, if only a small amount. Struggling mightily, he sat up farther and looked around the hold.

The ship had slipped into an easy routine. The horses were in their stalls at the far end of the hold, apparently now acclimatized to shipboard life. Most of the crew, except for those on watch, were asleep in their section of the hold. Of Prince Ahmad and El-Hadar there was no sign.

With Cari's help, Jafar al-Sharif got shakily to his feet. He felt every bit as wobbly as he had inside the circle, except now there was no fear that tragedy would strike if he fell. The gentle rolling and pitching of the boat only exaggerated his unsteadiness, and he had to lean on Cari's shoulder several times as he staggered to the ladder leading to the upper deck. Once there it was a simpler matter to put one foot up to the next rung and pull himself along, climbing slowly up to the top. Cari flew to join him on the deck, and Selima followed up the ladder behind them.

The night air was cool and crisp and fresh, with the invigorating tang of a salty breeze. El-Hadar himself was handling the rudder, while a couple of sailors tended to the sails. Prince Ahmad stood in the bow, looking pensively over the rail; Verethran the monkey stood near him, clinging to the rigging of the foresail.

The prince heard Jafar coming when he was a few steps away, and turned to face him. Surprised and pleased that it was Jafar, Ahmad reached out his arms to clasp the older man's shoulders. "It's good to see you back on your feet again, O marvelous wizard," he said. "We were all quite worried about you." Verethran the monkey chittered his agreement.

"I was quite worried about me, too," Jafar admitted. "That was a most difficult spell, and I'm afraid my talents are rather spent for a while. In a way it's good that we have a long sea voyage; it will give me some time to recuperate."

"The voyage may not be quite as long as we feared," said the prince. "We may reach this Isle of Illusion within a week. El-Hadar tells me we are traveling at an unheard of rate. It seems the winds are all perfectly with us, blowing in precisely the direction we need with just enough strength to fill the sails completely and not enough to threaten ripping them. El-Hadar thinks you have bewitched the wind." He smiled, and Jafar joined him.

"It was the other way around, as I recall," Jafar said. "We will have to offer a particularly good yasht to Varyu in thanks for this help." He turned and faced into the breeze. "We are most grateful, Your Excellency."

Even this little bit of activity so exhausted Jafar that he excused himself from the prince's presence and returned to his pallet in the hold, accompanied by Verethran. Selima stayed up on deck with Ahmad, gazing at the stars with him and talking about nothing in particular. In this dark, clear night she was almost invisible, and the prince could only tell where she was by the sound of her voice.

In the morning, Jafar was so ravenous that he ate three hearty helpings of the flatbread, rice, and dried fish that was the staple diet aboard the ship. The crew stood apart from him, regarding him with awe. A prince and a priest were one thing; they were just men, though of a higher station. But a wizard who had a Jann for a servant, and who commanded Afrits to his will—this was a creature from another world, whose reality touched on theirs in only the most capricious ways. They gave him wide berth when he walked, and spoke to him only when he spoke first to them.

Late that afternoon they reached a small island known as Pedhal, where they put in for the night. Pedhal was right on the edge of the portion of the Central Sea ruled by this new empire, and was small enough to have so far escaped enslavement. Most of the people on the island had heard nothing of this conqueror, and those that had were not particularly worried. In its long, boring history, Pedhal had paid allegiance to many empires, kingdoms, and petty princes. The people raised their sheep, grew their food, and paid little attention to whatever government was placed over them. They knew how temporary the whole situation was, and they refused to become excited about it.

Hauvarta's Shield took on more supplies here and, since there had been no rain during the voyage so far, replenished its supply of fresh water. Jafar al-Sharif and Prince Ahmad went ashore briefly, just to get the feel of solid ground under their feet again, but stayed on the ship overnight. The tide would be taking them out early in the morning, and they did not want the ship to leave without them.

Hauvarta's Shield sailed exactly on schedule, and once again the winds were precisely what they needed to take them rapidly on their course. El-Hadar gave his passengers strange looks and muttered vague remarks about transporting wizards—but he was careful not to make any criticisms loudly enough that his passengers might take offense. Ahmad and Jafar looked at one another and smiled, and said their yashts to Varyu for his blessings.

Late that afternoon, Leila and Umar regained consciousness briefly. Both were incredibly weak and frankly astonished at finding themselves still alive. When Ahmad explained to them what Jafar had done, they looked at Jafar with new respect and deepest gratitude. They drank some water and a little fish broth the cook had made for them, then went back to sleep again so their bodies could continue repairing the damage done by the rimahniya poison.

Prince Ahmad, too, was suffering a little during this voyage. His left leg, wounded in the battle against Kharouf's army, was throbbing because of the cold sea air, forcing him to limp slightly and occasionally wince at the pain. Twice the ship lurched at just the wrong moment, causing his leg to give out from under him and making him fall to the deck, though he quickly regained his feet. "We are a ship full of convalescents," he joked, but no one thought it was very amusing.

True to the training Umar had instilled in him, Prince Ahmad was treating this voyage as he would a new lesson at the madrasa. Everything was unfamiliar, everything was worth knowing, and he asked questions of every crewman who was not urgently needed somewhere else. There was much singing and dancing aboard the ship, and beating of drums and the playing of the flute. There seemed to be a song for every chore, and the men proceeded about their tasks with enthusiasm and laughter. For a time Ahmad could put aside his worries about his mission, since there was nothing further he could do about it, and regress to his happier days as a student again. Selima stood beside him at these times, also learning eagerly the things that life could offer—though in her case it was seeming more and more like an exercise in futility as she continued to fade from the world of life.

Jafar al-Sharif was learning things, too—not how a ship worked, but how it looked and felt. He had a number of sea stories in his repertoire, and this voyage gave him his first opportunity to know what it was like to live on a ship. The details of daily life, the descriptions of ordinary things on board, would add color and depth to his stories, and make them all the more real to his listeners. In walking across the deck as the ship rolled between the waves, he realized why sailors always had that stereotypical bowlegged sway to their gait, and he became far more sympathetic to their condition. Verethran the monkey became his almost constant companion during this time, and his clever antics helped cheer Jafar still further.

Jafar also spent more time reading the grimoire of Kharouf the yatu. Now that he had proved he could really do it, the subject of sorcery fascinated him. He rationalized that this gave him additional practice in reading, and that he might need some of the other spells in case the group ran into trouble. There was enough truth in both reasons to disguise the fact that he was also beginning to enjoy the feeling of power he got from performing his wizardry.

The day after they first woke up, Umar and Leila were able to stay awake longer and hear about the ship's progress. They were cheered by the news that the voyage was being made so speedily, and were particularly happy that their infirmities had not slowed down the course of the mission. They had both lost a considerable amount of weight, appearing gaunt and frail, but their stomachs still could not tolerate much food. They ate what little they could, then went back to sleep to recover their strength.

The next day the recuperating pair were in better condition yet, and feeling well enough to go outside. They could not yet even stand, let alone walk, but they felt the need for fresh air away from the stuffy interior of the hold. Several of the sailors carried them and their pallets up onto the ship's deck, where the brightness of the afternoon sun almost blinded them at first. Once they grew accustomed to so much light, however, Leila and Umar both agreed that lying up here was far preferable to lying in the dark hold with nothing to look at but the horses and each other.

Wanting some diversion—and also legitimately curious—Leila brought up the subject of Atluri. "I know as much about the place as is common knowledge," she said, "but sea stories are not enormously popular in Tatarry, where they have little bearing on life as we live it. I never heard the complete story, and what I did hear I've mostly forgotten. I wonder if anyone could fill me in on this place before we arrive, so I'll know more about it."

She was looking straight at Jafar as she made her request, and there was the slightest curl of a smile at the corner of her lips. Jafar cleared his throat and said, "Well, I do know the story in some depth and have been able to recite it upon occasion."

He was immediately beset by requests from all sides to tell the story. Sailors, he knew from previous experience, were always a good audience for a tale of magic, and it turned out this was particularly true when they were at sea in the middle of a long voyage with no pressing duties to perform. His being a wizard was momentarily forgotten in view of the fact that he was about to regale them with a yarn that, while familiar to most of them, never lost its basic appeal.

Jafar made himself comfortable, sitting on a barrel on the deck surrounded by an eager audience. Selima stood off to one side, smiling; she knew her father would be completely happy while he was working at his true craft and, while she'd heard him tell this tale before, she was nonetheless looking forward to the pleasure *he* would get from its telling.

As the storyteller let his professional mood come upon him, he realized anew how much the ritual of the other night had drained him. Try though he might, he could not work himself up into his normal spellbinding state to entrance the audience. The words were all there, the story was all there, but some of the spirit would be missing. No one in the audience—except Selima—would ever know the difference, but *Jafar* would know, and it frustrated him. He decided to tell a slightly abbreviated form of the story, without all his usual embellishments, so he could go through it without draining his energies still further.

With hands spread in the air for his expansive gesticulations, Jafar al-Sharif began his narrative:

* * *

The tale is told of a time when the island of Atluri, also known as Atluri of the Western Sea, Atluri the green land, and Atluri the charmed, rested upon the surface of the waters just as any other island in man's knowledge. And to all repute, this land well earned its gracious titles, for it was a land of abundance, a land of beauty, a land of wealth and ease. Legends have it that all a farmer had to do was scatter seeds about his land, without benefit of ox or plow, and a full, fair crop would rise to be reaped. Fishermen had merely to cast their nets into the sea and pull them back laden with fish. Nuggets of gold were as common as pebbles and silver streaked the ordinary rocks. The cows gave twice as much milk as those elsewhere, and the hens laid eggs twice as large.

The people of Atluri, so the historians tell us, were all fair to look at and pleasant to talk to, for they were as blessed as the land around them. They worked, but not to exhaustion, and they studied, but not to excess. Many of the people became quite learned, but few became very wise—and this was the whole of the tragedy that befell Atluri.

The citizens of this enchanted realm did not deny Oromasd. They prayed to him faithfully and extolled him as the creator of the wonderful world that surrounded them. They honored his divine laws to a great degree, for there was seldom anyone in so great a need that he coveted anything of his neighbor's, and there was seldom any problem so dire as to cause dissension and bitterness between people. To all outward appearances, this was Oromasd's most perfect realm, and the citizens were quick to remind other lands of how much better things were in Atluri than elsewhere.

Because things came so easily to them, they started to take Oromasd's bounty for granted. Of course the winters would be mild and the summers balmy. It stood to reason there would be no plague, no drought, no famine, no storms to ravage the land. Obviously the herds would increase and the fields would flourish. Atluri was far enough from all other lands that war never touched them, yet close enough to benefit from liberal trade across the seas.

Because the world did not challenge them, the people began to challenge one another. There was no evil in this, for the challenges were made out of a spirit of sportsmanship, rather than out of greed or petty vindictiveness. They staged contests of strength, contests of speed, contests of wit, contests of skill, and contests of daring. The people of Atluri loved to compete, not only among themselves, but against champions from other lands as well. There was nothing Atluri loved more than a game—unless it was to gamble on that game. Atluri became known as the home of people who would wager on anything, from the winner of a race to the day a given leaf would fall from its branch. The rest of the world thought Atluri was crazy, but the people were good-natured and harmless, so they were tolerated.

At the time of which I speak, during the Third Cycle of the world, Atluri was ruled by a king named Phinomexian, who had in his service a wizard named Calazar. As part of his official duties, it was Calazar's job to devise an increasingly difficult series of contests to challenge the skills of the best athletes, puzzle solvers, and games players in the world. Calazar was so good at his work that these contests gained fame around the world, and soon became so complex that it was said no individual would ever be able to win at every part of the entire contest.

One day Calazar came to his king with a series of games so difficult and convoluted that the king was beside himself with joy. "I shall make the offer," said Phinomexian, "that anyone who can complete the entire contest perfectly may have half my kingdom."

The wizard Calazar was immediately concerned. "I beg Your Majesty not to do this," he said. "While I am outstanding at creating these contests, there may yet be someone in the world just as outstanding at winning them. Offer gold, offer the rank of wazir, offer your daughter's hand in marriage if you must, but do not be so rash as to offer half your land. If you should lose, you and your descendants would ever regret it."

"Do not be so cowardly," bellowed the king. "I know a sure bet when I see one."

The king and the wizard argued thusly for over an hour, and the end result was a falling out between old friends; the wizard Calazar proclaimed he would never work for King Phinomexian again. He then retired to his green tower, covered with climbing ivy, and refused to take part in the worldly affairs of the kingdom. He became a philosopher, spending his days in search of knowledge and disdaining the daily doings of the land in which he lived.

King Phinomexian, the while, took the contest that his wizard had created for him, and proclaimed it to the world as the most exhaustive and challenging test ever conceived by mind of man, and he issued his promise of half his land if anyone could perfectly complete each part of the test. But, as a prudent afterthought, he added that anyone who tried the test and failed would have one foot cut off as punishment. This, he correctly reasoned, would deter some challengers and thus decrease the odds of anyone succeeding and claiming half his kingdom.

Over the next two years, there were half a dozen brave people who dared take the challenge—and the number of one-footed people in Atluri was increased by that amount. Those of the challengers who were strong enough and fast enough to pass the physical tests were not smart enough to solve the complex mental puzzles Calazar had created; those with the wit to solve the puzzles lacked something in strength and stamina, and fell behind in the contests of physical prowess. As time went on, it seemed less and less likely that a challenger could be found who could master all parts of the contest successfully—and King Phinomexian's bet seemed more and more a safe wager.

After two years, a man appeared at the castle, a stranger to the island, and demanded the opportunity to challenge this supposedly unwinnable contest. This man was ugly, with a twisted spine, unkempt hair and no turban, eyes that were at odd angles to his nose, a scar down the side of his cheek, and warts covering large portions of his face. He spoke with a lisp, and drool dripped from his mouth whenever he opened it. He hobbled with a cane, and had such a terrible tic that his head would scarcely hold still. He refused to give his name, but simply repeated that he wanted the chance to try the wizard Calazar's contest.

Everyone tried to dissuade him, from the lowliest servants to the wazirs, to the king himself. This poor man was crippled enough, they said; it would be a pity to further handicap him by cutting off one foot after he failed at a contest so far beyond his skills. But the man insisted on trying, and eventually King Phinomexian gave in to his entreaties and allowed him to challenge Calazar's contest.

The tests were all to be held in a single day, beginning in the morning. Few people showed up, at first; most claimed they didn't want to watch such a pitiful spectacle and stayed away. Certainly such a twisted, deformed creature had no hope of winning where the best and brightest in Atluri had all failed.

But to everyone's surprise, this lame, twisted man ran the obstacle course that Calazar had so painstakingly laid out; once he was in motion his infirmities mattered not at all, and he moved with such speed that he appeared almost a blur. In dexterity, strength, and endurance no man had ever matched his performance. By noontime he had conquered every one of the physical tests devised by Calazar, and was preparing to solve the intellectual puzzles that were the second part of the test.

People had heard by now of this prodigious contestant, and by afternoon the viewing stands were filling. As King Phinomexian watched this challenger work through the puzzles, he said to himself, "Surely this must be my old friend Calazar himself in disguise, out to tweak me for my foolish bet by showing me up. But I shall have the last laugh in this matter, for the creator of a contest cannot be expected to compete in it and win. I will let him finish and then disqualify him as a fraud."

And as the afternoon drew to a close, it was no longer a great surprise to anyone that this ugly, bent stranger finished all the puzzles perfectly, thereby completing the contest that everyone had heretofore thought unbeatable. Then it was that King Phinomexian called the new champion forward to stand before the throne, and addressed him thusly:

"You have performed these demanding tests with skill and daring and wit, and have shown yourself to be the best of all competitors on this island. To the winner of this contest I have pledged half my land, but I suspect fraud was involved in this competition. I contend you are not the man you appear to be."

"Indeed, I am not," replied the stranger.

"I challenge, then, that you are the wizard Calazar who created this contest, and as such you are not entitled to win the offered prize."

The stranger merely threw his head back and cackled, and as he did so his body increased three times in size until he stood nearly as tall as the ceiling in the king's throne room. His body became even more twisted, even more skeletal, and his eyes glowed with the fires from the Pits of Torment. "I am no puny wizard," said this horrible creature, "but the daeva Pairimaiti. You foolish Atluriya have made Rimahn smile with your self-importance and your grandiose challenges, and I have now come to collect my reward for winning your bet."

And then did King Phinomexian realize just how foolish his wager was, and on that spot he gave his soul over to

Oromasd for forgiveness and compassion, for he feared the day of his death had come. But the king was also an honorable man, and knew that he must keep his promises, even to a creature of Rimahn.

"I promised half of my land to the winner," said the king, his nervousness putting a tremor in his voice. "I will divide it in any equitable manner, O mighty daeva. Which half do you want?"

And the daeva cackled back at him with fiendish laughter. "The bottom half!" And so saying, he disappeared from the throne room.

And as the sound of his words died in the air, there came a great rumbling to the ears of the people of Atluri, and the ground beneath them did shake and tremble—for Pairimaiti had removed the rocky base upon which the island rested, and now the land was sinking slowly beneath the waters of the Western Sea.

The trembling of the earth did even affect the green tower within which the wizard Calazar had closeted himself. Calazar quickly ascertained what had happened, and realized too late that he was as much to blame for this situation as King Phinomexian, because he had created the foolish contest and he had withdrawn himself from the court where he could have given the king sounder advice on how to deal with this matter. Soon his beloved homeland would be lost to the waves, and he knew there was nothing he could do to save it.

But in his wisdom he knew he could at least save the people of Atluri, and so he began his last, and greatest, spell. Using all the strength that Oromasd gave him, and all the wisdom and learning he had amassed through the years, he cast an enchantment over the people of Atluri, that from this day forward they would be half as fish, half as human. They would breathe seawater naturally as though it were air, and thus would survive the tragedy that had befallen their land.

The power it took to complete this spell drained poor Calazar of all the life he had left in him. But though he died, it was a noble death, for he died so that many others could live. And on that day did the waters of the Western Sea rise up and swallow the land of Atluri, which vanished from the face of Parsina as though it never existed. But because of Calazar's spell, the people survived—and it is reported that their descendants live, even to this day, beneath the surface of the Western Sea in the sunken city known as Atluri.

17

The Isle of Illusions

The small audience was silent as Jafar al-Sharif finished his tale of Atluri's fall from grace. As was true for any good story, each listener was contemplating the sins of King Phinomexian and his people, and was weighing them against his own transgressions.

"There are no further official reports about Atluri," Jafar concluded.

"But there are plenty of unofficial ones," said their captain. "El-Hadar has heard many stories from other sailors on other ships traveling out into the Western Sea, about strange creatures that look like people swimming among the waves like porpoises. But none would ever approach when hailed."

"Can you blame them for being leery of strangers?" Leila said.

"There is also the report from Ali Maimun," said Jafar, "that he visited this place all those ages ago. Although he's played many tricks on us, he's never lied—and his words drive us onward. If Atluri really existed in the mage's time, we can only hope it continues to exist in ours."

And, he continued to himself, *that I can keep my wits about me and not get caught up in their carefree games that Ali Maimun warned me about. If they consider the Crystal to be part of some cosmic game, how can I beat them at it?*

They had already gone past the island of Korluf, the landmark mentioned in Ali Maimun's journal, and had not stopped there because El-Hadar said they had plenty of provisions and Prince Ahmad wanted to sail as quickly as possible. The winds were so favorable to them that, on the second day after Jafar told the story of Atluri, just as dawn was breaking, the lookout spotted an island off to their starboard side. This was a small island not marked on any of El-Hadar's charts, and it was in the proper location to be the Isle of Illusions to which Ali Maimun had referred. As *Hauvarta's Shield* slowly circled the island looking for the best spot to anchor, Jafar al-Sharif had a hard decision to make—but his recent success at conjuring the Afrit had increased his self-confidence manyfold.

"I must make the journey to this island by myself," he announced to his comrades. "I've given the matter much thought, and find that conclusion inescapable."

"Surely you don't think it's so simple that one man alone can face its dangers," Prince Ahmad protested. "I will come with you and offer the strength of my sword to complement your wizardry."

"That would needlessly risk both our lives, Your Highness," said Jafar. "You would only endanger yourself, and your sword would avail us little. Ali Maimun tells us that only wizards dare visit this island because of the illusions used by the native creatures to lure unsuspecting travelers to their deaths. If I would have taken anyone, it would have been Leila, for her ability to see past illusion would save me from those snares. But she is so ill she still cannot stand on her own, and we dare not wait for her to recover her strength. No other nonmagical beings—not even you, Verethran—would fare any better on this isle."

"One spell, and he thinks he's a real wizard," Leila muttered very quietly to Selima standing beside her.

"Surely, O master, you'll want me to accompany you," Cari said. "I can—"

"No!" Jafar said harshly, cutting short her words. "I want you to wait for me here."

"But you will need protection," the Jann protested.

"I have Kharouf's amulet. No magic can harm me."

"But don't forget, as Kharouf did, that swords can harm you, clubs can harm you, the sharp teeth of vicious beasts can harm you—"

"I'll have my cloak of invisibility with me. If anyone attacks me, I can vanish and escape them."

"But master—"

"This is an order, Cari. You are to wait for me here on the ship. Do you understand?"

"Hearkening and obedience," Cari said. There was a sullen tone to her voice and a quiver to her lower lip, but she had no choice other than to obey the orders of the man who wore the brass ring.

Jafar al-Sharif looked at her, and his heart was near unto breaking. He wanted her to be with him at least as much as she wanted to go, but he dared not allow it. The journal of Ali Maimun had said he would need to bribe this special tree with one of his magical implements in order to get the piece of its bark he needed to breathe underwater. He had no idea what this tree's tastes were like, but he did know his stock of magical implements was severely limited. He would offer the tree everything else he had first—but if the tree did not accept one of them, he knew he would have to offer it the ring of Cari. As much as he'd hate losing her, Oromasd's mission would have to come first. And if he did have to give up the ring, he did not want Cari to be there, watching him surrender her to this "tree which lives as does a man." For her own sake, and his, she had to be left behind—and he didn't even dare tell her why.

Hauvarta's Shield sailed into a natural cove on the northwest side of the island, and there El-Hadar dropped anchor. Jafar al-Sharif gathered up his magical implements; he carried the staff of Achmet the terrifying, tucked the cap of truth and Kharouf's grimoire into the pocket of his kaftan, and wore all the rest. The only things he left behind were Ali Maimun's journal and the two pieces of the Crystal of Oromasd, all of which he needed to complete this mission. One of the sailors rowed him ashore in the dinghy, then returned to the ship. The rest of the crew and passengers could only watch as Jafar got out of the little boat, waved back to the ship, and began trudging inland toward the center of the island where this special tree was supposed to exist.

Cari stood at the rail, staring at the spot where Jafar had disappeared into the underbrush. Her hands clenched and unclenched in frustration, knowing she should be there to protect her master from whatever evils he faced. Leila lay on her pallet a short distance away, watching the Jann. There was a very thoughtful expression on the blond woman's face.

Finally, Leila spoke. "If you want to go to him, then go."

"But he ordered me to wait here."

"Did he tell you how *long* to wait? It must be a full five minutes by now, at least."

The Jann jerked upright from her depressed slouch. "Such an interpretation never occurred to me."

Leila's mouth twitched slightly. "You know my skill for seeing falsehood. When our wizard said he wished you to stay here, he wasn't telling the truth—or at least, not the whole truth." She paused while the righteous Jann considered that. "We know that, without you, he may never escape the island—and so does he. He needs you there."

Cari narrowed her eyes as she stared back at Leila appraisingly. She spoke with exaggerated slowness as she said, "I thank you, O lady, for helping me interpret my master's order correctly. But—"

"Go keep our wizard safe," Leila said. "That's all the thanks I need."

Cari looked at her again, then vanished and flew off to the island.

Selima, who had watched this interchange, came over to Leila's side. "I still don't think Cari approves of you."

"That's not what matters," Leila said.

Despite his bravado aboard the ship, Jafar al-Sharif was quite cautious as he walked into the brush. Cari's reminder of how overconfidence had led to Kharouf's death was much on his mind, and he was not relying solely on the amulet for his salvation. True, it would protect him from spells that meant to harm him, but that was not what he feared here. The amulet did nothing against spells that merely fooled the eye—otherwise, Kharouf would have seen him on the hilltop despite the cloak of invisibility. And spells that fooled the eye seemed to be the chief hazard on this island, according to Ali Maimun.

He walked with his right hand always near the hilt of his saif, prepared for any danger that might come. He took small steps, each one slow and tentative, lest the very ground ahead of him be an illusion to hide a pit full of sharpened stakes. His eyes were constantly darting back and forth, looking for any suspicious movement that might indicate an enemy. He used the magical staff of Achmet much as a blind man might, to feel out the territory ahead of him. Briefly, he envied Akar, for the blind wizard would not be taken in by the island's illusions. Jafar considered closing his own eyes to feign blindness—but then he realized he needed to see in order to find this tree named Raffiliz. Better all around, he decided, to keep his eyes open and just move slowly and cautiously. It was still early in the morning. He had plenty of daylight left to him.

He had not seen a forest so overgrown since traveling through the jungles of Indi. This was not a tropical rain forest, though, but just ordinary brush left untended and gone wild.

Tree branches snatched at his clothing and thickets raked at his skin. A profusion of tiny insects flew into his face and darted around him. His probing staff revealed several small traps laid by burrowing predators, and he managed to avoid them.

But there were also pleasant things about the island. There were birds in the trees singing their bright, cheery songs. Sometimes he disturbed a small forest rodent that scampered quickly out of his way. The air smelled deliciously fresh and invigorating, and Jafar had to slow himself down deliberately lest it put too much of a spring in his step and make him careless. Of all the dangers he might find here, seduction by normality might be the most insidious.

The ground he'd been walking across was overgrown, but level. Suddenly, pushing past one dense thicket, he found himself in a clearing some fifty cubits across, in which there were no trees or bushes, merely tall, waist-high grass and a few large stones. Beyond the clearing was more forest, going up the side of a hill that was maybe a hundred cubits high. Near the top of the hill the ground grew rockier until it was all but barren of vegetation, and there was a dark hole that looked to be the entrance to a cave.

This change in the land was suspicious. The clearing could hide any number of disguised traps. He was wary in the forest because too many things pressed in on him from all sides; he must be wary in the clearing because he stood apart, exposed to view. He didn't like the looks of that hill ahead of him, either; it would be difficult to climb, and there was no tree at the top. Ali Maimun's journal hadn't mentioned a cave, either.

He decided to go around the hill for the time being, to bypass it and hope to find the tree Raffiliz on some more accessible part of the island. If he had no luck that way, *then* he could try the hill.

He turned to his left and started walking cautiously through the clearing, when suddenly he heard something from the top of the hill. It was a voice. A familiar voice. A familiar voice calling his name. He looked up again, and—

He looked away quickly. He closed his eyes and shook his head to clear it of all error. Then he looked again.

"Jafar! You've come for me at last!"

"Amineh!" he cried in a plaintive bleat. "You're dead."

His wife shook her head. "No. An evil wizard envied you my beauty, and vowed to have me for his own. He stole me from you in the night, and left a homunculus in my place. The yatu held me here on this island against my will—but he died a year ago, and I have been alone since then. I have prayed you would find me, and now my prayers are answered. Come, rescue me, take me back. My love is ever yours."

Jafar could not take his eyes from this vision. A part of his mind—a cool, detached part far in the back—questioned what he saw and heard, and found it remarkably strange. But his heart believed his eyes and ears, and would not listen to these cold, painful doubts. How could he continue to hurt himself, torture himself, with the lie that Amineh was dead, when here she was in front of him—alive and breathing and caring and loving. Amineh would be his once more. All he had to do was go to her and take her.

He turned back toward the hill and approached it, walking ever faster across the clearing with all caution abandoned. Amineh was at the top. He could not keep her waiting.

Cari the Jann followed invisibly behind her master as he made his way slowly through the forest. She greatly approved of the caution he used as he moved, and as she saw him avoid the predators' burrows she started to feel a little more optimistic that perhaps her help would not be needed here after all. If Jafar remained as careful as he was now, he would not be fooled by anything the creatures of this island could throw at him.

Then they came to the clearing, and the appearance of the woman on the hilltop. Cari saw and heard all that Jafar did— plus her magical senses saw and heard beyond that. She saw that the image of Amineh was but a phantasm, a magical show with no substance. And she heard rumblings from within the cave—pleased rumblings, *hungry* rumblings.

When Jafar turned back toward the hill, she knew she could remain invisible no longer. She had to protect her master; she had to stop him somehow from walking into the snare of whatever was in the cave, luring him to destruction.

This was no time for being coy. Cari materialized in front of him, saying, "Don't go up there, O master."

So lost was he in his trance that Jafar did not even question her presence here when he'd ordered her to stay on the ship. He merely said, "I must go. Amineh needs me."

"That is not Amineh."

"You don't know her. You never met her." Jafar's voice was cold, and his eyes were glazed over, veiled from all possible reason, lost in his heart's dearest dream which this illusion so cruelly simulated.

Cari grabbed her master to hold him back. She was far stronger than he was; if necessary, she could lift him up into the air with her and carry him back to the ship, away from the danger, until he recovered his senses.

"Let me go!" Jafar bellowed. "Let me go to Amineh!"

It was a direct order. The spells on the brass ring he wore constrained her to obey him. As much as she hated to do it, she released her hold on him, and, without any further acknowledgment of her existence, Jafar al-Sharif continued to walk across the clearing to the forest at the base of the hill.

The spells on the ring also compelled her to protect him if at all possible. She tried to think of how to do this. The way that came first to mind was to go into the cave and do battle with whatever lurked in there. If she could kill it—assuming there was only one creature in there—her master would be freed of his compulsion, or at least rescued from its consequences.

But the very thought of that made her shiver. She had no idea what lay waiting within that cave, but she could sense that it was old and mean and powerful. If it was some creature like an ogre, she could become invisible and it would never see her; she could take her master's saif and stab the fiend before it knew she was there.

But if it was some djinn, she would have no such advantage. It would see her coming, and had probably developed many magical ways of protecting itself during its lifetime. She knew she had to risk her own life to save her master, if that was what was called for, but—

But perhaps there might be some other way. Jafar's order had been to let him go to Amineh—but Amineh no longer existed. He had to have meant the *illusion* of Amineh. Cari was not used to thinking in such terms—she was straightforwardly innocent of such lawyer's reasoning—but Leila's example was enough for her quick wit to follow. And the hungry rumblings from the cave were becoming much louder.

Like all djinni, Cari had the power to change her outward form, though the shape she normally used was the easiest and most natural for her. While all young djinni played and experimented with different shapes, doing this in a realistic manner was a skill she had practiced only within the last twenty years—and not much at all in the last ten or so, as slave to

Akar's ring. She was not sure how successful she would be—
but she knew she had to try.

Jafar had reached the base of the hill, now, and had started
into the forest on the other side of the clearing. From where he
was, the trees blocked his view of the cave at the top, so Cari
would not have to compete with that more perfect illusion.
She'd had a glimpse, a short one, of the image Jafar had seen.
Working quickly, she tried to fashion herself into a duplicate of
that. She had no mirror available to see how well she was
doing; she would just have to do her best and hope it was good
enough.

"Here I am," she said, materializing behind a tree and
stepping forward into Jafar's view. "I ran down from my cave to
meet you."

Jafar stopped and stared at her. At first Cari was very self-
conscious, wondering whether he noticed some tiny flaw in
her shape that would have him condemn her as a fraud. But his
gaze was so uncritical it soon eased her fears. His eyes drank in
the vision of her, as a drunkard gulps greedily at his wine, and
he grew intoxicated on the sight. There was unquestioning
love, tenderness, and devotion on his face as he looked at
her—and his caring expression sent a strange thrill through
the Jann's soul.

I'm doing this to save my master's life, Cari reminded herself. *Nothing else matters*.

Jafar's hand reached out, oh so tentatively, to touch her, as
though that act alone would cause her to vanish—or, worse
yet, as though he feared finding her as insubstantial as Selima.
The trembling fingers of his right hand delicately touched her
cheek, and Cari smiled at him and put her own hand up to
touch his. "Amineh," Jafar whispered. "It really is you."

Cari just continued to smile, afraid to say anything that
might break the spell and spoil her illusion. She took a step
nearer to him, hoping to further steal him away from that other
illusion at the top of the hill.

Then suddenly Jafar's arms were around her, holding her
tightly to him, and his head bent down to hers. His lips
pressed to hers in a passionate kiss, and Cari's eyes widened;
she hadn't expected this. Fortunately, Jafar's own eyes were
closed, so he could not see her reaction.

I can't push him away or tell him to stop, Cari reasoned.
That would spoil the illusion. Besides, she didn't want to push
him away. The body she had manifested was enjoying the sen-

sation of being crushed against him, of being held and kissed. She carefully told herself, over and over, that it was only this form that was so pleased, not her true being, and it was all part of the illusion she had created for her master's sake.

Jafar's hands were caressing her now, producing pleasant sensations and arousing all sorts of strange new feelings within her body. It became harder and harder to think, harder to separate herself from the illusion. She'd never had a material body before that presented her with so many wonderful distractions, and she knew not quite how to cope with the flood of sensations assaulting her mind.

Jafar's lips kissed not only her own, but her cheeks and the hollow of her neck as well. He fumbled to remove the kaftan she appeared to be wearing, and Cari corrected her form so that it seemed to disappear as her hands moved up and over her head. In his current state, through his tears, Jafar didn't notice it vanishing.

As his mouth moved down and found the hollow cleft between her breasts, Cari discovered her hands under his turban, clutching his hair and pulling him tighter to her. There was a buzzing in her ears, and she closed her eyes against the suddenly-too-bright sun as her neck arched back and her rapid breathing swelled the breasts he now tantalized with his tongue. Without quite knowing how she got there, she found herself lying on her back on the cold, slightly moist ground. Jafar was beside her, and his hands were stroking her, gently exploring every curve, every hollow of her recently assumed body. He moaned softly and Cari tried to think of something tender she could say to him, but all her body would do was moan just as softly in response. She began to undress him, enjoying the new sensuous feel of his skin against hers. Part of her remembered the lectures every young Jann hears about the dangers of such encounters, but this was quickly lost in the flood of emotion and sensation, of fulfillment and release. Her kisses became as impassioned as his, her hands every bit as hungry.

Djinni did not make love in quite the same way humans did, but Cari was nonetheless prepared. She had watched Jafar and Leila, many times, when they did not know they were being observed. She knew what to do. She would not allow her illusion to be left incomplete.

* * *

It was Jafar's snoring that finally convinced Cari he had broken free of the compulsion placed on him by the illusory spell of the creature in the cave. She looked at his face, so handsome and so relaxed now, more at peace than she'd ever seen him. Gently she stroked his shoulder; he muttered lightly and turned over, finally releasing her from his embrace. She felt as though she must be glowing, as though her body were filled with a million fireflies. There was something special about this moment, something she would remember for thousands of years, if Oromasd so granted she should live that number. For a short eternity she watched him sleep, a smile still evident on his face.

But the time had come for other things. They had yet to find the tree Raffiliz and bargain with it for a piece of its bark. The sun was now past noon, and who knew how many other dangerous creatures were lurking about the island? As much as she hated doing it, she would have to waken her master and get him on his way again.

She took care to resume her normal shape, then knelt and shook him by the shoulder. Jafar's snoring ended in a snort, and his eyes fluttered slowly open. There was a silly smile on his face that vanished when he saw it was her, but his warmth did not disappear as well. "O Cari, I had the strangest dream—"

He looked at himself and the ground around him, and his eyes suddenly widened. "That was no dream. That was here. I don't understand. Amineh—"

"There is some evil creature living in the cave at the top of this hill. It cast a spell on you to make you think Amineh was here, so it could lure you into its hole and eat you."

"But Amineh *was* here, and I'm still alive. How could . . . unless . . . It was you!" he suddenly accused.

Cari looked away. "I had to counter his illusion, to free you from his spell. I hope you're not angry with me, O master."

"Angry? No, I . . . I . . . ." A flood of conflicting emotions surged through Jafar's mind, but anger was not among them. He, too, looked away. "I didn't mean for anything like this to happen. I didn't want to take advantage of your servitude—"

"You did not take advantage," Cari was quick to say. "I am bound to protect the life of the wearer of that ring, however I can. I merely did what was necessary."

"Merely what was necessary," Jafar echoed. "But how did you feel about it?"

"I felt I was doing my duty," Cari said slowly.

"Do you resent me for what happened?"

"You did nothing wrong, O my master."

Jafar al-Sharif stood up and quickly donned his clothing. "Well then, uh, we'll pretend it didn't happen. I do thank you for saving my life yet again."

"I did only what I had to, O my master."

"No," said Jafar, shaking his head. "You did more than that. Much, much more. And I . . . I thank you for that, too. But now I must find this tree Raffiliz—and I must do it without falling prey to any more illusions."

"May I suggest, O master, that I help you now that I am here. I can scout the island and find the tree much faster than you could."

At that moment Jafar needed time alone to consider what had happened. He felt ashamed and exhilarated by what he remembered. Eagerly he put aside his fear of the bargain Raffiliz might make. "Very well," he said. "Scout the island to find this remarkable tree, and then report back here to me."

"Hearkening and obedience." Cari flew off on her search, leaving Jafar standing alone, still very embarrassed by what had occurred. He knew something had changed; he could feel it in the air. Their simple relationship of master and servant could not continue as it had—but how it would develop from here, he had no idea. And this was not the moment to think about it, either, even though he couldn't ignore it.

Cari returned after only a few minutes. "I have found the tree, O master."

"Are you sure?"

"There can be no doubt. May I suggest you let me fly you there, to avoid any further unpleasant surprises along your path?"

"Yes, that sounds wise."

Cari grasped him under the arms and carried him into the air. She had flown with him before in such a manner and had thought little about it; but now, after what had happened, both of them were acutely aware of the closeness of their bodies, the nearness of their faces. They neither looked at one another nor spoke as they flew over the woods and toward the center of the island.

The island was not a large one, and after only a few moments Cari pointed to their destination. Her gesture was totally unnecessary, however. Jafar had already spotted it. Anyone with eyes could have spotted it.

The tree Raffiliz was at the top of a hill, the highest point on the island. From base to top it measured perhaps fifty cubits, but its height was not its most spectacular feature. Its thick, heavy branches seemed to radiate outward forever, tangling and interweaving, and even though this was the middle of winter, there were plenty of green leaves upon its boughs. Raffiliz stood like an enormous umbrella covering the land, with a diameter of at least a parasang. As Cari had said, there could be no doubt that this was the tree they had come to see.

Cari descended, but the branches were so thickly intertwined that there was no way she could have taken Jafar through them. She had to land, instead, at the perimeter of the umbrella, and they would have to walk the rest of the way in to the base.

Only a dozen paces within the canopy, the light from the sun was so blocked by the interwoven branches overhead that broad daylight was no lighter than nighttime with a full moon. The ground was bare, for nothing else could grow where Raffiliz took all the sunlight. Small animals scurried away as the two walked past them, until suddenly they found themselves confronted by a high wall of bramble bushes.

"How do we get past these, and how do they grow where nothing else can?" Jafar wondered.

"The brambles are but another illusion, O master, though with a less sinister purpose. They mean not to snare you, but merely to keep you away."

Jafar al-Sharif recalled the magical fire he and Prince Ahmad had encountered in the corridor on the way to see the prophet Muhmad—the fire that burned hot without consuming anything. Walking through it had caused him to review and evaluate his life, but had caused him no great physical harm.

Without hesitation he walked confidently forward into the brambles. The branches seemed alive, trying to grasp his clothing while the thorns and needles stung deeply into his skin. Jafar cried out in surprise and pain as he pulled himself roughly back, away from the menacing bushes.

"I thought you said they were illusions," he moaned.

"They are, O master, but illusions can have layers of reality to them. Look at your clothing and your skin."

Jafar looked, and indeed there was no effect. The branches had not torn his clothing, the thorns had not pierced his skin. His mind still remembered the pain, but his body showed no evidence of it.

"This is not merely an illusion of sight," Cari continued, "but an illusion of touch as well. You could walk entirely through the bramble bushes and not be harmed."

"But I'd be screaming in pain every step of the way. Can't we chop down these bushes to make a path?"

"The bushes don't exist, O master. You can't chop down what isn't there."

"Not even with an imaginary axe?"

"It doesn't work that way," Cari insisted.

"And yet I must get through," Jafar said. He stood and pondered the situation for a moment. He recalled the story of the hero Nansoch, who deliberately blinded himself so he would not be fooled by the fearsome images of evil King Paralat's protectors, and marched right past them to kill the king. Plucking out his eyes seemed a little extreme to deal with this problem—he didn't want to rival Akar as another sightless wizard—but perhaps he could just close his eyes and walk through the brambles as though they weren't there.

Screwing his eyes tightly shut, he walked deliberately forward. One step, two steps, still safe. On his third step, though, he hit the brambles, and again felt them tearing at his clothing and his skin. He opened his eyes and found himself surrounded by the thicket, from which he only barely managed to pull himself free. He fell down onto the ground, panting from the exertion.

"It's no use," he said. "Even with my eyes closed, my *mind* knows the bushes are there. As long as my mind is convinced, I'll never make it through."

"And yet it is possible. Ali Maimun did it—so must you."

Jafar al-Sharif was becoming very tired of having to live up to the exploits of the greatest wizard in all of history. Surely a beneficent god like Oromasd could have found a simpler role model for him.

"Ali Maimun did say that only wizards dared visit this island because of the illusions. That means wizardry must be able to combat them. I don't know any spells to do that, but perhaps a spell isn't necessary. As you've told me so often, magic is merely imposing my will on the world in special ways. Perhaps if I will these brambles away, they will no longer be there."

Jafar stood up again and closed his eyes. He concentrated on bringing into his mind the feeling of power, the feeling of his storytelling—the feeling he had called upon before to aid him in times of crisis. He was still worn out by his efforts with the Afrit several nights ago, and the power did not come upon him as strongly as it had in the past—but still it was there. He could feel it warming him.

He took this power and wrapped it around himself, like a cloak of iron, tough and impenetrable. *This power separates me from the brambles*, he thought. *This power protects me. I am a wizard, and no illusion can touch me.*

Slowly, step by careful step, Jafar al-Sharif walked forward into the illusion, visualizing nothing but the cloak of invisible iron he had encased himself within. He refused to think about the painful needles he'd felt before, the clinging branches, the stinging thorns; they could not hurt him now. He was a wizard following in the footsteps of Ali Maimun the mage, and he would not be stopped by imaginary brambles.

"O master, you are through. The bushes are behind you." Cari's voice came from far away, as though she were on a hill on some other island, shouting across the gulf. Jafar heard her and understood her words. He opened his eyes, but did not unwrap himself from his magical protective blanket. In that moment he was not completely of the world, but instead, of some plane beyond. And in that condition he walked forward to his meeting with the tree Raffiliz.

There were no further illusions, no barriers to his progress. It was as though the tree—or whoever cast the illusions—realized the futility of that course. Jafar al-Sharif walked unhindered across the plain, bare ground up the hill to the base of the tree with which he must deal. Cari was beside him, but, realizing what he had done, did nothing further to distract him. Her master would be the one to deal with Raffiliz.

"Approach no further!" boomed a commanding voice when Jafar drew to within ten cubits of the tree's thick trunk. "Curiosity induced me to let you draw this close, but I will tolerate no more."

Jafar al-Sharif looked at the tree before him, a tree whose trunk was so thick that ten men with their arms linked could not have encompassed it. He marveled at this tree, which was obviously old when Ali Maimun had stood here before it many centuries ago. "Have I the honor of addressing Raffiliz, the tree that lives as does a man, the tree fabled in story and legend as the wisest and most benevolent of Oromasd's creations?"

"I am Raffiliz," said the tree, though there was no mouth for the words to come out of.

"And I am Jafar al-Sharif, wizard of the southern provinces and heir to the legacy of the great Ali Maimun. As my predecessor treated with you, so do I propose to do now."

"Your predecessor was a man of great power and wisdom. I do not sense such strength in you."

"Such power and wisdom as I have are granted to me by Oromasd," Jafar admitted. "He has seen that they are fit to the occasion."

"And what is the present occasion?"

"I needs must visit the sunken city of Atluri. Ali Maimun has written that a piece of your bark will enable a man to live underwater for some time. I have come to ask such a piece of you, in the name of our most glorious creator."

"And would you give a piece of yourself if someone asked it?" the tree said. "A toe, perhaps?"

"I would if I knew it would grow back, as my hair and your bark certainly will."

"Ali Maimun gave me a gift of great magic in exchange for my bark. What can you offer me to match his gift?"

Jafar al-Sharif had been raised in cities all his life and knew how to haggle in bazaars. He would try his least thing first, the one thing he had that was a total mystery to him and he didn't know how to use anyway. Perhaps Oromasd had given it to him specifically to trade with this tree.

Taking the leather thong with the mysterious key from around his neck, he held it out and said, "This is a key I took from the treasure trove of the Jinn Estanash, a key with the engraved symbols of wings. It is an item of strong import, and I offer it to you in return for your favor."

"I know of this key," said Raffiliz. "Yes, I find it to be quite acceptable." A thick branch of the tree bent down in front of Jafar to accept the key.

Perhaps I was too hasty, Jafar thought. *If Raffiliz is so interested in it, perhaps it is valuable.* But he had already made the offer, and it was too late to refuse. Reaching out, he strung the thong around the proffered branch.

As the metal of the key came in contact with the wood, it suddenly began to glow, until it became so hot the limb began to smoke. "Remove that key at once!" Raffiliz bellowed.

Jafar grabbed it and pulled it away before it set fire to the great tree. Even as he took possession, the metal of the key cooled once more. "A thousand pardons, O venerable Raffiliz. It never did such a thing to me."

"Perhaps because you were meant to have it," the tree growled with displeasure.

I can't even give the accursed thing away, Jafar thought. *This Raffiliz knows what the key is, but I can't even ask him about it without showing myself up as a liar. Oh well, Oromasd will provide an answer in his own time—I hope. At least now I know it has some value and is worth carrying.* Meanwhile, he returned the thong to its accustomed place around his neck.

"What is that you carry in your hand?" Raffiliz asked.

Jafar hadn't wanted to offer the staff next; it was too valuable a tool to him. But if Raffiliz expressed an interest, he had to bend to that suggestion. "This is the magical staff of Achmet the terrifying, a tool of great power. If you wish it—"

"Bah! You would offer wood to a tree? Do you also pour salt as tribute into the sea? What else have you to show me?"

Jafar was fast using up his inventory. Reaching into his pocket, he said, "I have here a magical cap of truth."

"Now that intrigues me," said Raffiliz. "A cap of truth on the Isle of Illusions."

"There is a certain irony about it that a person of your excellent perceptions would doubtless cherish."

"Provided it doesn't burn me to a cinder," Raffiliz said cynically.

"I shall pray Oromasd chooses to bless this gift."

"Very well. I shall provisionally accept this cap of truth as payment for a piece of bark." The branch bent down near Jafar once more—a little slower this time, it seemed. Jafar could not blame the tree for fearing fire.

Jafar gingerly hung the cap on the branch, but this time there seemed to be no ill effects of the transfer. When, after a moment, no dire results occurred, a piece of bark fell to the ground at Jafar's feet. The storyteller bent down to pick it up.

"Will my companions be able to accompany me under the sea?" he asked Raffiliz.

"No. That piece of bark is enough only for one."

"Would you grant me more pieces?"

"The price would be higher than I think you are willing to pay."

Jafar could believe that. His remaining magical implements—the protective amulet, the cloak of invisibility, Kharouf's grimoire, and the ring of Cari—were all things he was glad he'd been allowed to keep. Parting with any one of them would be painful, and possibly foolish. Kismet must have decreed he would make his undersea journey alone.

"How should I use this bark to achieve my goals?" he asked.

"You must swallow the piece whole," Raffiliz explained. "Once you do that, you and any objects you take with you will be impervious to the sea for two days, and may exist under the water as though it were air. After two days, things will return to the way they had been."

"I thank you, O mighty Raffiliz, for this gracious gift that will enable me to fulfill my holy quest. May Oromasd and the Bounteous Immortals grant you even longer life than they already have, so that you may live to see the day of Oromasd's glorious victory over Rimahn."

"You have the bark you sought, O Jafar. Please depart now. One of the secrets of my longevity is that I've seldom bothered to listen to the dronings of foolish men."

Your manners leave something to be desired. Jafar thought, *and you would not well survive in a city bazaar. I definitely think I bested you in this bargain, costly though it was.*

18

The Seduction

Unlike Princess Oma, who was burdened with too much spare time, Shammara found herself with very little in the weeks following her son's marriage. She attributed most of her continuing success to her careful attention to details, and there were now more than enough details to demand the attention of two Shammaras. One set of demands came from the day-to-day administration of the Holy City. As though it were not hard enough to rule over a kingdom with the size and complexity of Ravan, Shammara had to do it all without appearing as though she were doing any of it. The regent still held titular power; he still sat at the courtly diwans and made pronouncements that became less and less comprehensible with each passing week. Shammara had to sit behind her screen in the great hall and "interpret" his decrees in the language of her own dictates. She greatly looked forward to the day, just over a week away, when she would no longer have to salve the feeble brain of a senile regent.

The coronation and transfer of power accounted for the even larger number of details with which Shammara had to cope. True, the chamberlain and his staff handled the most excruciating business of the coronation, but even so it seemed that Shammara's attention was often needed in at least three places at once. Haroun grew moody and often had to be pushed to perform even the most trivial functions correctly. Shammara's servants, fearing her displeasure, refused to make even the most minor decisions on their own, referring everything to her for approval. Messengers were constantly arriving from monarchs in neighboring kingdoms, who often demanded certain courtesies during their upcoming visit to attend the coronation, and Shammara had to weigh each demand against that ruler's importance in her own personal hierarchy of power.

She had worked hard to gain this position, and she would not have traded it for anything in the world—but even so she awaited the day after Haroun's coronation, when things would begin returning to normal.

And always, always, among the details were conferences with the wali of police to ensure that there were no counter-plots against her takeover of the city. She had not worked this hard and come this far only to be toppled so soon.

"My spies report no significant threat," the wali assured her. "There is no organized opposition. There are some dissat-isfied people—but then, there always are, no matter who's in power. People enjoy complaining, and the government is al-ways a convenient target. If you wish, I could silence the worst of the critics—"

"Don't bother," Shammara said with a wave of her hand. "As long as they remain isolated complainers, I don't fear them. They even serve a social purpose, for their complaints allow them to vent frustrations without exploding, like cutting holes in the top of a pie. Keep an eye on them, certainly, but take no action without checking first with me."

And of course, there was the perennial problem of Prin-cess Oma. Shammara was pleased that her scheme for divert-ing the princess's sharp mind was working so well, and she called her agent Rabah before her once a week for reports on the girl's attitude.

Rabah stood tall and straight before the most powerful woman in Ravan with no bending, no subservience. Outside these chambers she must act the role of a humble concubine, but here, alone with her employer, she was as she should be—an officer of the rimahniya, well-trained, strong, and proud, owing fealty to no temporal authority. She recognized the strength in Shammara, and respected her as an equal—though she wondered at the aberration that prevented Shammara from accepting Rimahn as her ultimate lord, since she clearly did not follow the path of Oromasd. But that was not her business. Rabah was paid well, and had performed her services admira-bly.

"And how has your royal charge been doing?" Shammara asked her.

"You must realize, Princess Oma has never been a girl to do anything by halves. Now that we have taken the trouble to

bring her sexuality to full blossom, she is devoting all her
restless energy to it. Even I have trouble keeping up with her."

"Everyone needs a hobby," Shammara smiled. "This
keeps her from becoming involved in more consequential matters—and if we should ever need to be rid of her, there'll be
plenty of evidence to convict her of adultery."

"I could attempt to convert her to the ways of Rimahn,"
Rabah said. "With her quick mind, she would be a natural, and
then she could be allied with us instead of an obstacle to be
dealt with."

"No," Shammara said firmly. "I don't want her as a religious fanatic, which is what she'd become. I want her more
. . . tractable, more flexible."

"I guarantee," said Rabah, "she is learning to become
more flexible every day."

Within the palace of Ravan was a small room near the
women's section. For many years it had been left in disuse, and
occasionally served as a storeroom. There was apparently only
one door leading to the rest of the palace, and no windows, but
the room had a further advantage that Rabah had shown to
Princess Oma: a hidden doorway that opened from a secret
passage leading all the way to the women's quarters. Even as
far back as the days of good King Shahriyan, architects had
realized that intrigues would always be a part of palace life, and
had laid their designs accordingly.

With Rabah's help, Princess Oma had completely redeco-
rated the chamber to suit her newly found needs. All the dust
had been cleared away and the room scented with flower petals
and incense. Carpets of deep pile covered the floor, with a soft
mattress in one corner, and plush satin and velvet pillows scattered about the room. A brazier stood in the corner diagonal to
the mattress, and oil lamps stood on discreet stands out of the
way to provide a soft, seductive light. Gauzy fabrics had been
hung to cover three walls of the room—and incidentally to
hide the secret door—while the fourth wall held erotic paintings on either side of the regular door. These paintings were of
orgy scenes, showing men and women fornicating in a large
number of combinations and positions. Oma and Rabah had
joked about trying all of them in turn some day—although as
Oma studied the paintings in more detail, the thought became
more an ambition than a joke.

Princess Oma was taking great delight in her sexual awakening. She no longer required Rabah to accompany her on every tryst, and she was learning which servants could be trusted to help her discreetly achieve her aims. She had begun to peer from the palace windows at the people below and point out men who looked interesting. She would then have her servants arrange for them to be brought into the palace on some pretext and shown to her special room.

Today a nervous, handsome young man entered the room, a new recruit within the palace guards named Murad ibn Kalem. Oma had spotted him on the palace walls patrolling in the early morning hours. His beauty and nervousness had aroused her. It was time to see whether what she had learned from the men she could teach to this boy.

Murad was tall and muscular, with clear skin and dark eyes. At seventeen, his beard had only started to form, but showed great potential. He came through the door very nervously, unsure why he had been summoned—and he grew even more nervous as he heard the door being bolted behind him from the outside.

Princess Oma reclined on the mattress across the room, her body scented with her favorite jasmine perfume. She wore a light blue sidaireeya with no Sadre under it; wine-colored sirwaal trousers covered the lower half of her body, and her feet were bare. She wore a sheer blue milfa and her head was uncovered; her fine black hair hung down her back in a thick braid. Her eyes, outlined with kohl, looked up and down his handsome form, and she smiled hungrily.

"Do you know who I am?" she asked.

The young man gulped, not quite sure whether to believe what was happening. Belatedly remembering his manners, he made a deep salaam and averted his eyes. "You are Princess Oma," he said. "I saw your procession pass my house on your wedding day."

"Very good. And you, I am told, are Murad ibn Kalem, the newest member of the palace guard."

"Even so I am, Your Highness."

"As such, you are sworn to serve me."

"To serve you and your husband, yes, O my princess."

"Well, my husband doesn't have need of you right now," Oma said, "and I do. Come kneel beside me."

Young Murad walked slowly forward, still unsure of what he was doing here. He had never had a princess speak to him

before, and especially not such a beautiful one in such intimate
surroundings. He knelt beside her as she requested, and bent
his head so he would not offend her modesty. The hair that
strayed from under his turban curled at the base of his neck
like an ornament atop the muscled back.

Oma's smile broadened as she unfastened her milfa and
let it fall to the floor. Reaching out with one delicate hand, she
took his chin and raised Murad's head until his eyes met hers.
"Am I so offensive to look upon, then, that you turn away from
me so?"

"No . . . oh no, Your Highness. Quite the contrary. You
are entirely too lovely—"

"Then why don't you appreciate my loveliness?" She
sighed deeply and slid her legs against each other, thus accen-
tuating her strength and grace.

"Your Highness, you are the wife of my prince, who is
soon to be my king. It is not right that we should be together
this way." With a sudden effort he stood, turned away, and
walked to the door—but he could not leave with it locked from
outside.

"If I am your princess, soon to be your queen, then I have
the power to say what is right for us and what is not. You are
sworn to obey me, and I order you to return to my side."

Many factors warred within the young man's soul, but
Oma's tone was so imperious that he had little choice but to
obey. At her gesture he knelt once more beside her mattress,
his body stiff and tense. She reached out to touch him once
more, and he trembled as her fingers caressed the side of his
face and neck.

"Your Highness, this is not right," he said in a shaky voice.

"Are you a priest, that you can lecture so conclusively on
morals?" Oma asked. Both her arms were reaching out behind
his head, now, stroking the back of his neck. Her long, delicate
fingers played with the bit of hair that strayed out of the bottom of his turban, and slowly insinuated themselves under the
wrapped cloth.

"I don't have to be a priest to know—"

"And I don't have to be a princess to know a woman's desire. Can you not see that this moment is meant for the two of
us?"

Her hands were wandering lower than his face, now,
downward across his chest. Her long fingernails made little
circles on the front of his uniform.

Murad's voice went higher as it took on a tone of desperation. "Your Highness, if you don't wish to honor your own marriage, at least consider mine. I, like yourself, am a newlywed, married but four days after you were, to a girl of good family and rare virtue. Oromasd orders us to be faithful—"

"Oromasd tells us a man may have many wives and concubines, that he may enjoy the favors of many women. Why do you so reject what our lord has granted you?"

And now her hands wandered even lower, inside the tops of his sirwaal and downward toward his thighs. Though Murad did continue to protest weakly, yet even so did his body betray him at the caressing touch of the princess's fingers. His manhood sprang to life under her ministrations, and her seductive voice drowned the sound of his conscience. Her words, her lips, her delicate fingertips, all conspired to overwhelm his sense of propriety—and as she felt his responsiveness, her own passion grew until it enveloped them both.

Her sidaireeya seemed to fall away of its own volition, exposing her beautiful young breasts with their nipples standing erect. With sudden greed he grabbed them, then let his hands begin to trail toward her belly. She pulled his shirt over his head so her fingers could luxuriate in the feel of his tightening muscles, and she drew him to her, on top of her, and crushed her firm breasts to his chest. She writhed beneath him, her legs reaching up as he fumbled with his clothing. Unable to control himself, he clumsily tore their clothing away—and together, alone in that small room, they consummated their passion with grunts, and sighs, and wild, enraptured cries. And Princess Oma's heart felt rich with triumph that yet another challenge had fallen before her, and the men of the world were hers for the taking. She never bothered to recall the tears of remorse he shed afterward—only the way her hands and mouth aroused him again and again to service her needs. Rabah had been right again about the stamina of youth.

It was two days later that Kalem bin Ali came to the Royal Temple seeking an audience with its high priest, Yusef bin Nard. As the wealthy and noble bin Ali had always been a generous donor, Yusef bin Nard took time from his schedule to grant him a personal audience.

Bin Ali was so angry he ignored the opening civilities. "I have come about my son, Murad, who is too ashamed of his actions to come himself."

"Your son is in the palace guard, is he not? What is so shameful that he dares not confess it to receive the absolution of beneficent Oromasd?"

"He claims he was summoned into the presence of Princess Oma and seduced by her into performing many and varied sexual acts. He was in tears as he confessed this to me yesterday, and he even pleaded with his bride for forgiveness. He is threatening to resign from the guard as punishment for his sin.

"My son is not an evil man, and I cannot believe he would fall so far on his own. Indeed, I have heard rumors of others in much the same straits—"

"I, too, have heard these rumors. They are most disturbing."

"Then what do you intend to do about them?" bin Ali fumed. "The laws of both men and Oromasd are very precise on the subject of women who commit adultery."

Yusef bin Nard took a deep breath and let it out slowly. "There are certain realities of the situation that must be taken into account. The laws of both men and Oromasd have always been interpreted with flexibility where royalty is concerned. In just a few days, Oma will be queen of Ravan—"

"We've been told repeatedly this makes her no different in the eyes of Oromasd."

"Of course not, and when Rashti judges her at the Bridge of Shinvar, she will be made to answer for all her sins, the same as you or I. But a man of your wealth and position knows the delicacy with which royalty must be treated."

"In other words, you intend to do nothing."

"I did not say that. In fact, my upcoming sermon for this week is in praise of fidelity and a strict admonishment against unlawful fornication."

"Sermons!" bin Ali snorted. "What good do they do? The righteous will nod agreement and the wicked will ignore them."

"Is that not always the way of the world? Did not Oromasd make us all fallible—"

With a sound of disgust, Kalem bin Ali stormed out of the room, leaving the high priest talking to empty air.

Indeed, Yusef bin Nard was a troubled man, more so than he dared admit to any member of the lay community. He had heard far more than idle rumors, and had already spoken to Shammara about the matter. She had sounded shocked and promised to speak to her daughter-in-law, but bin Nard sensed beneath her words a lack of interest that he knew he could never change. Oma would continue with her wicked ways until such time as it was in Shammara's interest to stop her—and bin Nard knew he dared not act against the princess unless he had Shammara's full permission.

Other matters, too, concerned him. Attendance at the Royal Temple was falling off drastically, and those who did attend—more out of habit than conviction—were lackluster in their devotions, to say the least. In part, bin Nard knew this was due to an unfavorable comparison between himself and his illustrious predecessor. Umar bin Ibrahim had been well loved by the people of Ravan, and even bin Nard had to admit the old man had possessed a degree of charisma that he himself could never hope to achieve.

Even so, this comparison did not account for the listlessness he saw within the Holy City. The death of Prince Ahmad, and his replacement by Shammara and Prince Haroun, had left the people feeling as though Oromasd had deserted them, as though virtue no longer mattered. Oma's behavior was not the cause, merely a symptom of the malaise that had overtaken all of Ravan.

Yusef bin Nard pondered the problem for a long time, and decided to try something radical. He would do a reading of the stars, not for any person, but for the Temple of the Faith itself, to see what the future held in store for it. He was not at all sure that such a thing could be done; he had never heard of anyone trying it. But the temple was almost as much a living entity as any person, and certainly it had a future that interacted with people and the history of the world. This decline in its fortunes was surely a temporary one, and Yusef bin Nard wanted to learn how long this unhappy time would last.

Deciding how to cast the chart for the temple was difficult, for it did not have a specific time of birth as did a person. After much thought, bin Nard decided to use the date of the temple's dedication, back at the beginning of the city of Ravan. He combed the temple records to determine the moment as accurately as he could, and took into account all the minor calendar reforms that had been made since that date. Then he made his computations and arrived at the answers he had sought.

But the answers made no sense to him. They said, quite simply, that the Temple of the Faith *had* no future—and that was patently ridiculous. It was far more likely, he reasoned, that his entire supposition was wrong, and that—as he had feared—it simply was not possible to cast the chart for a building. This was why no one ever did it, and he had simply wasted his time trying.

He could almost hear the voice of Umar bin Ibrahim whispering over his shoulder, telling him what a fool he was to depend on the stars when the answer to his problem lay with people and their behavior. Bin Nard sighed. There would be no easy answer to this dilemma. He would simply have to play Shammara's game of politics and trust in Oromasd to preserve the sanctity of the Holy City.

Kalem bin Ali and his wife Barakah paid a call on the house of Alhena. Umar's wife showed them graciously into the qa'a, and the three of them sat together on the mats, exchanging the formal pleasantries for half an hour as they sipped coffee from Alhena's silver service. Alhena could tell that her visitors were nervous about something, but her manners forbade her from bringing the subject up herself.

Finally, when the coffee and the conversation had relaxed him sufficiently, bin Ali broached the topic that was on his mind. "Ever since the deaths of Prince Ahmad and your respected husband, the city of Ravan has been in decline. People do not speak freely for fear of Shammara's vengeance, and people lack confidence in the Royal Temple because that fool, Yusef bin Nard, lacks the qualities of moral leadership that made your husband so beloved. People of good families are abandoning the Royal Temple for smaller temples where Oromasd still is more revered than Shammara, or else are abandoning their faith altogether. The Holy City does not feel holy to us right now."

"I have seen this problem for myself," Alhena admitted. "These matters are indeed sad, but I know not what I can do."

"We need somewhere to go that pays no homage to Shammara, a place where Oromasd still listens. I know your house contains a small shrine, Umar's personal place to commune with Oromasd. We were wondering whether our family could come by occasionally and have private services within your home."

"My husband always said that no one who worshiped Oromasd could be a stranger under our roof—and you, O my friends, are far from strangers. This home always has been, and always will be, a haven for prayer. Oromasd needs no special place to hear you from, but if you feel most comfortable here, then this is the place where your prayers will be their most heartfelt. You and your family are welcome at any time."

As she spoke, Alhena felt a warm glow throughout her body, and she knew she was doing the proper thing. She dared not tell anyone that Umar still lived—but by carrying on the principles he had so well established, by following the example he had always given, she could ensure that his spirit never left Ravan and that his message for good and for hope would not be abandoned.

At the same time, she knew she was embarking on a dangerous course, one that could risk a confrontation with Shammara. The woman who ran Ravan would brook no opposition to her authority—and Alhena would have to take care not to appear rebellious, or any good that she did would quickly be nullified by the jealous uncrowned queen.

19

The Undersea City

Jafar al-Sharif and Cari turned and walked away from the tree Raffiliz. This time they encountered no barriers, no bramble bushes or other obstacles to delay their departure. When they reached the periphery of the tree's overhanging umbrella, Cari lifted her master up into the air once more and flew him all the way back to *Hauvarta's Shield*, thus avoiding any further dangers the Isle of Illusions might have in store for the unwary. The two of them again felt the embarrassment of such closeness, and their mutual discomfort compelled them to silence on the journey back. Fortunately, Cari flew quickly, and they reached the ship before the silence became too painful.

They were welcomed back on board by their friends, who had been nervously awaiting the outcome of Jafar's journey. The storyteller gave a censored account of his adventure, saying of the deadly encounter only that some powerful creature had indeed snared him with its illusions, but that timely action by Cari had rescued him from a dire fate. He described the encounter with Raffiliz in slightly more detail, and most of his companions were satisfied with the account. Jafar did notice, however, that Leila was giving him and Cari strange looks. He knew he could not fool her forever, and would eventually have to tell her what had really happened. But not now. He was still trying to figure it all out for himself.

Hauvarta's Shield pulled up anchor and sailed westward, away from the Isle of Illusions. Their course now called for them to sail through the Jibrali Straits into the Western Sea, and westward still until they reached the vicinity described in Ali Maimun's journal where they hoped to find the sunken city of Atluri. Once again the winds blessed them, blowing at the maximum strength their sails could hold in the perfect direction for them to travel. The crew was now taking such marvels

almost for granted, but El-Hadar could still be seen occasionally shaking his head and muttering about wizardry.

Since Jafar al-Sharif had spun for them the tale of Atluri,
the ship's captain felt it incumbent upon him to tell other stories to pass the time on the quiet nights as *Hauvarta's Shield*
slipped peacefully through the waves. He boasted that he'd
had adventures in strange waters that would test the mettle
even of the heroes in the legends of old, and told his passengers of the city of gold, of the wizard with the giant turtle,
of the waterspout that took him to the sky city, of the sorceress
who had changed his crew into animals, of his encounter with
the daughter of the sea monsters, and hinted that there were
other stories as well he could tell that would truly strain their
credulity. Jafar al-Sharif listened avidly to these tales, occasionally questioning El-Hadar about details and making sure he
could repeat the stories himself at some later date.

To Jafar, it was the stories themselves that mattered; he
couldn't have cared less whether they were true or not. El-
Hadar swore the tales were true, and some of his crewmen
backed up his claims, asserting they had been along on one or
more of those adventures. Prince Ahmad checked with Leila,
who said that, while El-Hadar was given to some embellishments, the kernels of those stories were indeed factual. This
gave the passengers a new respect for the background and intelligence of their captain.

Leila and Umar bin Ibrahim continued to improve. Their
strength and stamina increased daily, and they were now eating food with ravenous appetites to replenish the energy their
bodies had lost while they were ill. The monkey Verethran
stayed with them most of the time, performing cute antics and
helping relieve their minds of worry so they could recuperate
faster.

Within two days after leaving the Isle of Illusions, the convalescents were walking around without assistance, and even
starting to complain about the limited space aboard the ship—
something they hadn't even noticed before in their pain. The
sailors were used to such close confines, but the passengers
were starting to itch for more freedom of movement. After riding so rapidly across vast stretches of Parsina, they felt suddenly imprisoned within the hull of this vessel.

Another day of sailing brought *Hauvarta's Shield* to the
Jibrali Straits, and here it was that the travelers confronted

another problem. "We cannot risk voyaging into the uncharted realms of the Western Sea without a full stock of provisions," El-Hadar explained. "If we were going north, paralleling the coast, there would be plenty of places to put in and replenish our supplies—but out to the west we'll find nothing but fish, seaweed, and whatever rainwater we can catch on deck. We must resupply in Jibral.

"Even in normal times, the Jibrali are thieves and pirates, and their merchants charge exorbitant prices for even the most basic wares. In these times, from what you have said, the Jibrali are doubly treacherous, for they are controlled by your enemies, the forces of Rimahn. We must place ourselves in their hands if we are to reach your objective."

"Perhaps not," said Jafar al-Sharif, thinking of the sparrow that kept the hero Argun fed during his captivity in the castle of Brabant. "I think my wonderful Jann can once again be of great service."

Calling Cari to him, Jafar explained the problem—though he still could not look directly into her face when he talked to her. "I would like you to fly into Jibral at night and bring us back some supplies to keep us provisioned."

"I must do it if you order it, O master, but it is not normally the way of the righteous Jann to steal."

"Who said anything about stealing? You'll leave the merchants money in exchange, a fair price for what you take. We'll just cut out all the face-to-face haggling and eliminate the risk."

To everyone but me, Cari thought, but of course she said nothing of this aloud. "Hearkening and obedience, O master."

There were limits, though, to how much Cari could carry when she flew, and as a result she had to make twenty-six separate trips over the course of the next three nights before the ship was fully restocked. This strenuous activity taxed even the Jann's magical strength and endurance to her limits, and Jafar realized how much hard work he'd been having her do for him.

"You have labored mightily on my behalf, O wonderful Cari, with very little rest," he told her.

"It is but my duty, O master."

"Nevertheless, a good master does not abuse his servants. We will yet need all your wits and all your skill before our adventure is done, and you must be fresh for the task. I will give you a respite away from us."

"But I ask for none, O master."

"Nevertheless, I order you to return to your homeland until I summon you again."

The crestfallen look on her face almost broke his heart, but she simply said, "Hearkening and obedience," and vanished from view.

With Cari gone, Jafar at first experienced a strange sense of calmness that he hadn't known since the incident on the Isle of Illusions. The disquieting presence of the Jann was no longer felt, and he would now have a chance in peace to assimilate what had happened, to evaluate their relationship and decide what he was going to do about it. It was only later he let himself feel the empty place in his heart that Cari filled.

The enemy had a large fleet scattered across the Jibrali Straits, but El-Hadar proved expert at running blockades. They sailed through the channel at night with all their lights out on deck. The moon was not to come up until nearly dawn, and thick, black storm clouds blocked even what little starlight might have given them away. Passengers and crew were all silent, repeatedly holding their breaths in suspense each time they neared an enemy ship. El-Hadar had to do a pinpoint job of steering in and out of the paths of the naval vessels to avoid detection, and sometimes they came close enough to hear the crews talking and laughing on the other ships. But they made it through the blockade, and by the time the moon rose, they were safely past the straits, well into the Western Sea.

The course laid out by Ali Maimun now directed them west southwest—and yet again the wind blew favorably. To El-Hadar, this was nothing short of miraculous, for the winds were always reputed to be northerly in the Western Sea. "Such phenomenal luck might almost tempt El-Hadar to become a religious man," he exclaimed at one point.

"That is a fate you need not fear," Umar bin Ibrahim replied with a smile. "But don't worry, O gallant captain. There are more ways to serve Oromasd than simply by praying, and you are doing your share now."

For five days *Hauvarta's Shield* sailed along the thirty-fifth parallel of latitude as Ali Maimun had instructed, and on the morning of the sixth day the lookout gave a call that brought everyone up on deck. Circling a spot of ocean was a vast flock of seagulls, terns, pelicans, and other birds of the sea, all screeching at one another and occasionally diving into the ocean for food.

This sight was unusual to the passengers, but to the captain and crew of the ship it was as miraculous at the ever-beneficent wind. "There should not be this many birds so far from any land," El-Hadar explained. "In open ocean, all you expect to see in the air is an occasional albatross."

"This is what we were told to expect," said Jafar al-Sharif. "We have reached our destination."

As *Hauvarta's Shield* sailed closer, a school of friendly dolphins splashed around them, leaping out of the water in excited playfulness. Even the most hardened of the sailors could be heard muttering prayers under his breath as they all realized they had reached some special spot, and none knew what would become of them. The sea played too many tricks on mariners, and most of them were unpleasant.

"This is the spot where I must go into the ocean and seek the sunken city," Jafar declared.

"El-Hadar cannot drop anchor in water so deep," the captain said. "We will try to maintain this position, but—"

Even as he spoke, the wind suddenly died completely, leaving the air heavy and still. "I don't think the ship is going anywhere," Jafar said with a smile. "But I must."

Prince Ahmad turned to face him and placed his hands upon Jafar's shoulders. "I wish I could accompany you and help you deal with the unknown dangers of this city and its strange people. I'll feel so useless just sitting up here on the ship while you face mysterious perils below the waves."

"No more useless than I felt while you were fighting in Estanash's cave," Jafar replied. "We all do what we can, when we can. Oromasd has designed our roles, and they all play a part in his ultimate plan. Don't worry, Your Highness; I have a feeling you'll be busy enough before our mission is over."

"I will pray for you, nonetheless," said Umar. "You are going to a place alien to men, and Oromasd alone knows what you may find."

"Your prayers will be a welcome comfort to me, O my friend," Jafar said. "At least these people are probably not hostile. Atluri, even at its most foolish, was never an evil land, so I may hope for a better reception than we got in Punjar. If anything, I may have to fear too warm a welcome; Ali Maimun himself describes the people as sportive and carefree."

"But that was many centuries ago," Leila pointed out. "Things can change in that time."

"I'll have my magical cloak to help me vanish from their sight, and I'll have Kharouf's amulet to protect me from magical mischief. If anything more serious threatens, I can summon Cari in an instant to help me escape. I should be fairly safe."

"If the magical bark works," Leila said.

"We'll find that out quickly enough." Jafar took the piece of tree bark from his pocket and popped it into his mouth. It smelled vaguely of cedar and left a dry, bitter flavor on his tongue. Raffiliz had said he needed to swallow it whole, but as he tried to do so, it lodged in his throat and he started choking. One of the sailors alertly brought Jafar a cup of water, and after several deep gulps the storyteller managed to get the bark down.

"No one warned me the cure might be worse than the condition," Jafar rasped hoarsely. "I don't feel any different, but I'll give it a try."

He embraced Umar and Prince Ahmad, clapping them on the back in good fellowship and letting them do the same to him. The monkey Verethran gave him a comical salute, while El-Hadar and the crew gave him a rousing cheer. Jafar embraced Leila in quite a different manner than he'd embraced Umar and Ahmad, and received a long, passionate kiss in return. He could not embrace poor Selima, much as he would have loved to, so he had to settle for giving her a confident smile. She was getting harder to see these days, even in daylight, which served all the more as a reminder of what he was about.

I must hurry, Jafar thought. *It's getting late for her.*

Standing at the side of the ship, he said, "If I start to drown, that's the signal to pull me out." Then, wrapping the cloak of invisibility around him, he jumped into the sea. His friends on the ship could only watch as he sank immediately beneath the waves on his way to a land beyond any they could possibly imagine.

Jafar al-Sharif felt the splash as his body hit the water, and knew a moment of panic as it completely engulfed him. He tried holding his breath, but knew that could work only so long. Meanwhile the cold of the wintry water was soaking into his body, and he was glad he'd brought the cloak along—for warmth, if nothing else. As he wrapped it even more tightly around him, he noticed that it felt dry. The bark must be working, then. As an experiment, he opened his mouth a tiny bit and tried to suck in just a few drops of water, figuring he could still swim up to the surface if this failed. But no water entered his mouth. As Raffiliz had promised, it felt as though he were surrounded by air, even though his eyes told him differently.

This is like walking through those bramble bushes, he thought. *I am protected from what I know is around me—for two days, at least. I hope that will be enough.*

Something bumped him from behind, startling him out of his confident mood. Jafar whirled quickly in the water, frightened that some sea monster might be attacking him, and stared instead into the silly, smiling face of a playful dolphin. The creature nuzzled him with its snout and swam off a bit, then looked back as though expecting him to follow. When Jafar just continued to sink, the dolphin returned and nuzzled him again.

Jafar felt no fear of this creature; it was rather like a large, friendly dog, eager to play. He petted it alongside its head, and the dolphin chirped out some high-pitched whistling and swam exuberantly around him. Jafar continued to descend, and the dolphin continued to follow him.

Other dolphins, attracted by the noises of the first, were starting to circle him, too. Jafar's amusement at their antics quickly wore off and turned to annoyance. These creatures might be harmless, but if they continued to pester him, they could hinder his efforts to find the sunken city and its piece of the Crystal of Oromasd. Fortunately, though, the dolphins' attention span was short; when Jafar did not join them in their games, they soon lost interest and swam off elsewhere in search of diversion, leaving the storyteller to continue his descent alone into the icy waters of the Western Sea.

The sea around him rapidly grew darker as the light from the surface failed to penetrate this deeply. He knew there were fish of all sizes and colors swimming around him, but it grew harder and harder to see them. He detected their presence as much by the disturbance they caused in the water as by sight, and he began to get worried. How could he deal with the inhabitants of Atluri if he could not see them?

His fears soon were eased, though, as he continued to sink and he saw around him fish that seemed to glow of their own accord, as though they had each swallowed a small fire. There were whole schools of them, again in different colors and sizes, and this gave Jafar hope that not everything this far under the sea was dark and inky.

After a while he saw three shapes approaching him from below. At first he thought they were more dolphins, for they were about the right size and swam with the same humping of their bodies; but as they came closer, he saw that they were people—or at least reasonable facsimiles of people.

Their front halves were very human, and looked perfectly normal. Two were dressed in vests of soft eelskin leather, with small shells sewn on as decorations; the third wore a coat of shark's skin. None wore turbans; they all had long hair that was braided down their backs so it didn't float around in the water and get in their faces. From their waists down, however, they wore nothing at all—for from their waists down, they re-sembled fish. They had smooth skin, like the dolphins, rather than scales, but the streamlined curves and the fins were un-mistakable.

The trio approached, and the one with the shark's skin coat hailed Jafar with open hands apart. "Welcome to Atluri, O mighty wizard."

Jafar looked at him suspiciously. "How did you know who I am?"

The fish-man looked amused. "I don't know your name, but few men who aren't wizards ever manage to come here."

That would certainly be true, Jafar thought. Without real-izing it, he had come to one of the few places in all Parsina where his credentials as a wizard were bound to go un-challenged.

"I am called Jafar al-Sharif," he said, "the wizard of the southern provinces. I travel now to your lovely and interesting land on the most urgent business of our lord Oromasd. I most humbly request an audience with your noble king on a matter that concerns the fate of all the world."

"That does sound important," said the man in the shark's skin coat.

"As you love Oromasd and the Bounteous Immortals, you will grant my request."

"We will certainly take you to the palace. The king likes to be apprised of anything new in his realm, so he'll surely grant you an audience. As for any help with your petition, that will depend on how successfully you entertain him. Follow us."

The trio moved off and began swimming rapidly down-ward, but Jafar could not match their pace. When they realized they were leaving him behind, they returned; the two men in the eelskin vests took his arms gently, and together the group swam through the murky waters toward the sunken city of Atluri.

At first, all was blackness around them except for the few luminescent fish, and Jafar wondered how his escorts knew which way they were going. He supposed, after all these millennia of living under the sea, they must have developed inborn senses of where they were in relation to given landmarks that his own eyes could not detect. At any rate, these were the people he had come to see, and they claimed to be taking him where he had to go, so he gave up worrying and left himself in their hands—and Oromasd's.

Some lights appeared to be glowing dimly ahead of them now, brightening the surrounding gloom. Jafar first thought they were more of the fish, then realized they were too stationary. As they continued swimming, the lights got brighter only gradually, indicating they were farther away than he had imagined—and therefore much brighter. His pulse began to race as he realized he was about to catch a glimpse of something few surface-living men had ever seen—the sunken city of Atluri.

The city appeared out of the gloom like a ghost village fading slowly into the world of mortals. Jafar saw it first as strings of lights, like a Sinjinese city decked out with lanterns for a festival. Strings of lights were everywhere in concentric circular patterns around a center, with other strings as radii connecting the circles, so that the effect was of drops of morning dew reflecting the sunlight on a spider's web. It was not until Jafar and his escorts came closer that he realized the lights defined streets and buildings for the city's inhabitants.

The word "buildings" was only an approximate term for the structures of the city, for in most cases they were actually grown rather than built. The majority of the dwellings that had existed when Atluri was on the surface of the earth had long since rotted away, but over the ages, colonies of coral had been sculpted and encouraged to grow in the desired forms, until today they formed the basis of the city. The "architecture" was sometimes practical, sometimes whimsical, often some combination of the two. Low, sturdy structures stood next to fragile-looking spires reaching upwards for fifty cubits or more from their base. Most rooftops had gardens on them, with strange and colorful undersea flowers showing off their blooms. Sometimes delicate bridges spanned the gap between

one building and another—though the effect was purely deco-
rative, since the inhabitants could easily swim across. The very
fragility of the scene made it all the more exotic, all the more
beautiful.

Jafar wondered where all the light was coming from, and
how these citizens of the sea could have brought fire under the
water. But as he entered the city itself he saw that the "lanterns" were actually cages holding different numbers of the
phosphorescent fish. The bars of the cages were woven of pro-
cessed seaweed, and the spaces between the bars were too
small for the fish to escape, yet wide enough for them to be fed
through. When some fish died, others could be trapped or
raised to take their place, thus providing Atluri with a constant
source of light.

And all through the city swam its inhabitants, the fish-
people of Atluri. Most of the men wore coats or vests of leather
similar to the ones Jafar's escorts were wearing, while the
women wore more delicate garments of woven sea grass or
other plants. In addition, the women's clothing was gaudily
adorned with seashells of all colors. They wore rings of coral;
some of the poorer women wore necklaces of seashells, but
most had several strands of pearls around their necks. Braided
long hair was the universal fashion for both men and women.
Apart from the fishy portion of their bodies, the Atlurim
looked just like people of any city—young, old, fat, thin, handsome, and homely.

Fish swam regularly through the streets of Atluri, just as
birds flew through the air of a city on the surface. Most of the
time the people ignored the fish, but Jafar saw one man's arm
dart out and grab a fish before it could escape, then start to eat
it raw as he continued to swim casually along with his companions. *It must be interesting to live in a city where the food so
obligingly comes to you*, Jafar thought.

Jafar's escorts swam with him past the outer circles of the
city, in toward the center. As they passed more and more people, the public curiosity grew and a crowd began following
them. Although no one made a hostile gesture, Jafar began to
worry about the size of the mob he was attracting. He still
remembered all too well the attention he'd commanded in the
city of the apes. As a performer, he enjoyed playing to an audience—but too large an audience could be unpredictable,
and it made him nervous.

Ahead of them, as they swam, loomed the palace of Atluri, rising out of the ocean floor like a towering titan. This was one of the few structures remaining of the old days when Atluri was an island; its massive stone walls—strengthened during construction by the spells of the court wizards—had survived the shock of sinking beneath the waves. Even it, however, had not altogether escaped the changes of time, for coral and sea plants had grown up around it, giving it a look of being almost alive. The wood of the doors had long since rotted away, leaving the palace gate yawning open for anyone who wished to swim in. There weren't even any guards to keep people away. This was the most relaxed, informal monarchy Jafar had ever seen or heard of.

Jafar's escorts led him straight into the palace, and the crowd behind them followed right inside. Apparently Jafar was going to see the king, and the populace was going to see Jafar. Well, he had no secrets from them; it just had never happened this way before.

The walls of the long hallways did not have paintings or tapestries on them, as he might have expected in a palace on land, but they were not barren of decoration. Niches in the walls held statues, and the walls themselves were often covered with mosaic murals inlaid with brightly colored sea pebbles, pearls, and precious stones. The Atlurim had adapted wonderfully to their environment and used their ingenuity to improve their surroundings—as men everywhere did. Most of the statues and murals depicted athletes and games of various sorts, and Jafar had to suppress a wry smile as he remembered the story of how Atluri had come to be here.

At the end of the hall they went through an arched entry-way into a large chamber, quite obviously the throne room. The high, domed ceiling was supported by a double row of columns that once were bare marble, and now were encrusted with shells and entwined with sea vines. The floor was a plush carpet of algae, and all was brightly lit by large cages of the glowing fish.

At the far end of the room, reclining on a silver diwan, was the ruler of Atluri, King Harnex. He was a pudgy man of cheerful face and robes of a fabric Jafar could not identify, but which glittered and glowed as though with a life of their own. On his head was a tall crown fashioned of mother-of-pearl in odd, yet dignified, shapes. He smiled as the procession entered, and he beckoned them all forward.

"Greetings, O wizard. The news of your arrival has preceded you. Come in, come in and introduce yourself, and explain why you have made the long and hazardous journey to visit our out-of-the-way realm."

Jafar's escort released his arms; he swam forward on his own and made a deep salaam—an act that was somewhat awkward under water, but still respectful. "Your Majesty, may you live forever, I am Jafar al-Sharif, known to some as the wizard of the southern provinces, and I have come to ask your assistance in a matter that affects all of mankind."

He then went on to explain about the release of Aeshma from his ages-old imprisonment and the coming battle against the forces of evil. He told of Muhmad's vision that he, Jafar, must gather the pieces of the Crystal of Oromasd to combat Aeshma's legions, and that one of the pieces had been left here in trust centuries ago by the great Ali Maimun. As the successor, however unworthy, to Ali Maimun, he asked the king's help in recovering the Crystal.

"I know about this Crystal of which you speak," King Harnex said when Jafar had finished. "For many ages, it has been the sacred duty of the kings of Atluri to guard it until the day it is needed again. In this way, humble Atluri—forgotten by the surface world—still plays its role in the game that pits Oromasd against Rimahn, the game with the entire world as its stake."

"Then you will give me the piece I seek?" Jafar asked, hardly daring to believe this part of the quest would be so simple.

"We will talk of that soon enough. You must understand that time as it is measured on the surface of the world is meaningless down here, where the sunshine never reaches and hence there is no day or night. We were preparing what you might call our midday banquet here, and we were hoping you would care to join us in our repast."

"I would be deeply honored, Your Majesty," Jafar said with great diplomacy, even as his mind recalled the image of the one fish-man who snatched his dinner as it swam past. He hoped he would not be expected to catch his own supper, or this meal would quickly become embarrassing.

But as King Harnex led the way into the dining room, Jafar was relieved to find that the table was already set and the food was already prepared—though it turned out to be one of the odder meals he'd ever eaten. Because there was no fire here on the floor of the ocean, all the food was raw, but still it was plentiful and tasty. There were filleted pieces of raw fish that tasted like rare beef, infused with a variety of different sauces to enhance the flavor. There were oysters, clams, and fish roe, and a seaweed salad that had a deliciously spicy tang. The food made Jafar thirsty, but he noticed that none of the other diners drank anything—they probably didn't need to— so he did not bother to ask. There was nothing insincere about the compliments he lavished on the chef at the end of the meal, for the food was all delicious even if it was unfamiliar.

As they ate, King Harnex talked to him about life in Atluri. "We lead a much different existence from the surface folks, as you can tell. We can't worship Oromasd in the regular, prescribed manner because we can't have fire under the sea, so our priests are sometimes at a loss for something to do. We try to keep to the practice of good thoughts, good words, and good deeds, and trust that Oromasd will take into account our special circumstances.

"You are doubtless familiar with the story of Atluri before we sank under the ocean. Well, sorry as I am to admit it, life in the sea—once we adapted to it—is even less challenging than it was for us on land, and so we are even more dependent on our diversions to keep us occupied. We avidly seek news of what is happening in the world above us. Anything you can tell us will be greedily seized and repeated for years."

At last, Jafar had found the most appreciative audience of his life. But where to begin? Atluri had sunk beneath the sea millennia ago, long before even Ali Maimun had visited it. There was so much history to cover that all the stories Jafar knew could barely scratch the surface—and Raffiliz's bark would protect him down here for only two days. "Your Majesty, it would take years—"

"Let me explain something to you, O Jafar," said the king, seeing his guest's indecision. "We are not ignorant of the world's events since our island sank. Our priests have learned to duplicate the spells of the ancient wizard Calazar; they can, on occasion, change men of the surface into men of the ocean, like us. They use this power sparingly, of course, but every so often there is a shipwreck nearby, and good sailors would drown if we did not save them. We cannot bring them back to their homes and loved ones, but we can give them new homes with us, and many finish out their days happily in our city. Whenever we chance to take in someone new, he is always questioned for news of the surface world, and he is made to tell all the stories he knows over and over again until we all know them, too. In this way do we keep ourselves informed of life in the upper world."

King Harnex paused. "So you see, as starved as we always are for entertainment and diversion, we would consider a new story to be a necessary payment for relinquishing the Crystal to you."

Jafar al-Sharif could hardly believe his ears. All they wanted was a story. This would be simplicity itself.

"I must caution you that we've heard a great many stories, and only a new one will satisfy us. If you think you know one, tell it to us now."

"There are stories of the Age of Heroes—"

"Ali Maimun told us most of those when he visited us; the rest we learned from others. I do not think you know anything new there."

Jafar's mind boggled at the idea of hearing the stories of Argun, Shiratz, and the rest of the great heroes from the lips of Ali Maimun himself, a man who knew them all personally and fought at their sides against Rimahn's hosts. But if the Atlurim weren't interested in those heroic epics, that still left him a vast repertoire to try.

He checked first the obvious ones: the milkmaid and the Jinn; Ali Kadar and the peri queen; Achmet bin Khazar and the city of gold; the thirteen ghosts of the Indi temple; Goha and the invisible woman; the enchanted heron; the fisherman and the magic net. But at each suggestion, King Harnex shook his head and said his people already knew that one, and Jafar would have to find something else.

Jafar dipped deeper into his vast repertoire. He suggested the lion and the bean farmer, King Mamluk and the giant of the Bitter Sea, the twelve journeys of Haroun the merchant, Faisal and the enchanted gourd, the wedding night of Hussain ibn Hamal—but at all of these, the king again replied regretfully that the people of Atluri were familiar with the tales.

With each story he mentioned, each one King Harnex rejected, Jafar became more desperate. He reached further into his memory for stories remembered out of the dim past, stories of horror, stories of humor, stories of reason, and stories of passion—all to no avail. The bawdiest stories that he scarcely dared tell in the presence of women were old and stale in this land. Even the tales that he himself had only recently learned from the Badawi storyteller were well-known to this audience.

Despite the chill of the winter sea, despite the water all around him, Jafar al-Sharif felt himself starting to perspire. These people knew all the stories that he knew, and probably more besides. If there was one they didn't know, it had to be one that hadn't been told yet. And if it hadn't been told yet, how could he be expected to know it?

Then, in his moment of desperation, kismet was again kind to him by reminding him of a story that indeed had never yet been told. A smile spread across his lips as he said, "Your Majesty, citizens of fair Atluri, I have for you a story that no ears have ever heard, that no lips have ever spoken, a story so fresh it has not yet a title. Prepare yourselves for a tale of wonder and wizardry, of mystic realms and exotic adventures."

And with this preface, Jafar al-Sharif began to tell the Atlurim the tale of the poor storyteller who outwitted a wizard and escaped on his magic flying carpet, of how the storyteller then encountered an exiled prince, and how they defeated the Jinn Estanash, and how they traveled to the land of far Punjar where they outwitted the evil king with the help of his enslaved wife and stole the king's most valued treasure, of how they fought the army of the dead and traveled to the city of the apes and visited the king of the winds.

Jafar realized as he was telling the story that there was as yet no satisfying ending for it, so he improvised one about how Varyu used the power of the winds to defeat the prince's enemies and return him to his throne, whereupon the prince made the storyteller his chief wazir and all dwelt thereafter in peace and contentment.

He spoke with his usual eloquence and gesticulations, and he felt the power surging through him as strongly as ever. It was an interesting sensation, now that he knew more of the origin of the power, to use it just for storytelling once more, for no magic greater than enchanting the ears of his audience. It was a strangely relaxing and, at the same time, exhilarating experience, and he knew it was going to help him succeed in this mission.

There was silence for a full minute as Jafar completed his tale. Then King Harnex clapped his hands and exclaimed, "Well done, O talented Jafar. You have the tongue of a storyteller as well as the skills of a wizard, and you have bound us all within the spell of your words. You have performed a feat we feared might be impossible, and for that you must be rewarded. Bring forth the crown."

At the king's command, two servants swam forward bearing between them another crown of mother-of-pearl, slightly smaller than the king's, in the center of which were set some large sea rocks. They placed this crown awkwardly atop Jafar's own turban, where it balanced somewhat precariously.

"For providing us with such exquisite entertainment," the king continued, "you shall henceforth be named as one of my wazirs, and be entitled to sit and advise me at my diwans."

"Your Majesty honors me more than I can say," said Jafar, "but if you so welcome my advice, then I must tell you such an honor is hardly appropriate. I am here among you for just a short time, and then I must return to the world of the surface. I would hardly make a fitting wazir."

"There are those who would say that the best wazir is an absent one," smiled the king.

Jafar smiled in return. "There is much truth in that—but in Oromasd's name, I swear that the only reward I seek is the piece of the Crystal you hold in trust. If you give me that, it will be payment and honor enough."

"Before that happens, O Jafar, you must tell us that story several times again, that we may learn it in all its fine detail and have it ever at our disposal. In such ways do we alleviate the boredom that would otherwise make our lives under the sea utterly unbearable."

Jafar started to object, then saw it would be pointless. He could well imagine how tedious life down here could be, and how desperately the people would cling to anything new. Repetition of the story would still be a small price to pay for the piece of the Crystal of Oromasd.

Thus it was that Jafar al-Sharif told his story a second time, and then a third, and then a fourth. By then the audience, which had swelled with each telling, agreed that they knew enough of the details to repeat it for themselves. As for Jafar, his voice was nearly gone, his strength was all but depleted, his wits were all but vanished. He could barely keep his eyes open, and knew that more than a full day had gone by in this pursuit. As much as he loved storytelling, it was punishing to go about it for so long without a rest.

"Your Majesty," he said in a harsh, croaking voice, "I have acceded to all your requests, and now I ask that you, in return, give me what you promised: the Crystal of Oromasd."

King Harnex paused and looked away. "I did not quite promise you the Crystal in exchange for a story. I said a story was necessary, but I did not tell you it was sufficient."

Jafar stared at him with growing anger. "In Oromasd's name, what more then must I do?"

"We have yet one more diversion, a little game you must play, a puzzle you must solve."

"What is it?" Jafar asked from between clenched teeth.

"You must, unaided, find where the Crystal has been hidden."

Jafar exploded. "I can stay under the water for only two days, and surely more than one of them has already elapsed."

"Well over one," the king agreed. "I would estimate, in the units of the surface dwellers, that you have approximately five hours left to you. Since it will take you about an hour to return to the surface, that gives you four hours to find the Crystal."

"You know as well as I, Your Majesty, that it would be impossible for even your fastest swimmer to completely search Atluri in a mere four hours."

"I will give you a clue: the Crystal is within this palace."

"You miss my point, O duplicitous king," Jafar railed. "I doubt I could search even that much within the allotted time."

"And you miss *my* point, O Jafar," said King Harnex, suddenly becoming serious. "The person who would be the successor to Ali Maimun must prove he has the wit and intelligence of his illustrious predecessor. The task I have set for you is not impossible. You could have the Crystal within your hands in a minute if you but used your head. If you would have the Crystal, you must find where it is."

Jafar stared in anger at this submarine monarch. He wanted to grab him by the throat and beat him, to force him to reveal the Crystal's location, and risk the anger of Atluri's population, but he also realized how futile that would be. The king would probably only become more stubborn, and Jafar would then never find the piece before his time down here ran out.

He glanced about at his appreciative audience, and saw only children eager for the game. In his heart he cursed Ali Maimun, whose example and book were impossible to live up to for a mere storyteller and apprentice wizard. He felt the minutes tick away, and began to hunt for a chest or box near the king's seat; he found nothing like that in the room. He thought of Selima, now more translucent than the fish-scale filters over the lights, and he began to panic.

He swam frantically around the dining room, examining the floor, the ceiling, the walls, the furniture, all corners where the Crystal might be hidden. If this piece was the same size as the other two he'd gotten, it would be about as large as a man's clenched fist. That would make it difficult to hide out in the open, but very simple to place within or behind something else.

The king and his subjects followed Jafar about as he hunted for the precious Crystal, whispering and laughing amongst themselves. They seemed to be enjoying this sport tremendously; Jafar wished them all a speedy trip to the Pits of Torment as his eyes darted around the room, seeking any possible hiding place that he might have overlooked.

Jafar spent half an hour fruitlessly searching the palace's dining room, then moved his search into the throne room. He spent nearly an hour there, with equally little success, then dashed out into the long corridors, searching up and down the length of their colorful mosaics for the special stone that was the Crystal of Oromasd. His audience was with him here, too, laughing and having fine sport with his desperation.

Finally, Jafar's exhaustion wore down his panic, and his wits returned. This frantic prying into the corners of the palace was getting him nowhere. He was trying to solve a puzzle through physical means when his best, and only real, asset was his mind. He had let desperation drive him into a panic, when what he really needed to do was sit and think the matter through. He settled into a corner of the hallway and tried to ignore the spectators watching him so intently.

The purpose of this game, King Harnex had said, was to determine whether Jafar was a worthy successor to Ali Maimun. King Harnex was not an evil man trying to prevent him from getting the Crystal, and he had said the solution was not impossible. They were trying to test his mind, not his eyesight. This had to be a problem, then, that could be reasoned out by a clever man.

Jafar searched his memory for everything King Harnex had told him. This was a contest of wits, and the Crystal was within the palace. That was comforting but not very helpful, since the palace was too large to search thoroughly in the allotted time. But the king had said something else, too: "You could have the Crystal within your hands in a minute if you but used your head." That must mean Jafar already knew where it was, if he could only recognize it as such. All things considered, that was the greatest clue of all, and Jafar started to feel excited.

The question now became, where had he been within the palace and what had he seen? The answer was slightly frustrating; he'd been in the halls leading to the throne room, the throne room itself, and the dining room. He had already looked most carefully in all those places, with no success. Could his hosts be moving the Crystal from one place to another after he'd already searched? But Jafar ruled that possibility out quickly. From what he knew of the Atlurim, they loved games, but they loved them played fairly. They would not cheat against him in that way. Besides, he would not then be able to find the Crystal simply by using his wits.

He stopped as a new thought occurred to him. King Harnex hadn't told him to use his wits; he'd said to use his *head*.

Slowly and deliberately, Jafar reached up and took from his head the wazir's crown the king had bestowed on him. Within the outer layer of mother-of-pearl was a small arrangement of what he had thought were sea stones. He'd paid them little attention before, but now he looked at them more carefully. One of them was clearly bigger than the others, though still smaller than the pieces of the Crystal he already had. Ali Maimun's journal had never said how big this piece was. It *might* be smaller than the rest. . . .

He plucked that stone from its place in the crown, and suddenly became aware that the audience was cheering, filling the entire hallway with the noise of their approbation. King Harnex, too, was smiling as he swam over to the storyteller, clapped his hands to Jafar's shoulders, and said, "Congratulations, O Jafar al-Sharif. You will indeed be a worthy successor to Ali Maimun."

And in that instant when Jafar al-Sharif took possession of the third piece of the Crystal, a mighty shaking took place on the magical web that underlay the world. Aeshma, who sensed such things naturally, looked to discover the source of the disturbance; but, as had been planned, Cari's uncle Suleim had organized the righteous Jann into a frenzy of activity, and they interposed themselves between Jafar and Aeshma so the king of the daevas could not tell the true source of the disturbance.

Jafar al-Sharif knew a moment of triumph, but it was a fleeting moment indeed—for in the back of his mind he knew he still had one more piece of the Crystal to get, perhaps the hardest piece of all. That was the piece that lay buried within Mount Denavan, the home of the daevas themselves. And even if he managed to get that, he still had no idea how to use the Crystals to save mankind from the power of evil that was marching eastward and threatening to overwhelm the entire world. But Oromasd had ordered him to try—and in his trying lay Parsina's only hope.

GLOSSARY

abaaya: a cloak or mantle worn by women

abdug: a cold yogurt drink

Adaran: the second-highest class of sacred fires; must be tended by priests

adarga: plain round or oval shield, covered with leather or metal

Afrit: a member of the third rank of the djinni

alif: the first letter of the Parsine alphabet

Atluriya: citizen of the sunken city of Atluri; *pl.:* Atlurim

ba: the second letter of the Parsine alphabet

Badawi: (pl.) tribes of the desert nomads

Bahram: the holiest class of sacred fires; must be tended only by highly purified priests; the king of fires, overhung by a crown

baklava: pastry rolls filled with chopped almonds, flavored with cardamom, and drenched in honey after baking

bazaar: an open-air market of many individual stalls

burga: a stiff mask worn by women, often embroidered or embellished with coins and other decorations

cadi: a judge or civil magistrate

camekan: the outer room of the hammam, where clothes are taken off and piled neatly

caravanserai: an inn providing merchants and wayfarers with shelter, food, and storage facilities for their beasts and goods; fee is generally based on one's ability to pay

chelo: a steamed rice preparation

cubit: a unit of length, approximately twenty inches or fifty centimeters

Dadgah: the third-highest class of sacred fire; may be tended by laymen

daeva: a demon, spawn of Rimahn, created to torment mankind and promote chaos

dahkma: a tower of silence, on which corpses are placed for vultures to eat the dead flesh

dhoti: a loincloth fashioned from a long narrow strip of cloth wound around the body, passed between the legs and tucked in at the waist behind

dinar: a gold coin of high value, equal to 1,000 dirhams; one dinar could buy a small village brewery

dirham: a silver coin of moderate value, equal to 100 fals; 1,000 dirhams equal one dinar; one dirham could buy a pony keg (150 glasses) of beer

diwan: a couch for reclining; also, an official audience or court held by a king or other ruler

djinn: a descendant of the illicit union of humans and daevas in the early ages of the world; mortal, but magically powerful and long-lived; *pl.:* djinni

druj: (s. & pl.) an evil creature who worships Rimahn and the lie; may have some magical abilities

durqa: a square, depressed area in the center of a qa'a, usually paved with marble and tile and containing a small fountain

emir: a nobleman ranked below a wazir

fal: a copper coin of low denomination; 100 fals equal one dirham; one fal could buy one glass of beer

fauwara: an ablutions fountain in the center of a sahn

fravashi: a person's heavenly self, to be reunited with the soul after the great Rehabilitation at the end of time

ghee: clarified, browned butter

gnaa: a rectangular headcloth for women, usually worn over the top of the shayla

grimoire: a magician's book of incantations, runes, and magical formulas

hammam: a public steam-bath house

haoma: the ephedra plant; grows on mountains; is ritually pounded and pressed to yield a fluid that is tasted during rituals, symbolizing man's eventual gaining of immortality

hizam: a waistbelt to secure weapons to the body, hold money and other items

homunculus: a creature of clay made to resemble a human being and magically given life

hookah: a water pipe

hosh: the central courtyard of a house, off of which other rooms open

hummus: a mixture of ground chick peas, garlic, and spices

Jann: (s. & pl.) a member of the fifth and lowest rank of the djinni

Jinn: (s. & pl.) a member of the fourth rank of the djinni

kaftan: a long, floor-length overrobe with full-length sleeves

khandaq: a sewage sump, a pit for gathering the city population's bodily wastes

khanjar: a curved bladed dagger, worn in a sheath in the hizam

kismet: unavoidable Fate

kohl: a powder of antimony, used as makeup to darken the eyelids

Kushti: (s. & pl.) a ritual rope or thread given to a child at investiture; its interwoven threads and tassels are highly symbolic; used during prayers

leewan: a paved platform about one-quarter of a cubit above central floor level, usually covered with mats or carpets

madrasa: a school, usually attached to a temple; teaches both secular and religious topics

maidan: a central square or plaza within a city

Marid: a member of the second rank of the djinni

milaaya: (s. & pl.) a colorful sheet worn by women as a mantle

milfa: a semitransparent black scarf drawn over the lower part of the face; worn in public by women

minaret: a tall, slender tower attached to a temple, where an everlasting flame burns in tribute to and as a symbol of Oromasd

minbar: a high, raised pulpit with a flight of steps, from which sermons are preached in a temple

musharabiya: a carved wooden grill of close latticework covering the street-facing windows of a house

nan-e lavash: a thin, dinnertime bread similar to flour tortillas, but crisper

niaal: (pl.) thonged sandals

parasang: a unit of length, approximately three miles or five kilometers

peri: a descendant of the union of humans and yazatas in the early ages of the world; mortal, but magically powerful and long-lived

pilau: a boiled rice dish, often with other spices and ingredients such as almonds, raisins, etc.

qa'a: principal room of a house, where guests are entertained

rahat lakhoum: an expensive confection of lichi nuts, kumquat rind, and hashish

rimahniya: (pl.) fanatical cult of assassins who worship Rimahn and welcome chaos

riwaq: a covered arcade with pillars dividing it into open sections surrounding on three sides an open area (sahn) in the center of a temple

rukh: a gigantic, magical, flesh-eating bird

saaya: a jacket with gold embroidery, worn by men

Sadre: a white shirt given to children at their investiture, which they are supposed to wear always next to their skin; putting it on symbolizes donning the Good Religion

sahn: an open courtyard in the center of a temple where the faithful gather to pray and hear sermons

saif: a sheathed short sword worn in the hizam at the waist

salaam: a word of greeting, meaning both "hello" and "peace"; also, a deferential bow of greeting or respect

sari: a full-length dress wrapped around the body

satrap: a provincial governor

Shaitan: a member of the first, and most powerful, rank of the djinni

sharbat-e porteghal: an iced drink of orange and mint

sharshaf: an oversized shawl worn when a woman leaves her mother's home for her future husband's; also worn at prayer

shaykh: the leader of a tribe, profession, or other group; usually elected for his age and wisdom

shayla: a rectangular, tasseled headcloth worn by women as part of a two-piece headgear; the tassels at the top dangle on either side of the face

shish kebob: a dish of beef or lamb and vegetables, cooked on a skewer over an open flame

sicakluk: the inner room of the hammam; the steam room

sidaireeya: a high-collared, open-front, waist-length jacket with elbow-length sleeves, worn by women over the Sadre; often highly decorated

simurgh: the magical bird who perches in the Tree of Knowledge

sirwaal: (pl.) long baggy trousers, gathered at the ankles, with a sash to draw in the waist; worn by men and women

sofreh: a cover placed over a carpet or over the ground while eating to give stability to the plates and protect the carpet; usually one of stiffer, waterproof leather is covered by another of cloth

soguluk: the middle room of the hammam where bodies are washed and massaged

taraha: a rectangular, black gauze scarf with beaded, embroidered, braided, or tasseled ends; worn over the head by women

thawb: a full-length, long-sleeved garment similar to the kaftan but fuller cut; also a capacious overdress worn by women

turban: a fine cloth worn wound around a man's head

wadi: a ravine formed by runoff rainwater

wali: a superintendant

wazir: a royal minister and political adviser

yasht: a special hymn composed to a yazata

yatu: an evil magician

zarabil: (pl.) cloth slippers, often embroidered

zibun: an ankle-length outer garment opening down the front; closes right over left at the waist, forming a waist-deep open vee in front; slits upward along each side from the hemline and slits at underarm seams from the edge of the short sleeve to the shoulder seam, to allow the decorated robes underneath to show through

ziyada: an outer courtyard surrounding a temple on three sides

THE PARSINE PANTHEON

THE GOOD DEITIES

Oromasd: the world's creator, ultimate power of light, truth, and goodness

The Bounteous Immortals: seven powerful spirits who sit on golden thrones in the House of Song and advise Oromasd. These include:

>*Spentaman:* The Bounteous Spirit
>
>*Vohuman:* The Good Mind; sits at Oromasd's right hand; protects useful animals and keeps a daily record of men's thoughts, words, and deeds
>
>*Ashath:* Truth; the most beautiful of the Immortals, she preserves order on earth, protects the fire, and smites disease and evil creatures
>
>*Kshatravar:* The Desired Kingdom; personifies Oromasd's might, power, majesty, and dominion; helps the poor and weak, and allots final rewards and punishments
>
>*Armaith:* Devotion; Oromasd's daughter, she sits at his left hand and personifies obedience, religious harmony, and worship
>
>*Hauvarta:* Integrity; represents wholeness, totality, and the fullness found in salvation; she protects water
>
>*Amerta:* Immortality; the protectress of plants, she represents the deathlessness found in salvation

Yazatas: Worshipful Ones; lesser heavenly beings who are prayed to and often act as intermediaries for Oromasd; their ranks include:

>*Varyu:* the king of the winds; dwells in the void, produces lightning, and makes dawn appear
>
>*Anahil:* the source of all waters on the earth and of the cosmic ocean, as well as the source of all fer-

tility; she is tall and beautiful, pure and nobly
born

Athra: the guardian of the holy flame

Verethran: the warrior spirit of victory who defeats
the malice of men and daevas; he punishes the
untruthful and the wicked

Rapthwen: the lord of renovation; protects the sun

Sraoshar: the lord of holy rituals; protects the world
at night, and protects the soul for three days
after death, until it reaches the Bridge of Shinvar

THE EVIL DEITIES

Rimahn: destroyer of all that is good, lord of darkness and the
lie

Daevas: personifications of evil aspects; act as Rimahn's emissaries on earth. Their ranks include:

Aeshma: the ultimate personification of Rimahn; king
of the daevas and satrap of the Pits of Torment

Akah Manah: Vile Thoughts, Discord

Az: Wrong-Mindedness

Azhi Dahaka: three-headed dragon, imprisoned in
Mount Denavan

Indar: Spirit of Apostasy

Jahi: the Great Harlot, symbol of debauchery, who
seduced Gayomar, the first Man

Nasu: the daeva of death, corruption, decomposition,
contagion, and impurity

Pairimaiti: Crooked-Mindedness

Saura: Misgovernment, Anarchy, Drunkenness

Taromaiti: Presumption

THE DJINNI

The djinni are descendants of ancient illicit unions between daevas and human beings. The five ranks of the djinni
include, in descending order:

Shaitan
Marid
Afrit
Jinn

Jann

Most djinni are worshipers of Rimahn, although some—
notably the righteous Jann—follow the path of Oromasd.
Though they are long-lived creatures of magic, their human
heritage makes them mortal and gives them souls—but those
souls are lost at the Bridge of Shinvar if they are deemed unworthy to enter the House of Song.

ABOUT THE AUTHOR

STEPHEN GOLDIN is the author of more than 20 science fiction novels, including *A World Called Solitude*, *And Not Make Dreams Your Master*, *Assault on the Gods*, *The Eternity Brigade*, and the Star Trek® novel *Trek to Madworld*. He has a bachelor's degree in astronomy and has worked as a space scientist for the Navy. He currently lives in Sacramento, California, with his wife Mary Mason and his stepson, Kenneth.

Hakem Rafi steals the Sacred Jewel of Oromasd
for the riches it promises.
What he is promised and what he gets are two
different things . . .

The Parsina Saga
by
Stephen Goldin

Kismet draws together Hakem Rafi, a small time thief;
Jafar al-Sharif, a simple storyteller; his daughter Selima
and Prince Ahmad of Ravan when Rafi steals the most
sacred relic of their country. Its disappearance puts into
motion the wheels of a war which will forever change
the earth, the gods and each one of the people involved.

☐ Volume One: **Shrine of the Desert Mage**
  (27212-8 • $3.95/$4.95 in Canada)
☐ Volume Two: **The Storyteller and the Jann**
  (27532-1 • $3.95/$4.95 in Canada)

And don't miss volume three of *The Parsina Saga:*
Crystals of Air and Water, to be published in
January, 1989.

Buy **Shrine of the Desert Mage** and **The Storyteller
and the Jann** on sale now wherever Bantam Spectra
books are sold, or use this page to order: